Light *of the* Moon

Elizabeth Buchan lives in London with her husband and two children and worked in publishing for several years. During that time she wrote her first books for children, including *Beatrix Potter: The Story of the Creator of Peter Rabbit*. Her first novel for adults was *Daughters of the Storm*, followed by *Light of the Moon* and *Consider the Lily* — which won the 1994 Romantic Novel of the Year Award — *Perfect Love*, *Against Her Nature*, *Secrets of the Heart* and *Revenge of the Middle-Aged Woman*. Her most recent novel is *The Good Wife*. Elizabeth Buchan has sat on the committee of the Society of Authors and was a judge for the 1997 Whitbread Awards and Chairman of the Judges for the 1997 Betty Trask Award. Her short stories have been published in various magazines and broadcast on BBC Radio 4.

For further information go to www.elizabethbuchan.com

Also by Elizabeth Buchan

Novels

DAUGHTERS OF THE STORM

CONSIDER THE LILY

PERFECT LOVE

AGAINST HER NATURE

SECRETS OF THE HEART

REVENGE OF THE MIDDLE-AGED WOMAN

THE GOOD WIFE

For children

ICE DANCER

BEATRIX POTTER: A LIFE

A DASHING YOUNG TIGER NAMED
JACK AND OTHER SILLY LIMERICKS

Light
of the
Moon

ELIZABETH
BUCHAN

PAN BOOKS

FT
Pbk

First published 1991 by Macmillan

First published by Pan Books 1991

This edition published 1995 by Pan Books
an imprint of Pan Macmillan Ltd
Pan Macmillan, 20 New Wharf Road, London N1 9RR
Basingstoke and Oxford
Associated companies throughout the world
www.panmacmillan.com

ISBN 0 330 34346 7

5 7 9 10 8 6

A CIP catalogue record for this book is available from
the British Library.

Printed and bound in Great Britain by
Mackays of Chatham plc, Chatham, Kent

For Adam, who built the Lysander so carefully,
with love

I am the enemy you killed, my friend.
I knew you in this dark; for so you frowned
Yesterday through me as you jabbed and killed.
I parried; but my hands were loath and cold.
Let us sleep now . . .

'Strange Meeting' *Wilfred Owen*

Acknowledgements

Although I have tried to set this book accurately, this is a work of fiction and should be taken as such. Anyone wishing to familiarise themselves with the events in the soe during the Second World War should refer to the documents and primary sources. Any resemblance to living persons is coincidental.

The areas in which some of the events in the story take place will be known to some but neither the farm at Castle Cary, the *château*, the convent, nor the Café Mas exists. Equally, as far as I am aware, there was no tyre factory at Ribérac or a radio station at St Aulaye during the period covered by the novel.

The first woman F-section soe agent went into France in July 1942, followed by other brave women, some of whom never came back. Their courage speaks for itself and slotting forward that milestone by nine months for the purposes of this novel is in no way meant to undermine their achievements.

My particular thanks are due to Debby and Dorian Bond for their terrific hospitality; Suzanne Bargett, John Bullen and Mark Seaman from the Imperial War Museum for their time and expertise; Herrn von dem Knesebeck for answering vital questions on German intelligence; Lisa Buchan for unearthing *La Bonne Cuisine de Périgord*; Mary S. Lovell for being so generous with her knowledge and research materials; and Mary Moore for her report on the French landscape and for her support. Any mistakes I have made are entirely mine.

There are many fascinating books on the subject and I have made use of incidents and drawn on materials from the following: *'Jacqueline': Pioneer Heroine of the Resistance* by Stella King (Arms and Armour Press, 1989), whose details on training proved invaluable. *Maquis* (William Heinemann, 1945) and *Horned Pigeon* (William Heinemann, 1946) by George Millar, two wonderful books that give the feel of the French *maquis*; *Duel of Wits* by Peter Churchill; *S.O.E. in France* by M. R. D. Foot (with thanks for Simon Cobley for finding my precious second-hand copy). I read and consulted dozens of books while I was researching this novel and the following were especially interesting or useful. *No Cloak, No Dagger* by Benjamin Cowburn (Jarrolds, 1960); *Who Lived to See the Day* by Philippe de Vomécourt (Hutchinson, 1961); *Undercover* by Patrick Howarth (reissued Arrow Books, 1990); *The German Home Front* by Terry Charman (Barrie and Jenkins, 1989); *Histoire de la Résistance en Périgord* by Guy Penaud (Pierre Fanlac, 1985); *The Abwehr* by Lauran Paine (Robert Hale, 1984); *The Order of the Death's Head* by Heinz Höhne (Secker and Warburg, 1969); *The Berlin Diaries of Marie 'Missie' Vassiltchikov 1940–1945* (Chatto, 1985); *The Past is Myself* by Christabel Bielenberg (Chatto and Windus, 1968); *We Landed by Moonlight: Secret RAF Landings in France, 1940–44* by Hugh Verity (Ian Allan, 1978); *Secret Warfare: Arms and Techniques of the Resistance* by Pierre Lorain (Orbis, 1984).

I owe a special debt of gratitude to my aunt and uncle, Margaret and Otto Soltmann, for their support. Their own story gave me the idea for mine.

To Fanny Blake, Caroline Sheldon, Laura Morris, Jane Wood and Hazel Orme, thank you. To Kate Chevenix Trench for her patience, rigour and for her skill at turning hieroglyphics into English, an especial thank you. To Adam, Eleanor and my husband, Benjamin, thank you for putting up with chaos for so long.

PART ONE

May 1941–December 1941

Extract from the diary of Evelyn, née St John

I thought that loving someone was simple. It isn't. Glorious, yes. Painful, yes. Unforgettable, yes. Simple, no. It took a war for me to find out.

The war stained our spirits. No one who lived through it could shake off what they learned, and some of us are so marked that we can never live 'normally' again.

I try.

If I had known about the deception and the degradation that human beings can inflict on one another, would I have gone into a field where such knowledge was unavoidable? If I had known I was going to encounter the once-in-a-lifetime kind of love and meet the man who belonged to me, yet who was forbidden, would I have chosen to do something else? Perhaps. Hindsight is easy. I was young and badly wanted to play a part.

In this more cynical age it is easy to forget how vehemently my generation believed that something was expected of us – unquestioning sacrifice, discomfort and hardship, certainly. We had been taught to revere the word 'duty' by our elders. We were accountable, if not to God then to our fellow human beings.

Adolf Hitler never seemed a joke to me – the caricature that figured in newspaper cartoons and pranced in newsreels. To me Hitler was a crazed, demonic force, a demagogue spawned from Germany's defeat in the First World War. Dispossessed nations can become greedy or be driven mad: Austria, Poland and Czechoslovakia were victims of a mad greed. So was France.

Because I loved France so much, this last was the most painful. I minded that the towns and villages of the Touraine were full of uniformed men. In the summer of 1940 I thought

3

about it constantly, picturing those sunlit fields and woods I knew so well, bristling with guns and soldiers in the German Wehrmacht. I returned to it again and again.

But here I must be honest. Had my choice been so noble? Was my so-called sense of duty only a convenience because I was at a loss in my personal life? I was not fully a woman, nor any longer a girl. I was unsure of my direction. What is true is that once I had taken my decision I never doubted its rightness – only my capacity to live up to it. I learned to question even a handshake, but I also learned to take full measure of myself and others. Never again will I look on anyone with innocent eyes. That kind of simplicity went for ever.

CHAPTER ONE

'Name?'

'Evelyn St John.'

'Any middle name?'

'Violette,' the girl said reluctantly. 'I never use it.'

'We like to be precise,' said the man who had introduced himself as Captain Fuller. 'Your age?'

'Don't you know?' Evelyn replied without thinking and realised she had been rude. She had not meant to be, and she wanted this job – whatever it was.

Captain Fuller extracted a paper from his file and began to read out details from it in a level voice. 'Age twenty-one. Daughter of John and Eugénie St John of Manor Farm, Castle Cary, Somerset. Paternal grandparents dead. Maternal grandparents French and live near Tours. Brother, Peter, aged eleven. Educated at a girls' school in Bath. Obtained matriculation. Unemployed since then. Bilingual and regular visitor to France. Interests include hunting.'

Flushing at this bare catalogue of her life, Evelyn clutched her brown crocodile handbag. She could have added a few things for Captain Fuller: her father's assets (considerable, but mostly in land), her mother's confidential visits to a Harley Street consultant specialising in nervous depression, that their marriage was unhappy and that she and her father fought at regular intervals on everything from the rights and wrongs of the recent war in Spain to whether Evelyn could go to university or leave home to take a job. If Captain Fuller was interested in the fine detail, she could throw in several unflattering photographs of herself in the *Tatler* attending hunt balls and cocktail parties in an expensive but particularly hideous taffeta dress which her mother insisted she wore. She could also add the list of social occasions on which she had

5

failed to shine and retired to read in the powder room, the painful episode with Arthur Jayford, and the titles of the books beside her bed – mostly French novels, chief among them *Madame Bovary*, the eponymous heroine of which, in her search for the delights of a grand and gaudy passion, fascinated Evelyn. She might have added that, in her most depressed moments, Evelyn felt she had been born cloven, an uneasy, unsettling mixture of French and English, belonging in neither country and suspected by both.

This was her second interview in three days. At the preliminary interview a uniformed officer took details of her family and childhood and tested her written and spoken French. He then read out passages from the Official Secrets Act and asked her to sign them, enjoining her to tell no one about their conversation.

Still mystified as to what it was about, Evelyn returned to her Aunt Fanny's pretty house in Thurloe Square and asked if she could stay on for a few more days. 'Goodness,' said Aunt Fanny. 'We'd better get you some decent town clothes.' Pleased with the way her plan was developing, her aunt proceeded to plunder her daughter's wardrobe in order, as she put it, to 'refurbish' the girl. It was she who had mentioned to a friend with influential contacts in the FANY organisation that she had a bright, healthy, bilingual niece kicking her heels at home and could she help? Fanny was fond of her brother John, but considered positively medieval his idea of keeping a daughter cooped up at home until she married. Evelyn needed to widen her horizons, and the war needed girls like Evelyn.

So, dressed in a Harris tweed costume which was a little too tight (Evelyn sighed at the size of her hips), one of her cousin's linen blouses, a straw hat and her only pair of silk stockings, Evelyn faced Captain Fuller in the Victoria Hotel, room number 238, in Northumberland Avenue. She still had no idea about the work on offer but imagined it was perhaps translation work of an important and confidential nature. (The secrecy and vagueness surrounding the job increased its attraction.) She had been expecting to find a Captain Prader,

6

but as Captain Fuller explained when he rose to greet her, he was standing in for his colleague who was indisposed.

The room overlooked a quiet inner courtyard and was furnished with a table covered with a grey army blanket, two chairs and a filing cabinet. The grate was empty. The only note struck against its unredeemable impersonality was Captain Fuller's leather briefcase and his copy of *Picture Post*. Evelyn wished she did not feel so awkward and unsure.

Captain Fuller got out a pipe and made a play of tamping the tobacco down into the bowl while he considered Evelyn. Tall, dark, green eyes, a trace of puppy fat. Very nervous. Captain Fuller was not at all sure he approved of this experiment to recruit women into the organisation. Captain Prader, however, was very keen: women put up with loneliness much better, he argued. They do not require company in the way men do. They will make good agents.

'Your maternal grandparents,' he asked, switching to French – fluent but careful and correct. 'Where exactly do they live?'

Recovering from her surprise, Evelyn took a deep breath and wished she did not find the face opposite her so unfriendly. A smugness, lack of humour and a touch of arrogance overlay the strong, well-structured features. It was a pity . . . Captain Fuller might have been handsome in a dark, rather interesting way.

'In a village ten miles east of Tours.' She answered him flawlessly.

'What does your grandfather do?'

'He farms and also runs a small printing business as a hobby. My uncle, my mother's brother, helps him.'

'Do you have any cousins?'

'André. He is twenty-two. Madeleine, who is twenty. Yvonne is now sixteen, I think.'

'And you are known in the area?'

'Yes, indeed. My mother's family have lived there for generations. We are an important part of the village.'

'I see. Are *you* well known there?'

'Oh, yes. I have been there every summer since 1934. Including 1939. I was there when war was declared but I

7

managed to get a passage home quite quickly. My mother was anxious that I grew up speaking French. She sometimes came with me.' Evelyn began to relax a little. 'I have quite a few friends there, but, of course, we haven't been in touch since— '

'Tell me about your background.' He did not look particularly interested. Evelyn dutifully recited more facts. Born at the family home in Castle Cary, her father joined up in 1916, was wounded and sent home. Her parents married in 1919 and she had been born later that year and sent to boarding school at the age of eleven. Her father forbade her to go to university ('Damn fool stuff') and refused to allow her to work ('Your place is at home, my girl'). It was only the advent of another war that persuaded John St John to allow Evelyn to answer Aunt Fanny's summons.

'How does your mother feel about the situation in France?' Captain Fuller was edging closer to Evelyn's political opinions.

'My mother?' What had her mother to do with the job? 'My mother has found it difficult to settle in England and is deeply grieved about the fall of France.'

Had Evelyn been entirely honest she would have admitted that Eugénie had made a mistake in leaving her native France. She found it impossible to settle to a life where the high spot of the year was the hunting season: those busy, noisy meets when the sun shone through the bare trees in a red haze and frozen mist steamed in layers like a ballerina's skirt. At these times, Eugénie felt her foreignness and tasted the isolation of the outsider. A life where children were to be seen but not heard, where the talk was of converts and spavins, and dog hairs a necessary accompaniment to interior decor. Where any woman over thirty suspected of attending to her looks was considered a little odd. Where the old, secure ways stretched complacently into the future. How very different from the society in which she grew up, where women took trouble with their appearance, refining the process into an art. Where to hold opinions on books and politics was considered necessary – vital, even. Where on high days and holidays the family gathered to celebrate their religion, their food and to follow the national pastime, the cultivation of love.

8

Far, far better if John St John had chosen a woman who would have fitted into the squire's life he knew. Perhaps it would have made the relationship between him and his 'infuriating, rebellious daughter' easier if he had been more happily married.

'How do you occupy yourself at home?'

A good question, thought Evelyn. I help run a large, rather dilapidated farmhouse. I deputise for my mother on her bad days and I dress myself up occasionally and drive to similar large houses where I am supposed to enjoy myself. Sometimes I do – but mostly I wish I was somewhere else. 'I help my mother with our social commitments,' she replied and met his blank gaze.

'Reasonably discreet,' Captain Fuller wrote on his form. 'Not over-forthcoming.' It was a promising trait. He looked up at his subject. He could not warm to Miss St John. She was the kind of girl his passionately Northern, working-class Quaker mother had distrusted when she was alive. Jack had seen plenty of the type when, a scholarship boy from grammar school, he had gone up to Oxford. Tallish, big-boned girls with plummy vowels, who turned him prickly and envious at the same time.

'You have no other commitments, Miss St John?' Captain Fuller's implication was quite clear.

'No.' She sounded a little uncertain.

'Are you sure?'

Evelyn thought of the fleeting but intense crush she had developed for one of her cousin's friends in France. She thought of Arthur Jayford. Newly commissioned into the local regiment, Arthur had accompanied her to several dances. Once, at a hunt ball, she had permitted Arthur to kiss her because she was curious and had imagined she had found a kindred spirit. She tried hard to give him what was required as he crushed her bulky taffeta dress against his starched shirt, and failed. The feel of his lips and intrusive tongue had been disgusting and she pushed him away. Arthur repaid her rejection by dancing for the rest of the evening with Sophie Quinlan Jones and ignoring Evelyn, who went home and wept tears of despair.

9

'If you mean, Captain Fuller, do I have any attachments of a personal nature, then no, I do not. But I confess I find your question a little strange.'

He had the grace to look down at the grey army blanket. 'My apologies, Miss St John. But I can assure you these questions are necessary.'

'Snooty mare.' He could hear his mother saying the words. Miss St John was a snooty mare. He wrote, 'unattached' in the file and blotted the ink. 'Damn,' he said to himself.

Jack Fuller's real name was Pickford. (Fuller was the pseudonym he had given Evelyn for security reasons.) His mother died when he was ten, leaving him alone with an ambitious father in the little Yorkshire town of Ripon. Being a solitary boy, there was no one to whom he felt he could turn to help him deal with the hot, stifling grief he felt at her loss. It was not just the misery of a small boy longing for the comfort of a parent; his mother had been his guide to the world. He saw it through her eyes. The 'them' and 'us'. 'Us' signified a magic intimacy, and the rest were either shiftless, snobbish or, casting the net wider, too rich for their own good. Or, the worst insult of all, 'Southerners'.

His father had not understood Jack's real needs. He was too busy to see that a child requires an unselfish adult to render his world safe. Mr Pickford was more interested in his own ambitions for his son. Pickford's was a small grocery shop which made almost no money, but he knew what he was doing when it came to his only offspring. He sent Jack to elocution lessons (paying for them with his tobacco money), arranged for private tuition in maths and Latin and ensured Jack went to grammar school. After an initial rebellion, playing truant from school, Jack performed perfectly. He won a scholarship to Oxford with no trouble, dominated the Union and electrified his peers with passionate speeches in defence of socialism.

He was spoken of as an up-and-coming young man, with a brilliant political career ahead of him. At Oxford, the plummy-sounding girls who went to bed with him, risking their reputations, thrilled to this young and fascinating student – and congratulated themselves on their social pioneering. Once,

Jack took back a slim, wanton, impeccably bred beauty to his room and allowed her to seduce him before he knelt above her and took over. Afterwards they talked, and Jack began to expound his ideas of a free and equal society emerging from the ruins of the upper classes. She slapped him on the cheek.

'If you practised what you preach, you wouldn't be so disgustingly eager to take me to bed.'

Jack never saw her again but he remembered her words and the unpleasant moment when he realised that he had been as guilty as any of social climbing.

Captain Fuller was taking his time writing his notes, every so often snatching covert glances to help him ratify his impressions. An agent should never be too striking, should melt into the background – the sort of person who is never noticed in a crowded room. Miss St John, he had to own, was striking. As he watched she shifted in her seat, one long leg placed decorously beside the other, and he had a sudden, disconcerting vision of what she could become – a swan-necked beauty with a tender, generous mouth.

'What is your opinion of the German nation?' Jack tamped down the tobacco in his pipe.

'I hate . . .' Evelyn tried to formulate the correct words. 'I hate what it is doing to itself and to the rest of Europe.'

'But you don't hate the Germans?'

'Not all Germans agree with Adolf Hitler.'

He looked up quickly from the file. 'But they do, Miss St John, they do. Germany is intent on establishing a thousand-year-old Reich. Surely the lessons of Czechoslovakia and Poland are obvious – let alone events since then?' He added the wounding rider, 'Even to the unsophisticated mind.'

Evelyn reddened. Why, she wondered, is this man deliberately misunderstanding me? Since she had followed political developments avidly since Hitler assumed power, she needed no reminding of Poland's agony. 'We should have gone to her aid,' she said. 'The Poles believed we would.'

'Really? Even with the Russians just waiting for an excuse to cross the Polish border?' Jack stopped there, disconcerted. As a socialist with Communist leanings, he still found painful the memory of the Nazi-Soviet pact made in August 1939.

Evelyn pulled on her gloves, hoping that he would bring the interview to a close. 'If you will excuse me, Captain Fuller, I have another appointment,' she lied.

Jack ignored her. 'What about France? What do you feel about her?'

The closed, slightly sardonic face across the table began to infuriate her. 'What *are* we doing for France, Captain Fuller? Perhaps you would be good enough to tell me. You seem to be well informed.'

Despite himself, Jack suppressed a smile. Miss St John seemed less flat a character when she was angry and her hostility set up a satisfying crackle between them. Evelyn leant forward on her seat. 'We fled back across the Channel after Dunkirk, and we have sunk the French fleet. For months now she has been under German occupation. I know we are suffering at home. I know our troops are fighting in Greece and in North Africa. But what are we doing to help the French?'

Instead of answering her, Captain Fuller gave two quick nods as if he agreed. He articulated his next question with care. 'Would you ever commit murder, Miss St John?'

'*Murder?*'

'Yes, murder. And would you be capable of lying to and deceiving even your closest friends and relations?'

In reply she shoved her arm through the shoulder strap of her handbag and rose to her feet.

'Captain Fuller. I think I really must go.'

'Would you?' For the first time, Captain Fuller smiled, a smile that indicated some sympathy. It made him seem much more human, even approachable. Her mind racing, Evelyn struggled to assume the expression she often adopted at social occasions to mask her real feelings. 'Certainly not,' she said, coolly.

Jack was impressed by the reaction. After all, it was not an everyday question. Perhaps he had underestimated this girl. He reached into his pocket and held out a cigarette case. 'Would you like one now?'

She shook her head. 'Look here. What exactly is all this?'

Although he had prepared his answer carefully, Jack took

his time. The firmness she had shown decided him that it was worth proceeding. 'Sit down, Miss St John,' he insisted and waited until she did. 'I will explain.'

The prudent half of Evelyn urged her to go, to leave at once without ceremony or apology. The other half was curious.

'To be brief, Miss St John, I represent an organisation, the Special Operations Executive, that has been set up to fight the war with . . . well . . . unorthodox methods. It is a very secret organisation, backed by the highest authority. If you were to choose to become a member, your total discretion and silence would be demanded. You would be forbidden to talk to anyone, ever, about your work.'

'Could I have a cigarette?' she asked.

Jack moved the cigarette case towards her and came round the desk to light the cigarette. 'The indirect approach, Miss St John, is what I'm talking about. This organisation is going to act as a gadfly on the German hide by putting agents inside enemy territory all over Europe. From there, they will cause as much chaos and disruption as seem appropriate. My section is concerned with France, and this is where you come in.' He noticed she had settled back into the chair. 'We need men and . . . er . . . women who are willing to go into France and work for us in the field. It is a job that requires nerves, dedication and a willingness to face the fact that you might never come back.'

Evelyn hoped her mixed feelings were not registered on her face. She puffed inexpertly at her cigarette. 'Are you allowed to tell me more?'

'No. Except that my organisation and its undercover work is a new science, I think it's safe to say. We will be discovering things as the war progresses, and possibly making mistakes. But mistakes are expensive. They will cost lives. We must, therefore, be sure we choose the right people.' Jack leant back against the desk. 'Only very special people can do this job. One of their qualifications is better than excellent French.'

Evelyn coughed as she inhaled. Jack leant over and picked up her file thinking: This is where she bows out.

She surprised him. 'Yes,' she said, stubbing out her half-smoked cigarette. 'Yes, I'm interested.'

He thinks I should be dishing out tea and sticky buns at the local vicarage, she thought (accurately) and felt unreasonably angry with him. She looked up at him: he was leafing through the file. Probably from the north, she concluded, detecting the accent that lay under the smoothed vowels. None the less, he was obviously well educated.

'Oxford or Cambridge?' she asked.

'Oxford,' he replied, absorbed in a paper. He frowned when he realised his blunder.

'I was curious, Captain Fuller,' said Evelyn sweetly, enjoying her tiny triumph.

Jack wrote the word 'sharp' in his notes. 'You must think carefully about this, Miss St John. It is not a light matter.'

Evelyn felt she was owed a little more. 'How do women fit into this work?'

'They could be very important. Carrying messages, liaising, jobs like that.'

'Jobs like that' sounded depressingly familiar – a wartime version of the tea and buns routine, only with a novelettish flavour. 'Oh,' she said, disappointed.

He caught the inflexion. 'I hope I am making myself clear. What I want you to do is consider putting yourself behind enemy lines in France and to disappear. You must merge so thoroughly into the community that no one suspects you haven't lived your entire life in France. Once there, you are under orders and will put into practice the training we will have given you. What we ask demands the highest courage . . .' Jack heard himself becoming pompous. 'It may be that sometimes you have to take steps to protect yourself. Do you understand?'

Evelyn looked at the gloves folded in her lap and then at her sensible shoes. Did she understand? She raised her eyes and encountered Captain Fuller's. A few days ago she had climbed onto a train that took her to Paddington Station. She had spent the intervening time with her aunt, inspected her cousin's wartime wedding dress and breakfasted in bed. All perfectly normal. Now she was being faced with a proposal that was anything but normal. She tried hard to think about danger and the idea of death, but they proved elusive. What she did understand, and with increasing excitement, was that here was a hand thrown out to rescue her from boredom, restlessness and a creeping disgust at her inadequacies.

'I would like to put my name forward,' she said.

'Are you sure?' Jack could not help pitying her ignorance.

'I'm sure.'

'As you wish.' He crossed something out in the file. 'I will recommend that you see Captain Prader. If he agrees with you, then you will be contacted about preliminary training. After that, you will be assessed to see if you may proceed. May I remind you that not one word of this interview must pass your lips. We usually suggest that you say you have been discussing confidential translation work.'

Evelyn rose in a flurry of lavender water and brown crocodile handbag. 'Agreed,' she said and, feeling light-headed, held out her hand.

Unwisely, Evelyn opened the letter during breakfast at Manor House Farm. Peter seized his cue and launched into the attack.

'She's got a letter from a boyfriend,' he sang out.

Eugénie St John looked up from her tea and her face tightened. 'Be quiet, Peter,' she said.

Peter winked at his sister. He had not finished with the subject and Evelyn, who could never resist Peter, only smiled. 'Go away. It's none of your business.'

Eugénie gazed out of the window towards the slope of the hill to the south of the farm. Patched onto its sides, the trees were rimmed with a late frost and white pockets were scattered in the north-facing hollows. 'No doubt Evelyn will tell us when she's ready.'

Evelyn looked at her mother and wondered for the hundredth time about the disaster of her parents' marriage. What had possessed John St John to walk into that village near Tours during the summer of 1919 and ask for the hand of Eugénie de Soubervielle? Certainly not common sense – but as she grew up, Evelyn began to understand its context a little better. If she had been a young, wounded and war-weary soldier, she, too, might have succumbed to an uncharacteristic impulse.

Some sort of magic must have drifted into those months after the Great War, Evelyn fancied. Either that, or the fragmentation of lives it had brought about had been so shattering that people willed themselves to forget by falling in love. For John mistook Eugénie's neurotic tendencies for shyness, and Eugénie mistook John's inarticulate and clumsy wooing for gentleness.

One hot afternoon they were married. Evelyn's grandmother often described the wedding feast spread beneath the limes in the de Soubervielle garden. Well dressed and at ease, the French guests wandered the lawns and terraces. The English, uncomfortable inside their starched collars and clumsy dresses, decided to make the best of it for the dear bridegroom's sake. John sweated copiously into his frock coat and beneath the ivory veil Eugénie flushed pink with happiness. Later, when the lanterns glowed in the trees, John took his bride in his arms and waltzed through the soft aura of light.

Ah, well. Evelyn watched her mother tug at her tortoiseshell hair combs. It had ended badly for them, but the consequences had not stopped there. Both she and Peter had been born into this mess of disappointment, as well as into a genetic muddle that caused them confusion too.

'Has your father had breakfast?' asked her mother, who had arrived late in the dining room.

'Yes.' Evelyn took a piece of toast. 'Peter, why don't you go away?'

'Aren't you going to read your letter?'

'Yes,' she said. 'When you've gone.'

'Run along, Peter,' Eugénie ordered.

Evelyn watched her brother disappear as she buttered her toast, remembered half-way through that butter was rationed and scraped some of it off.

'Is it a boyfriend?' Eugénie spoke so softly that Evelyn made her repeat the question.

In reply she opened the letter and read it. 'No,' she said at last, laying it down, wishing that she was alone to savour the excitement its contents engendered. She watched Eugénie relax. It was always like this. The anxious question, the perceptible relief. Lacking any other anchor, Eugénie was terrified

16

that Evelyn would fall in love, marry and leave home. Evelyn bit into her toast: sometimes the burden of her mother's fragile mental equilibrium weighed very heavily. 'It's all right, Mother. I'm not interested in anybody at the moment.'

'Not even Arthur?'

'Certainly not Arthur.' She finished her toast and poured out a cup of coffee. 'About the war,' she began. 'Mother, I've go to do something, whatever Father says, and . . .' Evelyn paused.

How often had Eugénie looked at her daughter and thought how perfect she was? Hundreds, thousands of times, from that first, heart-stopping moment when the baby had been placed in her arms and Eugénie, still shocked by the discovery that her marriage was a mockery, had fallen properly in love.

Evelyn fascinated her. The lovely skin that turned golden brown in summer and pale olive in winter. The long legs, the beautifully shaped mouth and dark shoulder-length hair. The endearing traces of puppy fat Evelyn still carried and worried over, and the ugly nails which, like Eugénie's own, were bitten to the quick. Eugénie recognised that Evelyn had been born with a bolder spirit than hers, and she both loved and was frightened by it. Evelyn challenged things and sought out new experiences in a way that she had never dared. Eugénie knew Evelyn's English sense of fair play, her compassion, her physical courage, her depressions and her need for privacy. But, above all, Eugénie recognised an imaginative spirit which left her behind and which she envied. And she was empty and bereft at the idea of Evelyn leaving home.

From over her coffee cup, Evelyn watched her mother and braced herself. She replaced the cup in the saucer.

'Mother. Please listen,' she said gently. 'I've been offered a job and I think I'm going to take it.'

Eugénie burst into tears.

CHAPTER TWO

A covered army truck waited at Guildford Station for the two women and four men who climbed into the back and were hidden from view. It headed in the direction of Wanborough Manor, a journey which normally took ten minutes but, for security reasons, the driver deliberately spun it out into an hour so that his passengers lost all sense of direction. Eventually, he climbed up the Hog's Back and dropped down over the brow towards the seventeenth-century manor house, flanked by a medieval tithe barn and a Saxon chapel.

The drive was sandbagged at the entrance, and the estate surrounding the manor – which included several acres of garden, woodland, a lake and two chalk quarries – was tightly enclosed. Once inside, the inhabitants were not encouraged either to stray beyond the boundary or go on leave.

The arrivals were ushered into the panelled hallway, dominated by a fine Jacobean staircase where they waited for the commandant to greet them. Very conscious that they were the only women, Evelyn and her companion, a girl named Mary, stood a little apart. Tall and thin with a black moustache, the commandant made a brief welcoming speech, outlined the rules and scrutinised the girls.

'We will be sharing a bedroom overlooking the front garden,' said the female conducting officer, who had been specially brought in to look after the women agents. She was as new to the job as Evelyn and Mary. Her name was Katherine, she said, but everybody called her Kitty. She was large, dark and smiled a lot. Kitty ushered them into a room under the eaves with an inadequate Victorian grate in the corner. Even in summer the room felt cool, almost cold. Three iron bedsteads took up most of the space. 'You are marked on your tidiness,' Kitty warned and Evelyn sighed at the coming upheaval in her domestic life. 'We will also lock the door at night. The chaps here are very high-spirited, and you never know . . .'

During the following days, Evelyn woke up to a world of intelligence tests, oral questioning, hard physical exercise and the strain of being under constant surveillance.

'Can I stand it?' she groaned on the third evening as they prepared for bed. The day had begun with a training run up the Hog's Back. After breakfast she had been invited to climb one of the huge beech trees in the garden and descend via a rope. After lunch, she practised target shooting in the quarry and sharp-shooting in the chalk pit with a .38 pistol. Training did not even end with dinner. An instructor sought her out in the long drawing room after the meal and plied her with whisky. Evelyn accepted two and rued it, afraid she had fallen into the simplest of traps.

'Can *I* stand it?' asked Kitty. She was lying on her bed in her cami-knickers and brassière, too tired to undress. 'You two are quite a responsibility.' Evelyn dropped her hairbrush onto Kitty's stomach and her conducting officer gave an unprofessional yell. Mary said nothing but during the night Evelyn woke and heard her crying.

In the morning Evelyn got up early and went to sit in the tiny chapel where Kitty eventually discovered her.

'Having second thoughts, old girl?'

Evelyn shook her head. 'No,' she said firmly.

The training continued for three weeks. 'Number Fourteen is an interesting candidate. She has formed a friendship with the conducting officer and consults her regularly. She reflects on her tasks and tries to achieve objectivity. She does not always succeed, and has a tendency to underestimate herself. She tries hard, even at the end of a full day's training, and possesses natural good manners. Physically adept. Promising shot. Perhaps not yet sufficiently mature to be trusted with this sort of job . . .'

The report on Evelyn went back to Baker Street to be studied. The chiefs evidently overlooked the reservations expressed in it. Their verdict came back: Evelyn was to proceed to the next step.

Arisaig was inaccessible except for one road and a single-track railway. It lay between Moidard and Mallaig among some of the most lovely but lonely landscape in Scotland. It was designated a restricted area, and anyone leaving or entering had to be in possession of a pass. SOE commandeered five houses in the area and each one housed a selection of potential agents plus an instructor.

Dark, gloomy and badly heated, Garramor accommodated the French agents. Evelyn was lucky, sharing sleeping quarters with Mary and Kitty while the men were crowded five or six to a room. The plumbing arrangements were inadequate and the numbers in the house ensured that the bathroom was always occupied. Downstairs was equally Spartan, only marginally cheered by a fire and bookcase filled with carefully chosen volumes such as Geoffrey Household's *Rogue Male* and John Buchan's *The Thirty-Nine Steps*. Garramor was run by a fair-haired chain-smoking instructor nicknamed 'The Wasp'.

'Fieldcraft . . . Number Fourteen, are you listening?'

'Yes, sir.' Evelyn was shivering with cold from the stiff breeze off the sea, and exhausted from a night-time hike. It was 8 a.m.

'Well, you didn't look like it . . . But females are forever day-dreaming.'

'Get your own back,' an agent who had been introduced as John whispered in her ear. Evelyn wrenched her attention back to the lecture and tried to concentrate.

Fieldcraft. Silent killing. Unarmed combat. Knife work. Rope work. Map work. Morse code. Raiding tactics.

'Get two rounds away, gentlemen and er . . . ladies. Never rely on one bullet to do the work. We are not proud here, we don't employ classical shooting techniques. But we do want results. Don't stop to think of anything or you're dead. Until you shoot straight by instinct – from under the bed, out of your pocket or round your arse if need be – you are no shot. Regard your pistol as a pointing finger. Remember "the double tap".'

At this point, the students were tested with electronically wired figures dressed in German uniform that bobbed up unexpectedly out of the undergrowth.

'Shoot 'em, you blighters,' yelled the instructor. 'Don't hang about. Change mags. Let them go like belches . . . You have three and a half seconds to kill. I don't want anyone being bloody intellectual about it!'

Evelyn found herself up trees shooting downwards, shooting by torchlight, shooting while she ran, shooting while she crawled over the heather. Surprise lurked in every corridor and in every nook of Garramor's grounds: without warning figures dressed in black raincoats and wide-brimmed hats sprang up. Once she came upon a group of three enemy 'soldiers' sitting at a table in the garden shed. She shot all three with the .32 Colt slung from her waist.

Later, two expert instructors in the arts of self-defence and silent killing joined the team. Nicknamed the 'Heavenly Twins', their work was anything but celestial.

'We are here to show you the possibilities. They are endless. Did you know that a matchbox or an umbrella is a very useful weapon? No? Ladies, do you know how to get rid of someone who puts his hand on your knee in the cinema? No? It's simple. You turn him upside down and stuff his head under the seat. It's done like this.

'In a war you have two objectives. Either to kill or capture your enemy. If you wish to kill him, do so at once.

'We hope it will never happen, but if you find yourself being interrogated, ladies and gentlemen, you must understand that you may be tortured. To prepare yourself, you should consider my suggestion to study yoga. Another method is to count while they torture you. It focuses the mind and, if you are to survive, you must promote mind over matter.'

Between the silent killing instruction and the course on explosives, Mary decided to throw it in. 'I'm terrified and horrified,' she explained to Evelyn and Kitty. 'I could never do this and I don't think I could stand it in the field.'

The two girls said goodbye to Mary with genuine regret and she departed by boat for England. Kitty saw her off and came back very thoughtful.

'You know we must see that the organisation recruits more women,' she said to Evelyn. 'We can't have only one.' She

21

gave her delightful laugh. 'What happens if the chaps get overtaken by sheer, unstoppable lust?'

'Can't say, Kitty, dear. But if I were you, I would lie back and enjoy it.'

If there was any lust directed at her, Evelyn was not aware of it. She was too exhausted and too busy assimilating the knowledge being crammed into her. Never before had she been required to stretch all her faculties simultaneously and found it exhausting but addictive.

'Plastic explosive – PE – ladies and gentlemen, is cyclonite mixed with a plasticising medium. It is considered one of the safest explosives, but it requires a detonator. It can be moulded into any shape – rather like bread dough for the cooks among us. Choose the most appropriate, according to your chosen target. A factory. Railway line. Bridge. No electricity pylons. They are a waste of time. Most towns and villages have emergency electrical supplies. We are now going to practise working with this medium up the valley. By the way, I am sure I do not need to tell the *bon viveurs* that it is not to be used on the salmon in the river.'

'Number Fourteen,' went the Garramor report, 'is an interesting agent. She analyses her work but needs reassurance. Maturing rapidly. Very friendly with her conducting officer, which suggests she is not quite self-reliant. Expresses anti-Nazi views and is obviously distressed by the situation in France. Sometimes acts a little girlishly. For instance, she has been known to giggle in classes. Has lost her temper once, under provocation. Liked by the men, but she does not go out of her way to attract their attention. However, the subject is very good-looking and is often discussed in the men's quarters. Appears to have developed a friendship with Number Five (John Dunne) which is surprising as they come from entirely different backgrounds. Shaping up well physically.'

'You're going to "finishing school",' Kitty announced towards the end of the Arisaig stay. 'In the south of England.'

'You mean I've got through to the next stage?'

'Yes, dear girl. You have. The final lap.'

Evelyn threw a copy of *Rogue Male* onto her bed and waltzed around the room in her underwear. 'Phew. Congratulate me, Kitty.'

'I do, I do.' Kitty's face darkened a trifle.

'What is it?'

'Nothing.' Kitty shook her dark head. 'You will be careful, won't you? I keep thinking.'

Evelyn laughed and propped herself up at the window sill so that she could look over the still, heathery sweep of the moor outside. 'I will.'

Kitty looked in her handbag for her diary. 'First of all you have to join up as a FANY. This is your cover in England. We will go to London tomorrow to sign the papers and organise details such as pay. You'll need a uniform. Then the chiefs will see you at Orchard Court, where they will brief you and I'm sure they will emphasise your particular responsibility to succeed as a female agent. If you do well then we can begin to recruit more.'

A wistful note in Kitty's voice touched Evelyn. She spoke without turning her head. 'Do *you* want to go, Kitty?'

Her conducting officer grimaced. 'I can't, much as I'd like to. I injured my knee in a skating accident when I was seven and it simply isn't strong enough. At least I'm coming with you as far as "finishing school".'

Evelyn watched a kestrel hover over its prey and swoop down into the heather. 'I'm sorry.' The kestrel rose, holding a black speck between its talons. 'Cheer up. I'll send you some lovely perfume and a Dior evening dress.'

'Don't you dare,' said Kitty. 'You'll get yourself caught. Nice thought though, Number Fourteen,' she added.

'Finishing school' was a house on Lord Montagu's estate at Beaulieu. The agents were not told where it was and only the trusted staff were aware of what was going on. Training was carried out in utmost secrecy, and security was rigid.

It was sweltering and the heat made it uncomfortable in the back of the canvas-covered lorry conveying Evelyn and the others from the railway station to their destination. The agents joked with each other to help pass the journey, carefully avoiding all reference to their previous lives as they had been taught. John sat next to Evelyn and recited passages from

23

Shakespeare in a Texan accent until she was weak with laughter.

On arrival the men were shipped to a house called Vineyards on the grounds of which still grew ancient monastic vines. Kitty and Evelyn were taken to Boarmans, a modern Danish-designed family home complete with pink roses, a tennis court and a horseshoe-shaped lake. From the beginning it was obvious that the instructors at Beaulieu held a strong prejudice against women agents. Or so Evelyn felt. She was conscious that she was being tested harder, watched harder, judged harder.

During the day they learned how to use codes, passwords and disguises, why they needed to be immaculately tidy – to see at a glance if their room had been disturbed – and how to use talcum powder, cotton thread or a dead leaf in a lock to detect intruders.

Instructors showed them how to evade a tail, down subways, side streets and in crowds, and how to use shop windows and mirrors to check if they were being followed. They learnt how to break and enter and were given a crash course in safe breaking.

Agents were taught how to disguise themselves: sponge pads stuffed into the cheeks alter the shape of the face; teeth can be discoloured with iodine, wrinkles emphasised with a lead pencil. With a little ingenuity an agent could appear sunburned one day, pale the next, tall for one occasion, stooped for another. He or she could alternate brands of cigarettes, change mannerisms, adopt different walks and accents.

'I'm enjoying this bit,' John informed Evelyn. For a joke he had made up his face with rouge and a deep red cupid's bow mouth. 'I'm very good as the tart with the heart. Want to look at me knickers?'

'No,' she said, laughing. 'I can't think of anything I'd like less.'

'Well,' he screwed his face into a caricature of Lady Bracknell, 'aren't we hoity-toity?'

Five minutes later he came back dressed as a French peasant, complete with a day's stubble and nicotined fingers.

'How did you do it?' Evelyn was amazed.

'As they say, easy if you know how.'

'German security forces,' students were cautioned by the instructor, 'are confusing because they are several overlapping organisations. The *Abwehr* is the wing attached to the German army, dedicated to military intelligence. The ss is the name of a separate Nazi Party organisation headed by Herr Himmler. Under its umbrella comes the *Sicherheitdienst*, the intelligence department which frequently clashes with *Abwehr*, and the Gestapo, the Party's secret police. ss officers accompany the German army into occupied territory and are responsible for dealing with civilian unrest. The ss also runs its own private army, the *Waffen*-ss, whose soldiers are trained never to surrender.'

The instructor said, 'If you are arrested by the Gestapo or the ss, do not despair. Their reputation is founded on brutality, not on intelligence. But beware their tactics. They will tell you they know all about your training and your colleagues. This is not necessarily so . . .

'Nobody,' the instructor handled this point with care, 'can be expected to remain totally silent under torture. But you must try for at least forty-eight hours. That way you give your circuit time to disperse.'

There were copious notes to take and read through in the evenings – on sending coded messages written in egg white, lemon juice, saliva or urine, how a wireless transmitter worked, Morse, how to organise a network and run the cells within it. Who best to recruit? (Never recruit members from another resistance organisation.) Security procedures. How to find safe houses, *boîtes aux lettres* for messages and how to operate the 'cut-out' system between the cells.

At four thirty one morning Evelyn was woken by men in ss uniform. She was dragged out of bed and made to stand for two hours in the cellar with her hands raised above her head. Each time her arms began to sink she was hit with a truncheon. A barrage of questions was thrown at her. Her nerve almost gave way.

The next night an instructor took her out alone into the New Forest. He showed her how to 'snake crawl' with the body flat on the ground, to 'bear crawl' on hands and knees and to 'commando crawl', a compromise between the two. Each of these had to be done without disturbing the wildlife. He taught her to listen with her mouth open, that night vision is deceptive and that it takes thirty seconds to establish normal sight on coming out of light into darkness. Then he led her round in circles, and left her with the injunction, 'Now get back on your own.'

The night was dark with banks of cloud obscuring the moon. Down in the undergrowth it smelt warm and peaty. Evelyn felt in her battledress pocket for her compass but could not see to read it. She propped herself up against a tree and tried to work out which direction to take. She made out that she was sitting in a clearing surrounded by thickly growing beeches and oaks. To reach a road, any road, it was necessary to walk through them. But which way? Still bruised and stiff from her 'interrogation', she got to her feet.

That walk through the wood was terrifying. Noises in the undergrowth – the rustling of small animals, a stick snapping underfoot – sounded abnormally loud. Convinced that someone was following her, Evelyn kept whipping round. Once she was sure she heard a gun being cocked and flung herself to the ground. It was like her childhood nightmares of being trapped in a pit. Sweat-covered yet cold with fear and nearing exhaustion, she wove through the tree trunks, praying to reach an open space. At last she emerged from the trees, knocking her sore shoulders against an overhanging branch. She sank to her knees against a moss-covered boulder and cried.

When she arrived back at Boarmans, it was with the intention of giving up. But Kitty, wearing striped pyjamas under a man's Paisley silk dressing gown, was waiting up for her. 'Here,' she said, after a shrewd look at her charge. 'Drink this.' She poured some soup out of a Thermos. 'You look as if you've seen the proverbial ghost.'

'I think I have,' Evelyn whispered into the mug. 'My own.' She looked up. 'I'm giving up. That was too much.'

'Nonsense,' said Kitty.

* * *

'For a woman, Number Fourteen has survived a rigorous training very well. She has matured during her stay and demonstrated that she has learnt her lessons thoroughly. We have been surprised by her physical endurance. We are still not convinced that she is capable of undergoing the serious nature of the job or realises what she is going into. We are worried by her age and feel that an older woman would have been a better choice. But she possesses guts, has a convincing French persona, is very willing and has tried hard to curb her faults. Still very friendly with Number Five. We recommend that she progresses to parachute training.'

In the French (F) section at SOE headquarters Evelyn's report was perused and minutely discussed. (Evelyn was not aware that the final decision as to whether or not women agents were to be allowed to go into occupied countries had yet to be taken by the Joint Chiefs of Staff. There were many who felt strongly that women belonged in the house and should confine their non-domestic activities to ambulance-driving and nursing.)

Meanwhile, after a short course near Manchester where she learned to parachute, Evelyn went down to Castle Cary to say goodbye. She was, she explained to the family, being posted to a remote station in Scotland on a hush-hush job. Security made it impossible for her to write to them. But they were not to worry.

'Not to worry!' said Eugénie, her sad eyes filling. She pulled at her hair combs, and her wedding ring slipped round and round her thin finger. 'Oh, Evelyn. Please don't go.' She inspected her daughter. 'You seem different,' she commented. 'Thinner.'

It was true. Evelyn was at peak fitness: the last traces of puppy fat had slithered away, routed by the back-breaking exercise. Aware that her body had changed, Evelyn was delighted by her firmed-up waist and taut thigh muscles. She caught herself looking at men in a new way. Whilst on training she had observed a variety of male knees and thighs, usually hidden beneath trousers. Liberated from their shirts, waistcoats and jackets, male chests seemed much less authoritative and, in some cases, considerably more attractive.

'Do you have to go?' Eugénie was insistent and on the verge of hysteria. 'I don't know what I'll do.'

Evelyn sat down beside her mother. 'Darling. You must make an effort and not give up. Promise me.'

Miserably, Eugénie averted her face. 'You're all I've got,' she whispered.

For the remainder of Evelyn's leave Eugénie took to her bed.

At Orchard Court in Portman Square, Evelyn was given her final briefing and her cover story checked. She would be parachuted in with a wireless operator. They were to join a circuit being set up by an old friend of one of the staff, the Comte de Bourgrave, who lived just inside the occupied zone in the centre of France and had managed to contact the staff via an escaped prisoner-of-war on the run back to England.

An intelligence officer checked Evelyn for incriminating evidence – cinema tickets, letters, photographs – and took charge of her personal possessions. She was issued with her identity papers and ration cards and changed into her carefully prepared French clothes. Then she was driven to Station 61, a house in Huntingdonshire commandeered by SOE, to wait for the flight.

On the journey there was time to reflect. Evelyn thought about how she hated leaving her mother but nevertheless longed for her freedom. She thought about what had happened in the past few months and what was to happen in the next.

She shivered, whether from nerves, fear of the job that lay ahead, the enormity of what she was taking on or disbelief that it was really she, Evelyn St John, embarking on this fantastic enterprise, she did not know.

CHAPTER THREE

'Intense young men', Alison, Lady Chalmers said, leaning over her grouse in red wine sauce, 'are all very well, but they do have this teeny-weeny tendency to be tedious.' The laughter that greeted her observation caused Paul to flush. There he sat, at a silver-laden, linen-draped dining table in a Scottish castle, eighteen years old, visiting Britain for the first time and suffering a pointed social put-down.

'We need to laugh at ourselves more,' Lady Chalmers continued. 'Live with grace. All this nonsense about honour has nothing to do with the real business of living.' She stretched out her neck, well aware that the elasticity of her under-chin was beginning to go, and that she had arrived at an age where her witticisms counted for more than her beauty. 'It's an excuse. It's too simple to fling yourself away. Much cleverer to stay around and make it work.'

Paul had annexed the dinner-table conversation for some time on the subject of dying gloriously for one's country. Lady Chalmers, in a single wounding blow, silenced him, and made him appear a fool. Deep red from humiliation, Paul made an excuse, got to his feet and left the room. However, when he returned he sat down quite coolly, picked up his napkin and began to talk about deer-stalking as if nothing had happened.

It was a manoeuvre that required courage and Lady Chalmers approved. She watched Paul unobtrusively as she sipped her wine and concluded that he had distinct possibilities. She ticked them off: tall, very blond, sensitive face, rather passionate-looking, almost certainly a virgin. She decided to make up for her ruthlessness in her own way, and proceeded to do so later that night.

For ever afterwards, Paul associated Huntley and Palmer's Rich Tea biscuits with his first seduction, which took place in

29

Lady Chalmers's shabbily luxurious bedroom. He remembered very well the white linen sheets that were growing thin and soft with age, a tartan covered day bed, huge eiderdowns, the arctic perimeter of the four-poster bed and, of course, Lady Chalmers herself, extravagantly scented in a peach *crêpe-de-Chine* nightgown.

She had given Paul generous lessons in lovemaking. 'No, no, Paul, you're not storming the Reichstag,' she admonished. 'Not like that, like this.' And Paul had learnt to laugh at himself. He listened and obeyed, and was grateful. Afterwards, Lady Chalmers passed him a plate of Huntley and Palmer's biscuits and said, 'You must be hungry after all that effort.'

Paul forgave Lady Chalmers but did not forget the embarrassment of the dinner table. Never again, he promised, would he make such a fool of himself. Thinking it over, he realised that Lady Chalmers had rendered him a great service. He had committed the cardinal social sin of boring his listeners. Dogmatism and humourlessness were no recipe for life. He set himself to perfect his social manner, and by the time he reached his middle twenties, Lady Chalmers would have considered her lessons well learnt.

There had been three markers in Paul's life. The day of his tenth birthday on which his father handed him a book containing the story of Roland and Oliver, the Lady Chalmers affair, and 5 September 1939, when he regained consciousness on a Polish dirt road with a shattered leg.

Roland and Oliver: the names assumed mystical qualities in Paul's mind. The tale of two medieval knights, bound so strongly in friendship that they perished together at the Ronceval Pass, acted as a powerful stimulant on an imaginative ten-year-old. It generated potent daydreams in which he, Paul von Hoch, became as invincible in battle and as wantonly sacrificial with his life as those knights in the service of the Emperor Charlemagne.

When he discovered the extent of his son's obsession, Graf von Hoch, Paul's father, had not discouraged the boy's ambitions for a military career. He remarked merely that it was harder than Paul supposed to be a good general or even soldier. It took self-discipline as well as physical force.

The Führer took power in January 1933 when Paul was nineteen and fresh from his stay in Britain. Then the Tiergarten in Berlin had been ablaze with white ribbons of fire, marking line after line of brown-shirted, jackbooted men marching in synchronised rhythm to the drumbeats. The torches spluttered, and shouts of 'Führer!' rose above the tumult. Paul had watched, excited and hopeful, imagining that the old divided Berlin – a city of plump bankers and cream cakes, hungry prostitutes plying their trade in cast-off army boots, dazzle and blinding despair, politely applauding opera goers and pitched street battles – was vanishing.

He had been wrong, as his father told him many times, accusing Paul of being taken in by brass bands and cheap sentiment. The young Paul had attended several of Hitler's theatrical rallies and returned deeply impressed. 'But you don't understand, Father,' he argued, still stirred by the drama and the quasi-mysticism of the Chancellor's appeal to the German nation. 'This man can make our country great again.'

'Rubbish,' said Graf von Hoch. 'You'll grow up.' By 1941 a wiser Paul had witnessed the rise of the Nazi state and the surrender of German society into the arms of National Socialism and war. He realised, not without a fight with his pride, that Hitler's dreams were not Germany's salvation.

When the telephone rang on his desk for the nth time that day, Paul allowed it to continue until he had finished writing his sentence. Eventually, he picked it up.

'Paul,' said Ingrid. 'What about dinner?'

'I said I would join you at eight thirty.' His mind on what he was doing, Paul was not really concentrating.

Ingrid was aware that Paul hated to be disturbed at work and she hesitated. 'If you wish,' she said doubtfully. There was a pause while Paul crossed out a word and made a neat substitution. Her voice carried down the line. 'I think we should attend Count von Hummel's reception. It would be wise.'

Ingrid was not going to give up. Paul looked at his watch.

31

Ever vigilant over what she perceived to be his interests, Ingrid was constantly reminding him that he needed to be seen if he was to keep his contacts oiled. She was, of course, right.

'Paul,' she said with a hint of reproof. 'Are you listening?'

'I am,' he replied and put down his pen.

As Count von Hummel was fêted for the manner in which he mixed the political, financial and artistic coteries of Berlin at his lavish receptions, Paul knew it was not sensible to ignore an invitation. He smiled at the image of Ingrid's quivering social antennae, just as his secretary, Fräulein Mitter, put her head round the door. The Fräulein allowed herself to think that Paul's smile was intended for her, and then realised her mistake. She advanced into the room, picked up the pile of papers in Paul's OUT tray and retreated hurriedly.

'Will you pay attention, Paul. Shall I meet you there?'

The telephone had the effect of deepening Ingrid's voice and Paul, lulled by its sleep-inducing timbre as she described the people they would be likely to meet, closed his eyes. Then he roused himself. 'Yes. All right, Ingrid, I'll see you there.'

'Don't forget: dress uniform.'

'Ingrid!' he said with some exasperation, and controlled his urge to put down the telephone. As usual she was pushing at the boundary between intimacy and possessiveness – and in their case, between the possible and the impossible. Paul understood the emotional time-bomb ticking in Ingrid and recognised it as a symptom of war. 'I will see you there,' he said.

But the phone had gone dead. He replaced the receiver, knowing that she would be disappointed by his lack of enthusiasm. The phone rang yet again. Paul picked it up and replied briefly before replacing it and getting up.

He looked round the door to Fräulein Mitter's office. She was typing hard, surrounded by piles of papers coded into different colours. Unclassified. Need to Know. Secret.

Never a beauty and well past the age of romance, Fräulein Mitter had arranged her plaits in a coil around her head. She looked, and was, a perfect product of the local branch of the women's National Socialist organisation, and, as such, he did not trust her. Nevertheless, Paul went out of his way to be kind to her as he pitied what he imagined was a dreary existence.

'You look very charming today, Fräulein Mitter,' he said. She handed him some additional messages and Paul went over to the window to read them. The Tiergarten lay below and he glanced at it as he read, wishing he was outside, strolling past the statue of Empress Augusta Viktoria.

He replaced the messages on the desk and left the room. Fräulein Mitter gazed after him. She always knew when Fräulein Sturmbakker had been bothering him on the phone and she relished a dart of hatred before returning to her typewriter.

Number 76–8 Tirpitzufer, nicknamed the 'fox hole' by its intimates, was not the most suitable building for the headquarters of the Intelligence Service of the Supreme Military Armed Forces Headquarters, the *Abwehr*. Nevertheless, it was the wish of the *Abwehr*'s head, Admiral Canaris, to remain there and, in one important respect, the Admiral's obstinacy was justified. From the Tirpitzufer it was possible to reach the *Wehrmacht* headquarters in neighbouring Bendlestrasse without crossing the street, and it was also strategically placed for access to various foreign and civil bureaux.

Paul knew better than to try the antiquated elevator in the 'fox hole' (the Admiral refused to modernise his headquarters). Instead, he made for one of the badly lit staircases that ran up through the building. Except for a slight limp, he was more or less fit again from a determined programme of summer hikes but by the time he had negotiated the warren of passages, which seemed designed to confuse even those who knew the building well, he was out of breath.

Lieutenant-Colonel von Bentivegni was head of the *Abwehr*'s Section III, responsible for counter-sabotage, counter-espionage and security in matters relating to the armed forces. His brief included the recently formed Group II-N, the detection and prevention of sabotage in all areas of communication, such as the radio, telegraph and postal services. He looked up as Paul entered. He was, as usual, immaculate.

33

'I apologise for calling you up,' he said, removing his monocle, 'but I wished for a private word.'

Paul waited. Von Bentivegni was an old friend of his father, and theirs was a friendship that never ceased to amuse those who knew them. On the one hand, his father, an outspoken liberal, utterly opposed to Adolf Hitler, on the other, von Bentivegni, a Potsdamer with substantial military connections and a Prussian's sense of duty.

It was a friendship that yielded practical results, in that it benefited Paul, who at twenty had taken his father's advice and set about establishing a military career. Von Bentivegni was able to put in a word for him after he passed out from cadet school close to the top of his class, and ensured that his protégé was sent to train in wireless and radio communications. It has been astute planning. Paul had chosen to specialise in the area where the greatest developments were taking place.

After the course he was assigned a post under the command of General Guderian. An innovator and military genius, the General, by grasping the simple truth that communications were the key to victory in a modern army, transformed the strike power and the effectiveness of the new German army. By now a junior officer in a Panzer division of the General's 19th Corps, Paul witnessed just how devastating was a division of fast armoured tanks in constant radio contact.

When Germany invaded Poland on 1 September 1939, Paul was commanding a Panzer tank in one of Guderian's ten divisions, which struck hard across the base of the Polish corridor towards Kulm. The Poles fought like gladiators, suicidally brave, defending their border on horseback and on foot but were no match for the flexible radio-controlled units that harried and wheeled, encircled and destroyed.

One evening, the corps had halted near a cornfield whose late crop was still standing. The waist-high corn was beginning to rot. Behind it lay the remains of a farmhouse. Paul climbed out from the Panzer and walked a little way up the road to make a reconnaissance when the explosion occurred.

The Pole had used the corn to hide his progress as he inched his way forward, belly down and clutching a grenade.

At the last moment he leapt to his feet and ran towards the tank. He threw his missile into the open turret and in the resulting explosion was himself blown to bits.

One minute Paul was checking a map reference. The next he was on the ground, his head pillowed in his corporal's lap. Stranger still, his mind was crystal clear. He knew who he was and where he was; he knew his head was covered in blood and that something serious had happened to his leg.

Poor Father, Paul often reflected as he convalesced. How will he reconcile himself to the flaws in his beloved sons? First Otto, with a weak chest that left him unable to fight, and now himself. At least he had the Iron Cross to show for it.

'You have received your orders?' Von Bentivegni had now finished what he was doing and was ready to talk to Paul.

'Yes, sir. I am going to France at the end of the week.'

'Are you happy about that?' Von Bentivegni was shrewder than he sometimes looked. He understood very well Paul's disappointment at no longer being active.

'Sir, I'm delighted.'

'Never mind the waffle,' said the Colonel. (Paul had always admired his lack of humbug.) 'I know you're disappointed that you are no longer an officer in combat.'

Von Bentivegni was not a man to waste time over regrets. When it became clear that Paul could not return to his old post, he summoned him to dinner, lectured him on making the most of what there is, and recruited him into the *Abwehr*. 'Why ever not?' he had said to Graf von Hoch. 'The boy has a first-class brain and natural logic. He should get on with it and stop moping.'

'Yes, sir,' said Paul.

'I expect some good results from you, Paul,' said his mentor. 'There will be plenty to do. You understand that it is unlikely that all the French will settle down and say "thank you for coming". In fact, quite the reverse. Lots of them will be plotting away in their garlic-smelling cottages and *châteaux* to make life as difficult as possible. If by any chance these types know what they are doing, they will go for the obvious targets – railways, etc. But they will also consider targets in your brief – radio communications. Naturally, your cover as officer in charge of radio communications for the garrison in Ribérac will allow you to keep an eye on these potential dangers. I realise you might have wanted Paris but I need a first-class man in the centre of France. You are to be promoted to major.'

'Yes, sir.'

The Colonel went over to the cabinet by the wall and extracted from it a bottle and two glasses. 'In memory of a fine Moselle I drank with your father, we will share this bottle. Congratulations, Paul.'

The wine was bitter yellow in the glass but tasted magnificent. Von Bentivegni poured himself a second glass. 'Loyalty is the primary duty, wouldn't you agree, Major von Hoch?'

Paul hesitated. 'Yes, Colonel, but it is not so simple. I am loyal to my country and to my commanding officer. But as a patriot—'

'I see.' Von Bentivegni cut him short. He was not going to allow Paul to voice dangerous sentiments. 'In my opinion there is a distinction to be made between "positive" intelligence, such as we in the *Abwehr* specialise in – the gathering of information about armed forces and in wartime about foreign political and economic affairs – and "negative" intelligence, such as monitoring the activities of the civilian population. Intellectuals, Jews . . . Ours, I would say, is the more legitimate work for a German patriot.'

'Of course,' said Paul. Von Bentivegni was giving him a warning: coded, oblique, but insistent none the less. It said: we in the *Abwehr* must beware the SD, the *Sicherheitdienst*, created as the security section of Himmler's SS with particular responsibility for promulgating Hitler's National Socialism in the Third Reich. Primarily concerned with controlling the private thoughts of citizens, it acts in conjunction with the Gestapo as a guardian of Germany's moral well-being. It is also destined, in the ambitions of SS-Obergruppenführer Reinhard Heydrich, the Reich's Central Security Department chief, to become the all-embracing intelligence service of the Third Reich.

'Our colleagues in the SD,' Paul said carefully, 'are not our natural allies.'

'Quite,' said von Bentivegni. 'The SD are watching us. It is my opinion that they wish to take control of all foreign intelligence matters, swallowing the *Abwehr* in the process. I wished you to know that.'

Ingrid had been waiting in the ballroom of the Kaiserhof Hotel for well over half an hour before Paul arrived. To all appearances she was engaged in flirting with a couple of admirers but she was waiting all the same.

As Paul was taller than most, it was easy to catch sight of him as soon as he arrived. He stood in the doorway looking round him and she was reminded for the hundredth time of a drawing she had once seen but could not remember where. She had searched for it in books and in galleries. Its memory, tantalising and elusive, haunted her for she had the extraordinary conviction that it contained the key to Paul.

Ingrid was the sort of person who held many such superstitions: 'If I wear this dress, I'm bound to win at cards.' 'If I find this picture, Paul will marry me.'

Tonight Paul looked blond and tanned from a holiday at home in Koblenz to which she had not been invited. Ingrid's hand strayed to the gold embroidery on her dress (Strassner's black crêpe and a sweetheart neckline, bought in an extravagant moment and at the cost of her coupon supply), and rubbed the thread between her fingers until they smarted.

As she was born into circles where beautiful interiors were commonplace, the magnificence of the setting was of secondary interest. She was far more interested in assessing the social composition of the evening. While she chatted to an aspiring novelist who was trying to impress her, her attention focused on who else was in the ballroom tonight: the Metternichs, Loulou de Vilmorin, Gottfried von Bismarck, Ulrich von Hassell. Ingrid possessed superlative and predatory social skills – a word here, introduction there, flattery precisely aimed – and she deployed them instinctively. Few could resist the combination of her seductive voice and fragile blondeness when she turned her attention on them. Her name was seldom absent from the best guest lists. The older, married men liked her and told her stories, insisting on inviting her to their dinners. Their wives tended to concur at Ingrid's sweetness. The younger set invited her skiing, to weekends in *Schlosses* and sought invitations to her informal parties at her chic apartment.

Ingrid had only once made a big mistake, which was to fall in love with a married man. The liaison had been public and stormy. Her lover had not wished the affair to end but Ingrid, sensing shrewdly that time was not on her side if she wanted to make a good marriage, had been adamant. The episode had left her considerably more wary.

Her peace of mind had been further shattered when she met Paul. She knew instantly that he was the man she would like to marry.

'Fräulein von Sturmbakker.' A voice broke into her conversation. 'You look ravishing.'

Ingrid automatically deepened the hollows at her collarbones by pushing forward her shoulders. Then she saw who it was. 'Hauptsturmführer Gehrbrandt! How nice. Are you well?'

'In excellent health, Fräulein. I was hoping I would see you.'

Ingrid repressed her distaste and kept on smiling with practised ease. She did not want to see Siegfried Gehrbrandt. His glacial presence visibly deflated the would-be novelist, who withered and bowed himself out of the conversation. Ingrid turned to Gehrbrandt. 'That was unkind.'

'Speak for yourself, Ingrid. You were obviously not enjoying the poor man's company, and I thought I would rescue you. You should be grateful.'

As he spoke, the insignia on his black uniform caught her eye and reminded Ingrid that the young man whom she had once helped with a timely introduction to a member of the Nazi Party was now a rising member of the ss. In days gone by, Ingrid would have shaken him off with a curt dismissal, but now it was different. Instead she asked, 'Have you seen Paul? I was about to go in search of him.'

'Aha,' said Gehrbrandt. 'A dinner arrangement, no doubt, and I was about to ask— '

'*À deux*, Siegfried, I'm afraid.'

'Poor Ingrid,' said Gehrbrandt, who divined many of

Ingrid's wishes and was malicious as well as ambitious. 'Ever hopeful.'

Paul brought out the worst in Gehrbrandt. Even so, Ingrid put all her art into maintaining her smile and prayed that he would not see that his words had found their mark. Gehrbrandt, however, was in a mood to tease.

'A second son, Ingrid, and not much money. Some brains I grant you, but only a staff officer. It won't do, dearest girl. Now look at me. Money,' he was the recent beneficiary of the estate left by an aunt, 'a trusted member of the Party and an ss officer with prospects. Wouldn't you rather it was me you were seen dining with?'

'No, she wouldn't,' said Paul, appearing at Gehrbrandt's elbow. 'Shall we go, Ingrid? I'm hungry.'

Gehrbrandt did not appear to hear what Paul said for he hailed a waiter and handed them both fresh glasses of champagne. 'Then we must drink to the progress of the war. May the best man win.' Paul raised an eyebrow at the crudeness of Gehrbrandt's challenge and slipped his arm through Ingrid's. 'Of course,' went on Gehrbrandt, after he had drunk half his wine, 'it's no contest. Look at the war in the west. The French are too venial to resist us and the British have been neutralised and have no allies. Anyway, it'll take them a long time to recover after their poor showing at Dunkirk.'

'Actually,' remarked Paul quietly, 'I think the Führer admires the British. Tell me, Siegfried, what do you think about Soviet Russia?'

Gehrbrandt shot him a look. 'My dear Major von Hoch, the Russians are our enemy. *Untermenschen*. We will soon beat them.'

'Yes,' replied Paul. Hitler's attack on Russia, his former ally, in June of that year had been a surprise to everybody as well as to Stalin. Ingrid gave his hand a warning pinch which said: Don't go on.

'We all have faith in the Führer.' Gehrbrandt was alert and fox-like beside Paul's slightly rakish elegance.

'You know as well as I do, Siegfried, that we have to consider the practical aspects of war. Germany will have to supply her armies, maintain her fronts, fuel her tanks and machinery and still keep the factories running and feed her population. Our resources will be at full stretch – particularly as we no longer obtain supplies from Russia.'

Ingrid broke in. 'Paul, it is getting late.'

Gehrbrandt knew precisely why Ingrid was trying to finish the conversation. He was quite used to people becoming nervous in his presence. With a snap of his heels, he bowed over her hand. 'I trust he is taking you somewhere suitable, my dear.'

They left Gehrbrandt standing in the colourful crowd, his black uniform etched against the gold and white of the elaborate Kaiserhof interior.

'I don't like him,' said Ingrid in the vestibule as Paul draped her evening wrap around her shoulders.

'Why should you? Just because you helped to advance his career doesn't mean you should like each other.'

'It's more than that.' Ingrid snuggled into the wrap and checked that no one was listening. 'I think he's dangerous.'

'Don't worry about him,' said Paul, who understood Gehrbrandt. Almost certainly the man was looking for an eligible wife who would help him in the realisation of his ambitions. 'Incredible though it may seem to someone as beautiful and well connected as yourself, one does encounter hostility from time to time.'

'Be serious, Paul.' Ingrid was uncharacteristically sharp.

'I am serious,' he replied, refusing to be taken by her mood. 'I'm seriously thinking of dinner.'

She allowed him to settle her into the passenger seat of his Mercedes and remained quiet while he drove them very fast to the restaurant. She did not want to pick a quarrel tonight.

Horcher's was full of diners allowing themselves rein over the restaurant's famed cuisine. Ingrid sat down and waited for her napkin to be put in place by the waiter. On their left, a uniformed ss officer attacked a lobster while his heavily ringed companion toyed with breast of chicken. Paul raised a finger in acknowledgement to a couple of colleagues across the room.

He moved the vase of lilies from the centre of the table so that he could see Ingrid properly. He enjoyed taking her out to dinner for very simple reasons: they shared a common interest in good food, she was a charming dinner companion and, of course, she was beautiful.

Tonight she had taken particular pains, and he was aware she had on a new dress. It complemented her white skin, red lipstick and the golden hair covered in a gold net. A beautifully crafted study in black and gold.

Ingrid was aware of the effect she was achieving; the only jarring note was the anxious expression in the blue eyes under their Vaselined lids. Not for the first time, Paul found himself thinking that she would inevitably be hurt. She did not deserve it. She was kind, loyal and capable of great love.

'Fish tonight?' he asked her.

Ingrid laid down her menu. 'It's not true,' she said suddenly. 'You do have money.'

Paul leant back on the red plush. 'Ingrid, you mustn't let Siegfried nettle you,' he said, rather amused. 'Yes, my family have been lucky, and I've no need to worry. Unless things go wrong, of course.'

Ingrid picked up the discarded menu. 'I think I will have the sole.' She paused while Paul made up his mind. 'Darling, what will you do after the war?' She looked at the gold signet ring he wore on his little finger, and then at her own ringless fingers. She was holding the menu so tight that her knuckles had whitened.

'I might study law,' he replied, 'or I've been thinking I might venture into politics.'

'And if we lose the war?' she asked under her breath.

He took his time to reply. 'Let's just say, Ingrid, that we must not lose the war.'

Ingrid had never been able to read Paul's thoughts or even get half-way to divining them. The knowledge depressed her and made her feel lost. It shrivelled the confidence she displayed with others. Paul was generous, unfailingly courteous, attentive, polished – and somehow utterly detached. He never allowed Ingrid to glimpse what he was really feeling or told her his thoughts. On the rare occasions when she felt she *had* negotiated a way past the barrier, such as the first time they slept together, she failed yet again to reach the hidden Paul.

41

'Do you love me?' she had asked into the dark, feeling that she had earned the right.

'I think you are one of the most beautiful women I know,' he had replied, and Ingrid had turned her face away into the pillows.

'Then why aren't you with one of Berlin's other beautiful women?'

Paul did not respond immediately. 'Because you attract me very much and we are honest with one another.'

She had not dared tell him how much this hurt her. Because she loved him, Ingrid was determined that if suffering was necessary, she would suffer. She possessed several advantages: her body, her social poise and her family home, and she planned to use them.

'Paul . . .'

He put down his knife and fork and drank some wine. Over the glass, his eyes quizzed her face. 'You want to talk to me about something, I can tell. The new dress.'

The kindness in his face made Ingrid wince.

'Von Hoch.'

One of Paul's colleagues came across to their table. 'Come and see me before you leave, my friend.' He laid a hand affectionately on Paul's shoulder. 'I have a report on the French situation which I would like you to read.'

Holding his napkin, Paul half rose. 'Will it keep me awake at night, Franz?'

'A riveting bedtime story of Communists, Pétainists and an upstart general called de Gaulle. You'll be kept busy working it all out. The Communists are the worst. Personally, I feel you should watch de Gaulle. The British may come round to him and give him their backing.'

He gave a bow in Ingrid's direction and returned to his table. Ingrid picked up her evening bag and felt for her cigarettes, managing at the same time to take a quick look at herself in the mirror on its inside flap. Paul leant over with his lighter and she blew a stream of smoke into the air.

'Paul, as I am older than you – '

'Good God, only by two months,' he interrupted.

Two months can seem like two decades, and Ingrid was,

as she often told herself, a woman of twenty-seven years and two months. 'I have decided to exact the privileges of the elder,' she continued, before her nerve vanished.

'Ingrid,' said Paul quickly, 'are you sure you want to go on?' He knew at once what was coming. They had held this conversation a couple of times during the last six months and both times she had been badly upset.

'I want you to marry me.'

He held up his hand to make her stop. Ingrid reached over the table and pushed it way. 'You will listen to me, Paul. Just this once.' She was almost ugly with determination. 'When I inherit Silberbirchen from my parents . . .'

Silberbirchen was the Sturmbakker estate. Paul knew it very well. Built around a wide courtyard containing a three-tiered fountain, its gardens were so perfectly designed that to move one shrub would destroy the whole. There was a panelled dining room and a library. There were marble statues in the garden, English chintz curtains in the windows and ticking clocks on the mantelpieces. The smell in the house was of wax, tobacco and juniper mixed with rose and leather.

'I know,' he said.

'I have never asked you this straight out before, Paul. My parents are getting old and Silberbirchen will need a new master. Not just anyone – but someone who will love it. I think that person should be you. I, of course, come with Silberbirchen.'

Ingrid needed to go no further. She lit a second cigarette and waited. 'No,' Paul said, and took one of her hands between his. 'No, Ingrid, it just isn't possible.'

She pulled her hand away with a jerk and traced a circle on the white cloth with one red nail. 'Can I ask why?' She saw that he was retreating behind his polite mask. Determined to prevent him, she demanded, 'You at least owe me the truth.'

She looked up and knew with a sick feeling that she had made a mistake. The familiar inscrutable expression had slipped back over his face.

'Why, Paul?' she almost cried. 'Why can't you marry me?'

'Ingrid, there is a war on. It isn't fair to embark on marriage at the moment. Anything might happen.'

'Is that the truth?' she persisted, knowing that it was not.

'I am touched that you have made me the offer of Silberbirchen— '

'Why reject it, then? Paul, think. We come from the same sort of background, we move in the same circles, our tastes are similar— '

'Ingrid, marriage can't be just a question of property or business interests.'

'Very often it is,' she flashed back at him.

'Not for me,' he said and picked up his wine glass. He was angry and she knew it. The urge to rub salt into her wound became too much for Ingrid.

'It's because you don't love me, isn't it?'

He had once told Ingrid that their relationship was an honest one. Tonight it should be no different but he hesitated to inflict more pain. 'Not enough, Ingrid,' he said, very gently. 'What we have is delightful and I treasure it, but it does not include marriage . . . I thought you understood.'

How could she ever change the smooth, impenetrable face that Paul chose to turn on her? How could she puncture that detachment? What art, what spell, what black magic could she invoke to bring him to his knees? With the desperation of a trapped animal, Ingrid realised she had nothing.

'Paul, stop!' she blurted, terrified that she had gone too far.

'Wouldn't it be better if our affair ended, Ingrid? If you are thinking like this, then I must not allow it to continue. It would not be honourable.'

'Well, if you imagine no woman thinks of marriage, then you are stupid,' she said, on the verge of tears. 'Damn honour.'

Paul gave a shout of laughter and pushed back his chair. In the candlelight his hair turned darker gold. He reached for his cigarettes. Ingrid took a deep breath and lit another, proud that her hand did not shake. The smoke grazed its way down to her lungs and she welcomed the sensation.

'You win,' she said. Pain was infinitely preferable to the

thought of losing Paul. 'I understand the rules. We're both adults.'

They went back to the Rauchstrasse after the meal, which had ended with both of them drinking their cognac in silence. Ingrid had taste and her apartment was decorated with a charming mixture of antiques and modern paintings. She had chosen pink silk lampshades for the bedroom and they threw a rose light on her skin as she undressed. In contrast to her small waist, her buttocks were full and her thighs white and heavy. Paul lay back on the bed.

'Ingrid, if you find anyone else when I am gone, you must forget about me,' he said.

Ingrid climbed onto the bed and straddled his body. He relaxed. She had learnt her arts from a skilled lover and he allowed her to have her way. Her face hung over his, the lipstick on her mouth running into little lines which gave her a blurred, sensual look. Her hair streamed down over her shoulders. He ran his fingers up the damp arms and pulled her down towards him. Her mouth hovered above his.

'Please, Paul. I will love and honour you, and even allow you to have your distractions. I won't mind.'

For a second he was sickened by her need and considered leaving for good. Then he rolled over, pushed her down into the pillows and bent over to silence her.

CHAPTER FOUR

The twin-engined Whitley banked. Evelyn felt sick but tried to smile at her companion. Since the feeble lights in the fuselage went out at that moment, her efforts were lost on him. A burst of gunfire from the rear gunner juddered through the plane. She had been warned by the young pilot at the secret RAF base at Tempsford to expect a few high jinks over the Channel, and this she supposed was them.

'We'll fly low till we reach the coast, and then I'll shoot the old girl up to seven thousand feet to avoid the flak. We can't go higher without oxygen. After that I'll drop low again to avoid enemy fighter planes. Also, the rear gunner will test the guns over the drink just to make sure everything's in working order,' he had said, pulling on his flying jacket over a jersey and dark trousers.

They had been briefed in the farmhouse at the end of the runway and kitted out with parachutes and overalls in the adjacent barn. The briefing officer checked Evelyn's cover story. 'Your code name is Alouette, to be used only in communication with us. Your field name is Violette, and the alias or cover you are operating under is Evelyn Liegaux,' he reiterated for the final time. He took a small box down from the shelf. 'Here are tablets to keep you going if you need to go without sleep. These are knock-out ones and this . . .' He handed Evelyn a single colourless capsule. 'This is lethal.' She stared at it, with a tight feeling at the back of her throat, and then put them all into her bag. 'One more thing.' The briefing officer held out a small package. 'This is from the staff. It's a good-luck present.'

It was a gold powder compact, carefully dulled and bearing no incriminating hallmark. 'Thank you,' she said.

'You are to pawn it if you need to.'

'Maps. Francs. Compass. Chocolate . . . all there. Just in case,' the pilot explained. 'That's why I wear civvies under my uniform.'

Evelyn imagined that the dim electric light in the room would hide her expression, but he peered forward and scrutinised her face.

'Don't worry,' he said. 'Nothing will go wrong.'

She had busied herself with the harness, not wishing him to see her fright. 'I'm not used to flying.'

Nothing will go wrong, Evelyn repeated to herself as she climbed up into the Whitley's long flat fuselage, holding a packet of sandwiches and a Thermos of rum-spiked coffee.

The plane dropped height and her protesting stomach was left far behind. A torch flashed beside her in the gloom.

'Coffee?' enquired John. Evelyn stretched out her hand and a beaker was pushed into it. 'Not quite the Ritz,' he said, 'but not far off.'

They were lying on top of the bomb bay of the specially adapted Whitley. Wearing parachute harnesses over flying suits and their clothes, Evelyn and John were propped up against the side of the aircraft like beached whales. Since it appeared to fly with its nose slightly dipped, their position was not comfortable. The fuselage reeked of oil and had an odd, tinny smell which did nothing to alleviate Evelyn's nausea. Swaying from a hook above her was John's radio set packed into its foam-rubber bag. Stacked underneath it were four metal containers expertly packed with guns, explosives, cigarettes, chocolate and coffee.

The plane banked to the left and banged up against an air pocket which set its body shuddering. At its stern, the rear gunner adjusted the revolving gun turret and scanned the sky for enemy aircraft. A partition hid the cockpit. A breezy dispatching sergeant, whose job was to prepare them to jump, squeezed up against the bodywork on her left.

She took a mouthful of coffee and burnt her tongue. It was an oddly reassuring sensation and brought her back to normality as she was in danger of suspending belief that she was on her way to occupied France. The coffee was good and the rum settled her stomach. She drank it all and kept the tin beaker between her hands for a minute to warm them.

'Where are we, do you think?' she asked.

The dispatching sergeant craned his head round towards the cockpit and then looked at his watch. 'About half-way there, ma'am, I'd say.'

Evelyn passed the beaker back to John and heard him pour some out for himself. He drank with gusto. 'All I need now is smoked salmon sandwiches and perhaps a touch of Blue Beluga.'

The sergeant laughed. Some of these specials were right cards. He leant over. 'I think you should try to sleep, sir, and you, ma'am. It's always wise.'

I quite like being called sir, thought John, enjoying his new rank. He had no intention of joining the army but since agents were required to have a British cover they were issued with a rank. John, much to his amusement, was not a full captain. He lay back on a pile of blankets. Evelyn felt for the canvas package to her right and pushed it under her head. She closed her eyes. The aircraft engines grew louder, and the creak of the wireless transmitter swinging back and forth on its straps more insistent. Then the noise faded.

In the cockpit, Flight-Lieutenant Quine adjusted the throttle. His hands were sweaty on the ivory control handles and he wiped them on the legs of his flying suit. Quine felt a great deal less confident than he had appeared earlier. He wished he had more experience of this sort of work. He leant forward on the green leather seat to look out of the window. Back home they would be plotting his flight – singletons, they were called, lone aircraft that nobody was supposed to know about, which pushed their way over to the Continent in unfrequented air corridors.

The moonlight was patchy tonight. Quine screwed up his eyes in an effort to sight the Loir and get his navigational fix.

'Come on.' He spoke to the moon as she slid away yet again. 'I need you to see the river. Give us a break.'

Quine had checked the flak map when plotting his flight at the Tempsford base and he was pretty sure that if he kept Angers (at the junction of the Loire and the Loir) to his right, he would be in the clear. He did not fancy the prospect of being brought down in France's occupied zone. Especially if there were 'bods' on board.

Captured 'bods' would result in nasty business for all concerned. Quine would have the advantage of being able to claim prisoner-of-war status but if you were a 'bod' in civvies Jerry reckoned he could do more or less what he liked with you. Quine had heard in the mess a few stories of what the Gestapo got up to.

As if on cue, the moon sailed out from behind her cloud cover and the river unfolded beneath the Whitley. Quine trimmed his speed and dropped height to fly low along the river until Tours was in his sights. Then he headed south towards Angoulême, keeping just inside the occupied zone.

The change in engine note woke up John and Evelyn simultaneously.

'Keeping the pecker up?' John pushed back the loose piece of webbing that flapped around his head.

'Fine,' she replied cautiously.

The webbing flapped forward into John's face.

'Blimey,' said John. 'This is worse than playing Oedipus.'

Nerves made Evelyn giggle. 'What *are* you talking about?'

'Masks, darling girl. I seem to have spent my entire bloody life hiding behind them.'

John sometimes considered ironing out the frequent expletives in his language but then concluded that nobody much minded. It was only to be expected from an actor as motley and mercurial as he and anyway, it was too much like hard work to erase the habit of a lifetime. There was no point adding to his problems, which had started young.

At fourteen John had not meant to make such a thorough job of running away from home. All he had wanted to do was give his mum a fright. After one of their fights he boarded the boat-train at Victoria for a lark, meaning to return that night. Fate ordained that a famous French actor-manager was on the train returning to Paris. He saw John and liked what he saw. A thin, mobile-featured youth, who would never be tall but who possessed a definite charm. The actor-manager cast forth a lure and John, not wishing to be chicken-hearted, made up a story about being an orphan and allowed himself to be swept to Paris.

In a not-very-successful theatre with stained red velvet curtains and disintegrating seats, he had been taught the trade – and also seduced by the actor-manager's wife. Since the episode was conducted with skill and sensitivity, and John was curious, he had enjoyed it. Over a time, he embarked on several affairs. One in particular. By the time he considered he should return to England, it was too late. He had written once or twice but the letters never seemed to get posted, and it appeared that his parents had packed up their two-bedroom terraced house and vanished, leaving no forwarding address. John had no idea how to trace them.

He had gone back to Paris. Working for his actor-manager in the Pigalle, he lived in a garret and rapidly became fluent in Parisian *argot*. He developed a Pollyanna-ish attitude: everything happens for the best. If he had remained at number 2, Louisville Road, Brixton, for example, Fate would never have thrown Minou at him.

How could you describe Minou? John sometimes tried to write about her, usually after the late performance at a table covered in wilting stubs of Leichner's 5 and 9 and always failed.

Minou appeared to model herself on the writer Colette in her earlier music-hall days. Sharp pointy chin, large fathomless eyes, hair cut in a thick fringe and a penchant for striped sailor's shirts. But John knew Minou would not have known about Colette because Minou was a prostitute who could barely read. Maybe it was the Colette-like composition in the blood of some French women – cat's eyes and an aura of flagrant sexuality.

Coming from a family of ten crammed into a tenement in the old port of Marseille, Minou had not been given much choice about how she earned her bread. It also had to be said that she took to her profession. She enjoyed it and did it well. Minou was always clean – her clients were made to wash too – perfumed with cheap scent, her clothes darned and her hair brushed. When she accepted a client she reckoned to give good value. She said the right things and moaned appreciatively in the right places. Clients loved her, felt better for their visit and returned. One or two tried to beat her up but they did not repeat the exercise. Minou was well guarded.

John had been hiking around Provence when he met Minou in a waterfront bar in the old quarter of Marseille. It was one of her rare free nights and she was sitting at a table eating *bouillabaisse*. He watched her little teeth nip the pieces of fish and suck at the squid in a manner that made him catch his breath. When she saw John standing rather awkwardly in the entrance, Minou waved as if she knew him. So he went over. Within moments he too was eating, picking over the bones in companionable silence. After the meal, Minou took him drinking; Pernod clouded the rest.

When John awoke the next morning, the sun shone through the latticed shutters in bright hard bars and his head felt as if it was about to drop off. Minou lay beside him, her pointy chin turned away, her feline eyes hooded by feathery lashes. She looked soft, young and peaceful. John bent over her sleeping body and kissed her uncovered shoulder. Minou woke up.

John put his case so fervently that he almost believed it himself when he told Minou that she would like being a housewife in England. She protested over and over that love did not come into it, but, if it helped, she loved him more than anyone. Nevertheless, she was not going to change her life on the streets.

Minou had not told him about Floret. Looking back, John should have known. Every whore has a pimp and Marseille bred a fine line in the latter. Pimps could be violent and they could weep over their sick mother but they never mixed business with pleasure. Love did not enter the arena. Money did, and Minou earned good money. Floret knew perfectly well there were a good few years in Minou before drink or disease took over and he wanted a return on his investment. When John found out about Floret, Minou begged him to leave. 'If you loved me you would do as I ask,' she screamed at him, frightened that Floret would do him some harm. 'Go. I don't want to live in London. I love it here, don't you understand? Here, with the water and the sun.'

'Please, Minou,' he begged. 'Give yourself a chance. Give *me* a chance.'

But Minou was adamant.

Ever after, John wondered if he had done the right thing, or indeed if it had been what Minou really desired. Years later, after a particularly dreary tour of the Midlands, he nerved himself to go back to Marseille. Nobody was eager to talk – they disliked strangers in the old town – but eventually a bartender released a snippet of information: *'Elle est morphineuse.'*

After that, it was back to provincial theatres and shabby lodgings. Edinburgh, Margate, Weston-Super-Mare, Birmingham. John's career never shone. He was competent enough, sometimes made his audience laugh and sometimes he moved them, but he never achieved fame. In a funny way, he was quite content; the episode with Minou had taken away much of his ambition. He was never again to feel so intensely about anything.

So the years went by until 1941. One night he was drinking in a Soho bar. He started to sing a risqué little French number – a ditty full of complicated sexual innuendo – and a chap in a grey pinstripe suit sat up. Within two weeks, John was travelling down to Wanborough Manor.

Once again the Whitley lurched and John fell against Evelyn. 'Masks? Oedipus?' she asked, puzzled.

'Oh dear! I shouldn't be saying anything about my torrid past,' said John. 'I shall fall as silent as Ligeia's tomb.'

Evelyn would have liked to know more. 'Any more sandwiches?'

John searched the sandwich tin. 'You're in luck.'

She ate it thoughtfully; it might be some time before they got another meal.

'It's no use.' John was fumbling at his layers of clothing. 'Close your eyes, darling.'

'What's the matter?'

'Nature calls. I'm sacrificing the Thermos.' After a few moments he sighed with relief. 'That's better. I think it's stage fright.'

John noticed Evelyn early on at Wanborough Manor. Sheltered upbringing, he concluded, sensing her insecurity. But he found her excitement infectious and rather charming and went out of his way to smooth over for her some of the more awkward surprises of being pitchforked into a crowd of strangers. In the evenings, they would take their whisky out into the walled garden to watch the sun disappear behind the Hog's Back. The skies were pink with early summer and the slopes of the hill were thick with cow parsley and rosebay willow-herb. A grassy smell rose from the warm garden. 'Will we remember this, do you think?' Evelyn asked one night.

'No,' replied John, teasing. 'I think we'll be dreaming of bacon and eggs.'

Evelyn giggled.

At Arisaig, one of the instructors – a big, brawny American who had wheedled his way into SOE long before the Americans came into the war – had fancied Evelyn in a mild way. He took extra trouble to ensure she could handle a gun with as much ease as a powder compact – Vickers, MG34 and 42 ('the Spandau to you guys'), Schmeissers, Lugers, the tommy gun and, of course, the Sten. John had enjoyed watching this shy, polite *ingénue* metamorphose into a brigand who walked off with the shooting honours.

Fire power was not John's forte. Neither had he felt attracted to the stabbing, garrotting and suchlike activities which seemed to be expected of him. Physical agility was not his bag either. Scaling walls, leaping up trees and trekking for miles up some bloody mountain were, in his view, counterproductive. Where he did score was at the wireless training. He even enjoyed working out the schedules – 'skeds', as they were known. He had a good ear and a natural gift for Morse configurations. Once he donned earphones, tuned the set and curled his index finger over the transmitter key, he felt at home.

He looked up at the swaying wireless set and wondered how soon it would be before he and Evelyn were put to the test. Judging by the preparations being made by the sergeant, it would not be very long.

'John . . .' Evelyn leant over. 'John . . .' She was giggling again. 'Don't forget to tell the sergeant.'

'Tell him what?'

'About the Thermos. They might fancy some coffee on the way back.'

Quine spoke into his headset. In response, the dispatching sergeant eased himself over towards Evelyn and indicated that he wished to attach the automatic-opening strop of her harness which would ensure her parachute opened. She watched him, knowing that she was about to jump out into the cold dark air a thousand feet above France. Having checked the strop, the sergeant fastened the line which held her extra baggage onto her leg strap and showed Evelyn that both were correctly in place. 'Remember that when the line slackens you will have three seconds or so before landing.'

He moved on to John and attached the wireless's webbing to John's harness. He gave the thumbs-up signal to Evelyn over the sergeant's head. The sergeant crawled towards the exit door and pulled back the cover. Moonlight flooded in and a stream of thin, cold air invaded the oily-smelling fuselage.

Evelyn wished she had been awake when they had flown over Tours. She would have liked to have thought of her grandparents and cousins asleep down below. Under her flying suit, she went cold and shivered. If any of them had the remotest idea of what she was doing . . .

John touched her arm. '*Merde*,' he shouted over the roar of air and engines, using the traditional French slang for 'good luck'.

Evelyn blinked back at him in the uncertain light. '*Merde*,' she mouthed back. 'All the best.'

'Good girl.'

The Whitley circled and a red light appeared on the roof above them. The sergeant raised his arm and Evelyn shifted into place behind John.

'There they are,' shouted the sergeant.

'Five hundred feet,' said Quine into the headset.

The red light turned to green. The sergeant brought down his arm and John disappeared. Evelyn swung her legs over the 'Joe's hole' and flexed her hands on the edge. Below her, three points of light were flashing.

'Go,' yelled the sergeant.

Forgetting to worry about her face hitting the opposite edge of the hole, she pushed against the plane's protective fuselage and fell into space. A blast of air caught her and the Whitley's underbelly slid away. The whine of its engines drifted back for a while as she dropped and then suddenly all was quiet. Almost immediately her parachute opened with a jerk. It sounded like sheets flapping on a washing line. Evelyn reached up with her hands as she had been instructed and grabbed the webbing.

Currents of air slapped her face and buffeted the harness, and she swung like a marionette on a string. The moonlight grew brighter and whiter and spread its silver over a silent landscape below. She squinted to get a better look and made out a shape floating on her right. After the plane, the peace was extraordinary.

The torches flickered through the darkness under her feet. Her panoramic view narrowed. She was floating down into a clearing surrounded by dark trees that sucked her towards the earth. The lights grew brighter. There was a burst of conversation and someone shouted 'Shush!' Then 'Attention!'

The line on her leg went slack. When she hit the ground she bent her knees and rolled sideways. For one gut-freezing second she thought that it was Germans waiting for her under the trees. A stone grazed her cheek. Her fingers scrabbled unsuccessfully for a hold as the parachute pulled her over the rough ground. The skin was ripped from one finger and she yelped. But she was safe and presently slithered to a halt. Two shapes materialised out of the darkness.

'Tout va bein, camarade? Vous n'êtes pas blessée?'

Evelyn sat up and reached for her harness clip. 'Tout va bien.'

'I can't believe it, you are here at last.' The speaker sounded breathless and excited.

Evelyn unclipped her baggage pack, wriggled out of the harness and undid her flying suit to reveal a camel coat over a blue cotton dress and wool headscarf. She struggled to roll up her parachute which continued to flap and billow.

'Here, let me.' The larger of the two men came forward and

held out his hand. He wore a short black jacket and a beret. 'I'm Jean-Claude and I'm in charge of the reception party here. We've been waiting weeks for you to arrive. Do you have the password?'

'The apples are ripe, and my name is Violette.' The new name rolled round her tongue.

Jean-Claude shook her hand lengthily. Since the reception committee had spent most of the waiting period fuelling themselves with brandy, he smelt strongly of drink. Evelyn's spirits lifted. Here was the France she knew and loved.

'We weren't expecting a woman,' Jean-Claude sounded dubious. 'We've had very little information to go on. I am afraid your companion has twisted his ankle.'

Evelyn finishing bundling the unwieldy parachute and stood with it clasped to her chest. 'Badly?'

'Yes, I'm afraid so. We will have to make alternative arrangements, but first we search for the rest of the *parachutage*. There were four containers, yes?'

She nodded.

'Right, give me your parachute and I will put it in the van.'

Feeling like a new girl on her first day at big school, Evelyn shook her head. 'Sorry, it's against orders.'

Jean-Claude sighed. 'The parachute is needed,' he said. 'Please, consider, we have nothing in France. No clothes, no material. You cannot expect me to bury such a valuable thing.'

Evelyn was not to know that Jean-Claude's current mistress was looking forward to a new set of underwear and he had been rash enough, during one lovemaking, to promise to procure the silk.

Before she could answer, he was diverted by a third figure running towards them, calling out that they had to go.

'I'm Antoine.' The man who had first spoken to Evelyn held out his hand in greeting. 'Pleased to meet you. Jean-Claude is the big man round here and he is used to getting his own way.'

Jean-Claude swung round and the moonlight highlighted a square face and a determined chin. 'Right. We must go. Load up the van. You, Violette, are to go with Antoine.'

There was no time to argue. Jean-Claude wrested the para-

56

chute out of Evelyn's hands and disappeared towards the gate. 'Come on.' An unmade-up lane skirted the field and a van was parked by the gate. Two men were lifting the heavy metal containers into the back when Evelyn joined them and a third was camouflaging the load with sacks. John leant against the gate.

'Bloody hell,' he greeted her, obviously in some pain. 'It can't be helped. I'm being taken to a temporary safe house. They don't think they can get me to the one they planned.'

Evelyn pulled the scarf from around her neck. 'I'll tie this foot first.'

'Thanks,' said John, and shifted the attaché case which held his wireless set into the other hand.

'Find the café in Ribérac nearest the main square,' Evelyn said as she wound the scarf around the ankle and tied a knot. 'I'll be there on Wednesday the first week, Tuesday and Thursday the second, between ten and eleven in the morning.'

'You leave at once,' ordered Jean-Claude. 'I will take your friend.'

'See you soon, Violette,' said John.

Antoine beckoned to Evelyn. 'Here's your bicycle. It's not a very good one, I'm afraid. You must be very careful. Not only are we breaking curfew but you have lights and that's an offence. Also the road is rough, so please follow me.'

As Evelyn rode off down the track after Antoine she looked back. It was a strange scene. Moonlight streaming over the field fringed with black trees, and at the gate the frantic movements of the men working to obliterate their traces.

One by one, the torches were extinguished. The last sack was pushed into place. The noise as the van engine wheezed into life was earth shattering in the silence.

'*Gazogène*,' Jean-Claude explained. 'It's rotten for engines.' He put his arm under John's shoulder and they lurched into the lane. 'I'm sorry I can't offer you a lift,' he explained. 'It is too dangerous. The Boches are everywhere.'

'Everywhere?'

'Did you study a map of the area?' John nodded. 'Well, as

far as we know there is a garrison of three hundred at Vauxains – that's apart from the contingents in Bordeaux and, of course, Ribérac. Anyway, it means all cross-over points on the line are guarded, and we will have to go through the forest.'

Jean-Claude handed John a bicycle. John looked at it and thought that if he could survive this, he could survive anything. He wiped the sweat off his face and leant experimentally on his feet, an exercise which proved pointless because he nearly fainted. Jean-Claude swept a torchbeam over the ground and rubbed out a footprint with a large boot.

'No sense in advertising our presence.'

John made a huge effort and used his good leg to mount the bicycle. Jean-Claude wheeled his into the lane.

'I'll take you to my niece, Mariette,' he said, as he strapped John's wireless onto the back of his bike. 'Not ideal, but it will have to do. She lives at the far end of Bertric-Burée, a village north of Ribérac. Her garden leads straight onto the demarcation line. After you have rested the foot, we will hide you properly.'

The distance they had to cycle was ten kilometres or so. In terms of sheer dogged endurance the ride was a marathon. At first, John tried brainwashing himself: 'It could be much worse.' When that failed, he pretended that the sickening pain in his ankle was, in fact, pleasure. This approach was not destined for success either.

'Hurry.' Jean-Claude's voice was made fainter by the increasing distance between them. John bent over the handlebars and invoked any god who might be around to help him. At one point Jean-Claude stopped to anchor John's attaché case more securely. 'We go over the line now,' he said. 'Don't make any noise.'

At last, he turned up a lane and a cottage came into view at the end of a narrow strip of land planted with rows of vegetables. 'Wait,' said Jean-Claude. 'I must talk to her first.' He dismounted and walked towards the cottage.

John slid off his bicycle onto the ground, almost weeping with relief. He saw a door open and Jean-Claude step inside. A light appeared in the downstairs window. Five minutes passed. Perhaps the niece didn't want him? He wouldn't blame her. Jean-Claude reappeared. He put his finger to his lips and jerked his head in the direction of the cottage. John gave him the bicycle and limped towards the door.

All his life he had been sensitive to smell – the stale sweat of the green room, the lingering whiff of fish and chip suppers in poky digs, the obscure tang of a herb in a good French dish. He was particularly familiar with the smell of poverty and this assaulted him as soon as he entered the cottage: the fungoid smell of clammy plaster, the mouldiness of water-impregnated wood and the unpleasant odour of damp clothes in airless conditions. The cottage possessed a single down-stairs room with a couple of cabin-like areas opening off it. It was very untidy. Clothing was draped over chairs and the remains of a meal littered the table. A girl in a nightdress stood by the table with no sign of welcome in her face.

As John limped over the threshold, a bed creaked upstairs and a child's cry sounded above them. Mariette went over to the staircase in the corner of the room and shouted up, 'It's all right, Jeannette. It's only me.'

John clutched the edge of the table for support. 'There are children in the house?'

'Yes,' the girl replied sullenly, pushing the oil lamp further into the centre of the table. 'Mine.'

'Then I shouldn't be here.' John was perturbed. 'I'm sorry.'

She jerked her head in the direction of the garden. 'If he says so then I don't have much choice.'

'I'm sorry,' he repeated, at a loss. 'I'll try and leave as soon as possible.'

She gave him a hard stare. 'Are you badly hurt?'

By now John was swaying with the effort of staying upright. 'Not really.'

She pulled out a chair, pushed John down into it and bent over to look at his foot. She was wearing a cardigan over a nightdress that was too short and her hair hung down over her shoulders in wispy strands. When she got up and went over to the oak dresser, her breasts and bottom swayed rather attractively under the thin material.

The dresser was the one piece of good furniture in the

59

room. Searching among a litter of glasses and odd china, she found a bottle. Handing John a glass, she filled it from the half-empty bottle.

'What is it?' he asked after its first shock.

'Pineau des Charentes. It's made round here.'

Jean-Claude let himself in. Tall, with a torso that had once been heavily muscled but was now turning to fat, his hair was very black in the lamplight. He seemed menacing, the sort of man whose energy never gave out and who was used to taking the lead. 'I've got to go,' he said, 'otherwise I might run into the dawn patrols. Let me see your papers.'

He riffled through John's papers expertly. 'I'm a policeman,' he explained. 'So I've more excuse to be about than most.' He studied the papers. 'Not bad. Have you got your *feuille semestrielle*? You need it to get food and clothing coupons. If you haven't got one we'll have to get it made. What's your cover story?'

At Tempsford, the briefing officer had taken away four typed pages detailing John's new persona. His job now was to flesh out those bare bones, and to make 'Olivier' come to life.

'I am Olivier Blanc, aged thirty-two. Former employee of SNCAS but unable to take up employment after 1940 as experiences on the battlefield have left me psychologically incapable of holding down skilled work. Now offering my services as a farm labourer.'

'Yes, but why is he in this house?' asked Mariette, with a note of triumph. 'Think up that one.'

Jean-Claude flicked at John's papers with a stubby finger. 'He is here, Mariette, because he fancies you? Got it?'

Mariette pushed back the strands of hair that flopped over her shoulders. 'Wonderful,' she said bitterly. 'Gone in the head and interested in me.'

Jean-Claude poked a finger at her. 'You just shut up and do what you're told.' Then he handed back the papers to John. 'Right, Olivier. I've hidden your luggage in the shed. Don't tell her what it is.'

'What makes you think I'm curious?' said Mariette, who had a fine line in ripostes when she felt like it.

Jean-Claude ignored her. 'When the ankle is healed, I will return. Meanwhile stay indoors and don't let anyone see you.' He transferred his attention to the girl. 'Keep your mouth shut, Mariette. There's no telling what might happen if you don't.'

She shrugged and looked resigned. 'My mother? What about her?'

'Tell the old woman he's a boyfriend, like we've agreed.'

Mariette turned her back on Jean-Claude. John caught a glimpse of her face, pale and rebellious. 'I don't like it. What happens if we are caught?'

'You won't be,' he replied with the confidence of someone who knew what he was talking about. 'I tell you, the Boches are stupid. If you act sensibly they won't suspect a thing.'

'All right,' she agreed reluctantly. 'You don't give me much choice. If the children are harmed I'll blame you.' She paused. 'Anyway, what do you think I am going to feed him on?'

'He's got a ration book.'

John was feeling very uncomfortable. 'Please,' he said. 'I don't think this is fair on her . . .'

The argument did not impress Jean-Claude in the least. 'She will do as I tell her,' he said. 'We will see that she's looked after.'

Whoever 'we' was, the idea of them did not appear to comfort Mariette. 'So?' she said. 'So what if he has got a ration book? That's not enough to feed a sick child.'

Jean-Claude pulled out a roll of francs from his pocket and peeled off a couple of notes which he gave to Mariette. She took them, stuffed them into the pocket of her cardigan and stood, rocking on the balls of her feet, to watch him leave. The door closed.

John dropped his head into his hands. 'It's very kind of you,' he said, 'truly.' The words were inadequate, but he did not feel up to improving on them.

'Are you hungry?' she asked with a sigh.

'No,' said John, who longed only to sleep. He finished his Pineau and allowed Mariette to ease off his shoe and untie Evelyn's scarf.

'Tsk,' she said. 'It's badly swollen.'

She pulled open a drawer in the dresser and extracted a strip of linen which she dipped into a bucket of water standing under the sink. The cold helped ease the discomfort.

'My two children and my mother also live here,' she said fiercely. 'They are upstairs. You must promise to say *nothing* to them.'

'Keep it,' John said.

Mariette had picked up Evelyn's scarf. She cocked an eyebrow. 'Thank you.' Now that she had seen the violent-coloured bruise and the surrounding skin puffed out like a *mille feuille*, she seemed to regard John more sympathetically. She got up and hung the scarf on a peg by the door.

'One thing.' Her back was turned. 'You will have to share my bed. Don't worry, my husband is dead. Jean-Claude is really his uncle, not mine.' She turned round to help him and her breasts rose with a quick intake of breath. 'Up you get.'

In her bedroom, Mariette threw back the faded coverlet and helped John to climb onto the bed. He lay back. The smell of old sheets, damp and dust was very strong. On the other side, Mariette settled herself and pulled the cover up to her shoulders. After a minute or so she fell asleep.

John remained awake, trying to ease his ankle into the most comfortable position. Relief at being safe and the Pineau took the edge off his discomfort.

Some time during the night he awoke to find Mariette had rolled closer to him. He shifted his ankle and fell asleep, only to wake a second time when she flung an arm across his chest.

Antoine was obviously used to cycling and before ten minutes had passed Evelyn was panting to keep up with him. Scattered with stones, unexpected cracks and tree roots, the road was uneven and difficult and more than once she almost fell off.

At a crossroads Antoine halted. 'We turn right here towards the main road and the demarcation line. There is a hundred yards or so of no-man's land and then we're over. I'm afraid I don't have a pass for you yet,' he said anxiously, and she felt guilty that he should be worrying about her. 'But it would be difficult to use at the moment. Once over the road, we are almost there.' He turned to look up the road and then flapped his arm for Evelyn to get down. 'There's someone coming.'

'Where?' she asked stupidly.

'Quickly, Violette.'

She did not need to be told twice. Antoine was already running towards a ditch with his bicycle. She pursued him, flinging her machine behind a bush where it lay with its wheels spinning. They sprawled in the ditch, breathing hard, face down in the grass.

'Head down,' whispered Antoine. 'It might be nothing, but it is better to be sure.'

They waited, listening for the car engine. Antoine raised his head and the lights of a very slow-moving car broke through the dark night. He ducked. Cruising smoothly on petrol, the car came into view, stopped while the driver apparently checked out the crossroads, and then continued.

'Vichy police,' Antoine breathed into Evelyn's ear. 'Line patrol.'

Fear is infectious. Evelyn swallowed and a treacherous thought surfaced that she had been a fool to get into this. She learnt later that Antoine had a lot to lose: a wife, small children and a job as a senior administrator in the town hall.

'The bastards often work hand-in-glove with the Germans.' The mild-seeming Antoine continued in a whisper. 'In fact, in some cases they are worse than the Germans. We'll get some of them one of these days.'

They waited for another ten minutes. 'They won't backtrack,' Antoine informed her, 'because they're stupid as well as collaborators.' Evelyn digested this information. It appeared that a section of the population was more hated than the official enemy.

'It's good to have you, Violette. For a time we thought we couldn't ever make contact with England. But a friend called Laroche got through on a transmitter with the help of the Count. Otherwise you would have been dropped blind and we wouldn't have been there to receive you.'

Crossing the main road proved an anticlimax after that. An easy dash over the tarmac and then off at top speed towards the village of Bertric-Burée. She was now in occupied France. After riding through the village, smelling comfortably of dry dung and not so pleasantly of rubbish tips, Antoine bore left onto a track which ran between two maize fields sloping up to the breast of a rise. The green spears massed thickly, almost taller than Evelyn. Antoine went on foot and Evelyn followed, her feet sliding on the dry, whitish earth. Every so often she was forced to catch her breath: once she lost her balance and her bicycle slithered into the maize. She retrieved it and toiled on.

At the top of the rise Antoine pointed to a path that ran off at a right angle. 'I leave you here,' he said, and Evelyn's heart missed a beat. 'Follow the path until you come to a gate in a stone wall. Go through this and turn right, keeping the wall on your right. Walk about fifteen paces and you will see a creeper hanging down. Behind this is an iron grille set into a stone archway. Pull the grille towards you and follow the passage inside. It is quite safe. Please hide your bicycle in the shed you will see nearby. Goodbye.'

Antoine held out his hand, and Evelyn noticed that it was trembling. He seemed too small and frail to be doing this sort of work. She listened to the dull sound of his footsteps going away.

The maize rustled. Banks of cloud were gathering and day-break, she saw, was imminent. She looked at the border of fruit trees beyond which stretched yet more maize. A cock crowed in the valley and the warm autumn night was heady with the smell of ripe crops. Evelyn's fingers tightened on the handlebars. At least she had got this far.

The path narrowed and a wall came into sight. It was high, built of flaking stone and in need of repair. A pair of wrought-iron gates opened through a stone archway into parkland and Evelyn had her first glimpse of the *château* set at the top of a gradient.

It was getting late. As instructed, Evelyn hid the bicycle and carried her suitcase to a massive vine growing down over the wall. She searched for the iron grille and found it with some difficulty. It was well hidden. It eased smoothly open when she pulled, allowing dank air to spill out. Taking a deep breath, she let herself down into the passage and pulled the grille shut behind her.

It was pitch dark. Evelyn felt for her torch and inched along the stone passage. The walls wept moisture and she noticed a strong odour of mouldy grapes. After a hundred yards or so, the passage widened, ran upwards and ended abruptly in a wall. She ran the torchbeam over it and discovered a wooden door set cunningly into the stone. Evelyn put down her suitcase and got out the pistol concealed round her waist before easing it open an inch. She peered through into a large barn-like structure with heavy beams, stone walls and a blacked-out window. On a table in the centre burned an oil lamp. A man was sitting at the table bent over some papers. Evelyn must have made a noise, because he looked up and got to his feet.

· 'Mademoiselle?'

Evelyn lowered her pistol. 'Monsieur de Bourgrave. The apples are ripe.'

CHAPTER FIVE

It must have been two years almost to the day since Hélène had last seen her own face. It had been accidental. On finishing evening surgery in the infirmary, she picked up the hand mirror sometimes used for patients with face injuries and, without thinking, looked into it. A stranger, and yet not a stranger, looked back. Hélène had run her hand over her cheek, tracing the new lines from her nose to mouth, pausing over the fatigue shadows and the little red veins flowing under her skin. The rest of her head was hidden under a nun's veil, and perhaps that was as well. She had put down the mirror, knowing she had committed the sin of vanity and thinking, being the least vain of women, how ironic that was. Nevertheless, Hélène had been interested to have caught up with her face.

When Hélène had lived at the Château Belle-Place, there had been mirrors everywhere. Great gilt-enshrouded affairs, with mockled glass and subdued reflections. She had passed her childhood and early twenties avoiding them and praying to the Virgin for a miracle. It went something like this: one day plain, skinny, difficult-to-deal-with Hélène de Bourgrave wakes up and discovers she is beautiful. As a result, her handsome cousin Charles de Bourgrave, who is mad with love for her, sets about obtaining a special dispensation to marry his first cousin and makes her his countess. Hélène even wrote it down as a story, but when she read it over the writing did not have any conviction.

While she had been studying to become a doctor in Paris, Hélène had undertaken to help with a research project into the possible relationship of childhood experiences to illnesses in the adult. It had been a huge, unwieldy topic, and the findings only began to dent its surface but here and there it yielded some interesting thoughts for the doctors. Hélène conducted some of the interviewing. She remembered one woman, suffering from a psoriasis over her hands, feet and face, saying to her, 'If I had been happier when I was a child I know I would not be ill.'

Hélène probed further. 'Why do you think that is, Madame?'

'Because it is when I dream about being a child again, which I do from time to time, that this begins.'

Hélène wrote it all down in her notebook and reported it. But it was not until the project had finished that she began to understand the link between a child and the adult. She, too, had been unhappy but the result was not a skin disease. It was a profound and constant unhappiness which she managed to conceal from everyone. Except, of course, God.

Hélène's father, Charles de Bourgrave's uncle, died soon after she was born and her mother, a fretful lady with a grudge against life who was not in the least interested in her only offspring, died four years later leaving her in the charge of Charles's parents.

Hélène now realised that being fond of a child is quite different from providing the instinctive, uncompromising love of a parent which can set a pattern of self-confidence and serenity for maturity. And so she grew up with this lack. The de Bourgraves tried their best and, indeed, went out of their way to be scrupulously fair and to give her a thorough education. It remained, however, that Hélène was not their daughter. Not that she blamed her uncle and aunt: Hélène knew she was not lovable.

Once she had overheard her aunt admit to a friend that it would have been easier if Hélène had not been quite so plain. Scrutinising her bony face and its slightly buck teeth and lank, brownish hair, even the most dispassionate of judges conceded this girl was not promising material. However much she ate, Hélène remained whippet-thin, which only accentuated her awkward waistline and large ankles. Miserably aware of her shortcomings, she ignored the interest and life that a natural intelligence lent to her features and developed a habit of staring at the floor when spoken to.

Hélène's want of beauty, however, made no difference to Charles, who chose to champion his cousin and saw to it that she did not suffer too much at the hands of the more socially adept children in their circle. In return Hélène idolised him.

'Skinny thighs,' Charles teased. Hélène was ten and he was thirteen. 'Just like the frogs in the lake.'

They had made a hideout in one of the *château's* outlying fields, and covered it with turf and leaves. Inside, it was gloriously intimate and private and they sat eating chocolate truffles stolen from the Blue Salon. Hélène was pleased to have Charles to herself and his insults rolled off her.

'You wait,' she retorted. 'I might be an ugly duckling.'

'That old story!' said Charles. 'I'm surprised you take all that seriously.'

'Why not?' cried fierce and determined Hélène. 'Why shouldn't I believe it?'

Charles finished a rum truffle. 'It's all right, I love you as you are, you know,' he said matter-of-factly.

Hélène knelt beside him. 'Will you love me for ever and ever?' she asked, her face raised to his in the attitude of a saint in a stained-glass window. 'Truly?'

'Truly.'

'I will remind you of that,' she promised, in a manner far older than her years.

Hélène had kept her promise. She had grown up and her love had turned into adult passion – but Charles had also grown up and changed his mind.

Sister Hélène put the hand mirror away without a second glance and looked up through the open window. It was a hot, clear day, and the October mist had vanished from the valley. Autumn smells drifted in through the window – warm, ripe fruit, musk rose and spicy pelargoniums. A German *mouchard* on reconnaissance duties droned through the sky, searching the landscape for anything suspicious.

She knew what the pilot would have in his sights. A road widing south-east from the town of Angoulême, its verges dotted with flax-blue campions and late poppies, turning due south at La Rochebeaucourt at the point where Pauline de Tourzel's *château* lay between the road and river. Still pushing southwards, it ran on to Verteillac, passing the manor of Lussac on its right and on down to the market town of Ribérac. To the east of the road lay a tree-fringed fretwork of tracks and minor roads, which unravelled into grey stone villages. Down by the rivers Euche and Donzelle the land was divided into small flat fields, and clumps of heavy woodland as far as Château L'Évêque and Brantôme. Further to the south-east lay Périgueux. To the west, the land opened into a wide plain stippled with walnut trees, poplars and cypresses. Later in the year, the wind would race across the grain fields and up the hills to the medieval villages that dotted its ridge. It was familiar country, with which she and Charles had grown up and knew as well as their own bodies – a landscape now dotted by border posts which followed the demarcation line between occupied and unoccupied France.

'*Les sales Boches*' was an expression with which Hélène had become familiar and she heard it from patients living on both sides of the new mark on the map. For many of them their lives had been literally cut in two. The disruption from the time-consuming business of obtaining permits to cross the line and the annoyance that the border imposed, for example, on the simplest of journeys, provoked the boldest among her patients into some unwise expostulations.

'*Les sales Boches*.' Hélène always turned away when she heard these things. It was not her business. She was there to heal the sick. Yet she understood these men and women and their feelings.

There was a knock on the infirmary door.

'Yes?' she replied. Morning surgery was over but sometimes a patient wanted to come and talk about a problem and Hélène never discouraged them. As a result the infirmary was permanently busy. 'Come in.'

'Why, Jean.' Hélène turned from the window, surprised. 'I wasn't expecting you.'

The boy let himself shyly into the room.

'Let me see,' said Hélène, falling back on the techniques learnt at many bedsides, 'it must be over a year since I last saw you. You will forgive me if I say you have grown.'

'So everybody tells me.' Jean was resigned to this comment

and also to his too-short jacket that nobody had any material to replace.

'Your parents are well?'

'Y-es.'

She marked the hesitation but did not comment. There are many reasons why an adolescent boy speaks of his parents with reserve. 'Well. Can I help you?'

He shifted from one foot to the other, and Hélène noticed that the fine hair on his upper lip was turning black. To make it easier for him, she sat down at the desk and folded her hands in her lap. Jean reached into his pocket and pulled out papers, string, a knife, and finally an envelope which he gave Sister Hélène. 'I've been told to give you this.'

Hélène stared at it. She knew the crest on the flap very well. Once she had torn up eight letters written in the same handwriting. Eight letters which had not said very much – the salvage from the wreckage of her unsuccessful love affair. Tearing them up had been part of the preparation for her new life.

'Remember, perfect obedience to the Rule,' Reverend Mother enjoined them, as she prepared the postulants to take their vows. 'Absolute. Unswerving. So precise that a hair's breadth deviation is a fault. Then, *mes soeurs*, you may see the radiance of God.'

Hélène held up the letter and Jean, trying to read her expression, thought perhaps she was angry. 'I'll go now, if that's all right,' he said. '*Au revoir, ma soeur.*' She looked up and through him and he, bewildered, backed out of the door.

Jean was gone and Hélène had not even risen to show him out. The envelope was in her lap, and the lessons of the hard, difficult years of struggling to be a nun threatened to dissolve. Instead she was Hélène de Bourgrave again, desperate with love for a man who was not prepared to go against the church in order to have her.

'I love you,' said the handsome, assured, rather autocratically inclined Charles at twenty-five. 'You know that. I've kept my promise to love you. But not in the way you want. It wouldn't work.'

'How do you know?' asked Hélène, twenty-two, an Hélène

whose plainness had been smoothed almost into those looks the French call *jolie-laide*. 'You're never tried.'

She began to unbutton her blouse and revealed a cream, lace-edged *crêpe-de-Chine* underslip that she had put on as part of her plan, and stood with bare arms. These she clutched across a chest that had never developed enticing curves. She realised she was not conducting the business of seduction very well. 'I'm not asking you to marry me. I know we can't because we are first cousins. But you can love me.'

'No,' said Charles with regret. But he reached out and touched her nipple under the satin slip and watched it pucker. Then he rebuttoned Hélène's blouse and looked into the face that he loved very well but not enough. 'No, it's not possible.'

After that Hélène had left for Paris and medical school to study to be a doctor and tried very hard to set her life along other lines – a course which had steered her to the position where she now sat, as infirmary sister at the convent of St Euphonie.

Picking up the paper knife, she slit open the envelope and read Charles's letter.

'Can we count on you? Charles.'

Her first reaction was of anger. How dare he, after all these years? Her second was: He has not forgotten.

'My sisters,' Reverend Mother warned them only the previous evening, 'our purpose must not be imperilled. You must cleanse your heart of all hatred and allow God's love to fill your souls. The world is suffering, and we must suffer with it. But it is not our place to take sides.'

Not to take sides! Reverend Mother had presumably gauged exactly the self-control she demanded from her sisters, who were, after all, French women as well as nuns. Even in a convent as poor and remote as St Euphonie's news trickled in. They knew when Poland, Belgium, Holland, Denmark, Yugoslavia and Greece were taken by the Germans. They knew there was fighting in Russia. They knew what was being said in Vichy to Maréchal Pétain and his government and they knew that Nazi flags flapped from every flagpole in Paris. They knew, too, of the secret traffic that went on over the demarcation line, which ran not so far from the convent, and

71

of its *passeurs* who arranged for everything – from food to weapons or people – to get in or out.

The sound of a trapped insect in the room attracted her attention. A hornet was banging against the window pane. Making a mental note to speak to Sister Jeanne as she was sure the hornets had made a nest in the wall outside, Hélène got up from the chair, folded Charles's letter and used it to brush the hornet outside.

The sun caught her hand as it rested on the sill and she let it remain. It had been an autumn as warm as this one, she remembered, when she had taken the decision to become a nun. Having failed her final medical examinations, Hélène returned to Belle-Place beaten and exhausted. She had failed because six months previously Charles had married his first countess and Hélène had lost all interest in becoming a doctor. It was stupid, contrary and destructive, she knew, and yet she was unable to prevent her retreat into the unhappiness that secretly she felt was her lot.

Then, on one of the first days of the grape harvest, which had been early that year, Hélène was praying for guidance in her luxurious bedroom in Belle-Place. The large mirror over the mantelpiece reflected hollow eyes, lank hair and a dull complexion. She got up and looked into it. 'What are you going to do, Hélène?' She remembered, suddenly, the story of Héloïse who, after the castration of her lover, Abélard, retired to a nunnery. Hélène stared harder at herself and, as she did so, her future fell into place.

Hélène left her room and went to watch the grapes being brought into the yard. It had been a good harvest, and the grapes were plump and luminous. She reached out, picked one and held it between her finger and thumb like a medical specimen, hoping that God would grant her a respite from feeling. The next week she applied to join the nursing order of the Sisters of St Joseph de Cluny at St Euphonie's.

Ten years later, the hand on the window sill was beginning to show the faintest patches of pigment under the skin and Hélène had still not managed to pour herself into the mould of a good nun. She still possessed too much obstinacy, too much independence of mind, and was still fighting bitter battles to achieve the perfect, disciplined serenity of a hand-maiden of God. Hers was a vocation that required patience, obedience and lack of pride – and Hélène possessed none of these naturally. Her response to Charles's letters showed that.

Hélène placed the letter into her pocket, went over to the steriliser and extracted the clean instruments. One half of her gave thanks that it was of the old-fashioned type which required only bottled gas while the other was irritated that St Euphonie's could not afford up-to-date electrical equipment. Still, it was better than nothing – and a lot better, she imagined, than the equipment available in the African jungle where she had once hoped she would practise as a qualified doctor.

Her instruments checked, Hélène proceeded to count the dressings. She noted the drug supply and sorted out some mixtures made up from her own recipes. Bertic-Burée and the nearer villages relied on the convent for medical treatment and, a welcome addition to an order that specialised in pastoral care, Hélène had been given permission by Reverend Mother to hold surgeries twice a day and to run two wards which acted as an overflow for the hospital in Ribérac where Dr Mazille worked. The previous winter of 1940–1 had been the worst in living memory and food shortages had taken their toll on the old and the very young. The dispensary at the infirmary had borne the brunt and supplies had never recovered. Hélène touched a bottle containing baby's gripe water with the tip of her finger and sighed. Winter would come again soon enough. She gave a final check. The room was as she liked it: pin neat.

The chapel bell rang in the courtyard. Hélène wrote a final note in her daybook and let herself out of the door that opened directly onto the courtyard and walked through the cloisters to the chapel. The sisters were already filing through the door and she fell into step, her head bowed and hands clasped under her scapular.

· The interior of the chapel was a dim, peaceful place, always cool, always overlaid with the smell of incense and candlewax. The statue of the Virgin rested in a niche before the altar and, looking at her, Hélène was once again struck by the intellectual conundrums she presented. This sublime Lady, the model for virginal life, so pure, so stainless, was the preeminent example of womanhood. Yet, for women to follow her example they had to deny their sex with all its fleshly functions. It was a strange paradox and Hélène had never truly understood it.

After the service, she was summoned to Reverend Mother's study. She knocked, entered and knelt for the Blessing. Panelled in dark wood, the room smelt of beeswax and Reverend Mother's rosary was arranged in a precise coil in front of the crucifix on her desk. Her touch on Hélène's forehead was not affectionate. 'Sister,' she said, 'I have sent for you because we need to talk.'

Hélène raised her head and waited, her knees flexed on the ground and her back very straight. Reverend Mother looked down at this obstinate nun and gifted woman, far more gifted than she was herself, and her expression was chilling. Hélène knew Reverend Mother suspected she held confidences back – her struggles, her rebellions, her despair at her lack of progress. Her spiritual secrets. The pride that made it impossible for her to trust such a woman as Reverend Mother whom, try as she might, she disliked.

'Sister, I wish to impress upon you yet again that we must strive for perfect obedience.'

'Yes, Reverend Mother.' Hélène paused. 'Have I failed you so badly, Reverend Mother?'

The older woman thawed a fraction. 'Not me, Sister . . . although God perhaps. You are not alone, we all fail God. But I am not concerned today with what may have happened but with what might happen.'

Under Hélène's habit lay the letter from Charles, a reminder of her disobedience. 'Yes, Reverend Mother,' she said.

Hélène had long ago schooled herself to accepting direction as if she were the humblest of medical students. Reverend Mother tried to read the features before her and for a moment hers softened. She, too, had fought battles with her pride and understood the struggle.

'Sister, I am speaking to you because I fear the present situation will try you in particular. Unlike many of your sisters, and I am referring to your past life because these are special circumstances, you know this area well and your family are renowned in it. You must not, therefore, be swayed from your chosen path because previous loyalties resurrect themselves. Do you understand?'

Hélène felt the lash of humiliation that Reverend Mother had singled her out from her sisters. I do not trust you, she was saying. Hélène closed her eyes and hoped that her expression did not betray her despair. 'Yes, Reverend Mother, I understand.'

Reverend Mother picked up the rosary and let it slide through her fingers. 'I often wish, Sister, that we understood each other better.'

Hélène knew that this admission had cost her superior some effort, so she spoke frankly. 'Reverend Mother, even in a convent it is difficult not to condemn the German occupation of our country. Some of the occupiers behave like brutes. Many have suffered, many will suffer. Is it not our place to help?'

'Help, yes. Take sides, no. Do not be distracted by specious reasoning. Remember, you no longer belong anywhere except here.' She motioned Hélène to her feet. 'Surely it isn't so hard, Sister, to follow the way of God?' Reverend Mother attempted to smile. 'I know you will not let me down.'

Outside in the cloister, Sister Hélène stopped to breathe in some fresh air. The main convent building was Gothic but the cloister, inspired by the twisted columns found in Italian churches of the Renaissance, had been added later. A similar one could be found at Moissac in the Quercy. A devil in the stone carving at the bottom of the pillar grinned as Hélène felt in her pocket for the letter to which she had not confessed. For that omission she would make herself forgo soup at dinner and offer to help the sister on meal duty.

She turned her face towards the sun and her lips tightened. Europe was at war, Charles had contacted her because he was evidently planning some kind of resistance activity and she was frightened for him – and God in His infinite wisdom was offering no comfort. She walked over to the waste-paper basket that the ever-tidy nuns kept in the cloister, removed

CHAPTER SIX

As he watched, Bessy threw out a hand and muttered in her sleep, and Charles de Bourgrave guessed that she was reliving her experiences in Vienna.

He was right. Bessy was dreaming: anxious dreams clotted with unpleasant memories. It was winter and dark, and there were the sounds of shouting and running along the rain-puddled streets. In her dream, Bessy hurried past the Wilczek Palace again and again with the pamphlets sewn into her underclothes, each time terrified that she might be caught.

One face kept recurring in her dream. It was Anna, the Jewish girl whom Bessy had helped to smuggle out of Vienna when things got really bad. Anna had been ill with TB and weak. She had been passed on to Bessy by student friends and Bessy had offered to hide her in her flat in the centre of Vienna, which was foolhardy but the only thing Bessy could think of to do. In her dream, she heard once again the authorities knocking on her front door and heard herself denying all knowledge of Anna's whereabouts, adding that since she was an American Austrian politics did not interest her. At this point Anna's cough sounded behind the cupboard door and Bessy coughed too, to hide it, simultaneously biting her tongue hard. She then waved her bloodstained handkerchief in front of the men. Terrified of contagion, they took a step backwards, and left.

After the Anna episode Vienna was no longer a place where Bessy wished to live or study. Raised on the precepts contained in Paine's *The Rights of Man*, she opposed Hitler's annexation of Austria in March 1938 and the persecution of Jews and socialists. She decided to get out and made the long cold train journey to Paris. The train had been packed with refugees and piled to the roof with suitcases. Bessy's carriage

77

smelt of must and sweat, of urine and rotting food. The majority of passengers – though Bessy was lucky and secured a seat – were forced to stand and watch through the train window as the country they knew as home disappeared.

Charles bent over the bed and rubbed his wife's cheek. Her eyes opened. Intensely fierce eyes, that could appear forbidding if Bessy was angry, surrounded by fair lashes which she insisted on darkening. Today, because she had been tired, they had escaped the mascara. Charles preferred them so, but as with many things Bessy went her own way.

'*Monsieur le comte?*' she said sleepily.

'How are my wife and heir?' He massaged the small of her back where he knew it ached. 'Did they enjoy their afternoon nap?' Bessy drew her knees up as far as possible under the silk coverlet, and felt the bulge of the baby tighten the skin on her stomach. 'Busy. At least, the heir is. I think he must be practising walking the estate.'

He smiled and moved his hand up her back to smooth her hair from her neck. Almost every day, Charles reminded himself how lucky he was to have Bessy. Not that he didn't mourn his first wife – or even sometimes regret Hélène.

'Have you met our new secretary, my darling?' he asked.

Thoroughly awake now, Bessy eyed her husband. 'I am most suspicious, Charles. I never heard you mention any Liegaux relations until last month.'

Charles sat down on the bed. 'A man must have some secrets from his wife, don't you think?'

Bessy looked enigmatic. 'Maybe. But, remember, the compliment can be returned.'

There *were* things from which she excluded Charles that she wanted to forget. She remembered throwing the incriminating anti-Nazi pamphlets into the sewer, when she became frightened that she was being followed, and castigating herself bitterly for her cowardice and for letting down the people who risked their lives to print them.

But Vienna was in the past, and Bessy did not want to dwell any more on the choices that had been forced onto her and her friends by the rise of the Nazis – or, when faced with the threat of violence, of the discoveries they had made about each other's courage and resolution. It was much better to put it behind her and if the past invaded her sleep, well then, she must endure it.

'Did you see her at lunch?' persisted Charles, who had been out.

'Yes, briefly. I was too tired to pay her much attention.' And she added, 'Miss Liegaux is rather beautiful.'

'If you like the type,' said Charles and paused. 'And, of course, I do.'

Bessy's mock outrage failed to hide her anxiety. Charles misunderstood, and reached for Bessy's hand. 'My darling, you have no need to worry. I couldn't possibly look at anyone . . .'

Bessy could not place her finger on it, but a nagging, obstinate presentiment told her that Charles was involved in something dangerous and that he was keeping it from her to protect her.

'I need a secretary,' he continued. 'The baby will be here soon and I don't want you overtaxing yourself. Remember, you have been ill and I think I have given you far too much to do lately.' He got to his feet. 'We can't let things go, even if there is a war.'

'No,' she said, knowing how much the *château* and the vineyards meant to Charles. 'Of course not.' With an effort she pulled herself upright on the pillows. 'Where does Miss Liegaux come from?'

'Near Tours,' said Charles, absently. He got to his feet. 'Her mother, my third cousin twice removed or some such, wrote and asked if we could give her work. They have need of the money, and we need help. *Voilà*.'

'Charles?' Bessy wanted to believe her husband. He was looking out of the window, and she turned to watch him.

'Charles,' she almost panicked, 'you won't do anything stupid, will you?'

Charles reached into his jacket for his cigarettes. 'If I did, you would understand, Bessy.'

Of course she would. The granddaughter of an Irish immigrant to America, who had made a fortune from canning foods, Bessy had been isolated from the common lot by a series of expensive governesses, a carefully orchestrated social life and a wardrobe that belonged in fairy books. But she had grown up possessed of a troublesome social conscience, perhaps the legacy of the Irish nursemaid who fed her a diet of Irish history throughout her childhood. Stories of violent political upheaval, Celtic magic, wild poetry, hunger and deprivation, which mixed myth, fantasy and fact. Bessy's veins, already running with the tough, Puritan tradition of the New Englander, were infiltrated by a heated romanticism and an outraged sense of injustice. Guy, her twin brother, who never listened to these stories, was troubled by no such encumbrance as an active conscience. His approach to life was considerably more pragmatic. Unsure and deeply worried by her wealth, Bessy escaped from her moneyed cocoon to study the still infant discipline of psychology. Here was something, she reasoned, which would help her to understand the real world. But to do so entailed being psychoanalysed and to prepare for this Bessy went to Vienna to attend a series of sessions with Dr Ruth Brunswick.

'You are a prig,' said Guy when she told him of her plans. They were sailing in the bay in one of her father's yachts. It was a hot sunny day, and they were attending a ball that night. 'It's the mental equivalent of gazing at your navel.'

'Nonsense, you are a philistine,' she replied, pulling in the mainsheet.

'Good,' said Guy promptly. 'I'm going to keep it that way.'

'Watch it,' she said, bringing the boat around. 'I'm in charge here and I could have you in the water.'

'It doesn't make you any the less a prig,' said Guy. 'But never mind, twin. I'll live for both of us.'

In Vienna, Bessy joined the circle surrounding Anna Freud, Paul Federn and the Krises and studied Freud, Abraham and Ferenczi. She decided to train as an analyst. Thanks to Hitler and National Socialism, her plans were curtailed, but she cut her political and moral teeth on the experience.

As the situation in Vienna worsened, her impulse to take a stand against the Nazis strengthened. It gave her the courage to take the huge risk of hiding Anna. It was not just a question of hatred, she explained to Charles when he was wooing her. 'One must be prepared to act. You cannot do nothing.'

Charles said nothing but privately agreed. He had discovered Bessy on Bordeaux station, seriously ill with a high fever. She was *en route* from Paris to Lisbon where she hoped to find a passage home to America. On failing to board a Spain-bound train, Bessy, too ill to care, had collapsed on a bench near the station café. Charles, struck by her looks, had naturally offered his help and taken her back to Belle-Place to recover. To his surprise, within a very short time he fell in love with her.

'Promise me, nothing stupid,' Bessy repeated. 'You have a baby to think of.' Charles took her hand and kissed each finger in turn. Normally a bad liar – he had never intentionally deceived the women in his life – now he was improving each day. He lied to Bessy because he wanted to protect her but also his honour as a Frenchman was being called into question and for that he was prepared to take the risk of losing Bessy's trust.

'I promise,' he lied.

'One other thing,' said Bessy. 'I don't think Louis Thiers should be trusted.'

'Why not?'

'If you talk to him,' Bessy sounded worried, 'you will discover he is pro-German. He is also greedy.'

A shuffle at the door terminated their conversation. Panting a little from the stairs, Katrine knocked and came in with the tea-tray. Bessy sat up and asked for her hairbrush.

'Mademoiselle Liegaux is waiting to join us. Will you show her up, Katrine?'

Charles went back to the window and sat down on the window seat. He watched Bessy brush her hair, pick up her powder compact and attend to her face. It was the kind of intimacy he enjoyed and which his first wife had not often granted. He understood Bessy's fears and recognised also her own dilemma. She was no coward but it was not fair to expect her to participate in something so dangerous. Anyway, he inclined to the view that these things were better left to men.

81

So thinking, he watched Bessy adjust the heavy lace cuffs on her bed-jacket.

It had taken all Charles's eloquence to persuade Bessy that the life he was asking her to share with him at the Château Belle-Place would not mean she was giving up her role as a useful, independent woman. 'I don't want to be a parasite,' she informed him, when he tried to kiss her into submission. (Bessy was a firm believer in the feminist ideology she had first encountered in Viennese circles.) Charles assured her that becoming the châtelaine of Belle-Place would be very hard work. 'We all depend on each other here,' he told her. 'I need my workers as much as they need me. Getting the wine back to its rightful category will ensure their prosperity as well as mine.' But the illness she had contracted in Paris, as well as her pregnancy, had weakened Bessy's superb physique and she had done less at Belle-Place than she had hoped. In her more honest moments Bessy realised that her illness had been of service. Charles was a conservative and responded better to a woman who required pampering than to one of sturdy self-reliance. Those battles, she anticipated, would come in good time.

She put down the powder compact and pulled the tea-tray towards her as Evelyn knocked at the door. Bessy held out her hand as she entered.

'*Madame la comtesse*,' said Evelyn.

'Call me Bessy. You will forgive me receiving you in bed but I have several anxious males, my husband and doctor to name but two, all in league against me. They keep telling me I must rest. What I say is, keep them happy.' Her smile was intended to draw Evelyn into an amused female conspiracy.

Evelyn smiled back, not too nervously she hoped. She was suffering from what she later recognised as 'early days phobia' – an almost paranoiac conviction that her true identity could be read from her face. It could not, of course; nor should she fall into the snare of categorising everyone she encountered as either resistance workers or informers. Most people – and the instructors at the Special Training Schools had emphasised this – were ordinary *attendistes*; people who were not sure what to think, who wished merely to get on with the business of everyday life undisturbed.

It was obvious to Evelyn at once, however, that Bessy was no ordinary housewife. Even in bed she radiated assurance and poise. Here was a woman who appeared to have found her niche and was content with it. Bessy looked pale and strained but Evelyn noticed at once the expensive *maquillage* and creamy antique lace on the countess's bed-jacket. Bessy's tawny hair, cut to shoulder length, was pulled back by a pair of exquisite enamel combs. The effect was of some elegant and gracious lioness who had wandered in from the savannah. Evelyn pulled discreetly at her own crumpled cotton dress.

'Will you have some tea? It is an English habit I've acquired. Has my husband told you anything yet? If I know Charles he hasn't.' Bessy smiled at Charles and he shrugged slightly.

'I am showing Mademoiselle around as soon as you have given her tea,' he protested. 'The poor girl was too tired this morning.'

At Wanborough Manor and Arisaig, they had emphasised how rough life might be in France. 'You will be constantly on the move,' they warned, 'sleeping in barns, making do with poor accommodation . . .' – predictions that some instructors, who knew they would be remaining on safe English soil, emphasised with care. Evelyn flicked a glance around the luxurious room and raised an eyebrow. Drinking her tea out of porcelain decorated in Angoulême sprig, Evelyn imagined her debriefing. She was sitting in a chair that could only be Louis Seize in a room furnished in faded brocades and chintz, with long, freshly painted shutters opening onto a balcony overlooking terraced flower-beds. The coverlet on Bessy's four-poster was silk, swagged with twisted gold braid that had aged and muted. Bessy herself was framed by bed curtains of gold brocade shot through with dusky pink and olive green. Thinking of what she would tell her instructors steadied her.

'Once upon a time,' Bessy was saying, and Evelyn pulled herself together, 'Château Belle-Place was one of the vineyards producing *premier cru* wine. Unfortunately, and I will not go into the details, the vineyard fell into neglect and the quality of the wine suffered. When my husband inherited it from the late Count he decided to devote his life to restoring the wine's reputation. It will take a lifetime, I'm afraid.' Bessy looked towards Charles for confirmation but he continued to smoke his cigarette, allowing her to continue.

'I am in charge of the secretarial side, dealing with customers, suppliers of materials, wages and all that sort of thing. You can imagine there is a lot of correspondence and record-keeping. But as you will have noticed I shall be out of action for some months. This is where you come in, Evelyn. How is your typing?'

'Good,' the girl lied.

'Now, *chérie*,' said Charles, deciding it was time to divert the conversation, 'I am going to show Mademoiselle Evelyn around. Then I will return her to you.'

'All right,' said Bessy, 'but don't let him frighten you, Evelyn. He can be quite fierce.'

Charles ushered Evelyn downstairs and into a room off the hall.

'This is the Blue Salon,' he said. He closed the double doors behind him and took up a position by the fireplace. 'Look around,' he invited, and watched Evelyn's reaction.

She obeyed him, admiring the long white stone room, its carved plaster ceiling, its huge sunlit windows and the walnut panelling. It was a lovely place, filled with row upon row of blue and white china. The curtains were of pale blue silk and the furniture upholstered in faded blue brocade. Evelyn walked over to a rosewood cabinet and inspected some of the porcelain, gently touching the glass pendicles of a crystal Napoleon candelabrum with her finger. She could see that the Count was proud of his house. A man of only medium height, with receding brown hair and a moustache, wearing a battered tweed suit and a slub linen shirt, he had the look of a thoroughbred. In command, at ease with his surroundings. She swallowed. Bessy was right; he did seem fierce.

'If you look over there between the windows,' he said, 'there is a letter written by Marie-Antoinette to her lover not long before she went to the guillotine.'

'Let's hope we don't lose our heads.' Lulled by her setting, Evelyn spoke rather dreamily.

'No,' said Charles. 'We won't.'

He opened a door leading off the Blue Salon and ushered her into a small cluttered room. 'This is my study,' he told her. 'It's where I keep the family records.'

In the centre of the room was a rosewood desk piled with papers. Elsewhere, on every conceivable surface, there were photographs in silver frames of people whom she took to be the family. Hanging on the wall were framed certificates, a huge beautifully decorated family tree, yet more photographs and earlier oil portraits. 'There is my father being presented to your King George V,' he said and pointed to a photograph displayed on the desk. Evelyn examined it and was surprised. The previous Count had a very weak-looking face. 'My father lost most of our money in unwise speculation.' Charles sounded bitter. 'So we are not what we once were.' He gestured at the certificates on the wall. 'I was forced to sell off quite a bit of a vineyard which was once as respected as Monbazillac. Enough of that now. One must take care where one speaks,' he said. He paused and looked at her. 'You are very young. Too young really. And I must be honest, Mademoiselle, I was not expecting a woman.'

Evelyn flushed at the implied slight. 'I am almost twenty-two,' she answered carefully. 'And fully trained.' She emphasised the last word. 'And here of my own free will.'

Charles looked very serious. 'Yes, of course,' he said politely. 'Still, this is not a game for juveniles.'

Evelyn looked up at him. She could see he was not convinced of her capabilities. Charles picked up a fountain pen from the desk. 'All my life I have been used to walking around the grounds of Château Belle-Place as I liked, as well as overseeing my other pieces of land in the area without hindrance. I have a house near Nantes. I have come and gone as I pleased. Now, if I wish to do that, I have to apply for a permit to get across the border. I have to wait my turn and, if I wish to go at the wrong time of day, it is even more difficult. Do you see?'

'Of course.'

Charles dropped the pen with a clatter onto a china ink-tray. 'When I wish to ask one of my regular workers if his son will help me out this year, as he did last year and the year before, I am told this cannot be because he has been transferred to Germany to work in a factory. Do I need to go on?'

'No,' she replied. 'I understand perfectly.'

Charles made up his mind. He went over to the bookshelf, reached up and took down a volume on the top shelf from which he extracted two cards. 'Let us begin the work.' He handed Evelyn the two cards, one blue, the other green. 'You will be acting as courier, a messenger if you like, for the organisation I am trying to set up. I gather you have been trained for this work.'

Evelyn listened carefully as the Count went into details about identity cards and ration books, regulations concerning bicycles, the importance of observing the curfew and the times of buses and trains.

'This one,' he pointed to the blue card, 'is your border pass. It is made out in your name but I think we should arrange additional false papers for you, perhaps as a sales representative for a pharmaceutical firm. It would account for any odd hours you might keep. Never carry both cards on you at the same time. If you are caught with two sets . . . I am afraid the Germans have got into the habit of holding spot checks, *rafles*, particularly at bus stops and stations.'

Evelyn put the cards in her pocket. 'How many people know about these papers?'

'Nobody except me and Antoine, whom you have met. He arranged the forgery. He has been a good friend. One more thing. Don't show them to anyone – they might be gossips or even informers.'

Evelyn did not need to be told. 'What about my contacts?' she asked.

Charles hesitated. 'There are three principal ones. The policeman Jean-Claude. Antoine. And Henri at the bicycle shop. Jean-Claude is very useful and appears to have the trust of his superiors. He is also in a good position to obtain information. He lives over by the village of Allemans. I am in the process of recruiting at the moment. Which reminds me – are you quite clear where we are?'

Evelyn had studied the map of the area thoroughly before she left England, but in the dark and confusion of the dangerous journey from the drop point, it had been easy to lose the exact orientation.

Charles got a map out of the desk drawer. 'Here is the town of Ribérac on the river Dronne. We are west of the demarcation line, outside the village of Bertric-Burée. The village of Verteillac is to our north. All right?'

'Quite clear, Monsieur le comte. I will need to contact Georges, the wireless operator, during the next few days.'

Once again, the Count seemed to be assessing her and Evelyn felt a twinge of resentment. He was so obviously doubtful of her suitability. 'It was made quite clear by London that I am in charge, I hope?'

'Yes.'

'I don't want anything going on behind my back. All messages will go through me, if you please. And, of course, any orders will come from me alone.'

'There is no need to worry, Monsieur le comte. I understand the situation.' Evelyn spoke a little defensively.

The Count gave a laugh. 'No, you don't, Mademoiselle. You are not a citizen of an occupied country wanting to retrieve its pride.'

'Is there anything else?' Evelyn endeavoured to fill the embarrassed silence.

'You must get to know the *château* intimately. Please use the wine passage whenever you come and go on difficult business and be careful to disguise your tracks. Some of the time, of course, you must be seen to work with me in the office.' He paused. 'My wife,' his voice changed, 'knows nothing of this, and will continue to know nothing. You saw for yourself that she is in a delicate state. It's possible she might guess but let us try and keep it from her at least until the baby is born.'

'What about the staff?'

'There is Katrine, the maid, who comes in daily, Marie, the cook, who lives in – a little hysterical perhaps, but loyal. Then there is Gaston, the butler. He has been with my family for forty years. Various people come in from the village, including Louis Thiers, the gardener.' Charles remembered Bessy's warning. 'He may be untrustworthy. None of my staff know anything of this work, nor should they. It would put them in severe danger.'

'Do any of them have any contacts in Tours which might put my cover at risk?'

Charles shrugged. 'I don't know.'

Evelyn cleared her throat. 'I shall hide my revolver in the *château* with your permission.'

He nodded and went over to the desk. 'Here, take this,' he said, giving her a typed booklet. 'I amused myself once, writing a history of the château. It might prove useful. And this book,' he handed her another, 'is a manual from which you might familiarise yourself with the basic principles of viticulture.'

She turned Charles's booklet over. The photo on the front was cracked and seamed with handling and obviously had been taken some years previously. 'The trees have gone,' she said, looking at it closely.

'Ah, the forest,' said the Count, softening. 'If the land is neglected, even for a short while, it returns to wilderness. But we managed to beat the trees back.'

'You make it sound like a battle.' Evelyn was intrigued by the idea of a forest as a powerful enemy biding its time.

'Holy Joe. I imagined you would be out in the grounds by now,' said Bessy from the doorway. 'The sun is about to set.'

Charles looked up. Bessy had got dressed in a soft tea-gown and put on lipstick. His expression registered pride in his handsome wife. 'Should you be up?'

'We have a great deal to do before tomorrow.' Bessy was indignant. Charles turned to Evelyn.

'Tomorrow we are holding our annual celebration lunch in honour of my birthday. Everyone is invited. It is a big event for us. But this year I am trying to prevent the Countess from over-exerting herself.'

'Charles!' Bessy brushed her hair back from her shoulders. A good inch taller than her husband, she slipped her hand through his arm, her fierce eyes now soft and full of laughter. 'You mustn't fuss.' His hand closed round hers protectively.

CHAPTER SEVEN

Almost the last thing Ingrid said to Paul was, 'You must rest your leg.' Kissing him goodbye, she had laughed and stripped off her expensive glove to rub the lipstick mark off his cheek. 'Promise me,' she insisted.

Paul ignored Ingrid's advice. He knew he must keep the leg flexible, otherwise he suspected it would set into stiffness. The surgeons had done a brilliant job but they could only go so far. The rest lay with him and depended very largely on his state of mind, as he had discovered during the ups and downs of convalescence.

Between thankfulness at being alive and bouts of debilitating exhaustion and depression, Paul learnt to accommodate physical pain. It was a question of detachment, he told himself as he lay staring at the hospital ceiling. Take the pain. Examine it as if it was under a microscope. Believe that it is becoming easier. Diminish its importance. As a mental sleight of hand, the trick worked some of the time, particularly when his leg began to heal. Otherwise, Paul learnt to endure.

After experiencing it, Paul did not agree that suffering ennobled the soul but he acknowledged that pain did bring one reward: an appreciation that its absence was an intense, to-be-relished luxury. Sometimes, when he was overtired, he recalled the first nightmarish days when, bumping by ambulance and plane on a stretcher back to Berlin, pain and fever had attacked him. The memory was a nostrum for the times when depression settled over his spirits and sucked away at the Paul of the past. The Paul who had to accept that his future was going to be very different from the one he had planned. He was maimed: the shot-up leg that had left him with a permanent limp meant his life as an active soldier was over.

'I have to make the best of my situation,' he told Ingrid one night when the leg was almost fully healed. 'I must talk to a few people.'

He was amused when Ingrid leapt into action and told him he must start telephoning the 'right' people at once. When Paul explained that she had not quite understood his meaning, Ingrid became very quiet. Tearful but resigned, she remained in Berlin where she consoled herself with non-stop social engagements. From her letters it was obvious that she was enjoying the role of 'one who had yielded up her man for the Fatherland'. Paul was ready to bet she played it to perfection. He imagined her swooping down on a willing victim, red-lipped and siren-voiced, to intimate with a tremulous *moue* of her mouth how much she was suffering.

Paul shifted his walking stick into his other hand and banished this image of Ingrid as he was ignoring the imprudence of walking alone in the French countryside. Pausing under a patch of trees to enjoy the cooler air under their canopy, he turned to look back along the valley. His father would have enjoyed this walk and would have noticed all the features of French husbandry – down, he had no doubt, to the piles of manure waiting to be forked onto the fields. Paul noted with approval the order and neatness with which the fields were tilled, and the precise lines of the crops – winter wheat, late maize, rows of fruit trees – and concluded that the French were among the first in the world when it came to agricultural skills. He moved on.

It was autumn and the low sun caught Paul in the eyes. Breasting the hill, he was dazzled by the light – and almost stumbled into the solitary figure in a blue dress standing at the top.

'Don't bother to help,' Bessy said to Evelyn. 'Everyone is much too preoccupied to show you what to do. Food is a very serious business – especially these days.' But Evelyn was trained to helping out at the damp June fêtes and village whist drives of her childhood and she made an effort, fetching and carrying china, knives, forks and glasses until her arms ached.

Then she decided she was better out of the way and took

the opportunity to familiarise herself with the locality. Nobody noticed as she walked down the gravel drive to the road.

The drive was bordered on one side by a drystone wall, well worn by weather and flecked with moss and clumps of wild dog rose. Built with care and satisfyingly mellowed with age. Evelyn leant against it and scrutinised Belle-Place, enjoying the feel of the warm stones on her back as she did so.

The *château* was built around an older building – Charles's family history told of its fifteenth-century origins – and traces of the original stone stood out against later additions. The main wing was three-storeyed, with long shuttered windows in the first two and smaller mansard ones in the attic. At each end of the house was a square tower tiled in a grey slate that shone like silk in the sun. Punctured by a stone archway which allowed for the drive, the remains of a crenellated wall continued round the house, encircled a stable block and ran, like a medieval battlement, towards the wine cellar where Evelyn had met Charles, terminating in the middle of a field. At each corner of the square formed by the wall was a pepper-pot shaped tower with slit windows. The tower walls were cracked and in need of repair but they were, none the less, a reminder of the lightness and sophistication of fifteenth-century architecture. To the right of the main house was a separate *pigeonnier* built in the same stone. In the past, doves and pigeons had signified wealth and this part of the Périgord was filled with buildings housing them, often as elegant as their owners' dwellings. At Belle-Place the *pigeonnier* was placed so that it overlooked a field beyond, at the point where a wooded rise of land joined the skyline.

Evelyn gave herself a couple of minutes to memorise the layout and then continued up the drive to the road. At this point the trees became thicker and the *château* was cut off from sight. With a sense of excitement mixed with apprehension she walked on, glancing left and right just to be sure that no one was following her.

At the junction she turned left and walked down towards the valley that ran behind the *château*. The valley, such as it was, dipped towards the river and flattened out for a mile or so before extending on either side up to a ridge. Along it and up on the ridge were square red-tiled buildings with stone archways leading into yards full of ducks and hens. The plain was well cultivated, the yellow and green of late crops alternating with the whitish-brown earth of the fallow. Thin dark cypresses, of the kind Evelyn had seen in reproductions of Italian paintings, rose perpendicularly and made a setting for the Romanesque church tower in the distance.

Seduced by the stillness of the autumn, Evelyn stopped to look. This area and its past appealed to her. She loved the fact that here seemed to be a turning point between the softer north and the harshness of the southern landscape. She could imagine the valley in summer, baking under the sun with tobacco and sunflowers in the fields and geraniums blooming in tin pots in doorways, or, when it was stripped bare by the winter, leafless trees outlined against the hill and ducks splashing through half-frozen puddles.

She shaded her eyes to see better and turned to see who was coming up the road. A man moved out of the sun and came towards her.

The fright of being caught unawares made Evelyn's heart thump and she took a step back onto the verge. Calm down, she told herself, while unprofessional panic made her want to run. Limping a little, the man walked up to Evelyn and stopped.

'Excuse me, Mademoiselle . . .'

Dressed in a worn corduroy suit and white silk shirt with a knotted silk scarf around his neck, he seemed very much at ease. The sun had tanned his nose and cheeks, and where the hairline met his neck the hair was bleached almost white. One very brown hand, wearing a signet ring on the little finger, grasped a stick; when he stopped he leant on it for support. To look at, he was different from the men she was used to: elegantly assured in his old clothes, a little rakish even, lean and glowingly brown and fair.

'Pardon, Monseiur,' she said, and moved back.

Paul found himself staring into a pair of defensive green eyes in a face from which all animation and pleasure at the scenery had drained away. 'Excuse me,' he repeated. 'Can you help? I want to get back to Ribérac. Which road should I take?'

Evelyn knew from the maps and postcards she had studied at Orchard House that there were two routes. She also realised that, despite excellent French, this man was not a native and she had better be careful – a refugee, perhaps, from Alsace-Lorraine?

'You could return to the main road, Monsieur,' she said, 'and then turn right. Or you could fork right at Bertric-Burée and go the longer route through Allemans.'

'I'm very interested in the architecture of the smaller *châteaux* and I have been exploring the area,' Paul explained while he sized up Evelyn and found himself wanting to keep her talking. 'There is a very good example over the hill.' He pointed in the direction from which he had come.

'You mean Lussac.' Evelyn was thankful she had memorised the area minutely. 'Yes, it is an attractive house. It's one of the better here.' She had no idea if that was true or not.

'Yes, I think you may be right.' Paul rolled his short sleeve up a brown forearm brushed with fine hairs. 'I particularly like the way the steps are placed by the main door. It gives the right balance to the building.' His obvious enthusiasm and knowledge was very attractive. 'But I imagine you know it well.'

'Yes indeed, Monsieur.' Evelyn made herself sound deliberately wooden. She moved onto the road. 'Good day, Monsieur.'

Without warning Paul leant forward and stopped her. 'Wait,' he said. 'Don't move. Look. On your shoulder.'

Evelyn squinted down at her dress. An Adonis Blue butterfly had alighted on her dress and, as she watched, it quivered and opened its wings.

'It's the same blue as your dress,' said Paul. 'Underneath, of course, he is a buff colour.' He put out a finger. 'Let's see if I can persuade him to come to me.'

His finger touched her shoulder, an unfamiliar, oddly disturbing touch, and she almost stumbled. The butterfly snapped its wings shut, opened them, and flew off into the distance between the trees.

'A pity,' said Paul. 'But no doubt he has things to do. It is getting late in the year.'

The sun shone directly into Evelyn's face and she put up a hand to shade her eyes. 'Probably,' she said, and found herself smiling.

Enjoying the picture she made, Paul leant on his stick and smiled back. Long legs, thin feet stuffed into worn leather shoes, a wide mouth in a serious face framed by shiny dark hair that curled in feathery wisps by her ears, a tiny mole at the base of her neck and the coltish look of someone who hadn't quite grown up. The girl was definitely not from the fields.

'I must go, Monsieur.' Evelyn was now sure that Paul was not French. His clothes, if well worn, were nevertheless expensive-looking and the signet ring indicated a good family. Perhaps – she dropped her hand and twisted the finger of one hand in the other – he was German, one of the officers from the garrison.

'Of course.' Paul looked sorry. He pointed at the road. 'Did you mean I should continue along here?'

Without meaning to, Evelyn fell into step with him and walked back the way she had come. Paul made conversation about the crops and the walnut harvest and the prospects for the *vendange*. Evelyn replied briefly as she dared, and they walked up the slope and into the shade of the trees. At the top Paul stopped.

'There.' Evelyn was panting slightly in the warmth. She pointed to the road. 'If you continue you will reach the main road. Turn right and follow it.'

But Paul was not looking at the road. He was looking at Evelyn. There was something about her that stirred up in him an odd reaction: a desire to preserve at all costs the funny young vulnerable expression on her face that he sensed could turn quickly into hurt or disappointment. Paul had never been given to quick seductions or Don Juanish impulses: he preferred more leisured, more satisfactory wooings, but he wanted now to bury his face in her neck and smell her warm body. Evelyn followed the direction of Paul's gaze and slowly began to flush.

Paul moved closer, and she noticed that a line etched into his forehead made him look older than she had at first thought and his eyes were very brown. Above them, the trees rustled in a breeze. Her hands fell to her sides.

'You had better go then, Mademoiselle,' Paul said, his foreign intonation growing more pronounced, and Evelyn knew then that he was German. Still, she did not move. The sun was playing tricks on her vision, and she felt slightly drunk on new sensations.

Paul came closer and, not knowing what was going to happen, Evelyn waited. Paul hesitated, reached out and touched her very gently in the hollow at the base of her throat where the sun was beginning to flush it brown. Neither said anything.

Then Paul began to walk towards the main road, limping a little. Evelyn watched his retreating figure, her hand clasping her throat. No one had ever done that before – touched her with such a mixture of lightness and sensuality – nor had she ever felt such a response.

Paul stopped abruptly, and turned around. 'Will you be here again?' he called.

Evelyn remained where she was, pleating her blue dress between her fingers. 'No,' she replied, feeling her way back into normality. 'No.'

Paul shrugged, and continued on his way. He turned for a second time to wave, but Evelyn did not respond.

By the time Evelyn returned to Belle-Place the tables had been arranged in rows in front of the house, with the top table nearest to the front door placed at a right angle to the rest. They had been set with knives, forks, sprigged china plates, a quantity of glass that indicated serious drinking and baskets of fruit and bread. Obligingly, the sun continued to shine on the first guests as they made their way up the drive and through the stone archway.

Earlier in the day Charles had warned Evelyn that she would encounter a good cross-section of the community. 'I like to invite everyone involved with me or the *château* and, of course, the vineyard workers. It is important for me that

we have an annual get-together, and very important for them.'
He paused, and she knew that he relished every moment of
being master of his house, estate and extended family. 'I don't
need to tell you to be careful. In past days, those wonderfully
simple days, it was possible to sit down at the table and not
question my guests' politics. Today, it is not at all like that,
and I am forced to entertain people whose loyalties are not
the same as mine.' He spoke with the arrogance of someone
who expected people to agree with him and yet also with real
regret, and Evelyn liked him better for it.

She posted herself behind one of the tables and watched
Charles issue last-minute orders. She was beginning to feel
that he was not a man with whom she was going to find it
particularly easy to work. It was only later that she realised,
with a flash of insight, that the Count reminded her of her
father.

Marie's menu for the day was anchored under a pile of
plates and Evelyn picked it up.

∞ ∞

Confit de canard aux petits pois nouveaux
Foie de volailles au vin
∞
Le Boudin à la mode du pays
Les Haricots à la Périgourdine
La Côtelette farcie de Ribérac
Les Châtaignes blanchies
∞
Les Croquants aux noisettes
Les Pruneaux fourrés
∞ ∞

She looked up at the scene. It was obvious that weeks of
careful preparation had gone into this lunch, including some
determined hoarding. Somehow, despite the privations and
restrictions, Charles and Bessy were going to make sure that
life continued as normally as possible.

Charles was dressed in a suit with a starched wing collar
and Bessy in a chiffon tea-gown that floated above her ankles.
She also wore a large hat covered in matching chiffon with a

cluster of dusty pink silk roses. She felt it made her look far too frivolous, although Charles liked it. They stood together in front of the main door, greeting each guest as he or she arrived. Evelyn turned her attention to the gathering company. One of the vineyard workers wandered past her table, a cigarette hanging from his mouth and a bottle clutched in one hand. He called out to one of his friends and took a swig. His wife, a stout lady dressed in black, pulled at his arm and told him to behave. Marie appeared from behind the house, looking harassed. Someone pressed a glass of wine into her hand and sat her down. Two children leapt out at Evelyn from under the tablecloth, and shouted, 'Got you!' and she nearly dropped a bottle. Smiling, she scolded them.

From the drive came the sounds of horses' hoofs, and presently a couple of riders picked their way through the arch. Charles waved to them and indicated the stables with his hand. The riders wove calmly through the guests and dismounted in the stable yard. Behind them came a horse-drawn cart loaded with hot-house peaches, nectarines and goats' cheeses wrapped in vine leaves. At the sight, Marie pulled herself to her feet and waved off all offers of help.

'No, I must do all this,' she said, retying her apron strings. 'It is my job. Bring the cheeses over here.'

How many times has this scene been played in this place? Evelyn wondered. Squinting through the sun made the different colours and groups blur into indistinct shapes and turned what she saw into something misty and tender.

Charles came over to her looking more relaxed than she had yet seen him. 'I've put you at the end of the top table,' he said. 'A little prominent perhaps, but it would be odd if I didn't.'

'Who's that?' she asked, discreetly indicating a man in a brown tweed suit with a gold watch chain and a swastika sewn onto an armband.

Charles said nothing for a moment. Then he sighed. 'Just take care,' he said. 'I'll explain later.'

Jean-Claude walked past, accompanied by a woman whom Evelyn took to be his wife: a thin, nervous-looking woman whose hair had thinned almost to the point of baldness. He ignored Evelyn and nodded to the Count. 'I must get my wife to send Madame a new hat,' said the Count. 'It would be a gesture of some sort.'

Antoine was also there, scrubbed and stiff in a dark Sunday suit. His wife had obviously once been beautiful but now, pale and worn, she held onto Antoine's arm as if she was too tired to care about her appearance. Curious, but keyed-up and a little self-conscious, Evelyn moved back under the protection of the trees. She did not feel quite sure of herself yet. How many of these people were potential resistants? How many would work for the Germans?

At lunch her neighbour was an elderly gentleman with false teeth who lived, he informed Evelyn, in a large house up towards Verteillac.

'No,' she parried his curiosity. 'I have always lived in Tours. This is my first trip here . . .' and 'No, I am not married.' She tried some questions for herself. 'Do tell me something about yourself, Monsieur. Has your *vendange* been good this year?' But when he leant over and applied his white moustached lips to her ear and whispered some mildly indecent anecdotes, she was rather surprised.

'You have a choice, Mademoiselle,' he said at last when the desserts were placed on the table, realising that Evelyn was not interested in his stories.

'Monsieur?' Evelyn wondered what was coming. She looked around for help, and wished that John was there.

'What will you have to drink, Mademoiselle? Monbazillac. Le Montsaguel. *Eau-de-vie. Le rhum blanc. La liqueur de genièvre ou les raisins à l'eau-de-vie?*'

Evelyn raised a hand in protest. 'Enough, Monsieur, I couldn't possibly drink another glass.'

Actually, she would have liked to have accepted a liqueur, and allowed herself to become hazy and sleepy. The elderly gentleman gave her a look which said, 'You haven't been worth the trouble', and turned to the woman on his other side. Full of good food and warmed by the sun, Evelyn propped her elbows on the table and rested her chin on her hands.

Across the table, Madame Jean-Claude scratched at her thinning hair. Evelyn's neighbour pushed back his chair, crossed his legs and revealed a grubby sock suspender. Bessy's lipstick was smudged onto her glass and she had taken off her hat. She leant back on her chair and sipped a dessert wine. Charles was engaged in conversation with a heavily made-up woman in a red and black suit. As the woman talked she fiddled with heavy gold bracelets on either wrists, flashed red nails and gesticulated to draw attention to herself. Further down the table, one of the wives got up to see to a child. Her dress had not withstood the strain of such a large meal, and a rolling expanse of pink corset was visible through the split seam.

If the wine had not been spilt at that point, the incident would have been avoided, Charles said later. The lid might have been kept on emotions. As it was, a glass of wine was knocked over by Madame Devereux's small daughter into the lap of Madame Angelot. It was an extra pity that Madame Angelot had chosen to wear her refashioned wedding dress, which now did duty as her best ensemble.

The red stain spread like blood over the white, very white, silk. Shocked that the one good dress she was likely to possess until the end of the war had been ruined, Madame Angelot, who cared excessively about her appearance, dropped her head into her hands and sobbed.

Matters were not improved when Madame Devereux threw a glass of vintage white dessert wine onto the stain to try to save the material. Her aim was bad and splashes of the liquid hit Monsieur Javaux, a man not noted for his patience. He sprang to his feet and called Madame Devereux 'a clumsy fool'. Everyone on the table was sucked into the argument that sprang up and, in the ensuing mêlée of insults and jeers, the phrase 'Fascist' was thrown at Madame Devereux. In response, Monsieur Devereux, he of the brown suit and Nazi armband, sprang up and called the company 'a lot of dirty Communists'.

There was complete silence. Bessy exclaimed, 'Oh no.' The guests measured each other up across the littered tables. Two of the men pushed back their chairs. Their wives held them back. Monsieur Devereux thought it best to retreat and gathering up his unsmiling wife and snivelling daughter he pushed them though the silent tables towards the drive.

Angry that his hospitality had been soured, Charles rose from his seat and hurried over to the Devereux family to try to smooth over the incident. Apparently he failed. The Devereux almost ran through the archway and down the drive.

'I'll kill you one of these days, Devereux!' someone shouted after their retreating backs, and the guests were left to pick over the ragged remains of the celebration.

It took a little time. The glasses were twice refilled before conversation picked up and the mood settled. Charles and Bessy worked hard to salvage the afternoon, and after a while their efforts were rewarded.

Throughout the incident, Jean-Claude remained seated. 'It was no use my interfering,' he explained to Evelyn. 'It was better the Devereux went. Now you know the way we are.'

Evelyn made a surprising discovery about herself: she was more English than she had supposed. She found such an ugly and public display of contrary loyalties unsettling.

Before she went to bed that night, Evelyn unpacked the suitcase that Charles had provided. He had thought of most things: a lawn nightdress, tooth powder, face flannel, stockings, which she fell on with delight, a silk blouse, a green wool skirt and jacket and a woollen cardigan. They were pleasing clothes, not too smart for her role as a secretary, and they showed a subdued good taste. She wondered how Charles had managed to obtain them without attracting anyone's suspicion.

Evelyn hung up the skirt by its tapes and the jacket over it on the coathanger. Her other clothes went into the rosewood chest of drawers and she spent a pleasant few minutes arranging them between the lavender bags that had been thoughtfully provided.

Next she searched for a suitable place to hide her pistol, rejected the bowl heaped with rose *pot-pourri* as too dusty, and decided instead on a packet of sanitary rags that she had parachuted in with. It wasn't perfect, but she judged men would look there last. She wandered around the room, patting a brocade cushion on the day bed, touching the silver-backed brushes on the dressing table and admiring the silk-swagged bed. The wallpaper fascinated her. It was an authentic Toile de Jouy, originally a deeper colour but now faded to a pale red and buff.

She unbuttoned her blue dress and hung it up, feeling that she owed it to many to take special care of it: the previous owner, probably a French refugee in London who had been persuaded, or perhaps needed, to sell it, the SOE staff workers who searched through the city for foreign clothes and luggage to make sure their agents went into the field French from collar to toe, the French tailor who altered the dress to fit Evelyn and who took enormous pains to ensure the seams were consistent with French dressmaking and the seamstress who sewed a false label into the neck.

These careful, expert people deserved her gratitude, down to the hairdresser who had cut her hair in the French manner, the dentist who had extracted her English fillings and turned them into French ones (not something she had enjoyed), and the cobbler who had attended to her shoes.

The mirror on the inside door of the cupboard swung open and she caught sight of herself in her cotton petticoat. Thin shoulders, dark hair and hands with bitten nails. She touched the place at the base of her throat where Paul had rested his finger and felt the pulse beat under her skin.

Of all the stupid, irresponsible things, to be diverted by a handsome face was the most dangerous. She fingered the strap of the petticoat before pulling it off over her head and reaching for her dressing gown. The man was almost certainly a German. Evelyn felt faint at the thought but with luck, nothing would come of the encounter and it had taught her a useful lesson. Evelyn tied the dressing-gown belt extra tight around her waist and switched off the light.

With what was now almost second nature, she approached the window from an angle, keeping to one side so that she could look out on the gardens without being observed. Her bedroom overlooked the back gardens. The view was of a series of terraces edged in box that descended to a ha-ha about three hundred yards away.

Moonlight flooded the scene and she remembered Captain Fuller's warning. 'You might not come back.' A little jab of fear went through her.

Captain Fuller and the other instructors had done their best to explain the dangers and to emphasise what could happen if she made a mistake. She closed her eyes and savoured the memory of the lunch under the trees, the feel of the sun – and her meeting with Paul. A curious impression that she had met someone who mattered sifted through her mind, and Evelyn was aware that she wanted very badly to live.

She knelt up on the window seat for a long time, watching the moon slide high over the garden.

CHAPTER EIGHT

A couple of days later Evelyn was at work in Charles's study, sorting through a pile of bills and correspondence. Some of it was weeks old and required immediate attention. She placed these in one pile. Other papers had his scrawl on them, often consisting of one word: 'Do', 'Nonsense', 'Yes'. These she had set aside to go through with him.

The door opened and Charles came in, dressed in riding breeches and smelling strongly of horses. Evelyn looked up and sniffed nostalgically. 'I shall have to ask you for some explanations of the technical terms,' she said cheerfully, wishing she had been the one out riding.

Charles dropped his crop into a chair. 'I want you to take a message to Françoise. Now, if you please.' A pair of English yellow string gloves joined the crop. 'You must stop what you are doing here now.'

Evelyn stacked the papers into neat piles and got to her feet, repressing a desire to say, 'You might at least be polite.' She was learning to put up with Charles's peremptory manner.

'You can use your cover as Evelyn Liegaux. Françoise lives in Chalais, and I have a business contact there who makes corks for the wine bottles. If questioned you must say you were trying to see him.' Charles searched through Evelyn's pile of papers and scattered them. 'Ah yes. Here is his bill. We can be querying it.'

Evelyn sighed at the sight of the disarranged papers. 'Yes, I see.'

'Chalais is about twenty kilometres west of Ribérac in the occupied zone,' said Charles, and gave Evelyn relevant details. 'You can either try and beg a lift with Chenier who works in the vineyard, or you can take the bus. Give Françoise my message and bring back any she may have for me.'

Evelyn pushed her chair underneath the desk. 'Yes.'

'Remember, the Germans like to spring *rafles* at bus stops.' Charles rummaged in a drawer of the desk. 'Where did I put . . . ? Ah.' He held up a couple of franc notes. 'You'd better take these for expenses.'

Evelyn put the bill and the money into her pocket. 'Thank you. I will account for the francs when I come back.'

'Nobody can tell who I am,' she reassured herself as she climbed up into Chenier's van waiting in the back yard. Even so, she pulled her headscarf further down over her face because she still couldn't quite believe that 'secret agent' wasn't stamped all over her face in black ink.

Monsieur Chenier smoked a very pungent kind of cigarette in yellow paper. Cloaked in smoke, Evelyn sat quietly beside him as he coaxed his ancient van along the D2 to Chalais. He was taciturn, but he glanced at Evelyn once or twice as if he was trying to work out just who she was. At Chalais he dumped her unceremoniously and drove off with a wheeze from the *gazogène* exhaust.

Feeling odd and conspicuous Evelyn moved over into the lee of a house. 'Nobody can tell who you are,' she reiterated firmly, 'unless you act suspiciously.' She looked around for evidence of German soldiers.

The first time Evelyn hunted – she was fifteen and it was Boxing Day 1934 – she had got up at dawn. After grooming her mare until she shone, she had spent a good hour in front of the mirror arranging her stock and adjusting her hair until she was satisfied. The hunt was a social occasion and interested observers would watch and comment sharply on newcomers and their performance. The morning was bright and frosty – nose-tingling, cheek-reddening weather. Evelyn's mare had been desperate to get going and she had been forced to stand apart from the main body of the meet while she attempted to control it. It had been a lovely, noisy diversion, enlivened by jokes and stirrup cups and the colourful motley of horses, people and dogs.

It remained a game as Evelyn allowed her horse its head

after the first sighting, and she gasped with pleasure as the cold air hit her face and the ground accelerated past beneath her. It was superb. It was magic. Never before had she experienced anything like it. Then, streaking through the scrub bushes to her right, Evelyn saw the fox, its brush flying behind its body; a small terrified panting animal. And what she had been so carelessly enjoying turned into something quite different.

Watching the faces in the street in this small French town, Evelyn was reminded of the hunted fox. The quick surging step and hunched shoulders of some, the anxiety written on the faces of others, the weariness with which they hefted bags of shopping from one hand to another. These people were bewildered and, in a less dramatic way, at bay.

Evelyn looked at her watch. It was eleven o'clock. After some trouble she located Françoise's house down a side street. The houses here opened directly onto the cobbled road. Since they had been built they had subsided so that their windows were not much above the level of the streets. As she passed, she could see inside into yellow-faded-into-cream painted kitchens with iron ranges and rows of blackened pots hung on the walls. She could hear a genial level of chatter, punctuated by children's cries of 'Maman'.

Eventually she found the correct door and knocked.

It was jerked open an inch or so. 'Yes?' shouted a woman's voice through a crack.

Evelyn explained who she was looking for, and the woman clicked her tongue. 'She's not here, you will have to go to Aubeterre and ask for Madame Degas's laiterie. She is working there.'

The door shut in Evelyn's face and she had no option but to make her way back to the centre of Chalais. Summoning a coolness she did not feel, Evelyn made enquiries about the buses. A woman with frightened eyes and a lined face told her she would have to wait for an hour so Evelyn made her way to a café, sat down at a table and pretended to read a pamphlet which she picked up, entitled: 'Why the Maréchal Pétain is working for you'. Every time someone approached her table her heart missed a beat. It resumed extra fast when they moved on.

It was only eight kilometres or so to Aubeterre, but the journey took well over half an hour. The bus was crammed with people – old ladies in shapeless black dresses and men in baggy trousers and serge jackets – as well as numerous baskets of fruit and vegetables. At Roufliac a man climbed on board with a protesting hen under his arm and sat down next to Evelyn.

'*Excusez-moi, Mademoiselle,*' he muttered through teeth black with decay. '*Excusez-moi.*'

In Aubeterre the *laiterie* appeared to be shut. Evelyn took a risk and peered through one of the windows into a tiled room stacked with empty bottles. It was dark and closed.

'What do you want, Mademoiselle?' shouted a man with a moustache from the back yard. Evelyn jumped.

'Is Françoise here?' she asked politely.

The man hesitated before walking over, wiping his hands on his apron. 'Who are you?' He pulled at his moustache while he looked her up and down.

'I'm a friend,' she said, wishing she sounded more convincing.

'Are you?' He was making up his mind whether to believe her or not.

'Yes. She's expecting me.'

'Well, if Françoise is expecting you, I'm sure you can wait. She's at lunch and won't be back for half an hour.'

Evelyn thanked him and retraced her steps back to the main square where she had seen a café. She was hungry. However, on searching in her shoulder bag she realised that she had forgotten to bring her ration cards with her. Charles's money did not stretch to a black-market lunch and she resorted to buying a packet of nuts – the only non-rationed food available. While she ate them rather miserably, she watched a couple at the next table eating plates of stew.

It was the little things that mattered, the details that made such a difference to comfort and peace of mind. Evelyn knew that. The instructors had tried to engender an ultra-cautious frame of mind. 'Do you have your papers? Where are you going? Why? That is not a good enough story . . .' They were right, and Evelyn, lunchless in Aubeterre, sent them silent recognition and awarded herself one mark out of ten for field-craft.

The *laiterie* was back in production when Evelyn returned, hungry and jumpy. On enquiry from one of the workers, a tall girl with a plait detached herself from a basin filled with milk bottles which she was washing. The two girls shook hands.

'Have you seen cousin Madeleine?' Evelyn gave the pass-word, keeping a wary eye out for the man with the mous-tache.

Françoise slipped her arm through Evelyn's. 'Only the other day,' she replied and led her out of earshot. 'She sends her love and says that Tante Marie-Thérèse is better.' Françoise produced two cigarettes from her apron pocket and offered one to Evelyn. 'You're in luck, I scrounged these off my friend over there.' She pointed to one of the men stacking crates. Both girls lit up and leant against the wall. They seemed to be gossiping – indeed, they discussed the difficulty of buying stockings. When they finished their cigarettes, Evelyn leant forward and stubbed hers out with her shoe. 'The leader asks if you could send Gilbert over to help,' she said.

Françoise held out her hand. 'You should catch the bus if you hurry,' she said, tossing back her plait with a wink, 'but you won't be back before dark.'

Françoise was right. It was dark and well after curfew when Evelyn let herself out of the wine cellar at Belle-Place, exhaus-ted and irritable. She had been on the move since ten o'clock that morning. At Ribérac she had been forced to walk back to Belle-Place, and it had been far from pleasant dodging into doorways and under hedges whenever she thought a car was coming. In the silent dark, half running, half walking, the loneliness of the job had struck her hard.

'Not bad,' said Charles when Evelyn reported the events of the day to him. They were standing half-way down the grand staircase, supposedly discussing one of the paintings that hung on the wall. He indicated a stiff, bejewelled figure in a family group dating from the *belle époque*. 'Many Germans around?'

Evelyn stared at the painted face, amused by the strong family likeness which ran through the de Bourgraves. 'I didn't see any,' she replied.

'Hm,' said Charles. This time he pointed to a picture in a gilded frame of a ravishing, sparkling-eyed lady in satin and ostrich plumes. 'My English great-great-great-aunt,' he said. 'Rather infamous.' Evelyn raised her eyebrows politely. Charles cleared his throat. 'Tomorrow you are going to Angoulême. I want money taken to a contact in the old town. You will have to spend the night at a safe house. By the way, did you hear anything interesting while you were out?'

'Only something on the bus coming back. Apparently there has been an incident at La Rochebeaucourt.'

Charles went downstairs into the hall. 'Ah yes,' he said.

She wondered what he meant, but decided not to probe. Instead, she went to the dining room and helped herself to an apple and a peach. Up in her room she lay down on her bed to eat them, but half-way through the peach she pushed aside the plate and fell asleep.

Angoulême shared the fortified appearance of many of the cities and towns in the region. Situated on top of a steep ridge overlooking a valley, the old quarter was dominated by a grey, ornately façaded cathedral and networked by a series of narrow, random-seeming streets. Otherwise Angoulême enjoyed the benefits of a major railway junction which handled the *wagons de grande capacité*, the special long-distance trucks now used to ferry food and equipment into Germany.

Evelyn passed the cathedral and turned down a street that led into the centre of the old quarter, following it until it opened into a small square. There were few people about and not many shops, except for a chemist and a book shop, the dusty-looking contents of which suggested that it had seen better days. At one point, Evelyn was convinced that someone was shadowing her and grew uneasy but resisted the impulse to look back over her shoulder. Using a shop window for its reflection she checked the street behind her. After a minute she was reasonably satisfied that the street was clear of tails but as an extra precaution she turned down a side street and began to zig-zag towards her destination.

Number 10, rue de la Harpe was situated at the corner of a square, next door to the Café Coquelot. Evelyn waited unobtrusively until the square was clear of pedestrians and then knocked on the door with the aid of a brass knocker in the shape of a woman's hand. Dressed in a thick tweed suit, the woman who appeared in the doorway had a pile of white hair done up in a bun on top of her head, rather like a brioche.

'Do you have any frogs' legs on the menu?' Evelyn asked. 'My aunt Marie-Thérèse wishes to know.'

'Dear me, yes,' replied the woman. 'Come in.'

She hustled Evelyn upstairs to an *appartement* on the first floor.

As soon as they were inside she took Evelyn by the hand and peered into her face. 'You are young,' she said after scrutinising Evelyn hard. 'It's a bad business.' She added as an afterthought, 'How is the dear Count?'

At first Evelyn felt rather discouraged. This bobbing, elderly lady was not the kind of person she had envisaged for this work. Until, 'These bloody Boches,' exclaimed her hostess, one hand on her hip. Evelyn was startled by the blunt language issuing from such genteel lips and bit back a smile. 'They are idiots to come here.' She darted around the room, fetching wine and biscuits while Evelyn looked at her mud-splashed shoes.

By the time she had finished her first glass Evelyn realised Madame Herier possessed a courage and determination that matched those of anyone she knew. The old woman had evidently taken some serious risks for Charles and she felt a little ashamed at her initial doubts.

'You will dine with me,' Madame Herier announced.

'Oh, no. I couldn't put you to such trouble,' said Evelyn without much conviction. She was hungry. The previous night she had missed dinner at Belle-Place and this morning had missed lunch because of the trip to Angoulême. She need not have wasted her breath. Madame Herier insisted on giving Evelyn the best meal she could produce and, sitting at a table over-large for the room, they ate onion soup, artichokes in garlic sauce and gritty bread.

'*Peste*,' said Madame Herier, biting into it. 'This is not good. Of course,' she explained, pouring another glass of excellent claret, 'now that my husband is dead, I don't have anybody around much.' She glanced towards a large sepia photograph of a military gentleman framed in black silk, then put down her spoon and moved across the room towards the window. Lifting the heavy lace curtain an inch or so she looked down into the square. 'I think we are all right, my dear,' she said, letting the curtain fall. 'Sometimes I've seen a man in a velour hat hanging around here.'

Evelyn stared at her in some horror, a coldness gathering in her chest. 'Madame, you must take care.'

'They can kill me if they like,' said her hostess without a trace of fear. 'I'm old.'

Evelyn finished her meal with a reduced appetite.

Evelyn did not sleep well. It was before dawn when she woke, and she went over and over in her mind what she would have to do that day. Determined not to expose Madame Herier to danger one minute longer than necessary, she got up early. But the old woman, her white hair neatly braided, was already up and waiting for her with a cup of coffee. 'May *le bon Dieu* keep you safe,' she said.

Evelyn's contact was due in the market square at nine o'clock, and she spent the interval moving unobtrusively from street to street, keeping a constant watch for tails. At the correct time she made her way down a long line of stalls towards the end of the row where the honey sellers congregated. She stopped in front of the one which displayed the notice, 'The best honey in Périgord'. She lifted a pot containing clear, light brown honey. 'This one,' she said, 'what sort is it?'

'*Mille fleurs*,' said the youth behind the stall.

'And this one?' Evelyn picked up a much darker honey.

'*Tilleul*. Lime, and that one is clover.'

'Ah yes. But I think I would prefer a pot from Bonnard's farm.'

The youth did not even blink. 'Yes,' he said, 'you'll want my father, then. Over there.' He jerked his head.

Evelyn approached a parked van and spoke to a man sitting in the driver's seat. After a minute, he got out, went round to the back of the van followed by Evelyn and opened the doors, shielding them from view. Evelyn extracted a roll of francs from her basket and passed them over. Bonnard immediately pulled aside a wooden panel at the side of the van and slipped them behind it. Then he handed Evelyn a pot of honey.

'One thing,' he said. 'We've got a parcel we must get rid of today. Can you help?'

'What sort of parcel?'

'English.' Bonnard flicked his eyes in the direction of a bench where, dressed in a badly fitting suit, a fair-haired youth was pretending to read a newspaper. He looked raw, out of place and scared out of his wits. Evelyn was dismayed by the savage RAF haircut, the uneasy posture and Anglo-Saxon complexion. She met Bonnard's questioning gaze and felt an unworthy desire to disappear into the crowd.

'Where's he come from?' she spoke in a whisper.

'Shot down near Poitiers.' Bonnard began to pile the jars of honey into a box.

Evelyn inspected her own jar. 'Sure he's not a plant? Did you check?'

'No,' said Bonnard. 'But we know he's genuine. Arrived yesterday. And the Boches have been searching the town for someone.'

The honey was a deep amber with a hint of orange. She peered into the jar as if the answer to her dilemma was inside it. She was well aware that sentiment or misplaced loyalty towards a fellow Englishman were dangerous – could force wrong decisions. Nevertheless she could no more leave the man – who was no more than a boy – than she could an animal in distress.

'Mademoiselle?' said Bonnard.

'All right,' she answered with a shrug. 'Can I have any help?'

'Too dangerous for me,' said Bonnard, finishing packing

his honey. 'But my son will get him into the station. I'm afraid you're on your own after that.' He closed the van doors. 'Thanks,' he said awkwardly. The two of them said goodbye. Bonnard rejoined his son at the stall and spoke to him.

Evelyn retired to the bench and sat down beside the airman. She bent over and retied her shoelace. 'I am your contact,' she informed him in an undertone. 'Don't say anything.'

Bonnard junior caught her eye and moved off.

'Follow him.' Evelyn straightened up. 'I will be behind you.' The airman put his hands onto his knees and made an effort to push himself to his feet. He was alarmingly white and shaky-looking but after a second stood upright.

Bonnard's son stopped at frequent intervals to allow them to catch up, leading them through the back streets, across empty yards and through gardens until he reached a high wire fence. Beyond it lay the station. Their guide lit a cigarette. 'You buy the tickets,' he said *sotto voce* to Evelyn as she passed him. 'I will deal with the parcel and give it to you on the platform. *Attention!* Boches everywhere.'

Evelyn bought two return tickets to Aubeterre and pushed her way through the queue of passengers onto the platform. Crossing the track, she spotted Bonnard and the airman hiding behind a stationary carriage in a siding. Evelyn strolled up the platform, taking mental notes of the station layout in case they had to make a run for it. Two German staff officers were holding a conversation by the ticket barrier. Evelyn's eyes widened but her step did not falter. Further down the line, a posse of *cheminots* was working on the points; the clink of their tools against the metal was clearly audible. Beyond them stretched a line of labelled freight cars. As she turned to retrace her steps, it occurred to Evelyn that the freight was an obvious target for sabotage.

A breeze got up and the afternoon was chilling fast. She pushed back the hair from her face and concentrated on how to get the airman to Ribérac unnoticed. When the train for Aubeterre arrived Bonnard pushed the airman out of their hiding place and disappeared. Uncertain of which carriage to get into, the airman hovered: a dead give-away. Evelyn, watching from a few metres away, signalled him on and the man grabbed hold of a door handle and pulled himself up into the train.

In the corridor she stumbled against him. 'Can you talk French?' she whispered.

He shook his head.

'Go into the first empty compartment. I warn you, if you are caught I will have to disown you.'

Inside the compartment she chose a seat nearest the corridor. The airman slumped beside her. His nose was running and he wiped it with his sleeve. Evelyn passed him her handkerchief, knowing it was up to her to get them both to safety. 'Are you armed?' she murmured.

'Yes.' He did not seem sure.

Evelyn flipped open the flap of her leather shoulder bag and pretended to scrutinise her face in a hand mirror. The corridor was clear. She closed the bag, leant over and nuzzled the airman's shoulder. 'Do exactly as I say. You must pretend you are deaf and dumb.' The boy – no more than eighteen or nineteen – flushed deep red, accentuating his sandy hair and unfinished features. Evelyn continued to whisper into his ear. 'It's only a short journey. When I get out you must follow me. On the platform, put your arm around me as if we were lovers.'

A fat woman pushed her way into the compartment. She settled herself by the window, from where she viewed Evelyn and her companion with disapproval.

Ten minutes into the journey movement in the corridor indicated that something was happening. Evelyn folded her gloves in her lap, disentangled herself from her charge and sat up. 'Tiens!' she remarked to the fat woman. 'The smoke today.' Once again she opened her bag, this time pretending to deal with a smut in her eye. Swimming into vision in the corner of her mirror she made out a man in a grey raincoat. He was standing at the entrance to the next-door compartment.

Evelyn's brain slotted obediently into action. To her surprise, she felt quite calm and made a great play of pushing and pulling at her eyelid. Eventually she closed her handbag and smiled at the fat woman. The door of the compartment opened and Evelyn's ticket was requested in a heavy German

114

accent. She handed it perfectly naturally to the Gestapo officer. After a cursory glance he gave it back to her. 'Your identity card, please.'

She gained the impression that he was not very interested. Perhaps he was tired, or bored by the business of monitoring sullen faces. He held the card up to the light with thick fingers and compared the photo with Evelyn.

'Your name?'

'Evelyn Liegaux.'

'Where were you born?'

'Tours.'

'Where are you going?'

'Aubeterre.'

'Why?'

The airman gave a phlegm-ridden cough. Evelyn glanced at him. 'To see my sister-in-law. She's a TB doctor,' Evelyn explained shyly.

'How much money have you got on you?'

'Only five hundred francs and some small change.'

His eyes streaming, the airman gave way to a paroxysm of coughing. The Gestapo officer turned down the corner of his mouth, handed back Evelyn's card, flicked his eyes over the airman and the fat lady and backed out of the compartment. Muttering under her breath about *'les mutilés de la guerre'*, the fat woman heaved herself out of her seat and left.

Paler than ever, the airman flopped back against the seat and Evelyn began to feel real concern for his health. She closed her eyes. So far, so good. For the moment.

On that Boxing Day meet, the fox had run for a long time: streaking across scrubland tangled with brambles and hips and carpeted with frost-crisp grass. Evelyn pounded behind it with the others. A mist settled over the afternoon and its wet droplets oozed over her clothes and face. There were so many reds: the berries in the hedgerows, the violent, dying sun, the pink-red of the huntsmen's coats, and finally the red of the fox's pelt, spread with scarlet. It gave a short, sharp scream as it died.

She kept her eyes closed for a moment longer and allowed the rhythm of the train to take her over. Then she thought of something. 'You must hide your gun,' she hissed into the airman's ear. She rolled over and pressed a kiss on his neck. He jerked awake from a half-doze. 'Push it down the back of the seat. Use me as a cover to do it.'

There was a glimpse of a black barrel, a hasty, furtive movement and the airman stuffed the gun down into the back of the seat.

'Pretend to be asleep.'

She turned her head as she spoke just as a second man in a grey raincoat walked down the corridor, looking carefully into each carriage. The door opened for a second time.

'Your bags, please,' said the Gestapo man.

Evelyn surrendered her handbag. The man opened it and searched inside. He caught her gaze and held it until she lowered her face with a soft smile. He hesitated, gave her back the handbag and moved on.

At Aubeterre Evelyn stood in the carriage doorway, blocking the view inside while the gun was retrieved. On the platform, the airman put his arm around Evelyn's shoulders as she had instructed him. It felt hot and dry against her neck and he was shivering.

'How do you feel?' she asked, after they had negotiated the ticket barrier and were out of earshot of other passengers.

The airman was beginning to shake. 'Not good,' he muttered. 'In fact, dreadful.' His eyes, registering shock at having been shot down and the terror of being hounded across France, filled with tears.

'Sorry,' he stuttered, and made an obvious effort to master himself.

'Only one more bus ride,' Evelyn encouraged, filled with sudden pity. 'And then you can rest. Don't give up.'

In the bus he slumped against her but eventually she was able to tell him, 'We are nearly there.' He almost whimpered and Evelyn felt renewed concern. The boy needed comfort. She took his hot, fevered hand between hers and gently stroked the fingers until they reached the bus stop.

Back at Belle-Place, Evelyn reported that she had hidden the airman in the wine passage and they needed Dr Mazille.

Charles took charge. 'Good. You did the best thing,' he

116

said, and, suddenly, Evelyn knew a trust had grown up between them. 'Now forget all about it. I'll do the rest.'

At least, Evelyn thought as she sank into a bath, at least I got through. And the knowledge sharpened and toughened the Evelyn that was beginning to emerge from the chrysalis of the old.

CHAPTER NINE

The question asked by the staff of the Special Operations Executive during the depressing months of 1941 was: Would the soe get off the ground?

It was a trickier question than might at first be supposed: soe was not popular with the older, established Special Intelligence Services. Their leaders' reaction to the birth of the organisation in July 1940 and to Winston Churchill's exhortation to its members to 'set Europe ablaze' was to mutter in their leather chairs in the clubs about blithering amateurs.

It was not entirely a matter of blimpish seniors reacting to the invasion of their territory by a young Turk. The sis knew the business. Their objectives were precise: they were after a steady flow of reliable, accurate information. They wanted everyday life to proceed as normally as possible. This allowed their agents – an old lady, a carpenter, a housewife – to meld into the background of a village in rural Italy close to the French border or a port in northern France with naval installations. The sis wanted no one to give it a second thought if their agents happened to wander close to interesting areas.

Considered, disciplined intelligence-gathering was put in jeopardy by those whose main objective, or so the sis had been led to believe by their grapevine, was to instigate 'bangs' – sabotage, derailments, road blocks, guerrilla attacks – in Nazi-occupied territories. In their view, 'bangs' were dangerous and made Jerry suspicious, prompting him to call for additional registration by the civilian population and hold interrogations. This rendered life extremely difficult for the non bona fide citizen. Jerry was also quite likely to shoot hostages in retaliation for resistance activity. In short, the waters became thoroughly muddy.

So the feeling ran in the clubs and comfortable rooms where

the well-bred, well-connected *éminences grises* of the clandestine took their decisions. The SOE staff experienced the full
force of establishment inertia working against them and had
to fight for transport, money, time and the confidence of
those who granted these things. They were not easily granted.
Added to that, keeping the secret of SOE was so important
that it was sometimes impossible to ask for supplies when
they were needed, because it imperilled this secrecy.

'Who are these blighters?' demanded one irritated civil servant in the Admiralty. 'Why do they keep on asking for
boats?'

'Don't know,' his colleague replied.

'Well, don't give 'em anything without a fight. We can't
have 'em wasting our resources.' The sentiment was echoed
in the Air Ministry and the War Office.

In the autumn and winter of 1941, the time and energy of
the overworked staff at SOE headquarters was being wasted
in fighting unnecessary battles at home and the situation was
too serious to permit such profligacy.

Former corporal and doss-house lodger, Adolf Hitler was
now the conqueror of eight European capitals: Warsaw,
Copenhagen, Oslo, The Hague, Brussels, Paris, Belgrade and
Athens. A war lord who had realigned the political structure
of Europe in less than five years and whose dominations
stretched from the grey-green Arctic tundra to the island of
Crete and yet further south to the frontier of Egypt.

In his political testament, *Mein Kampf,* Hitler inserted a clue
to his intentions into his glutinous prose. Germany, he wrote,
required more room and needed to expand eastwards.
Accordingly, on 22 June 1941 Hitler launched the most
ambitious phase of his plan for a thousand-year Reich: Operation Barbarossa. 'I have decided again today to place the fate
and future of the Reich and our people in the hands of our
soldiers,' he said, as the German army began to file along a
930-mile front into Soviet Russia. Simultaneously, Göring's
Luftwaffe attacked sixty-six Soviet aerodromes and bombed
Kovno, Minsk, Rovno, Odessa and Sevastopol. The lesson of
Napoleon and the retreat from Moscow ever fresh in the
minds of the military strategists, the move was received by

many German generals with professional horror. Russia, they felt, was just too big to conquer. Their objections, however, were temporarily silenced when the opening campaigns on the Russian front proved them wrong. The *Wehrmacht* proceeded to win a series of notable and decisive victories.

SOE had to grow up fast. Undercover warfare was a new science and demanded different attitudes. 'Give us this day lateral thinkers,' went Tony Turner's prayer, 'and grant us those who no longer behave like officers and gentlemen.' Survival meant being ahead of the enemy – unencumbered by scruples or sensibilities.

'There is a monster gobbling up Europe, Jack,' went Daniel's letter, 'and you are sitting on your backside doing nothing. Pacifism is a luxury.'

Jack Pickford winced when he got to that bit in the letter. As always, Daniel took his friendship with Jack very seriously and never pulled punches. Worse, Daniel had abandoned his own pacifism and was writing from the unimpeachably Olympian moral stance of having joined up as a rating in the navy where he was undergoing all the ritual horrors of service life.

'Come and join me in this hell,' finished the letter. 'We can talk about it in our old age.'

Jack shoved the letter into his pocket. Daniel was a dear friend, and in a slippery, increasingly chaotic world, Jack placed a premium on his affection. Nevertheless, the implications of the letter upset him.

With the lash of its contents fresh in his mind, Jack wandered into Tony Turner's office in SOE headquarters and requested a report just in from the debriefing section. 'God Almighty,' he said, after skimming the contents. 'We're just a flea on an elephant.'

'Make him scratch though.' Turner was putting his papers away.

Jack handed him back the report. 'Got any more news?'

Turner indicated the empty in-tray and shrugged. 'Not a squeak. We're waiting to hear from Alouette and her lot.' He sounded a bit worried. 'Marseille has gone quiet as well and we've got a few teething troubles with the BBC.'

'Jerry got them in Marseille, do you think?'

'Who knows?' said Turner, stuffing more paper into the files. (A rule at headquarters forbade leaving papers lying on a desk.) Turner was definitely troubled, Jack decided. 'We had in some good stuff from Benoit. An excellent run-down on petrol stores and oil dumps from Marseille to Bordeaux. But that's all.'

'Of course it might be very difficult to get the messages to the "pianist",' said Jack, 'particularly if the place is stiff with Germans.'

'Hmm,' said Turner. 'I gather the pianist is holed up with his wireless in a house in the old port. Nasty, really.'

Jack stared at the blacked-out window. Autumn always had a depressive effect on him, and this one was the worst yet. 'Damn,' he said, and thought unfairly: Damn Daniel.

There was, he thought, a link between his socialism and his instinctive pacifism strengthened by Quaker roots. Or, at least, that is how it had originally seemed. But as doubt muddled his reasoning, Jack was increasingly asking himself whether or not his pacifism was only an excuse to shift responsibility for beating Hitler onto someone else's shoulders.

Worse: had the establishment subverted him more thoroughly than he suspected? Had the defensive, prickly scholarship-boy-from-the-north-made-good been seduced by the symbols of King and Empire – a convert to the world of Kipling's *Kim* and the 'Great Game'? Had he, Jack Pickford, the man who wanted to change the old order, given in to its commandments to put King and country first?

The job, when it came, had been welcome – it avoided the problem of call-up papers. A friend from his Oxford days was employed by Slaughter and May, a firm of city solicitors. Slaughter and May had important contacts in SOE: Jack's friend had become involved. In turn, the friend slipped in a word for the brilliant linguist Pickford. The result: one excellent staff officer working at the SOE headquarters who appreciated the current joke that SOE was 'All may and no slaughter.'

Getting the job had been yet another call on the old-boy

network, and Jack suffered it with moderate grace. He suffered less gracefully some of his new colleagues, even though he knew that the upper-class accents often concealed a ruthlessness and intelligence that was hard to match.

'Poor blighters,' Jack said, imagining what it was like to be an agent sweating it out in an attic room in Marseille.

He picked up an edition of *Bottins* and riffled through the list of French factories and industrial complexes without really looking at the print. Then he put it down and went over to the window. Turner's office was very small and cramped.

Turner cast him a look. 'Getting fidgety, are we?' He himself was over thirty and considered himself settled and mature.

'Yup,' said Jack, and turned to look at the map of France on the wall. He ran his finger down until it reached Pau near the Pyrenees.

As a student he had spent the summer vacation walking along the pilgrim trail from Pau in France to Santiago de Compostela in northern Spain. Not in the spirit of religious discipline – Jack had rejected his family's Quakerism and all religion. No, it was more of an aesthetic exercise. He disliked the gaudy extremes of Catholicism but he was curious and wanted to test himself physically.

The walk had been long, hot and hard and Jack enjoyed every minute. He loved coming down off the road into villages smudged with summer dust and torpid with heat. He loved the clear exhilaration of the mountain air, and the heavier heat that sat below the ranges. He loved sitting outside village bars or cafés in the evenings, drinking red Rioja until he could stay awake no longer. Sweaty, stiff and blistered, he acquired a taste for the Latin way of life that clashed pleasurably with the sober plan he had set out for his future. He made friends with some of the pilgrims he met on the road and, in unguarded moments, even found himself envying their gift of faith.

Tony Turner was a shrewd man. He watched Jack's finger circle Pau. 'They would never let you go, Pickford. You're a security risk,' he said, thankful that he himself had got past the stage when one thirsted to go into action. There was honour in sitting behind a desk, and he was glad he was seasoned enough to appreciate the fact.

'They've let de Guélis go,' said Jack, referring to F-section's briefing officer, who had spent a month in France on reconnaissance, making contacts and recruiting. He had brought back precious information on ration cards, identity papers, railway timetables.

'Yes,' said Turner, 'that's different. You know as well as I do, we can only afford to do that sort of thing once.'

Jack turned back to the map. 'How many have we got out there now?'

'Well over a dozen, including Benoit and Alouette.' Jack's interest was aroused and he swivelled round to face Turner. 'Did you know them, then?' asked Turner, observing Jack's expression.

'I'm pretty sure I interviewed Alouette when I helped out for a couple of days.'

'Good material or not?'

'Very young,' said Jack sourly. 'I recommended her in the end. Just. But I'm not at all sure about her. Too young.'

'You should see some of the lot we've got now,' interrupted Turner. 'They need leading reins.' He remembered a snippet of information. 'Gossip has it that Alouette was a good shot.'

'Was she?' said Jack. 'Well, at least she's got that. Can't think why she volunteered. Very comfortable background.'

'Perhaps,' said Turner, meaningfully, 'she wanted to escape from something.' And more meaningfully, 'Some people do, don't they? Didn't you like her?'

'Not my type.'

Tony Turner screwed the top onto his fountain pen and glanced at his watch. 'I'll tell you one thing,' he said. 'Anyone who goes into France has my vote for courage.'

'Or lack of imagination,' said Jack, by now thoroughly disgruntled with himself. He knew perfectly well that Evelyn had not struck him as such. He stuffed his hands into his trouser pockets and hunched his shoulders.

'Now that,' said Turner, rising to his feet, 'is very unimaginative of you. Put it down to innocence rather, if you wish to persist in being unfair . . . or should I say jealous? I think you need a drink.'

Jack stared at Turner for a moment. Then he laughed. 'Reproof taken,' he said, hauling his hands out of his pockets. He brushed back a lock of dark hair that had flopped over his forehead and reached for his cap.

It was six o'clock, and chaotic, dirty, glass-strewn London was pulling herself together for the night.

The nights were kinder to the bomb-raddled city than the days, for they smoothed away the craters and the rubble and hid the splintered wood and powdered coal that half filled holes where houses had once been. Particularly when the sirens – 'Moaning Minnies, luv' – no longer sounded with clock-like regularity as they had during the terrifying months of the Blitz. No, when night came Londoners had a chance to forget that the Luftwaffe had attempted to reduce their city to rubble. At night, except for the whiffs of gas and the smell of water-soaked dust which infiltrated the oddest places, London looked and felt almost like old times.

In the evenings, hotels filled up. Nightclubs threw open their doors to all ages, all types, uniformed and civilians, gay and raucous, drunk, despairing, hell-bent on pleasure, who slept where they could: on floors, in hotel lounges and in Tube stations. Guests were invited to dinner and offered a bath as part of the hospitality. Children were packed up like parcels, labelled and bundled onto trains, leaving wet patches from nerves and tears on the platforms. Watching them depart, bewildered and frightened, for the safety of America or Canada, even Australia, many parents were forced to the discovery that this was the greatest war sacrifice of all.

Since the war began, sandbagged, entrenched London had expanded, contracted and expanded. Manners changed overnight. There were foreign uniforms in Mayfair and more foreign refugees than ever before in the East End, cluttering up clubs and boarding houses. There was dust and more dust, wedding cakes with no icing, stews without onions, cigarettes that left specks of tobacco on the lips and dancing to Lew Stone's band.

Outside number 64, Baker Street, the evening had thrown

its camouflage over the street. Jack enjoyed the moment of transition, when women exchanged bare legs and scrubbed faces for carefully hoarded stockings and lipsticks. (*'Il faut skimp, pour être chic,'* said *Vogue*.)

'Do they still have cosmetics in France, do you suppose?' Jack wondered aloud as they strolled down Baker Street.

'Sun gone to your head, dear boy?' asked Turner. 'Why on earth do you want to know?' He walked on. 'Aha,' he said, a light breaking. 'I see why you're so jumpy. You have a lovely waiting for you over in France.'

'No, Turner, I haven't. I only wondered,' Jack replied. He was, in fact, trying to imagine the conditions Alouette was working under. He rolled a satisfying picture around his mind of Evelyn St John living in an outhouse and sleeping under old sacks. 'French women mind about those sort of things.' He changed the subject. 'Do we know anything about conditions over there?' He moved aside to allow an elderly lady passage.

Turner lowered his voice. 'Curfew regulations, cigarette prices, bicycle regulations, that sort of thing? Trouble is, the rules on identity cards and work permits change every month or so, which makes it impossible for our chaps to work on them.'

Jack also lowered his voice. 'Won't the chaps in SIS help us out at all on that sort of thing?'

Turner shook his head. 'Stupid, isn't it?'

They walked on to the pub, wrestling with the problem of how to gather information about a country which, now that war had placed a black-out on communication, might have been at the other end of the globe.

'What about the French Secret Services?' said Jack. 'Some of them must be helping us, even if they're pretending not to. Surely they could get out the information we need?'

Turner shrugged. 'Who knows?'

As usual, the pub they had adopted as 'theirs' was almost empty, which was one of the reasons they liked it. Conducting conversations outside – which was a safe place – was not always pleasant in cold weather. Staff had been warned to be on guard against possible German spies and they took the warning seriously.

The pub was warm, filled with a permanent smoke haze and the two men sat down in the corner with their beer. Jack liked Turner and felt comfortable with him. Turner did not act superior. He was content to take Jack's brains and achievements for what they were.

'We have a new nickname,' Jack settled himself on the tatty plush. 'The Racket.'

Turner blew foam away from the side of the glass. 'Not an affectionate one, I fear.'

Jack hesitated before he imparted the next piece of information. 'Did you know that the Foreign Office have ordered that there must be no more "bangs" in the unoccupied zone without their permission?'

'I needed that,' Turner said, as he drained his glass. He put it back down on the table. 'You keep a close ear, Pickford. Yes, I knew about it. It's a serious problem.'

'It's outrageous,' said Jack hotly.

Turner got out his pipe. 'We'll just have to show them then, won't we?' he said, without rancour.

'I think the sis lot need their necks wrung.' Jack became infuriated whenever he thought of the establishment's hostility. 'I bet they make it their business to read our wireless traffic and to help themselves to any intelligence they fancy.'

Turner put the pipe down on the table and gave a quick look around the pub. 'Shut up, Pickford,' he warned. 'We're not in the office.'

Jack pushed back his hair with one hand and got up to fetch refills.

'What do we know?' He shoved the fresh glass towards Turner.

His companion raised his eyebrows in despair. 'This is supposed to be a relaxing drink.'

'There's a war on.'

Jack picked up his cigarettes, Turner's tobacco pouch and a beer mat and arranged them on the table. He began to talk very fast.

'France is divided into two – well, three. Unoccupied

126

France, ruled by Maréchal Pétain – but really Hitler – and a bunch of right-wing generals from their cosy hotels in Vichy. Occupied France centred on jackbooted Paris, plus a sub-section, the *zone interdite* that covers the northern coastline and is virtually impossible to penetrate. I imagine our friends from the SIS are working away at that one. We also know the French are divided politically. A percentage back Adolf. But there are also strong Communist loyalties, particularly in the industrial areas. The rest of the population get by and keep their heads down.'

Turner yawned. It had been a long day.

'The point is,' said Jack and swept the cigarettes and beer mat into a heap, 'we're working in the bloody dark, with a dozen agents, a few wireless and a couple of containers of arms. On top of that, our own bloody side won't lift a finger to help.'

'You need a dose of liver salts,' said Turner. 'And I am going back to work.'

As they were retracing their steps up Baker Street, 'You see,' Jack resumed the conversation, 'I've thought about it. You can't target sabotage, train resisters, arm them and lead them when the invasion takes place without proper back-up.'

'No,' agreed Turner. 'That's correct. But it takes time.'

'We haven't got time.' Jack's frustration was evident. 'The situation is frightful and all we can do is send out girls like Alouette.'

Turner stopped and knocked the bowl of his pipe against a lamp-post. 'Strikes me,' he observed mildly, 'you're obsessed with this girl.'

'Good God,' Jack was startled. 'Absolutely not.'

'All I can say,' said Turner, poking his pipe stem gently into Jack's chest, 'is she has an advantage over you, Pickford. She's in the field and you're not.'

Trust Turner to hit the nail on the head with little words that pricked and jabbed. Jack turned them over and over in his mind. It was true. Alouette was in France, dealing with loneliness, possibly hunger and fatigue – and even terror. He, Jack Pickford, sat stung and waspish in London, the only adventure in sight a binge at Kate Meyrick's nightclub.

How had it come about that a girl raised on milk puddings and 'nanny knows best', whose make-up was a compound of gentility and social accomplishments, who had been taught to say nothing of interest, whose father's politics, he imagined, were of the most rigid – how did a girl like that end up in the field, where she was tackling the Nazis, and he didn't?

He knew perfectly well why not.

During the next few weeks, Jack ate the sour bread of self-doubt. It took him some time to decide what he was going to do. His decision was precipitated partly by the report smuggled back to England of the massacre in November 1941 of forty-eight hostages in Nantes, shot in revenge for the assassination of a German colonel, partly by the news of the round-up of agents at the Villa des Bois in Marseille – which at a stroke halved the F-section agents in Vichy France – partly by the feeling that it was no longer morally admissible to sit in the wings and partly by the telegram.

The knock on the door sounded before Jack was properly dressed. A telegraph boy stood in the hallway and held out a yellow envelope. 'Telegram sir.'

Slowly, very slowly, Jack wiped his hands on the towel he was carrying. The telegraph boy thrust it at him, bobbed his head and turned away.

'Thank you,' Jack called after him. He went back inside and, very conscious of each piece of clothing he put on, finished dressing. He brushed his hair and polished his shoes; he even made a cup of tea. After that he knew he had to face the contents of the telegram.

REGRET DANIEL WENT DOWN WITH CONVOY, read the text from Daniel's mother. NO SURVIVORS.

The tea steamed on the kitchen table and Jack watched it, wondering why he felt nothing.

NO SURVIVORS.

Had Daniel known what was happening as the water washed over his frizzy brown hair and filled his mouth and lungs? Had he been screaming with pain? Would the fish, or whatever lived down there, trace his obstinate chin in a watery salute before he disintegrated?

128

What a bloody waste.

Jack endeavoured to drink the tea but his hand shook too much to insert his finger through the cup's handle. He tried to pick the whole thing up, burning his hand. The cup dropped back into the saucer. Tea sloshed over the table.

Why did Daniel have to have been on the convoy that sank?

He could not bear to touch the telegram, and left it where it lay, damp and soggy, on the kitchen table where he found it when he came back from work.

Grief, he discovered during the following weeks, was extremely selfish. It didn't admit anyone else into its exclusive territory. Angry and bitter, Jack missed Daniel more than he thought possible and he was not at all nice to the friends who, risking a verbal flaying, tried to comfort him.

One night he got drunk at Kate Meyrick's nightclub, resigned what remained of his pacifism to memory and applied the next day for active service in the field.

CHAPTER TEN

Darling Paul,

I have made a resolution to write to you every day – we have a duty to cheer the soldier on. I am writing this in my bedroom, watching the carts come in from the fields. It is dark so early now and it makes me feel even more depressed. Still, I will be going back to Berlin in a day or two. Of course, I wouldn't say this to my parents but it *is* awfully depressing here without you.

Do you miss me? Are French women very beautiful?

When can you come back? Let me know in good time and I will arrange a big party. Berlin is very gay at the moment – and I go to a reception every night. It's almost as if we weren't at war at all.

With all my love,
    Ingrid

Ribérac
15 November 1941

Dear Ingrid,

I don't have time to answer your letter in full. But this is just to tell you I will be writing to you properly as soon as I can, and I have settled in.

Yours,
    Paul

The rue de Théâtre in Ribérac was paved with grey cobbles and was so narrow that pedestrians went in danger of their

130

limbs – if not their lives – when vehicles forced a passage down it. Henri's bicycle shop was situated half-way along, beside a house with white shutters. Before the war, Henri had done well, but the shortage of materials and lack of money had seen his business change from a thriving to a declining one. Henri, however, was philosophical about the change in his fortunes. His situation was no better and no worse than that of his friends and associates – except for the black marketeers, of course.

The room John and Evelyn used was directly above the main shop. It was stuffed with bicycle impedimenta – wheels, spokes, pumps – and islands of grease discoloured the wood floor.

Evelyn pulled back a curtain which had seen better days. She was acting as look-out by the window which gave out over the rue de Théâtre.

'Date?' John spoke with his pencil between his teeth.

'November 20 1941.'

He wrote a group of numbers down on the pad. He took his time and Evelyn felt a familiar damp prickle under her armpits. 'I don't like it here.' She rubbed her hands on her skirt. 'It's too risky.'

'*You* don't like it here, my duck,' John was also sweating. 'I don't think either of us does.'

'We won't use it again.' Evelyn seemed more agitated than normal. 'Couldn't you use the place over by Belle-Place I suggested? It would be much safer.'

'Jean-Claude couldn't get hold of the van to drive me out of the town. I didn't fancy walking it in broad daylight, holding an attaché case. And my sked was due.' John's ankle was practically healed and he had been moving, so far successfully, from safe house to safe house. Jean-Claude had brought him into town to wait until it was convenient to convey him to a farm near Lusignac. 'I feel like a parcel,' he added, in an effort to divert her. Evelyn flashed him a smile.

'You know what I think.' John encoded his message and checked a vertical column of letters. 'We ought to have several sets in different hiding places. I'm going to ask for some more.'

131

'Ask for the moon rather, my friend. I don't think there are spares.'

'Those fancy lads sitting on their *culs* back home just have to be made to see,' said John. 'Pardon my French.' He tapped his pencil on the pad in a parody of Morse.

Again Evelyn checked the street. 'I might be persuaded to,' she said affectionately. Silence, while both of them concentrated. Evelyn allowed the curtain to drop back over the window. 'Always keep an eye out for fat men who are constantly checking their watches,' she recited. 'They are fat because they've concealed detector sets under their clothing and their wrist watches are portable detector dials.'

'Do you mind!' protested John. 'I'm trying to forget about them. Where are the scouts?'

'In place. One in the front. One at the back. Did you check the exits?'

John looked up from his work. 'Always ensure', he mimicked to perfection a school-masterish instructor at Wanborough Manor, 'that there is an escape route out of any building you may be in. Either by a back door, a window, fire escape or across the roof.'

With his hands he executed a little mime depicting the instructor, acknowledged Evelyn's amusement with a flourish of his beret, and pulled his transmitter set towards him. The wireless transmitter, known as a paraset, had been donated to SOE – under pressure – by the SIS. Fitted with a Morse key, covering frequencies between 3 and 7.6 megacycles, it was capable of transmitting and receiving for well over a 500-mile radius but it was heavy to carry and took a bit of getting used to. Yet John felt an affection for the old beast which, considering what would happen if he was caught with it, was generous.

After plugging in the valves and headset, he selected the correct crystal and connected the power pack. Using the calibration curve pasted onto the lid of the box, he began to tune the receiver into the home station frequency. Fascinated by the procedure, Evelyn watched from her look-out point. John switched the arrowhead knob in the middle of the set to 'transmit', depressed the Morse key and twiddled the 'Tank' and 'Aerial', turning the knobs until the bulbs on the set glowed at their brightest. 'Got you, baby,' he said, in exaggerated American.

'Can I help with the coding?' asked Evelyn, who knew John spent long hours enciphering and deciphering.

'Just keep calm,' he replied, shoving the pencil behind his ear. 'This is my bit. Anyway! '"Tis done." Who said that?' He quizzed Evelyn but she was not quick enough to remember *Macbeth*.

'Oh, never mind,' John wagged a finger. 'I forgot I was working beside an ignoramus.' He checked the configurations. 'In double transposition no less, incorporating the double security check. Neat, watertight and in the best Thame Park tradition.'

The problem of creating a code that the German crypto analysts could not decipher was one that continually exercised the minds of the experts. At Thame Park, SOE's wireless training school, they favoured – for the present – the double transposition method. Cumbersome and immensely time-consuming, it was nevertheless as foolproof a code as it was possible to devise. So far.

Evelyn checked the street for a third time. It was clear. 'We've got an operation tonight,' she confided to John.

'Aha. That explains the troublesome little nerves that I can detect underneath the perfect agent,' said John. 'Thought you were rather jumpy.' He adjusted his headset and twiddled the knobs for a final time until the familiar hissing came through the earphones. 'Time?'

Evelyn checked her watch. 'Three fifty-five. Our time.'

'Time to go . . .' John limbered up his fingers and tapped out his call sign. Across the room, the giveaway aerial balanced on the window sill of a second window, which overlooked the garden. The radio detection units searched constantly for evidence such as this.

'Wake up, you buggers,' John muttered to himself. 'Get off your tight little backsides and do some work.'

It was a difficult moment, raising home station. The call sign often did not get through at first and the conditions might be unfavourable. Tension did not help the wireless operator and any delay allowed the Germans more time to pinpoint the 'pianists' with their equipment.

Evelyn had grown used to John's language and secretly relished the decadent flavour it conveyed: a world of night-clubs, dance halls and backstage chat from which she had decided that John came. She went over to him and touched him lightly on the shoulder to show she understood. He looked up for a second, face contorted with concentration, and then returned to the wireless.

The headphone emitted a stream of Morse. 'Got 'em.' He whispered triumphantly, and sent out his call sign. DRT to BDQ, DRT to BDQ. QTC 1 (I have one message to send to you) QRK (What's my intelligibility?) K (Over). Home base answered: BDQ QRK QRVK (To DRT. Your signal is intelligible. I am ready. Over.) John began to send coded letters . . . XBVTS RTOLE VMYEX BPIKW QMMLU. When he had finished, he waited, pencil and paper at the ready to take down home station's message. QSL AR, he tapped on the Morse key. I acknowledge receipt. Over and out. He pushed back his chair and grinned up at Evelyn. 'Phew,' he said.

At the secret radio station 53-A, located at Grendon Under-wood in Buckinghamshire, John's 'godmother', a FANY with a disastrous perm took off her headset. 'He sounds different today,' she reported. She pulled at one of the too-tight sausage curls. 'I hope nothing's wrong. His touch didn't sound quite right.'

'He's probably transmitting under insecure conditions,' commented the supervising sergeant, picking up the pad and tearing the page off. 'But I'll ask them to vet the message and his fingerprint and security check.' Each agent was given a special security check to incorporate into their message. Each one's touch on the transmitter key was unique and easily identifiable.

Exhausted from the effort of listening and concentrating, the FANY tidied her equipment. She wondered where DRT was – which country even – and what sort of conditions he was transmitting under – a hayloft perhaps, or a garret in a big city? She felt quite maternal about him and tried, but failed, to imagine what he looked like. The fact that home station depended on her keeping watch and listening for any changes in DRT's radio fingerprint bothered her sometimes. It was even more unnerving to know that her seniors relied in part on her judgement as to whether or not this man really was DRT.

The FANY pushed her curls under her cap, and finished putting away her equipment.

Sister Hélène watched the candle on the altar burn lower. She had been praying for some hours. Her back ached and her knees hurt, calloused as they were from years of praying. The candlelight felt as if it was burning her eyes, although Hélène knew perfectly well that this was her imagination. The result of hunger, more like. She had been fasting in an effort to do penance for repeatedly failing to confess to Reverend Mother about Charles's letter.

Why had Charles sent it? Why had he stirred up the past, a sediment so full of anguish and unanswered questions that it should have been left to settle? Hélène had arrived at an explanation: God sets each man and woman temptations and the inducement in the letter was one. It was up to her to resist it.

She blinked and the dazzle of the candle assumed normal proportions and she decided that starvation was not a remedy for her confusion. Ste Thérèse, Ste Cathérine, Ste Brigitte, these were nuns who responded to mortification of the body with mystical revelations but Hélène, as she often reminded herself, was not one of these elect. Her role was practical, supportive and earthbound.

'Dear Lord,' she prayed, and folded her capable, bony hands under her chin, 'will you help me? The world has disintegrated into war. There will be the sick, hundreds of them. There will be refugees, those on the run and those who lose the will to live. I will need all the strength you may grant me to deal with these. Please help me to do your will.'

She wished sometimes that God could be direct and speedy with his answers. She wished she had the wisdom to know her own motives.

Hunger always made Hélène feel dizzy and when she

finally lifted her head, the chapel swung around in circles. She pulled herself up onto the pew and waited for her vision to return to normal. Two other sisters were also absorbed in private prayer and she watched their motionless, unswervingly straight backs and wondered if they were struggling as she was. They seemed enclosed by a thick, private wall of prayer, and she envied their apparently effortless intimacy with God.

To do and not question. This was an exhortation difficult to accept for someone trained to use reason and to analyse, but they formed the bedrock of religious life.

Hélène was beginning to feel better. She rose to her feet, stood under the swagged crystal chandelier which had been a gift from a rich patron and looked at the altar before making her way to the door. In the corner of the nave she paused by the stone statue of Ste Jeanne and contemplated it for a moment.

'La plus brillante et la plus douce fleur de la France chrétienne et paysanne.'

Against all the conventions of her day Ste Jeanne had put on armour, picked up a sword and ridden into battle. Driven by her inner voices and a conviction of her own rightness, she had led armies, survived an arrow wound in the shoulder and crowned a king. Short-haired, flat-breasted, Ste Jeanne discarded her femininity and died as much for the confusion it engendered in her contemporaries as for anything else. But she *had* gone into battle, buoyed up by an unshakeable conviction and driven by a chivalrous imperative – pity for the oppressed. Could Hélène – *should* Sister Hélène – follow her into battle?

Hélène let herself out of the chapel and into the sharp night air.

'Je tire ma révérence.' Charles did not often sing which, as Bessy frequently pointed out, was fortunate for his listeners. But tonight he was keyed up.

It was six o'clock and curfew was in force. He looked out of the window. The weather was holding. Cold, dry and overcast. As he watched, the last fingers of light were extinguished in the west and dusk took a grip on the landscape. If the plan was proceeding, as agreed, then his group would be getting ready.

Tonight's operation was taking place because of a local band of Communists. A couple of days previously they had raided a small German garrison billeted on the *château* at La Roche-beaucourt, where they captured a cache of weapons. The Communist resistants had transported their booty as far as Belle-Place before the arrival of daylight made it too dangerous to go further. This was the incident Evelyn overheard referred to on the bus. The Communists needed help, and quickly, to hide their capture and their leader did a deal with Charles.

The captured weapons now lay hidden in Belle-Place's wine cellars and the Communists wanted them transferred to a hiding place over the demarcation line. Although it irked him, Charles agreed on condition he took a rake-off. Stranger alliances had been forged in wartime, he reasoned, than between a fervent royalist, such as himself, and a group of mad Communists. If Paris was worth a mass, then twenty grenades, two Mausers and an automatic machine-gun (complete with ammunition) made it worth supping with those he considered the devil's accomplices.

Having dismissed his valet for the night, Charles was having to dress himself. He pulled open a drawer and searched in it for a dark shirt, which he eventually found. He did up the buttons and went over the plan for the night. Packing, loading and transferring the weapons should take two to three hours, allowing for any backtracking and hold-ups at the line.

Charles searched for his socks in another drawer. The trouble with Communists was not their lack of bravery, rather the opposite. Picking off German personnel and organising raids were all very well but they were tactics that were bought at a price. After the raid at La Rochebeaucourt, the Germans had shot two suspects from the village.

No, he needed to think about a tentative suggestion Evelyn Liegaux had made: 'Why not organise a secret council where we agree common guidelines on resistance activity in the area?'

He stared at the mess he had made in the drawer. It would give his valet a heart-attack but he shut it without attempting to tidy the contents. Only a short while ago, when Russia had been on Germany's side, the Communists advised their members to support Germany and Charles was not inclined to trust them, however sensible Evelyn's suggestion was. He pulled on a dark blue jersey, brushed his hair and wound a dark silk scarf around his throat.

Mademoiselle Liegaux appeared to have picked up the situation quickly. Either she was exceptionally observant, or exceptionally well trained. Both perhaps; she was very reticent when he asked her about her training in England. Charles had not been disposed to like her at first – she was too young, and his responsibilities were, therefore, that much greater – but he had grown used to her. She was proving quick and resourceful. Better than that: reliable. So far, Mademoiselle Liegaux did what she was told, did it efficiently and made no fuss about it.

His lambswool lined *canadienne* jacket hung in the wardrobe. Charles put it on and checked in the pockets for his torch. The wardrobe door swung back, and he caught sight of himself in the mirror. Quite a different image from the normally dapper Count stared back at him. A half smile appeared on his lips. Charles was enjoying his transformation: it made him feel young again.

He wished he could have kissed Bessy goodbye. She was visiting friends in the village – and appeared to accept without question his explanation that he would be away on business, possibly for the night. Actually, she had not really been listening. She was preoccupied with other things.

'Do you think I will ever feel normal again?' she had joked. 'I can't believe it's so uncomfortable being pregnant.' An American unencumbered by delicate European sensibilities, Bessy was not afraid to bring up the subject of pregnancy and childbirth with her husband. 'Would you believe how my fingers have swollen?' She held up her hand, minus a wedding ring. 'Too bad I had to take it off.'

Charles picked up their wedding photograph from the bureau. The photographer had caught the moment when

Bessy turned to him, almost crushing her bouquet of lilies between them. 'I'm so happy,' she told him. 'I didn't believe I would be.'

Dressed in a cream silk suit, wearing a string of large and beautiful pearls (a gift from Charles) and the de Bourgrave diamond on her finger, Bessy, her tawny hair coiled and tamed for the occasion, leapt up at him from the photograph. 'It will not be easy, the two of us,' she seemed to say. 'But I want our marriage to work.' Charles looked at Bessy's picture for a moment longer, replaced it on the dressing table and left the room.

Mariette ladled out the soup so ineptly that it slopped over the bowl onto the table. It was bad enough that Jean-Claude had invited himself to dinner ('I thought I would see how you are getting on,' was the excuse) but to bring his mistress on some pretext or other was too much. Who did he think she was to have to provide food for all and sundry? Sundry in this case being Renée Legrand. Jean-Claude must think her stupid. Didn't he realise that the fact he laid this woman at frequent intervals was written over both their faces?

'How is your wife?' she asked maliciously, hoping to make Madame Legrand blush.

'In Angoulême, visiting Odilla,' replied Jean-Claude, amused for the moment by the crudity of Mariette's attack.

Odilla was Jean-Claude's eldest daughter, and no better than she should be either. However, *she* had married a rich man, lived in style near the cathedral and got away with her behaviour.

Renée Legrand shifted into a more comfortable position on the chair. She had good legs tapering to thin ankles of the kind which made you think all of her was as delicate (which it was not) and she did not hesitate to display them. Mariette caught a glimpse of white silk under Renée's dress and her temper worsened.

One day, she thought, a rich, handsome man is going to take me away from Bertric-Burée.

'*Chérie,*' he would say, 'I love you. There is no one else, there never will be, and I am going to care for you always

139

and you can spend what money you like and you will never have to work hard again.' It was a favourite fantasy of Mariette's and had been known to occupy up to fifteen minutes if she elaborated on the bedroom bit of the scene.

'Monsieur, your husband?' she asked Renée. 'Is he well?' Jean-Claude's temper, according to Mariette's late husband, was legendary when roused, but Mariette was enjoying herself and had gone beyond caution. She need not have worried: Madame Legrand was fairly experienced in this kind of attack.

'Won't it be cold by now?' She deflected the question, eyeing the soup.

Mariette turned her head. 'Mother,' she shouted and waited until the old lady climbed slowly down the stairs before finishing serving the soup (twenty-four garlic cloves seethed for a good hour in stock). And another thing, she thought, flicking a glance at her mother easing herself into a chair, I will never wear black when I am old.

Mariette made the sign of the cross over the bread, cut the smallest piece she dared and stabbed it onto the end of the knife. Madame Legrand removed it daintily.

Renée ate her soup with little clatters of her spoon and genteel slurping noises. I expect that is how she makes love, Mariette thought, and hacked a large piece of bread off the loaf for herself and dipped it into the soup. It was very good, and she began to relax after a couple of spoonfuls. Perhaps it did not matter so much after all. Nothing did. Except survival – and the children, of course.

Jeannette chose that moment to choke, and Mariette got up to see to the child. Jean-Claude felt in his pocket for a handkerchief and a couple of identity cards fell onto the table. He grabbed them and put them back into his pocket without comment, giving Mariette the handkerchief. She felt a righteous anger stir. How dare Jean-Claude come to her house and involve her in his games? She was sure the cards were forgeries.

It had been bad enough giving shelter to the injured man with big eyes and cropped fair hair. Although he had been very nice. Polite, quiet and he had helped around the house. Fetching in the wood and that sort of thing. Mariette had been grateful for the company – sometimes the days went past without her talking to anyone except her mother and the children. Even so, she felt strongly that Jean-Claude should not put the children at risk.

To cap it all, she was expected to obey without protest, solely because she was the widow of Jean-Claude's nephew. Thinking it over, Mariette had decided that she would not put up with it in future. Jean-Claude could take his resistance and his blowsy mistress and put them where it stank.

She got up and went to the stove and extracted the *coeur de porc braisé* from the oven. '*Enlevez les parties blanches, salez, pouvrez, enveloppez-le dans la toilette et ficelez le tout . . .*' Even if she was a rotten housekeeper Mariette was, none the less, a gifted cook who could produce a succulent meal out of a hunk of sausage, two cloves of garlic and a tomato and, if pressed, could recite dozens of traditional Périgord recipes from memory.

Jean-Claude undid his belt a notch. A roll of flesh rippled under his shirt. 'Smells all right,' he said expectantly. 'Did you go to market this morning?'

Mariette straightened up. The dish was burning her hands through the cloth and she did not reply until she had put it down. 'I did,' she said.

Friday was market day in Ribérac. Since it was the biggest and most important market in the Périgord Blanc region, many people in the area made their way into the town at some point during the day. Held near the Palais de Justice, the market was more than a place where commodities were exchanged. Rather, it was a crossover point where old and new loyalties were discussed and local gossip and information were ratified. Its habitués tended to turn a cold shoulder on the intruder but if the Germans were at all interested in the undercurrents flowing under the surface of the town's chatter – and it was a fair bet that they were – then that's where they should plant spies.

'Extremely good,' said Jean-Claude, eating very fast as usual. He tore chunks off his bread, which he stuffed into his mouth with the meat. He was aware that Mariette was easily ruffled and thought it best to keep her sweet.

'That's the last meat I'll be able to buy,' she said, untruthfully, but she thought she would have a go at squeezing a bit more out of the old goat. 'I have no more money, and black market prices are impossible.'

'Don't worry too much,' said Jean-Claude, tapping his pocket. 'Did you notice, Mariette, what the Boches were up to?'

'Same as ever,' Mariette replied, who had been too busy trying to sponge a drink from an acquaintance. She spooned more gravy onto her bread and bit into it.

'À bas les doryphores,' sang Renée Legrand, in an irritating soprano. *Doryphores* was a slang expression for the Germans.

'If only they *were* potato bugs, my dear, if only they were,' said Jean-Claude, and Mariette would have done much to wipe the lustful expression from his face. He pushed aside his plate and reached for his cigarettes.

'A slice of Échourgnac cheese would be nice,' sighed Renée, a true Périgourdine. The sentiment so united the company that they went quiet, reliving memories of the food they had once taken for granted.

'Do you remember – ' Mariette began, thinking of one of the great celebration dinners for the *vendange* that had been held in Ribérac before the war, but she was interrupted.

'Will the English invade, do you think?' Renée was not interested in the past, only the future and how it affected her. She smoothed down her skirt over her knees, a self-satisfied little smile on her mouth.

One day, continued Mariette's private thoughts, I will get away. I will put a wreath on Jacques's grave and leave. Paris perhaps. Or Marseille. And I won't put up with people like Renée Legrand ever again.

'The English will come in the end.' Jean-Claude was confident.

How? wondered Mariette.

'But they are not our friends,' said Renée. She was flirting.

I'm so bored with all this, thought Mariette, watching Jean-Claude shape his fleshy lips into a kiss. I don't care who wins this war, as long as I am left in peace.

'How can you be sure?' she asked. 'They might not come.'

'I'm sure,' replied Jean-Claude. He got to his feet, hitched up his trousers and buckled his belt, revealing a hairy stomach. Mariette wondered if his pubic hair was as black as the hair on his head. She could, of course, ask Renée for confirmation and then shuddered at the thought. A naked Jean-Claude beside her in the bed was the last, the very last, thing she wanted.

'I must go,' Jean-Claude announced. 'Duty.'

The women stared at him. Jean-Claude's flat, solid features were impassive. Mariette's mother took the opportunity to help herself to the remains of the bread. She dipped the crust in the pork gravy and sucked at it. Renée rose to her feet and laid her hand on Jean-Claude's arm.

'Don't go,' she cajoled. 'You don't need to, surely?'

'I'm going on duty,' said Jean-Claude. 'Don't be foolish, Renée.' Both women suspected he was not telling the truth.

Mariette extracted a cigarette from the flimsy packet on the table and lit it. She jerked her head at Renée. 'You had better leave too.'

Renée obediently reached for her coat.

'You know nothing,' said Jean-Claude. He was breathing heavily and smiling down at Renée. The big ape, Mariette thought, watching as Renée pawed Jean-Claude's face, already peppered with stubble. 'Nothing at all,' he repeated. He bent over and kissed Renée. 'Keep well, my chicken.'

'Quite right,' Mariette said to the empty room when everybody had gone, and blew a stream of smoke to join the flaky patches on the ceiling. 'I know nothing. Nothing at all.'

Antoine held up his hands. 'Come on, then,' he said to his daughter.

The five-year-old butted her way onto her father's lap, and Antoine, who could never resist her, kissed the top of her head. 'Story,' she demanded.

As he read to her, Antoine held the too-thin body close to his, trying to deceive himself that it was becoming more solid. They both enjoyed storytime, and sometimes they spun it out for half an hour or more. Thérèse, Antoine's wife, moved around the room, seeing to the supper dishes. She was looking very tired and strained and Antoine wished above every thing else that he could take her away to safety. He shifted the child on his knee.

'Thérèse,' he said. 'I must tell you. Tonight I will be busy.'

She looked up from the sink and her face appeared more drawn than ever. 'Oh, no, Antoine,' she said in a dull voice.

Antoine put his daughter down and went over to his wife. 'It will be all right,' he promised. 'I'll take great care.' She sighed and tugged at his sleeve in a hopeless way. 'We did agree,' he said. 'We must do something.'

'I know.' Thérèse lowered her voice because of the child. 'But I'm frightened.'

'So am I,' he confessed.

Thérèse sighed. 'It's far worse waiting,' she said, wiping her wet hands. 'Imagining that every car that stops outside the house is coming to tell me that . . .' Her sentence trailed away and she brushed back a piece of hair that had escaped from her wispy brown bun.

Antoine put his hands on his wife's shoulders and pressed down. 'Thérèse, shall we send the children away?'

'Oh, no,' she said quickly, and her eyes became pools of distress. 'I couldn't bear it.'

'Why don't you go with them?'

Thérèse considered. 'I could. But that's a lot to ask, Antoine. Anyway, I don't want to leave you.'

'We are asking a lot of each other.'

She touched her husband's hand where it lay on her shoulder. 'I don't know what is best. I'm too tired to think properly.'

She leant against him, and he put his arms around her. They stood together until their daughter pulled at Antoine's trousers and said she wanted a hug as well.

' "Vengeance is mine, I will repay," saith the Lord.'

Vengeance, Paul reflected, putting down a copy of *Anna Karenina*, which was prefaced with this quotation, is the privilege of those who have been wronged. But where, Paul wondered, does God's mercy fit in? In the story, Anna Karenin does her son a great wrong when she abandons him for her lover, but Tolstoy makes her pay for it.

The author is wily however: it is Anna's guilt, rather than society's revenge, that drives her to suicide. In this case, it seemed, guilt proves stronger than love or duty – Paul found the conclusion depressing.

He put down the leather-bound French translation of Tolstoy's novel on the table. The character of Anna Karenin fascinated him. Here was a woman who thought she was daring enough, strong enough, to deny convention, only to discover she was neither of these things.

It was nine o'clock, and Paul got up to pour himself a cognac from a bottle provided by the owner of the house. He drank a mouthful and reckoned his quarters could have been a lot worse. The room he occupied was intrinsically elegant and not even the overstuffed furniture and potted plants could disguise its pleasing proportions. He had chosen this particular house as his billet, rather than a more imposing one down the street, because it overlooked Ribérac's Romanesque church. The owners, a family with young children, seemed reasonably civil. The linen was clean, the room aired and it was better accommodation than most of the men had to put up with.

Paul's gramophone, which he took everywhere with him, had survived the journey from Berlin and sat on the table by the window beside a stack of records. Piaf, Soustelle and the best recordings of Mozart and Beethoven symphonies Paul could buy.

He selected a favourite popular song sung by Lale Andersen, and as the first bars floated nostalgically over the room, he went over to the window with his cognac. The song, he knew from the intelligence reports back in Berlin, had become hugely popular with the Allies in North Africa. They called it 'Lili Marlene'.

There were people coming out of the church and a few stopped to listen, including one elderly woman who raised her hand to her face with a gesture that seemed to say: I can't bear it. Paul watched her uneven progress until she was out of sight and, feeling rather flat and cold, shut the window.

Disturbed by the rush of air, one of Ingrid's many letters fell onto the floor. Paul picked it up. 'Darling Paul . . . Miss you . . . parties . . . don't forget . . . etc., etc. Take care.' A couple of weeks had gone by since the meeting with the girl at the roadside – an enjoyable, strangely innocent episode that had left a persistent echo.

The substance of the meeting continued to reverberate through Paul's mind – the exact detail fading a little more each time – creating, nevertheless, seismic disturbances. Like ripples washing over hidden objects, like the stone lobbed into the stream, or an arrow, tipped with an unknown compound flying into the subconscious. And he still remembered the exact feel of the satiny skin of the girl's throat under his finger – and wanted to keep on remembering it.

He drank the cognac and extracted papers from his briefcase. The garrison at Ribérac was not a large one. Even so, the soldiers, plus the support organisation required to keep the men clothed, fed and operational, were enough to swamp and overburden the town's limited resources. However, they were well fed, reasonably well billeted (some grumbled at the standard of living in the villages) and well armed – one automatic machine gun to each platoon. More importantly, they were cheerful.

Paul's cover was to act as signals officer. His real role required the delicate bedding down of procedures designed to procure the undercover intelligence he needed. Tomorrow would see him combing the patrol reports, copies of radio back traffic, and a report in from the first of the civilian sub-agents, a butcher in the town, that Paul had recruited via his corporal. So far, so predictable. The next step was to target potential sabotage spots, and draw up a report for Berlin.

He glanced at Ingrid's letter lying beside his briefcase. There was a PS at the end which he had meant to decipher, jumbled into the 'loves' and 'missings'. There was a knock on the door.

'Come in.'

Corporal Werner Schwarz entered and saluted. 'Beg pardon, sir.' He was panting.

Paul put down the letter. 'Trouble?' He had worked out the PS, which referred to Siegfried Gehrbrandt asking Ingrid out

146

to dinner. Paul was amused. If that was her strategy, it wasn't going to work.

'Sir. I was having a beer with one of the locals, sir . . .' Corporal Schwarz was earnest and pregnant with information. He was a good intelligence operator and Paul trusted him. Schwarz was referring to the practice of 'tea stops' – which Paul encouraged – where locals were invited to drink with the men and chat. 'This Frenchman works at the Château Belle-Place. He thinks there is some kind of resistance activity planned for tonight.'

Paul folded Ingrid's letter and put it back in the envelope. 'Have you informed Major Blumberg? That is his department, not mine.'

'Beg pardon, sir. Major Blumberg has reported sick.'

'What about Hauptmann Hassell?'

'Sir, I'm afraid he's been called out on another matter.'

'Hm.' Paul stood up. 'Who is this man, did you say?'

'He works as a gardener at the *château*. He says that he overheard the Count planning to cross the demarcation line tonight. He thought we would be interested. Sir, before you make up your mind, I have to say this man was drunk.'

'Is there no other officer available who has the authority to deal with this matter?'

'No, sir.'

'Well, in that case . . .'

Paul reached for his belt and buckled it on. 'Where is the *château*?'

'About five kilometres north on the N708. It is situated between Lusignac to the west and Bertric-Burée. The demarcation line runs less than a kilometre away from its land.'

'All right, corporal. I think I know where it is. I walked past it the other day. I want two vehicles and a couple of sections to report to me in five minutes.'

Corporal Schwarz saluted and left the room. Paul turned off the gramophone, slid the record back into its paper sleeve and tossed Ingrid's letter into a drawer. His Luger revolver lay on the table. He picked it up, put it into its holster and left the room.

CHAPTER ELEVEN

The wine-cellar passage at Belle-Place smelt of mouldering grapes and fungus, and was lit by a dim oil lamp. Evelyn shivered: even though she was wearing an extra pair of socks the cold seeped into her feet.

Antoine and Charles worked in unison beside her. They lifted the weapons stolen by the Communists out of their hiding place in some empty barrels, and laid them out on a tarpaulin. As they handed them over, Evelyn took each gun, wrapped it in sacking, and then stacked the parcels in piles, ready for transportation.

'Have we finished?' Charles straightened up, his face bobbing in and out of the light like Lou Chaney's phantom. 'All right, Violette?' He seemed light-hearted and almost teasing. 'Your spirits are good?'

'Never better.' Evelyn wiped her top lip with the back of a hand. They were tacky with bits of sacking and the fibres stuck to her jersey and trousers. When she brushed them off, they merely transferred onto another part of her clothing. The feel of a gun in her hand was a familiar one. Evelyn brushed a finger along a barrel. She knew exactly what it took to strip, clean and assemble it. Not a big triumph perhaps, more in the nature of a thumbed nose at the enemy and people like Captain Fuller, but it gave her extra confidence. Some of the grenades were still smeared with the grease used to store them and she wrapped these especially carefully; the grease would act as a preservative against damp.

'It's half past ten.' Charles wanted to get on with the operation. 'Hurry.'

They prepared to set off. Charles lost his teasing manner and reverted to his peremptory self. 'Hurry up,' he ordered. 'Carry the stuff through the passage and down the field to the van. You, Mademoiselle, will help load, and then return to my wife.'

The bundles were heavy and awkward and they had to make several journeys down the damp and flaking passage to where they stacked them beside the grille door. His face criss-crossed by the shadow from the bars, Antoine peered and listened. Then he indicated for the Count to go ahead. Charles pushed open the grille and stepped up and into the open. He whistled a soft 'all clear' signal. Panting slightly from the effort, Antoine and Evelyn passed him the guns. Evelyn followed Antoine outside, pushed the grille shut and brushed the earth smooth of their foot-prints.

Charles divided the load. Evelyn heaved hers up onto her shoulder, but soon realised it was easier to carry them in her arms. The three turned left through the archway and walked down the path leading to the maize field. The cold made Evelyn's ears smart and her feet twice their normal size: softened by the winter rains, the earth in the ploughed field clung to her shoes in a clogged lump, slowing her down. They plodded on towards the road and Charles indicated that he would go ahead to reconnoitre.

He returned within a couple of minutes. 'Jean-Claude isn't here yet. Hide in the ditch until he arrives.'

Antoine and Evelyn settled into an irrigation ditch that ran along the side of the road. Evelyn put down her guns and eased her aching shoulders. Then she raised her head an inch above the edge. The road was empty.

'He should be here by now,' said Antoine nervously.

'How does he arrange his cover?' Evelyn was curious, although she knew she should not be. She scraped a large clod of the greyish mud off her shoes.

'Jean-Claude? He's probably put himself on night duty checking the demarcation line. He will have an *ausweis* to go over the line.'

Evelyn changed the subject. 'How are your wife and children?'

Antoine shrugged. 'I worry about them,' he said. He slid further down into the ditch with a flurry of stones and a lick of mud smeared his jacket. He seemed glad of the opportunity to confide in her.

'Yes, of course,' said Evelyn. She was conscious of how concerned about Antoine she felt and attributed it to the unexpected intimacies that spring up in wartime.

'If anything happens,' Antoine pushed his hands into the pockets of his jacket, 'it would be my fault.'

As she scraped away at her shoes Evelyn tried to imagine what it was like to worry continually about your family. There was no reassurance she could offer and, sorry to have raised the subject, she judged it best to say nothing. Charles darted across the road and crouched down in a clump of bushes opposite.

'Did the chief tell you the plan?' she whispered to Antoine, just in case there had been an oversight. 'You know you are to return with Jean-Claude?' She heard Antoine sigh into the grass verge. He still appeared puzzled by her. Perhaps working with a woman was bothering him? Perhaps he didn't like her having been trained in England? She could not decide. 'But, of course,' she said quickly, 'you will already know that.'

'D'accord,' Antoine concurred after a pause.

There was silence.

'Tell me,' said Antoine, 'did you meet General de Gaulle in England?'

'Good gracious, no.' Evelyn repressed a smile at the unexpected question. 'No, I'm afraid not.'

'Pity,' said Antoine. 'I want to know what sort of a man he is.'

'Why?'

'Well, we think he is the leader we want.'

In the dark, Evelyn raised her eyebrows. Definitely, Gaullist feelings were something she ought to report back to home base. Agents were encouraged not to side with one French faction or another – and most of them wanted to keep it that way. All the same, it was prudent to be aware of political developments.

With a scrabble of footsteps, Charles ducked out of the bushes and ran towards them. 'Listen,' he said, and held up a hand.

In the distance, there was the guttural chug of an engine accompanied by the regular clank of a loose exhaust. It grew closer and they saw Jean-Claude driving down the road towards them.

'What in God's name . . . ?' muttered Antoine, and grabbed at Evelyn's arm. 'Does he want to raise the saints? Every Boche for miles will have heard him.'

There was no time to speculate. Charles stood in the road and flagged down the van. Evelyn leapt to her feet, picked up the guns and swung the packages one by one up onto the verge at Charles's feet. Then she pulled herself up over the edge of the ditch and ran towards the back of the van. Jean-Claude pulled open the double doors at the back.

'What kept you?' demanded Charles.

'Bloody exhaust's fallen off,' Jean-Claude explained. 'I didn't have time to mend it.'

'I'll say,' said Antoine bitterly.

The back of the vehicle was empty except for a couple of boxes of turnips and potatoes. Jean-Claude shrugged his thick shoulders, his shadow splayed onto the road. 'A policeman gets given presents,' he explained. 'And I'm fond of Marais potatoes.'

Evelyn pushed the boxes aside and scrambled inside. She felt her way along to the driver's partition which was divided into wooden panels. She ran her fingers across the middle one and after a moment it yielded to the pressure. She eased it out of position and called, 'Ready.' Antoine took up a position beside her.

'Up.' Charles swung the first package up and pushed it along the floor of the van towards Evelyn. She stowed it in the space. The rest followed, and when the last one was hidden, she replaced the panel and tapped it back into position. Antoine pushed the boxes of vegetables up against it. Evelyn jumped down onto the ground.

Jean-Claude had crouched down by the back of the van and was trying to fix the rattling exhaust with a rag. 'That's all I can do.' His voice issued from a dark blotch of body and shadow on the road. 'There were no spares and no time,' he said and stood upright. He dabbed at the oil on his hands

151

with a rag. 'It's the best I can do.' In the dark he seemed even bigger – a black-jowled rather frightening giant in a policeman's uniform.

Charles squinted at his watch. 'All right, Jean-Claude, we understand,' he said. 'It's time to go.' He held out his hand to Evelyn and shook hers. '*Au revoir*. Now get back to my wife.' He swung himself up into the back to join Antoine.

'Do you have to go into the other zone?' Evelyn asked Charles suddenly. 'Wouldn't it be better to stay this side?'

'There are fewer patrols.' Charles was becoming impatient. 'Anyway, that was the deal with the Communists.'

Jean-Claude manhandled the doors shut. 'I'd better warn you,' he said through the crack, 'apparently four parachutists came down in the Bergerac region a couple of weeks ago and the border patrols have been strengthened. I saw a report today on the chief's desk.'

'Jesus!' said Antoine. 'Why didn't you tell us?'

Jean-Claude checked the fastening on the doors. 'It doesn't do to know too much, my friend,' he said, and got into the driver's cab. Evelyn winced as he started the engine and it clanged into life. The van wheels sprayed a shower of dirt along the road as it put on speed. Evelyn watched until it rounded the corner and the chugging of its engine trailed away.

After the noise had faded into complete silence she listened for a few moments to the sounds of the night, her eyes narrowed with relief. Hearing nothing, she picked a small branch and swept away the tyre tracks and footprints. Then she retreated to the *château* the way she had come.

Back in her bedroom at Belle-Place, she was startled by the entrance of Bessy. 'Evelyn, I insist you take this,' she said from the doorway. She caught Evelyn in her underclothes, trying to scrub the dirt off her face and hands. Evelyn made a grab at her dressing gown as Bessy advanced into the room and laid an evening frock on the bed. 'I've made up my mind that it is time you were properly dressed.'

Quite forgetting she was supposed to be someone else, Evelyn glared at Bessy. Did she mean to be so insulting? Then she remembered Evelyn Liegaux was neither likely to possess an expensive wardrobe nor should she glare at her employer.

'Oh no, I couldn't possibly,' she said. 'It is far too good. And you are far too generous.' All the same, she cast a covetous glance at the emerald velvet dress which had obviously been confected in one of the best Paris couture houses. An unworthy impulse to give in without a murmur stole through her.

'Nonsense, you must have it,' said Bessy, who reverted more often than she would care to think to the role of the bountiful American princess. 'It will suit you. I am too fat.' She paused. 'And am likely to be so for some months. Not that I mind, of course. This dress needs wearing, and you don't have one.' She added accurately, 'Or, at least, a nice one.'

Bessy had decided that championing Charles's country cousin was a project to which she could devote herself very happily. It would please Charles if she took an interest, and allow her an outlet for the do-gooding impulses that were frustrated by pregnancy. Bessy planned a productive campaign and she felt sure the girl would appreciate and welcome a helping hand. Besides, it wasn't her favourite dress.

Evelyn gazed at the material spread out on the bedspread. Bessy was tempting her with a grown-up dress, with the sort of wizardry sewn into its seams that left her, frankly, weak with envy. She sat down on the bed and lifted one of the sleeves.

'No,' she repeated, unconvincingly. 'No, really. I couldn't possibly.'

'Just take it.' Bessy was determined not to be robbed of a chance to act the Samaritan. 'Try it on. We are, or we were, about the same size.'

Evelyn gave in. 'Thank you so much,' she said, and meant it. 'I don't know what to say. I would love to have this dress.' She dropped the sleeve and looked up at her benefactress. 'But I shouldn't.'

'You should,' said Bessy with a satisfied smile. 'It needs a good home, if you see what I mean. See you at dinner.' She walked over to the door. 'What on earth have you been doing, Evelyn? Your nails are filthy.'

Without waiting for an answer she was gone, leaving the object of her bounty both chastened and curious to try it on. Evelyn scrubbed hard at her incriminating nails with what passed for soap, cursing at the grease that clung to them. Then she reached for the dress; it would make her far too conspicuous but she would wear it just once tonight.

As Bessy predicted, it fitted. More than that, it effected a transformation. Facing her was a woman whose hips and waist and curve of breast suggested words like 'beautiful' and 'desirable'. Evelyn inspected her reflection and felt a tremor of discovery. This was the sort of dress which made the wearer's most commonplace observation turn into something witty. In it, she could imagine holding her own in the chic, upholstered salons of the fashionable and clever or in the brocaded, gold-inlaid salons of the rich and titled. Men would look at her, and she knew that she would repay the looking. Gazing at the stranger in the mirror, Evelyn flicked up a questioning eyebrow. An element of fantasy was threatening to take over. What next? she asked herself.

She paused to pass her lipstick over her mouth, rubbed her lips together to give it an even gloss and descended the stairs.

Dressed in *café-au-lait* chiffon, Bessy was waiting in the Blue Salon. She held an extravagant lace-bordered handkerchief in one hand, the other played with the pearls twisted into a knot at her throat and anchored with a rose-diamond clasp.

'Oh, good,' she said. 'I was beginning to think you had disappeared off the face of the earth. Let me look at you.' Evelyn spun round for inspection. 'I was right. You are gorgeous.' Evelyn endeavoured to thank her again, but Bessy changed the subject. 'I was hoping Dr Mazille would join us. I thought you two should get to know each other, but he's had to visit a patient.' Good God, thought Evelyn, Bessy is trying to pair me off. 'So as there are no men, let's have dinner straight away.'

She led the way through the stone-flagged hallway which was tiled around the fireplace in uneven blue and white early Delft and hung with a Poussin and a Claude Lorraine landscape. In contrast, the dining room was panelled in light walnut, with bas-relief plasterwork running from waist height to the ceiling. An early Renaissance oil painting – Evelyn guessed it was School of Giotto – hung behind Charles's place, and a bronze candelabrum in the shape of Greek nereids was set on the oak table.

The two women sat opposite each other and Gaston placed the soup tureen between them. *'Bon appétit, Madame et Mademoiselle.'*

'That reminds me.' Bessy helped herself with a crested silver ladle. 'I want you to do some work for me tomorrow afternoon.'

Evelyn thought quickly. 'I'm afraid I will be out.'

Bessy's eyebrows drew into a straight line. 'This is very odd,' she said shortly. 'You are always busy when I want you. I shall speak to Charles.' She pushed the tureen towards Evelyn. 'I can't think why you have to go out so much.'

Evelyn helped herself to the soup. They should have crossed the demarcation zone by now, she reckoned, raising the first spoonful to her lips. Coasting without lights down the track. Jean-Claude and Charles knew the route intimately and, providing they got over the line, they should be safe.

'Goodness,' said Bessy, who had said something. 'I must be boring you.'

Evelyn put her spoon down and apologised. 'I am sorry. I'm so excited about my dress.'

'I was telling you about Guy, my twin.' It was obvious that Bessy was very fond of her brother. Her face lit up and her voice became animated. 'He is in Paris at the moment, painting. I think you will like him.'

'I'm sure I will.'

'He lives in an apartment in Montmartre, or likes to think he does, but every so often he escapes to the Georges Cinq and exists like a king for a few days. But he always goes back. Apparently, he needs the local colour to inspire him.'

She picked up her wine glass and twirled the stem between her fingers. Evelyn put down her spoon and pushed the soup away. 'You think his work is good?' she asked.

'Oh, yes,' said Bessy, glancing at Evelyn's half-finished

155

soup. She seemed surprised by the question. 'I think Guy is one of the best painters of our generation.'

'Tell me about your studies in Vienna.' Evelyn observed the plate of fish that Gaston placed in front of her with some dismay. Does the knowledge that your comrades are risking their lives at the precise moment you are eating fresh, black-market fish render it unpalatable? Using her fork, Evelyn pushed bits of it to one side and hid them under the cabbage which Marie had shredded thinly and fried in oil and garlic. Bessy continued to describe her studies and to explain that she had undergone psychoanalysis herself. It had taken three years and she had found it very painful. 'But worth it,' she added as an afterthought. She shifted her bulk in her chair and laid a hand on her stomach. 'Goodness,' she said. 'He is kicking tonight.'

'How does it work?' asked Evelyn. 'The principles, I mean.'

'You must go back into your childhood memories to find elements of yourself that have been hidden under layers of defence and deception.'

'Deception?'

'Oh, yes, we deceive ourselves all the time in order not to get hurt,' said Bessy and drank a mouthful of wine, thinking maybe if she drank enough it would help her backache. 'For example, I used to think that the good things in life were immoral. You know, the things I am sure you like too. Pretty clothes, jewellery. Good food. Or rather, I thought that to be useful and productive it was necessary to give them up. I still feel that sometimes, but I don't worry about it any more.'

'Why did you think that?' asked Evelyn. 'You couldn't possibly be worthless. You are beautiful, clever . . .' She did not finish the sentence, concerned she had gone too far.

'But that's it,' said Bessy. She was beginning to enjoy her conversation with Evelyn. 'People's perceptions of themselves are quite different from how others see them. My attitude was a result of my fear of being worthless. So I tried to deny my background. One year I gave away most of my income. It was an expression of my guilt at being born so well off.'

Evelyn's fork clattered against the plate. She drank some wine and her stomach churned. The silver on the table shone.

So it should – she knew Gaston had taken most of the morning to polish it. Hot-house peaches and nectarines were arranged in tiers in the fruit bowl, and the crystal salt cellars glowed in the candlelight.

'How did you live?' she forced herself to ask.

'Well,' Bessy was shamefaced, 'I managed rather badly, and was forced to borrow off Guy. Living in Vienna was more expensive than I imagined.'

Evelyn was rather touched by this admission. There was a tiny pause. 'Where is the Count tonight?' she asked politely.

Bessy wiped her mouth. 'Damn, my lipstick,' she said, scrubbing at the napkin. 'It's always coming off on things. Visiting one of our suppliers. He said he might have to spend the night if the business went on too long.' She rubbed her back. 'I hate it when Charles is away for one minute longer than necessary.' She spoke with passionate intensity. Knowing it was useless to try to eat any more, Evelyn indicated to Gaston that he should take her plate away.

Five kilometres away over the demarcation line, Charles opened the van doors and jumped down from the back.

'Stay there,' he said to Antoine.

Because of the trees it was very dark in the lane into which Jean-Claude had driven. Charles strained to see ahead. Nothing. He raised his hand and signalled to Jean-Claude. Bouncing over the ruts, the van followed the Count and after a hundred yards or so the lane narrowed and wound its way around to a field on the left. Jean-Claude stopped the van and turned off the engine.

'Did you ask Javaux to herd the geese into the top field?' demanded Charles through the window.

'Yes.'

Five minutes later the van was unloaded and the guns were lying in a pile on the track. The men worked in silence, each picking up a sacking parcel and carrying it over to the wooden structure by the gate which Javaux used to store maize for his cattle. Charles went to one end – the structure resembled a chicken house on stilts – and pulled back the wire mesh. He pushed the maize cobs aside and felt for a certain plank. The cobs slithered in an untidy fashion over the bottom of the henhouse and he swept them back, pulling the plank aside to reveal a space.

'First one,' he said.

Jean-Claude pushed his load into the false bottom of the hutch, and Antoine followed with his.

'Quickly,' said Charles. He looked around him. The field was filled with soft shadows and uneven light and very still. Charles pushed down on the last package and levered the plank into place. Then he raked the cobs back over the floor and pulled the wire mesh back into place. As he did so, the headlights of a vehicle coming from the direction of Ville-toureix cut into their view. The three men froze.

'The exhaust.' Antoine shrivelled with terror. 'They heard it.'

'Get into the van.' Charles sounded quite cool. 'Then wait to see which way it goes.'

'Get in the back,' said Jean-Claude. 'I can bluff the patrol if they don't see you.'

Charles and Antoine ran and scrambled into the back of the van. They pulled the double doors together and held them shut. Jean-Claude started the engine, and the van reversed back down the lane without headlights, leaving Javaux's field on their left. Unfortunately the geese, startled by the sound of the exhaust, set up a sleep-shattering honking. A light appeared in the window of Javaux's farmhouse and then went out. Jean-Claude craned to see the right and left before backing into the road. The headlights were getting nearer.

'Turn right,' shouted Charles through the partition. He had his revolver at the ready. 'Make for Chapdeuil and drop us there. We can hide in the *pigeonnier* of the big house.'

Jean-Claude did as he was told. He turned right and right again down a little-used road, but it became obvious that the vehicle was pursuing them. He pressed his foot down on the accelerator as far as possible.

'They may have several patrols out,' he shouted.

'How have they got hold of us?' Charles banged his fist on the van's wooden doors. 'Nobody else knew.'

Jean-Claude drove on. The vehicle behind them seemed to

be gaining and suddenly it came up behind them. Its headlights flooded the van's driving mirror and their dazzle made it impossible for him to see for vital seconds. There was a burst of bullets from behind. Charles knelt upright and balanced himself as best he could in the swaying vehicle. He pushed one of the doors open a fraction.

'It's German,' he shouted to Antoine above the noise, recognising the shape. Holding the door strut for support, he took aim at the headlights and shot. One side of the pursuing vehicle went black as his bullet found its mark. Charles took a second aim and, miraculously, doused the other headlight. The vehicle slewed across the road, and, in doing so, blocked a second vehicle behind it. Charles raised his gun for a third time. There was the sound of shattering glass followed by shouting. The Germans responded with renewed fire. Jean-Claude continued to try to pick up speed.

Sweat ran down Antoine's face. He reached over to Charles and tried to pull him away from the door. 'Get back, chief,' he shouted.

But Charles did not answer. Instead he slumped in slow motion against the side of the van. The door banged to and fro with the motion of the vehicle and Antoine edged towards it and pulled it shut. In the brief flicker of light that came through the opening he saw that Charles's skin had turned translucent.

The van accelerated. Antoine dropped his gun and touched Charles again experimentally. As he did so, Charles rolled over onto the floor and the shooting from behind began to grow fainter.

Panicked and not sure what to do, Antoine felt for Charles's pulse. It was very faint. Antoine dropped the arm and scrabbled towards the driver's partition. 'He's hurt,' he shouted through it. 'Badly.'

'*Diable!*' Jean-Claude swore. 'Don't panic, Antoine.' He swung the wheel. 'Look,' he shouted, trying to work out the best move, 'I know a route which the Boches won't. It will take us the back way to Verteillac and we'll get him to Belle-Place.'

Antoine leant over and prised the revolver from Charles's

hand. Then he felt under Charles's jersey for the wound, and stopped when his fingers encountered a massive wet patch on the right side of Charles's chest. With frantic fingers, he ripped off the Count's silk scarf, balled it up and pressed it as hard as he could against the wound. In this awkward position he held Charles as best he could as the van pushed onward along the unlit tracks.

At the Ribérac headquarters, Paul was trying to make sense of the map on the wall. He held a report in his hand. An enemy plane had dropped in agents on the night of 10/11 October. Unfortunately for the English, one of the parachutists had fallen straight into their hands – so had the containers. But the others were still at large.

'It's possible, and Major Blumberg would have an opinion if he was here, that this man Thiers is referring to some kind of escape plan.' Paul was giving himself time to work out the strategic implications. The lieutenant to whom he had addressed this nodded. 'There is probably some kind of escape network in the area.' The phone rang and he picked it up. 'Yes?'

He listened and looked up at the lieutenant. 'Apparently our patrol came across an illicit vehicle at a farm over the line. Shots have been exchanged. They are pursuing it. Map reference . . .' The lieutenant went over to the map and identified the correct area. 'The farmer's family is being questioned and the house searched. One casualty. Listen to me . . .' Paul instructed the caller on the telephone. 'Post a guard until first light. Report in at two-hour intervals.'

He put down the phone and looked at the clock. Ten o'clock. 'I don't think we will be having much sleep tonight, *Oberleutnant*,' he remarked. 'Can you get me the file on Château Belle-Place? I am sure Major Blumberg would not object.'

'Yes, sir,' said the willing lieutenant and put it in front of Paul.

Paul read the notes. They were neither painstaking nor informative. It was noted that the Comte de Bourgrave was known to be anti-German and the house was situated near to

160

the demarcation line. Major Blumberg had also scrawled the information that the Comtesse was American and therefore likely to exert anti-German pressure. None of the *château* staff had been approached for information. No surveillance had been mounted. Major Blumberg's Gothic script interposed comments here and there on the typed pages but nothing of much use to Paul.

'Yes, I see,' said Paul. 'The *château* must been important focus of the area, wouldn't you say? The set-up is still feudal and the Count a figure of note. He is the sort of figurehead that resisters would look to, provided he isn't too ineffectual a character.'

The lieutenant, who was young, nervous and not very clever, tried to follow the line of Paul's reasoning. Paul looked up, noted the confusion and raised one eyebrow. The gesture made him appear mocking, rather sarcastic, and the lieutenant's heart sank. 'I once spent a year travelling around Europe. It helps to understand the country you are trying to occupy.'

'Yes, sir, of course.'

That was the secret of effective military intelligence. A good *Abwehr* operative bedded down behind his cover to watch and observe minutely. It took a special watchfulness, the sort of watchfulness Paul had been forced back on in hospital. Stillness that absorbed. Stillness that a naturalist, for example, would understand.

'I wonder why the gardener betrayed the Count,' said Paul after a moment.

'He supports the Führer, *natürlich!*'

Paul glanced at the *Oberleutnant* and repressed a sigh.

The *château* was shrouded in darkness when Paul's staff car drove up the drive and through the stone archway. The lieutenant leapt out of the car and let the heavy iron knocker drop down on the door. Paul looked in through a window at an impressive interior, theatrically revealed as lights were switched on one after another.

'We don't receive visitors at this time of night,' said Gaston when he opened the door.

'Could you summon the Count, please?' Paul asked very politely, looking into the hall. For a moment he was reminded

161

of his own home. Château Belle-Place gave him an impression of a house that was scoured and burnished with beeswax, linseed oil and silver polish by devoted retainers.

'I'm afraid not,' said Gaston, omitting the courtesy *monsieur*.

'Then I am afraid I must insist.'

A woman called, 'Who is it, Gaston?'

Gaston showed signs of resisting his entry and Paul brushed him aside as gently as he could, walking into the hall. Several rooms opened off the hallway, and in one of them, standing between a pair of gilded double doors, was a woman whom he presumed was the Countess. She was tall, fair, elegantly dressed and when she moved forward at his entry he saw that she was pregnant.

'Who are you?' she said, extremely sharply.

Paul limped towards her. 'Countess de Bourgrave?' he enquired. 'I am Major von Hoch, and I am sorry to disturb you.'

'Then why did you?' Bessy was both cool and imperious. But under her poise a dreadful premonition was beginning to take shape. Had Charles deceived her? 'Is this really necessary?'

Paul stripped off his gloves. 'I would like a word with your husband. Could you fetch him, please?'

Bessy's smile contained a certain triumph. 'I'm so sorry, Major,' she said sweetly. 'Your journey has been wasted. I am afraid he is away.'

'I see. Are you sure?'

Bessy threw Paul a withering look. He raised an eyebrow.

'Major. I think I would know whether my husband was at home or not.'

Paul gave a little bow in acknowledgement. 'Of course, Countess.'

It was only then he realised that Bessy was not alone. Half concealed by the double doors was another woman and she stepped forward to put an arm round the Countess. Without knowing why, Paul knew for a certainty that she would be dark and slender with a mole at the base of her neck.

In the concealed passage between the grille and the wine cellar, Antoine and Jean-Claude were taking a rest. They had hauled Charles back up through the fields and pushed his limp body through the grille. It had been difficult and they had dropped him several times. Charles's face was bruised and his hair matted with earth. But he was still breathing.

'I'll check the wine cellar.' Jean-Claude was panting. He ripped off his jacket and felt the sweat spread damp and warm across his back. 'I hope there's no blood on my jacket.'

Clumsily Antoine levered Charles against the wall and leant back himself. He was shivering from exhaustion and from the knowledge that Marie was probably lying awake and frantic at home. Antoine had not wanted to bring Charles back to the *château*. 'Too obvious,' he said.

'Exactly,' said Jean-Claude, ever the policeman. 'It's obvious moves that sometimes get away with it.' Antoine was not convinced. He checked the blood-encrusted scarf over Charles's chest: at least that had stayed in place.

Jean-Claude scrambled back down the passage. 'I think the Boches are here already.'

In the back of Evelyn's mind there lurked a sentence, or a proverb perhaps, even a warning, struggling to take shape. It said: You are in danger.

'I would like to ask you a few questions,' Paul was insisting to Bessy.

'I'd rather you didn't,' replied Bessy. 'I am sure they can wait until morning.'

'I think not,' said Major von Hoch.

With a swirl of chiffon and *frou-frou* of silk petticoats, Bessy turned on her heel and indicated to Paul and the lieutenant that they should go into the Blue Salon. Her bearing made it quite plain what she thought of such an intrusion.

'I must explain,' said Paul. Bessy settled herself on the sofa and spread her skirts. 'There has been some trouble in the area and I need to check up.'

Evelyn sat down in the corner of the room on a spindly chair, a little apart from the others, every sense fully alert.

'How can I help you, Major?' Bessy managed to sound extremely unhelpful.

163

'Could you ask everyone in the house to come to this room, please?'

Bessy tugged at her pearls, thought better of denying Paul outright and got up to pull the bell.

While he questioned Bessy, Marie and Gaston, Evelyn watched the minute hand on the Tompion clock over the mantelpiece. Each tick sounded a leaden counterpoint. 'Where is the Count?' 'What has happened?' Each chime of the quarter hour thickened the ice in her stomach. She rehearsed the cover story. Major von Hoch was courteous and thorough. He and the *Oberleutnant* carefully checked the identity papers on Charles's desk. Evelyn observed the tanned wrists and the long fingers and remembered something. Rule number one: If you are questioned by the enemy in any other capacity than routine checks, consider yourself blown.

To be blown meant getting out, going back home. Leaving the one job she had held unfinished. It meant starting again. Evelyn was sure of one thing: she did not want that to happen. Here, in this place, was her business and she wished to finish it. Inconspicuously, she straightened her shoulders as Major von Hoch turned his attention to her.

He towered above her. 'How long have you been employed here . . .' he asked and glanced at her identity card, 'Mademoiselle Liegaux?'

The first time he saw Evelyn, she had been a dreaming innocent, an untouched girl. Now he found himself looking down into the face of a woman whose beauty had been civilised. The green velvet accentuated the colour of Evelyn's eyes and the soft electric lighting brought out the rose under the olive of her skin. The dress had been made to flow over curves, and yet to emphasise them. It was both decorous and utterly wanton, revealing by implication as much as it hid – and its wearer was a lifetime away from that simple girl in a blue cotton dress.

'I've been working here since September,' Mademoiselle Liegaux replied. Evelyn knew she should keep her answers as brief and as boring as possible.

'Why, Mademoiselle? You apparently come from Tours?'

The long thin fingers handled the papers with care – and for a second she relived his touch on the road under the trees.

'Because I needed a job, Monsieur.'

The clock ticked on. *Where is Charles? What has happened?*

'And you came south, like so many of your countrymen?'

'Yes, Monsieur.' Light, colourless, uninformative. That was how Evelyn should keep it.

'What is your job?'

'Secretary to the *château*.'

'Aha.' He nodded.

Did he believe her? Evelyn tried not to look at Major von Hoch, but the need to take stock drew her eyes towards him. This man was no longer warm and flushed from the sun, someone who took a liberty with charm and directness. Grey uniform, riding boots and collar patches were an effective way of changing an attractive stranger into the enemy.

Evelyn and Paul looked at each other. Regret, an apology in his expression. Reluctance, a hint of anger in hers. Between them, nevertheless, kindled an unmistakable spark. Evelyn felt its new and insistent burn flare through her body and its novelty and sweetness intensified the shock – and surprise at herself. With it came the instant check.

She folded her hands in her lap. Paul looked down on the eyelashes which fanned from the downcast lids, and at the line of her classically chiselled mouth, and noticed with an onrush of unexpected revelation that Evelyn's hands were not her best feature and that she bit her nails.

He handed back the papers. 'Thank you.'

Paul turned to Bessy. 'Madame la comtesse. I apologise again for disturbing you. Would you be kind enough to ask your husband to contact me first thing tomorrow. I would like to ask him a few questions. Then I will not bother you further.'

Bessy's furious expression did not lighten. 'Thank you,' she said, her mouth set into a hard line.

When the sound of the Germans' car had died away, Evelyn got up and sat down shakily beside Bessy on the sofa. 'It's all right, Gaston,' she addressed the butler. 'I will see to Madame. And you, Marie, please go to bed.'

Bessy grabbed at Evelyn's arm. 'I'm worried,' she said. 'I'm very worried. Why did they come here? What's going on?'

'Look,' said Evelyn, hiding her own anxiety. 'You go upstairs and I'll go and make you some hot milk. Let me just get into my dressing gown as I don't want to spoil my dress.' She left the room and ran upstairs.

She was lifting the pan off the stove when a muffled noise at the window made her whip round. Jean-Claude's large shape was outlined in the glass. He beckoned to Evelyn. She set down the pan and went to unbolt the door, dreading what she was going to discover. On opening it, she saw the two men with Charles sagging between them. 'I heard them go,' said Jean-Claude.

Evelyn took one look and beckoned urgently for them to come inside. 'He's wounded,' warned Antoine.

'Follow me,' she said.

Between them, they dragged the dead weight of the unconscious Charles up the back stairs, carried him across the landing into his bedroom and laid him on the bed.

'How can we get a doctor?' asked Evelyn, pushing back the sleeves of her dressing gown.

'Phone Mazille,' said Antoine. 'He's the doctor round here.'

'I take it he's safe?' Evelyn gently pulled Charles's legs straight on the bed and propped up his head. She went over to the phone.

The handle cranked into the hush. 'Hello. Can I talk to Dr Mazille? I know it's late . . . Is that you, Dr Mazille? Could you come to Belle-Place? There is a problem . . . No, I can't explain over the phone . . . a little problem with the Countess . . . Thank you so much.' She flung the receiver down. 'He's coming.'

'We must get out of here,' said Jean-Claude. 'I'll take Antoine back to Ribérac. If they ask why I'm late, I'll say I broke down.'

'You're leaving me!' Evelyn had a moment of utter panic when she realised she would have to take charge.

''Fraid so,' said Jean-Claude. He placed a hand on her shoulder. 'Sorry.'

Evelyn pulled herself together. 'Take care. It's possible they have staked us out. Remember to check the van for blood-stains.'

'Please God he survives.' Jean-Claude stared down at Charles.

'Go!' said Evelyn. 'I will let you know.' Scissors. She needed them to cut off Charles's bloodied jersey. Pulling open his bureau drawer, she searched inside and found a pair. She set to work, and winced when she saw the extent of the wound. Evelyn looked up at the crucifix on the wall. The anguished face of Christ was turned towards the window. Evelyn needed to decide now what to tell Bessy.

She went over to the connecting door to Bessy's bedroom and knocked. When Bessy answered she pushed it open.

'You haven't brought the milk.' Bessy was slumped uncharacteristically on a chair when Evelyn entered.

Evelyn dropped down beside her and took one of Bessy's hands in her own. Bessy paled. 'I have bad news.'

'I think I know what you have come to say,' the Countess replied.

'You must prepare yourself for the worst.' Evelyn was as gentle as she could be. Bessy pressed her fist into her mouth with a stifled cry. 'I'm afraid you must be brave.'

'I don't want to be brave. I want my husband.'

'You *must* try, Bessy.'

Bessy swallowed. 'You will have to help me.' She got to her feet and approached the connecting door. Then she stopped and said, 'What have you done, Evelyn?'

Inside his bedroom, Bessy gave a cry, 'Charles,' and flung herself awkwardly onto her knees by the bed.

All sorts of images ran riot in her mind: Vienna, Paris and Bordeaux railway station. She gave an uncomprehending little shake of her tawny head and Evelyn sensed Bessy's terror spreading, like a bloodstain, as if it were her own.

CHAPTER TWELVE

'Bessy, drink this.'

'Why?'

'Because it will do you good. You've had a terrible shock. Try.'

'No!' Silence. 'Just go away, Evelyn.'

'Think of the baby.'

'Did Charles consider the baby?' Bessy allowed Evelyn to prop her upright. 'He can't have done, otherwise this wouldn't have happened. I'm so angry with him.' She pushed aside the cup of tea that Evelyn was holding and turned away on the pillows. 'As for you, Evelyn, I don't know what you have to do with it all.'

'Hush, Bessy.' Concerned about Bessy's state of mind, Evelyn put down the tea and lifted the tray off the bed. The door to Charles's bedroom was open and she did not have to look through it to remind her what lay beyond.

At one point during the long night Dr Mazille drew Evelyn aside. 'I can't stop the internal bleeding,' he said in a low voice. 'You must warn the Countess.'

Both of them knew, without conferring, that to move Charles into hospital was out of the question.

Evelyn folded a towel while various possibilities chased through her mind, chief among them, how were they going to disguise the real cause of Charles's death? Dr Mazille returned Evelyn's look with despair and jerked his head in the direction of the Countess. Obediently, Evelyn crossed over to Bessy, who still knelt by the bed, crying quietly, and tried to draw her upright. Bessy shook her off.

'Charles . . .' Bessy began to cajole the still form on the bed in a low voice. 'Charles, listen to me. You are going to be all right. Please try, darling. I know it's difficult but try.'

Evelyn put her arm around the hunched and desperate figure. 'Bessy, come and rest.'

Bessy turned her head towards Evelyn. She was hostile and accusing. 'You don't imagine I can leave him *now*,' she spat at Evelyn. She was kneading Charles's hand with some force. 'Go away.'

Evelyn gave up and retreated with Dr Mazille to the other side of the room. 'Can you . . . could you arrange for the death to appear natural?' she asked, feeling her way over this delicate subject.

Dr Mazille wiped his scalpel on a bloodstained cloth and put it down on the bureau, which was now cluttered with instruments and surgical paraphernalia. Charles's photograph of Bessy had been pushed roughly to one side. The doctor was about the same age as Evelyn's father, a kindly, over-worked man, dressed in a formal grey tweed suit. Evelyn sensed he was wary of her. Cautious, prudent, appraising. Dr Mazille cleaned the rest of his insruments and said finally, 'I'll sew up the wound and write a death certificate saying that he died of a heart-attack.'

Evelyn let out her breath. 'Thank you, doctor.'

That was all that was said on the matter.

Around four o'clock, Charles opened his eyes. 'Bessy,' he said in a clear voice.

'I'm here, Charles, I'm here.' Bessy tore the hem of her dressing gown in her attempt to get closer to her husband. He turned his head with an effort. 'I'm sorry.'

Bessy's face streamed with tears and she wiped them on the corner of the bedspread. She kissed Charles's hand over and over.

'Sorry,' he managed to repeat.

'Listen to me,' Bessy stroked his hair. 'You are going to get better. Remember, we have a lot to do.'

Charles seemed to hear Bessy, for he tried to smile. Then he frowned and made a sound between a groan and a sigh. At Bessy's frantic, 'What's happening?' Dr Mazille hurried over and felt for Charles's pulse.

Bessy jerked at the doctor's sleeve. 'A priest,' she said wildly. 'It would matter to him. Get a priest.'

169

'Oh, Bessy,' Evelyn dropped to her knees. 'We can't. We mustn't.'

'We must. He can't die unshriven.' With a flash of inspiration, Evelyn pulled open the drawer of the bedside table and searched in it. Charles's illuminated missal was inside and she turned to the prayers for the dying. 'Read it, Bessy,' she ordered her. 'You read them.'

While Bessy stumbled and stuttered over the familiar, comforting words, Charles's pulse weakened and disappeared. 'He's dead,' said Dr Mazille, gently closing Charles's eyes and straightening up. He appeared very distressed.

Picking up his bag, he searched it and gave a bottle to Evelyn. 'I dare not prescribe anything too powerful for the Countess in her condition, but this will help to keep her calm. Give it to her every six hours or so, and watch her. I am afraid it's possible . . .' Dr Mazille paused '. . . it's possible she will go into labour. If she does, call me at once.' He appraised the figure crying into the crumpled, bloodied sheets. 'Have you any experience of confinements, Mademoiselle?'

'No. Only lambing.' Realising what she had said Evelyn hastily explained, 'I mean I have sometimes seen that sort of thing on farms near my home in Tours.'

'Well,' Dr Mazille had not registered the slip, 'I don't anticipate any problems. The Countess is in reasonable health. Now, we must put her to bed and then do what has to be done.'

'I'm afraid it will have to be quickly.' Evelyn looked at her watch.

'Of course.' The doctor was in complete agreement. He bent over Bessy.

'Please, you must calm down, Madame.' Speaking to her very softly, he managed to coax Bessy to her feet and to guide her through to her bedroom, still talking in his measured, patient way. Evelyn could tell, though, that Bessy was not listening. Or even understanding.

Evelyn set to work to obliterate the tell-tale evidence. The bloodied sheet needed to be disposed of, Charles's clothes destroyed, the instruments washed and the room tidied. She had just flushed a bundle of stained cotton wool down the water closet in the adjoining bathroom and was rinsing a bowl when Mazille returned.

'Good girl,' he said approvingly. 'Now you must go and sit with her until morning. Make sure her maid takes over when you leave. I will return after surgery. Try to keep the Countess in bed.'

Clearly at a loss for the right words, he extracted a surgical needle and thread from a leather case. 'But we will be discreet, Mademoiselle.' Dr Mazille was not going to enquire into the part that Evelyn played in the business.

He patted her rather awkwardly on the shoulder and she was touched to see that he had tears in his eyes. 'The Count was a good man,' he said. 'It's a waste.'

'Here, you can dress him in this,' she said practically, and proffered that clean shirt which she had found in the chest of drawers. Dr Mazille threaded the suture through the eye of the needle. 'Put it on the bed,' he said, and she obeyed. 'Now go and see to her. I can deal with this bit alone.'

Dr Mazille's sleeping draught ensured that Bessy slept until later in the morning. This meant that Evelyn had to deal with the shocked *château* staff, who mercifully had slept through the night. Both Marie and Gaston appeared to swallow her fabrication: Charles had returned from his business appointment early in the morning, only to collapse in his dressing room with a heart-attack.

When she woke, Bessy was very quiet and distant, refusing to eat or drink. Sitting by Bessy's side, Evelyn realised she would have to bully the answers to important questions out of her.

'Bessy. The funeral? When would you like it?'

'I can't think,' said Bessy. 'I don't want to think.'

And later, after Bessy had slept again (by this time Evelyn had consulted with Father André the priest, telephoned the solicitor and obtained a list of de Bourgrave relations to write to), 'Bessy. Father André, Gaston and myself felt it best if we buried Monsieur le comte the day after tomorrow. Would you like us to invite anyone in particular?'

Bessy's eyes were drugged and lost and their blue had faded to stone. There was a pale line around her lips.

'Don't ask me these things,' she begged Evelyn. 'You see to the arrangements.'

Transport being so difficult, and the de Bourgrave relations so scattered through the zones, it proved impossible to arrange for the requiem mass to be a grand family affair. Evelyn was relieved: it reduced her problems if curious de Bourgrave cousins were not around to ask questions or to demand explanations. Brief notices informing of the Count's death were therefore composed on the *château*'s thick white crested writing paper and sent out by Evelyn to the addresses she managed to cull from Charles's study. The note concluded with the information that at some time in the future a memorial mass would be sung.

During those three frantic days between Charles's death and his burial, cold weather settled over the Périgord. The body was removed from the bedroom to the library and laid in an open coffin with a candle at each corner and a mass of heavily scented lilies banked up under it. The door knocker was never still. From her seat in Charles's study, Evelyn could hear the sound of many feet treading through the hall as a procession of villagers came to pay their respects.

On the afternoon of the funeral the sky lowered a bruised, plum colour; rain threatened. Evelyn dressed in a black frock with a sweetheart neckline, a dark trenchcoat with a belt and a black felt hat which she tilted over her eyes. Outside, the cold made her gasp. Thankful that after the last hideous days Bessy appeared to be more in control, she helped her into the car and arranged a rug over her knees. She got into the driving seat and steered the big Hispano-Suiza behind the cortège to the grey stone church in Bertric-Burée, praying that the rain would hold off.

Bessy ascended the church steps. Half-way up she stopped and pressed her hand into the small of her back, a shrunken figure bulging grotesquely at the stomach, dressed entirely in black with a black veil thrown over her head.

'What is it?' asked Evelyn from behind.

'Nothing,' Bessy replied. 'It was nothing.'

The church was already full, and the congregation spilt over into the aisles and squashed into the space by the main doors.

The mourners were from the outlying villages – apart from the official deputation consisting of the mayor and his dignitaries from Ribérac – and many of them sat in silence. There was an air of shock, disbelief even. Evelyn ushered Bessy into the family pew and sat down beside her.

Candles burned in silver candelabra on the high altar and in the Blessed Virgin's chapel. The smell of burning wax overlaid the lighter, spicier fragrance from the chrysanthemums and late roses that Marie had arranged on the altars and in the window niches. Up at the high altar Father André checked the Bible and missals. He seemed pale and unsure, and his black mourning vestments were unkempt and unpressed.

A group of nuns, Evelyn presumed they were from the convent just below the church, entered in a crocodile through the main doors. They genuflected reverently and took their place. Evelyn's attention was engaged by one in particular. A tall, thin, slightly buck-toothed woman who fell to her knees as if she was feeling ill or very weak. Evelyn watched as the nun fixed her attention on the coffin lying in front of the altar and then pressed her face into her hands as if she wanted to obliterate the sight.

'Is there anyone I should greet for you?' Evelyn asked Bessy.

'No,' said Bessy, gazing into her lap. Anxious not to upset her, Evelyn left her alone with her thoughts.

To her dismay, she saw John had come to the mass. Obviously the news had travelled and he had come to find out what was happening. He stood by a pillar, dressed in a shabby grey suit with his shirt collar done up at the neck in the French manner, drawing as little attention to himself as possible. With a tiny widening of his eyes, John sent her a private signal that agents used.

'Ideally, wireless operators and couriers should never be seen together. Use letter boxes when you communicate.'

Dressed in a black, shiny-with-age suit, Monsieur Javaux blew his nose in the pew opposite. The sound trumpeted into the hush. According to Jean-Claude, who had passed on the information to Evelyn during a whispered conversation in the hall at Belle-Place, the Germans had not succeeded in wringing an admission of guilt out of him, nor in frightening him. Neither had they found the cache of arms. In the end, the interrogators decided to let Javaux off with a warning. Madame Javaux looked pale but composed. Evelyn realised she wouldn't be able to use the Javaux any more as the family had been compromised.

Behind the Javaux was the heavily made-up woman with gold bracelets who had flirted with Charles at the celebration lunch, swathed in a black veil and wielding a handkerchief. Under the black netting, her lipstick was a garish slash of carmine. Dr Mazille sat quietly with his family, his face impassive. The Belle-Place servants huddled in the middle pews, Gaston weeping openly. Someone else near the back of the church was also crying. One or two appeared bored by the occasion, others frankly curious, but mostly the congregation was grave and respectful. Evelyn turned back to Bessy. They could teach her all they wished in London about letter drops, safe houses and silent killing, but they could never prepare her for the muddle of feelings – guilt, grief, anger, helplessness and panic – that death brought.

'Did you manage to telephone Guy before we left?' asked Bessy. She pushed back her veil.

Evelyn hesitated. 'I left several messages,' she said. 'Katrine knows what to say if he rings.'

'I hope I can rely on her,' said Bessy, staring at the heaped flowers on the coffin. 'I want Guy more than anything.'

'Yes,' said Evelyn, and took Bessy's black-gloved hand. 'I am sure he will come as soon as he can.'

Father André raised both hands and began the requiem mass. There was no singing because it was a funeral, only the chant of the *Dies Irae* and the solemn antiphony between priest and mourners during the litany to the Virgin. The voices rose and fell and the circles of light thrown by the candles intensified as the afternoon grew darker. The tonic note of incense filtered through the dampening air. The mourners made the supplication for Charles de Bourgrave to enter heaven: *In paradisum perducant te archangeli* – let the angels lead you into paradise. Listening to the words Evelyn experienced a moment of unexpected calm. Outside, rain began to lash at the windows, in spurts at first, and then with increasing ferocity.

Intoning the appropriate Latin words, Father André processed in front of the coffin, down the aisle and out of the church doors into an ice-driven rain, towards the walled cemetery. Within seconds his vestments were soaked and the rain ran down his face and off his biretta in erratic rivulets. Holding an umbrella above them, Evelyn supported Bessy down the steps.

At that moment, a long black Citroën drew up by the cemetery. Evelyn took one look at it. 'I've left my missal in the church,' she announced. 'I'll be back in a minute.'

She discovered John waiting to leave the church. He was standing by the font. Evelyn walked past him towards the pew she had occupied. 'Boches,' she whispered under her breath as she passed. 'Use the side exit.' Evelyn pretended to search the place where she had been sitting and then returned down the aisle holding her missal.

'Let me know what's happening.' John was still by the font, waiting for her to pass him again. Evelyn dropped her missal onto the floor at his feet. 'So sorry.' John bent to help her pick it up. 'Message in letter box,' she said in his ear.

'Must know what's happening,' he said back and straightened up.

Evelyn did not look round again but hurried outside and ran down the steps, almost slipping on the wet stones. She rejoined Bessy by the graveside and pulled the brim of her hat well down. After a minute, unable to bear it any longer, she raised her eyes towards the blond uniformed figure that stood a little apart from the rest of the mourners – and knew that he had noticed that she was there.

Put off by the arrival of a German officer, Father André forgot bits of the service and had to be prompted. Dust to dust, he said, and Charles was lowered into the muddy grave now filling with brown rainwater. Freezing and merciless, the rain pinned hair onto faces, ruining hats, clogging the cheap powder on women's faces and invading the inside of collars and necklines. The earth around the grave lay in saturated clods. Bessy raised her arm and threw two white roses on top

175

of the coffin. Evelyn drew her away, the grave-diggers moved in, and presently the rhythmical sound of earth hitting wood joined the steady hiss of rain.

'You had better take over this case, my friend,' Major Blumberg had told Paul the day before. 'You started on it.' Blumberg's cheeks were criss-crossed with red and blue veins and his breath stank of stale cigarettes. 'Not in such good health, you know, my dear von Hoch. I'm being sent back to Berlin.'

Paul made no comment. Major Blumberg's love of the bottle had finally become too much of an embarrassment for the garrison, and there was little he could offer Blumberg in the way of consolation, except for conventional words of regret.

There was no question in Paul's mind that the juxtaposition of events — enemy terrorist activity and the Count's death — were linked. The coincidence was too great. Whether or not they were further linked with the concealment of the parachutists was not so straightforward. Paul considered ordering the examination of the body before the Count was buried. While he was doing so, the report came in that the funeral was scheduled for that afternoon. To examine the body was one thing: to incur deeper hostilities in the population by exhumation was unwise. Watching the desolate Countess at the graveside, he knew he had been correct.

'Countess.' Paul approached Bessy.

The now soaked black dress and coat accentuated the thin black-sleeved arms and the bulk of her stomach. Bessy resembled some primitive ebony statue. All colour had been leached from her skin. Gone was the tawny grace and creamy richness of her looks. Her face was white, the skin puffed around the mouth and eyes, and she had bitten her lips until they were sore. When she saw who it was, Bessy trembled visibly and then went into the attack.

'I was not aware that you had been invited, Major. I am burying my husband, and I wish to do so in peace.'

'Madame la comtesse,' he said, 'I quite understand. But I thought I should pay my respects.'

Bessy adjusted her veil with an unsteady hand. 'Please go away.'

Paul turned to Evelyn and found himself speaking to the

hat brim shading her face. 'I am afraid I need to ask the Countess some more questions,' he said. 'When would be convenient?'

The rain seeped into her inadequate shoes as she considered his request. Sooner or later the question was going to be asked by the Germans: where did Charles spend his last night? Evelyn needed to be clear whom she would name and she needed more time to check out the contact. Major von Hoch was waiting and Evelyn was opening her mouth to ask him to return the next day when Bessy gasped and clutched her stomach. She stood quite still, as if she were trying to puzzle something out. All eyes flew towards her.

'Evelyn,' Bessy said after a moment. 'I think you must fetch Mazille . . .'

'What is it, Madame?' As she asked, comprehension dawned on Evelyn. 'Don't be alarmed, we'll get you back.' She linked her arm into Bessy's. 'Lean on me.' Bessy grabbed at Evelyn and clung to her with a grimace. 'Oh,' she took a long breath, 'it's a very odd feeling. Please get me home. I don't like everyone watching.'

'My car is closer.' Major von Hoch indicated it with a gloved hand. 'Let me take you.'

'You know, darling,' John once commented to Evelyn at Wanborough, 'this kind of work involves a sort of mental chameleon act. I do it all the time. It's quite easy, you sort of burrow inside yourself, and assume the colour you're sitting on. If you see what I mean. You just do it.'

Evelyn schooled her features into complete expressionlessness. 'Thank you, Major,' she said. 'That won't be necessary.'

The rain sliced down between the graves and poured onto the headstones, creating islands of mud in the trodden grass. Evelyn's face was wet, and rain weighted down her eyelashes. Bessy's grip on her arm hurt. 'But could you help me get the Countess to the car, do you think?' she asked reluctantly.

'Certainly.' He took Bessy by the other arm, and accidentally brushed Evelyn's hand with his. Through the wet, slippery leather of her gloves she felt his touch once again and for a moment she could concentrate on nothing else. 'Thank you,' said Evelyn, when they had reached the Hispano and settled Bessy. 'We'll manage now.' She moved round to the front of the car.

Paul pulled up the collar of his greatcoat and spoke through the car window. 'I hope the Countess will be all right.' Evelyn fiddled with the gear lever and looked straight ahead. Drops of water fell into her lap from her hat brim. 'Are you sure I cannot do anything else?' he asked, concerned.

'Yes,' she replied, let off the brake and drove past the last few mourners who were walking away down the road.

Gaston met them in the hallway and helped Evelyn support Bessy across the hall and up the staircase. 'Madame,' he said, 'a Monsieur Guy has phoned. He has arrived in Rjbérac and is waiting at the Café du Terminus to be collected. I told him he was too late for the funeral.'

Bessy pulled off her veil and dropped it onto the landing floor. 'Guy,' she said with longing. 'Thank God. Fetch him, please.'

Gaston seemed distressed by this request. 'Madame,' he said, 'you forget I don't drive. The Count was the only one who could drive the car.'

'I'll go,' Evelyn offered when she was settling Bessy into bed, 'just as soon as I've phoned Dr Mazille.'

It was the last thing she wanted to do. 'You might as well,' Bessy said in a thick voice. She waited for another contraction to subside. 'You seem to have become so involved in my family.' She pressed herself upright and faced Evelyn. 'You have brought me bad luck, Evelyn. Be careful with Guy.'

Evelyn took several tries before she got the Hispano-Suiza into gear. The car seemed very heavy – Charles had liked his little luxuries. It was a car that, by rights, should be driven and tended by a chauffeur; it did not take to inexpert handling or to charcoal fuel. What was more, Evelyn was upset by Bessy lashing out at her so unexpectedly and nervous at driving on a wet road. At least the rain had stopped and the sky was making an effort to return to a more normal blue.

Fortunately, the road into Ribérac was mostly downhill. Evelyn shifted the gear lever into fourth. Driving an unfamiliar car was the least of her problems. Villetoureix, and beyond that Périgueux, lay to the south-east, Aubeterre and Chalais due west. She searched in her memory for any details of the area she might have forgotten. To the south of Ribérac, she remembered, was the terrain known as the Double. Partly covered in a medieval chestnut and pine forest and dotted with lakes, it was ideal territory in which to hide. After all this she might have need of a refuge.

It was a pity – and this she felt quite apart from her regret at the death of Charles – that Belle-Place had become a focus of German attention. It made problematic the assumption that the *château* was a safe house and that she could continue to operate from there. Evelyn needed to talk to John, and she needed to inform London.

At the crossroads just before Ribérac, the road narrowed and became a street bordered by houses and shops. Some of the buildings were decaying, but others were well maintained, sporting archways and balconies decorated with filigree iron-work. The road bore right and Evelyn coasted round the corner into the main street.

It was growing dark and the Place Nationale was choked with German vehicles, making her turn into the rue Gambetta difficult to negotiate. German uniform – both field grey and green – was evident in the streets. The Ribéracois, dressed either in the ubiquitous men's blue overalls or patched and flower-patterned dresses for women, wove in between them in a reasonable semblance of normal life.

Evelyn eased the Hispano into the Avenue Verdun. She brought the car to a halt and sat back in the leather seat.

Fact: A man had telephoned Belle-Place and said he was Monsieur Guy. Why didn't he say Guy Myers, his full name?

Fact: Bessy had not been there to verify the call.

Fact: Someone who did not know that Charles was dead might have been trying to draw him out of the *château* and into a 'mousetrap', either to kill him or to hand him over to the Germans.

It *was* possible; and each possibility must be dissected for its probability. Her doubts disturbed a layer of unconscious fears. Was the *château* under surveillance? Had anybody betrayed them? There was no avoiding the risk and she would only have the answers when she walked into the café.

A woman walked by the car, holding a boy by the hand. He was dark and too thin, and he reminded Evelyn of Peter. Her mouth tightened. She missed her brother and it was odd knowing that none of the family had the least idea where she was.

Evelyn trusted that the staff at SOE headquarters were sending the postcards that she had prepared before she left. 'Dear Mother. Working hard. The weather is holding . . .', anodyne and completely uninformative.

Evelyn swung her legs out of the car, pulled her headscarf on and walked towards the Café du Terminus. A train had just pulled in and passengers were being checked by two French policemen as they emerged. Two men wearing leather coats and trilby hats watched the proceedings, Evelyn recognised them immediately as the Gestapo.

One of the plain-clothes officers spoke to a policeman, who immediately singled out a man carrying two shopping bags. The man's papers were passed over to the Gestapo. Elderly, resigned and weary, the man waited while his possessions were extracted from the bags. A shirt. A book. A jar of pâté. A packet of Gauloises. The man was ordered to shake out the cigarettes from the packet and a couple fell to the ground. The smaller of the two Gestapo officers flicked them into a puddle with the toe of his boot. The elderly man looked up and, for a minute, Evelyn thought he would protest at the loss of his precious cigarettes. The man was told sharply to move. He started to put back his belongings into the bags.

Inside the café it was crowded and noisy. Men in overalls and baggy grey trousers and waistcoats were drinking by the zinc bar. Several more were sitting at the tables, holding conversations across each other.

With the same tawny-coloured hair as his twin Guy Myers was instantly recognisable. There was a pile of Louis Vuitton luggage stuck over with P&O labels standing beside him and he was sitting in a corner with a glass of beer talking with another man.

Evelyn drew back and went to sit down at a table by the

door. Who was the second man? He looked quite tall, although as he was sitting down she could not judge properly. He wore well-creased trousers and good silk socks, and a green felt hat sat on the table. He had grey hair brushed back from a high forehead and looked well-fed, prosperous. Pleased. He was talking to Guy in a soft voice in reasonable French.

Evelyn decided to wait until the man left. She did not have to wait long. After five minutes or so the man got to his feet and felt in his pocket. Evelyn was right: he was above average height. He took his time to count out the precise amount of change required to pay his bill and to stack the coins in a pile on the table. After saying goodbye, he moved towards the door and, as he left, flicked an appraising glance back at Guy.

Close to, the man appeared surprisingly seedy – as if he couldn't quite put his expensive clothes together convincingly. After he had left the café, Evelyn approached Guy. 'Monsieur, I have come from Belle-Place.'

With a quick movement Guy swung round to face her.

'It is Monsieur Maier?' Evelyn pronounced his name in the French fashion. 'I am Madame de Bourgrave's secretary, and she has sent me to fetch you.'

'Good,' said Guy. 'Delighted.' He shook her hand. 'What could be better?' His French was confident and fluent.

'I am afraid there is some problem at the *château* which I will explain to you in the car.' Evelyn indicated the luggage. 'Can I take something?'

Guy plonked an expensive leather portfolio into her hands. 'The key to my life,' he announced. 'Carry it carefully.'

Soon they were out of the café and beside the car. Guy stowed the luggage, strapped it in and snapped the boot shut in a decisive and capable manner. 'I'm driving,' he announced, opening the passenger door for Evelyn.

There did not appear to be much choice and she got in obediently. 'Turn round, up the street and left out of the town,' she said rather helplessly.

Guy whistled a snatch from a popular tune as he drove, revving the engine noisily, through Ribérac. Evelyn checked in her handbag for her identity card in case they met a road block. The meeting had not been a 'mousetrap'.

'Your companion, Monsieur,' Evelyn asked cautiously, 'is he visiting Ribérac?'

'Herr Fleischer? I met him on the train. He's on holiday touring the Périgord. He was quite an interesting guy in his way. German. I bought him a drink in exchange. We talked about painting mostly.'

Taken aback by the matter-of-fact way Guy referred to the German, Evelyn changed the subject. 'Monsieur Maier,' she said, 'I'm afraid Madame la comtesse has gone into labour. It is the shock. But it's only two weeks early and the doctor is quite confident.' Evelyn did not wish to alarm Guy.

Guy's whistle petered out. 'Sakes,' he said in English. He switched to French. 'Well, as long as she doesn't present breech or have any other complications.' Evelyn wondered if she was going to spend the whole journey back to Belle-Place in a mild state of shock. Everything Guy said held an element of surprise, not least his obvious acquaintance with mid-wifery.

'Poor sis,' Guy continued. 'I'm sorry I wasn't here for the funeral. The trains were delayed.' He had, in fact, been nurs-ing a hangover and missed his train.

'Madame is asking for you constantly,' Evelyn informed him.

'Yes. She would be.'

She tried again. 'Have you been living in Paris long?'

Guy took his eyes off the road and studied her for a couple of seconds. Evelyn would have been pleased to read his thoughts. Not very interesting, went Guy's verdict, but good eyes and mouth. Worth a try perhaps?

'Didn't my sister tell you all about me? She must be slip-ping.'

She had been told about Guy at dinner and Evelyn had not listened. She wished she had. Guy shifted and pulled out a hip flask from his pocket. 'Unscrew this for me, will you? I've been living in Paris for the last five years. I paint. Very well, actually,' he added. He took a swig from the flask and passed it to Evelyn. 'Take some.'

She studied him discreetly. Grey flannel trousers. Expensive cashmere tweed jacket. Silk tie. Gold cufflinks and hand-made leather shoes. Guy Myers did not believe in starving artistically in a garret. The tan leather shoes made his feet look narrow, but his fingers were large and square and, adding a jarring note to his appearance, were stained with nicotine and paint. Guy took another swig, keeping one hand lightly on the wheel. His blue eyes were similar to Bessy's but after the eyes and hair, the resemblance ended. His mouth, for instance, was cut on more generous lines than Bessy's and his face was broader.

'Paris was becoming too uncomfortable and expensive anyway,' he said. 'I can't be bothered any more. Eating on the black market has its charms but it's too much like hard work. So, as you will have noticed, I've come prepared for a long stay.'

'I've only been to Paris once,' said Evelyn. 'Tell me about it.'

Guy paused. 'You really wanna know?' he said in English. Evelyn faked puzzlement and he switched back into French. 'Well, I'll tell you about the important things. Coffee is three thousand francs a kilo. Olive oil has disappeared. Colza oil is a particularly nasty substitute. Butter is five hundred a kilo – it used to be twenty before the war. Les Halles is a wasteland except for the scavengers searching through the rubbish tips for turnip tops and cabbage leaves. Taxis have disappeared. The bicycle is in, but you need a number plate. Worse, it is forbidden for a Frenchman to enter the Ritz by the Place Vendôme. Only Germans may do so, and unaccompanied women are shown the door. Everyone picks up cigarette butts in the street and sawdust is *the* fuel of the moment. Do you want me to go on?'

Evelyn smiled. 'You are observant, Monsieur.'

'Of course I am,' he said, enjoying the impression he was making. 'That's my business. Fashion is divided into two cliques. *Zazous* affect an exaggerated English look, complete with the large dog. The swings – named after the jazz – favour the American. Wide trousers, two-tone shoes. Otherwise, the women wear ghastly wooden-soled shoes and shorter and shorter hemlines. And to rub French noses in it, a German brass band marches past the Étoile every day.'

'Turn left,' said Evelyn, pointing ahead. 'Have you not visited Belle-Place before?'

'Nope,' he said. 'Sister dear hasn't been well enough for visitors. I thought there would be plenty of time.'

He slowed the Hispano to a walking pace and the *château* came into view among the trees. Guy stopped the car and rolled down the window. 'Nice,' he said.

Below them, to their right, the valley glimmered brown and old gold under a layer of rainwater. Walnut trees moved in the breeze and patches of dead sunflowers with blackened heads ran between strips of fields harvested of their maize and tobacco. Over to the left, the vines stretched up and out of sight.

'Have you been here long?' asked Guy, pulling in his head and shutting the window because it was cold.

'Not long, Monsieur.'

'In that case we can make expeditions together.'

'Monsieur, I am very busy.'

'Nonsense. We will be excellent companions.' Guy snapped his fingers.

'I really don't have time for that sort of thing.' Evelyn managed to sound particularly colourless.

'Don't you?' Guy's eyes invited her to change her mind. 'Oh, well.' He looked out of the window again. 'I like the way the thrifty French farmer allows the walnut trees to grow right in the middle of his fields. He wouldn't dream of cutting down anything so valuable.'

With a sinking feeling, Evelyn realised that Guy was extremely sharp.

'One thing,' he said. He leant forward over the wheel and stared through the windscreen. 'I will have to trust you but I have a feeling that I can. Can't I, Mademoiselle?' She caught a good-humoured cynical look, which suggested he usually got his way. 'I'm going under the name of "Maier" here and I'm not going to let on I'm Bessy's brother. I think it would be prudent, just in case the old US of A decides it wants to tackle Adolf. So why don't we just say I am a Frenchman employed at the *château*?'

'Your accent?' she queried, conscious of an irony. 'I mean, Monsieur, your French is good but . . . there is just the tiniest suggestion . . .'

'We'll have to think about that. Maybe you could apply your mind to the problem.' He leant over and placed a finger under her chin and forced Evelyn to look into his face. 'On second thoughts,' he reflected, 'you are quite pretty.'

'We should go.' Evelyn removed his hand from her face. 'Your sister is waiting for you.'

Guy turned his attention back to the car. 'One more thing,' he asked. His voice was teasing. 'Do you have a husband or a lover?'

'What business is that of . . . ? I mean . . . excuse me, Monsieur.'

'Aha, a flash of spirit.' Guy's smile broadened. 'I always ask before I seduce a woman.'

'Monsieur,' she reproved him, 'we *must* continue.'

'Yes, of course.' Guy sounded matter-of-fact and twisted the key in the ignition. 'You haven't answered my question.' He steered the car into the drive. 'You can't wriggle out of it while I hold you a captive audience.'

'Well, I'm not going to answer it.'

'I'm patient.'

'What do you mean?'

'I suspect you are as pure as Snow White.' He sneaked a glance at Evelyn's hot face. 'Game, set and match, Mademoiselle?'

Gaston was waiting at the door of Belle-Place. 'Mademoiselle, will you go up at once? The Countess is asking for you. I will see to Monsieur and show him to his room.'

'Till later, then,' said Guy, and added, 'Snow White.'

As it turned out, Evelyn did not see Guy Myers for the rest of the day, nor the next. Bessy's labour continued throughout the afternoon and into the evening and she insisted that Evelyn sat by the bed. Towards midnight, Bessy became dehydrated and a little delirious. Dr Mazille did not dare to give her any drugs to help, and Evelyn was kept busy helping sponge her down.

This time when the dawn arrived it was to witness a birth. Bessy's son, the son she had always promised Charles, was born into the freezing half-light of a November morning.

Dr Mazille rubbed his eyes, for he was deadly tired. He examined the wet, slippery little body and bent over Bessy. 'Well done. You are both safe.'

Bessy answered through her bitten lips. 'I wish I was dead.'

Dr Mazille glanced up at Evelyn. 'You have a lovely son, Countess.'

'I don't want him.' Bessy shivered, gently at first, then with increasing violence. Dr Mazille thrust the baby at Evelyn. 'Here. She has gone into shock.'

Half an hour later Bessy was asleep, the baby washed, settled and ensconced with Marie. Evelyn took up a vigil by Bessy's bed. It had been another long night and she was drained of emotion. After a while, she went over to the window, drew back the silk curtains a fraction and looked down to the gardens. Picked out in white ice particles, the black masses of shrubs and bushes formed glistening, geometric patterns against an earth sprinkled with hoar frost like icing sugar on a cake. Evelyn blinked at the magnificence of the dawn: violet, soft pink and burning red. Her eyes pricked with fatigue and tension.

She was on her own.

PART TWO

January 1942–July 1942

Extract from the diary of Evelyn, née St John

A cartoon published in early 1941, I think, showed a lowering sky full of German war planes under which a soldier, a British Tommy, stands on a rock surrounded by sea. One hand clasps his weapon, the other is raised with clenched fist to the sky. The caption reads: 'Very well then, alone.'

I find that cartoon very moving. It represents the time before the German invasion of Russia, when we in Britain were fighting Hitler by ourselves. It also strikes a personal note. There I was at the Château Belle-Place, alone, still inexperienced, and, like the foolish virgin in the parable, crying in the dark.

The death of Charles meant that the Merrygoround circuit which he had started to build was leaderless. It was also blown. Without Charles's influence and authority, the attempt to unify the resistance forces in the area fizzled out and they splintered into factions: royalists, socialists, Communists and those who supported General de Gaulle in exile. It was a confusing situation to understand, even more difficult to work with.

To return to the cartoon. What other options did Britain have at that time? The answer, during those black and seemingly hopeless days, was not many. It made the work soe was trying to do even more necessary and I wanted to carry on. It was my duty.

Later the situation changed, of course. On 7 December 1941 Japan attacked the American base at Pearl Harbor. Both Britain and America declared war on Japan and Germany and Italy declared war on America. On a practical and immediate level, it meant that Britain could cease melting down iron railings and saucepans for armaments and call on America's huge industrial base. (The Americans had already been sending

189

over manna in the shape of powdered eggs, milk, cheese, blankets, children's clothing.) On a grander level, it meant there were men, guns, money and an international comradeship to soothe the ache of having been solitary for so long.

But it was a long time before the American involvement produced dividends – and at Christmas 1941 Germany seemed invincible.

Despite the demands made on the Germans to maintain their Russian front, the occupying forces continued to tighten security procedures in occupied France and the Vichy Government followed suit. Life became a tedious round of travel restrictions, curfews, demands for papers – you needed permission to pee, joked Jean-Claude. In the main, German troops behaved well. Most would agree on that point. The soldiers were sometimes frightened and often homesick. The Gestapo and the SD were another problem. Both organisations established large headquarters in Paris and began to terrorise the country and their agents were in all the big towns and garrisons. Technically, they came under the German High Command. In practice the SD and Gestapo did what they liked. They were often confused by their victims but if you are being beaten up it is a matter of academic interest who is doing it. Stories circulated of their interrogation techniques: how they disarmed suspects with coffee and cigarettes one minute and used cold baths and gun butts the next.

Charles died on 21 November, I remember. There was nothing we could do except pray the Germans did not investigate the circumstances. Bessy was ill from grief and shock. Merrygoround was compromised. A baby had been born. All these events rapidly converged – and I had to deal with them. And then I had the idea.

I remember thinking how strong and resilient I was becoming. How devoted I was to the job, how the restlessness in me was being usefully channelled, how nothing mattered more than to beat the enemy using the special knowledge I had been given.

That was my first mistake.

The second was not to admit a truth to myself.

CHAPTER ONE

DRT TO BDQ . . . DRT TO BDQ
REQUEST RETURN FOR BRIEFING STOP MERRYGOROUND BURNED
STOP PROPOSE PICK-UP SEVEN FIVE ZERO FOUR BOURDEILLES FIVE
ZERO TWO TWO STRAWBERRY STOP BBC PHRASE LE BOUCHER A DE
BONNE VIANDE? ALOUETTE

BDT TO DRT . . . BDQ TO DRT
YOUR MESSAGE ACKNOWLEDGED STOP PICK-UP STRAWBERRY STOP
BBC PHRASE LE BOUCHER A DE BONNE VIANDE STOP LIE LOW STOP

'Aha, this is what you get up to in your spare time!' Guy
Myers came up on Evelyn suddenly. She was sitting in the
library listening in to the BBC for her message. With a snap,
she turned the radio off and got up.

'I like to relax to the wireless sometimes,' she explained.
'But if I'm disturbing you . . .'

'No,' said Guy. 'Not at all. I'm interested, that's all.' He
smiled disarmingly. 'Was it a good programme?'

'Yes.' Evelyn fussed over the cushion in her chair.

'I see.' Guy began to inspect the pictures and books in the
library. 'Nice room you've got here, as they say.'

She glanced round. Nice was not the word she would have
used to describe the book-lined, somewhat chilly magnificence
of the library. Guy pulled out a book bound in the best green
Morocco, flicked through it and replaced it. 'I wouldn't have
thought my late lamented brother-in-law would have been
fond of Baudelaire. He didn't seem the type.' He pulled out
another book, and then made one of his swift conversational
pounces. 'I want to know why you are deserting your post.'

'My mother is ill,' Evelyn replied, peddling the story she
had concocted to account for her leaving Belle-Place. ('You
will promise to return quickly,' begged John when he trans-

mitted the request. 'I shall be ultra, ultra lonely.') 'She needs me. It will only be for a little while.'

'For Christ's sake, my sister needs you.'

The implication was clear. Bessy came before Evelyn's mother. Amused by Guy's directness, she plumped up a second cushion. Whatever else Guy might be, and she had not fathomed him yet – charmer? rogue? seducer? – he was fond of his sister.

'Will you stop behaving like a maid.'

She straightened up and caught his eyes. They were crackling with amusement, the sort of amusement, she reflected rather savagely, a man of the world would extract from teasing someone shyer and less assured than himself. 'Monsieur,' Evelyn calculated how quickly she could excuse herself. 'I will only be away for a little while.'

'Call me Guy,' he insisted. 'Since we are connected by marriage, I think we can use first names.'

'Guy, then. I am sure Marie can cope while I'm away.'

'We'll see, little cousin. My sister appears to rely on you. Evelyn's mouth tightened. She was unsure how Bessy felt about her. 'And since she is not at all well . . .' Guy patted her bottom and smiled. 'Miss Very Useful. Now have you thought up a reason as to why I should be here?' She pretended to hesitate.

'Yes, I have,' she admitted shyly.

'Oh, good.' He sat down and draped a leg over the arm of the leather sofa. 'Fire away.'

'Only if you promise not to mention my going away again.'

Guy's smile hardened a trifle, and Evelyn knew she had stepped over the boundary marked 'employer' on one side and 'servant' on the other. 'Please, Monsieur.' She steeled herself to plead.

Guy tapped his fingers on the leather and then said, 'A bargain. Now what is your idea?'

'I think you should be here at the request of the Count. He mentioned to me once he was thinking of having the *château*'s books and paintings professionally catalogued. But you will need to see to your papers.'

'Ah, yes.' Guy was thoughtful. 'Well, you must leave that

to me. I will make some enquiries. I don't suppose you know anything about that sort of thing?' He peered at the closed expression on her face. 'No. I wouldn't expect you to. You know, if you smiled more often you really would be very pretty.'

Anxious to terminate the conversation which, as ever with Guy, threatened to become too personal, Evelyn went over to the window, ostensibly to look at the view but really to check for cloud and fog cover. The pick-up might be that night. An early mist that had lain over the gardens was clearing but traces still hung over the fields. Guy swung his leg back onto the floor and joined her by the window. He extracted the damask curtain which she was absent-mindedly rubbing between her fingers.

'Naughty. This is old and valuable material, my dear. Treat it carefully.' Obediently, Evelyn let it drop. 'Yup,' he said, and cocked his head to one side to examine it. 'I should say Lyons circa mid-eighteenth century. Badly in need of restoration. In fact, they are a disgrace. Years of dirt and neglect.'

'Really?' Evelyn was fascinated by this side of Guy. She had not met many – any men – who took an interest in furnishings and colour schemes. It struck her as odd – and rather attractive.

'Bessy will tell you,' he said. 'Whenever we went to house-parties in Great Neck or the Hamptons, my hostesses made sure I spent most of the morning discussing interior decoration. I would advise antique Egyptian here. Shaker-look there. Italian Renaissance. Sometimes I couldn't help teasing a little. One lady has me to thank for her Cretan bathroom in a perfectly hideous thirties pile. I often think of how absurd her pink, wrinkled body must look wallowing in a replica of the Queen's bath – reproduced at enormous cost, of course.' Guy snapped his fingers. Snap, snap, his eyes bright with what looked like malice. 'Old bats,' he added and Evelyn laughed.

She thought about Belle-Place and its troubles as she crouched, terrified, in the passenger seat of the Westland

Lysander aircraft. It had dropped down precisely on target Strawberry, taxied to a halt and Evelyn, stifling a feeling of panic that she would never see any of them again, shook Jean-Claude's hand and kissed John.

'Give my love to Blighty. Go and see a good revue for a tonic. And get yourself dated by a handsome soldier,' he said into her ear.

The pilot slid back the cockpit hood. 'Just to warn you we will fly low over the Channel,' he shouted over the engine noise. 'The radar beams are fixed so Jerry will lose us in the mush at the bottom of the radar tube if we keep low. Not to worry if you think we're going into the drink.'

Evelyn negotiated the ladder up into the plane. 'Got it,' she shouted back and lied, 'Don't worry about me, I'm perfectly all right.'

'Tally ho, then.' The pilot gave the thumbs-up, shut the cockpit and taxied down the field.

Evelyn clung on to the seat and prayed it would soon be over. With a roar the plane bumped down the field, strained, rose and cleared – just – a patch of trees at the end. The subdued hum of the plane cutting through the darkness took over after that.

Would she ever come back to Ribérac? Would she ever know what happened to the inhabitants of Belle-Place? She left behind a seriously depressed Bessy who refused to look at or hold her three-week-old son and no one had been able to persuade her to feed him. 'Just take him away,' she repeated monotonously, each time an overture was made. 'Leave me alone.'

She left Gaston old and too demoralised by yet another war to be much help. Then there was Marie, loyal and concerned, who did her best to juggle caring for the baby and cooking – and, of course, Guy. Guy, who seemed to enjoy the crisis, who seemed thoroughly at home, and who was making it his business to find out as much as he could about Belle-Place.

The one outstanding, ominous, dangerous fact was Major von Hoch. Evelyn put up a hand to secure the passenger cockpit which was letting in a stream of cold air. Major von

194

Hoch had not returned to the *château* to find out where Charles had spent his last night.

Why not?

It was possible he had decided to put the *château* under surveillance. It was possible he was playing cat and mouse, waiting for them to make an incriminating move. It was possible he had believed the story of Charles's death. Whatever the odds for and against, Evelyn could only do her best and brief Gaston to act dumb and to say if asked that he had no idea of the Count's business activities. She was also sure that if Major von Hoch tried to question Bessy he would get nothing out of her in her present state.

Suspended in the thin, vinegar-sharp air, the Lysander's engines were earth-shatteringly loud, and Evelyn further terrified herself, which she considered shameful weakness, by imagining that every flak battery in northern France was springing into action. She wondered if you felt anything as you plummeted, free-falling and flailing, from a shot-down aircraft. Fear? Or did you accept your fate? Did you give in to it and enjoy those last moments of darkness and peace? Perhaps you lost consciousness? She began to hum: 'Au clair de la lune, mon ami Pierrot . . .' hoping it would divert her.

Later, the Lysander rose high into the sky over the French coast and then dropped in a stomach-churning trajectory to skim the sea, making for England.

For security reasons, field agents never visited SOE headquarters in Baker Street. They did not even know where it was. Even the strongest among them might be persuaded under torture to reveal its whereabouts. Agents, therefore, were seen by the home staff, who also took stringent precautions in case there were German spies tracking them, in outlying flats hired for the duration.

Nothing had changed in blacked-out Orchard Court, Portman Square, when Evelyn paused in the hallway to give her code name to Mr Lade, the doorman. Everything seemed as she remembered it. Outside in the street, lorries were taking people to work to help out the disrupted bus services, taxis were acting as auxiliary fire engines and pulling trailer pumps and the few cars there were sported headlight masks. Trapped by windows that did not let in enough air, smells lingered in the hallway, familiar and unforgettable – cigarette smoke, polish and damp clothes mixed with a whiff of stale sandwiches. After the early-morning breakfast of eggs and bacon at the Tangmere airstrip, it made Evelyn queasy.

'Morning, dear.'

Mr Lade at the door greeted her in the same cheery manner he greeted all the visitors. He was not deceived by the FANY uniform: he had seen enough incoming and outgoing agents to draw his own conclusions about the set-up that had come to roost under his roof. Lade was familiar with the far-away look some of them wore and the way they had of checking the street when they arrived. But not for the world would he ever confide his knowledge. He agreed with the Prime Minister. 'I also see,' Mr Churchill had broadcast, 'side by side with the devastation and amid the ruins, quiet, confident, bright and smiling eyes, beaming with a consciousness of being associated with a cause far higher and wider than any human or personal issue. I can see the spirit of an unquenchable people.' He waved Evelyn upstairs and sang under his breath as he watched her walk through the hall.

'My bonny is stationed at . . .
It's just as hush hush as can be
So nobody knows he's at . . .
Except his relations and me.'

Major Tony Turner was on the phone when Evelyn was ushered into the drawing room of the flat. When he saw who it was he got to his feet, wound up the conversation and held out his hand.

'Alouette. Good morning. Major Peters asks me to send his greeting and he will be with you as soon as possible. He will be very glad to see you.' Evelyn knew this was true – the staff cherished their agents and worried over their safety. Still clasping Evelyn's hand, Tony Turner gazed into her face as if he wanted to read what lay behind it. 'Hm. A little tired?' He pointed to a chair. 'Why don't we have a chat before Major Peters arrives?'

F-section of SOE (other SOE sections included Scandinavia, north-west Europe and south-east Asia) was sifting the implications and coming to terms with an unpromising situation. The round up of F-section agents at the Villa des Bois in Marseille left only a handful still working in Vichy France. True, the tally of arrests in occupied France was lower and several agents were still in place – one, for instance, was working as a dock labourer in Bordeaux and another was, for the moment, satisfactorily based in Paris. But Bloch's wireless had gone silent after 12 November and the staff suspected that it was for ever. In addition, this year winter had arrived early and it was viciously cold. There had been no drops, either, of men or supplies during November and December.

Evelyn produced a bottle of champagne from her bag and passed it over. 'A present,' she said. 'I thought all of you might appreciate it.'

Tony Turner most certainly did. 'I do,' he said. 'I'll look forward to it. It will remind me of many a good dinner enjoyed in France.' He examined the label; it was weeks since he had enjoyed the luxury of dinner. Then he placed it to one side. 'Now,' he said, pulling his papers towards him. 'You are expected to submit a report. I know you are tired.' Once again he scrutinised Evelyn's face for clues and gave a sympathetic smile which said, 'Of course I don't know what it's like but I will try. It's important that I understand.

Safe and increasingly sleepy, the adrenalin that had streamed constantly through her body since September began to seep away, depleting Evelyn's reserves of energy. The meeting was tiring, very tiring, and with each question, each painstaking sifting after facts, each examination of the smallest detail, she felt more drained. Afterwards he asked her to go over the material again so he could check the details. She faltered only when she described, without giving the full context, how she had made involuntary contact with a German officer.

'Hm,' he said, his face intent and concerned. 'A pity. We must consider the problem.'

Evelyn's concentration drifted.

'Now what are we going to do with you?' Turner was thoughtful.

The suggestion that he might plan something other than what she had in mind was enough to summon back the adrenalin and her determination. She shifted into a more upright position in the chair and leant forward.

'I want to take over as circuit head,' she found herself saying outright. 'If we discuss it, sir, under four headings, I think you might find it useful. One, military. How can the circuit help defeat the enemy? Two, political. Who is to hold the balance of power in the community? Three, security. How do we keep clear of the enemy and local police? Four, practical. How will it actually work?'

He picked up the champagne bottle and ran his fingers around the sealed cork. 'Go on.'

Twenty minutes later he said, 'You realise that this could be very dangerous, particularly in view of your contact with the German officer.' Forty minutes later, he told Evelyn to go away; he wished to think about her proposals.

Evelyn wrote up her report later that afternoon. Estimated strength of resistance, political affiliations. Where do they get their funds and weapons? Arms dumps. Position of local German garrisons. Strength. Armoury. Any tactics of note? Feasibility of railway and road sabotage. Local factories producing supplies for Germans or weapons. Morale of locals. Difference between situation of French in occupied and unoccupied zones. How to get across the line. Rationing. Strength of Gaullist sympathies. 'Wherever I go,' she wrote on that subject, 'I am frequently asked about the General. Many look on him as the potential Saviour of France.'

One of the junior staff officers at Baker Street was deputed to take her out to dinner but she refused, treating herself instead to coffee and a pastry at Papa Richoux's. Later she made do with a sandwich in the SOE flat in Wilton Court. The Spam was tasteless and Evelyn recalled with a pang eating bread rubbed in garlic and oil while overlooking the Belle-Place vineyards. Its remembered tang was as sharp as her homesickness for France.

Before she went to sleep, Evelyn considered the problem

of Major von Hoch and struggled to understand the turbulence and the ache that invaded her whenever she thought about him. Desire? The desire perhaps of the spoilt child who cannot have a toy on which it has set its heart. Or something dark and insidious?

Underneath the woollen blanket and feather eiderdown, her tired mind tangled into knots. What was she thinking of? Evelyn pushed the blanket back and lay staring at the ceiling with her hands tucked under her head.

When she returned to Belle-Place – if she returned – she would ensure that she never came into contact with Major von Hoch. And if she could not trust herself to do that, she must confess to Major Turner and jeopardise her chances of returning. The room was dark and stuffy because of the black-out and Evelyn would have liked the comforting light of a street lamp or a church clock to tell her the time. Five minutes passed, ten minutes. A relentlessly logical inner voice refused to stop. Evelyn must never again admit to herself that a breakaway part of her, a rebel part, urged her to say, 'What does it matter who he is?' Evelyn turned over and eventually fell asleep to dream of Bessy, John, Charles and Major von Hoch outlined against a pale winter-washed horizon like figures from a medieval dance of death.

Behind the black-out at soe headquarters in Baker Street the lights remained on all night: f-section was in conference while the staff debated the issues that Evelyn had raised.

'You know, these press chappies would have a field day if they ever got hold of the fact that we're dropping women into occupied countries,' said one of the staff officers through the haze of cigarette smoke. He was short and sported a sparse black moustache. No one felt equal to tackling that problem so his remark remained unchallenged.

'Is Alouette capable of leading a circuit as you say she could?' asked a conducting officer. 'We know the attrition rate is very high and the French resistance is in a mess. Is it safe to stake so much on a young girl?'

'Unfortunately, the war won't wait,' replied Major Peters. 'We must use the material we have to hand.'

Tony Turner coughed. 'In view of the developing situation in France, I would like to make two points. In future, we shall not train agents together who are likely to work at close quarters in the field. It is far safer if they know nothing about each other at all. Secondly, we are planning to send agents into France in parties of three. One, a circuit organiser. Two, a pianist who works solely to that head, no one else. Three, an arms instructor and, hopefully, sabotage expert. Obviously, enormous care will be taken to "fix" the cells, i.e., we don't want the men falling in love with the women or becoming jealous of each other. There are bound to be personality clashes.'

'That makes sense.' The conducting officer approved.

'Good.' Major Peters looked around the room.

'To return to Alouette,' Turner went on, 'a female circuit organiser is not an impossibility. After all, there may not be another candidate. However, it does present special problems with the men, who might react negatively to a woman.'

'And they are physically weaker,' added the staff officer.

'Not necessarily, old chap.'

'They get romantic notions.' The staff officer was anxious to make his point.

'True,' said Major Peters. 'So do men. And how can we, safe at home, judge what effect being in the field has on the emotions?'

There was a pause.

'How do our friends in the R/F section feel about the current situation?' was the next question. Major Peters took his time to answer. R/F section had been formed to work alongside General de Gaulle's Free French, who had escaped to London after the fall of France in June 1940 and were now settled in a London headquarters. Relations between SOE and the Free French were not plain sailing. For one thing, neither party saw eye to eye – and the French, beaten, defensive and in some cases bitterly ashamed of their country, were both hostile and suspicious of their English hosts who, in their turn, were inclined to tell them as little as possible.

'As you know,' Turner rubbed his eyes, 'the General is very sensitive, but in these matters he is coming round to our way of thinking. In fact, he is sending his own agent "Rex" back into France with the brief to co-ordinate the resistance. If Rex succeeds, then our work will be made easier, but we need *our* agents to be in place.'

'Who's Alouette's pianist?' asked the number two.

Major Peters folded his fingers into the church and steeple shape children sometimes make when playing finger games. 'Georges II. He's still operational. Skilled and reliable.'

'Arms and sabotage bod?'

Major Peters pushed a file towards Turner who began to read from it. 'There are two possibles. "Theo" who's just finished the sabotage course at Hatfield. He's ready to go. Or "Tomas", who some of you already know as he worked at headquarters. We decided to grant his request to go operational.'

'I don't like it,' said number two. 'He's a security risk.'

Turner's face appeared grey in the electric light. 'Look,' he argued patiently, 'we must use whoever we can get at the moment. There is a risk, yes, but Tomas understands and is prepared to take the necessary action should he be caught. I should also add, his training reports are first class.' Turner looked towards the conducting officer who had accompanied Tomas on his training. He nodded confirmation. 'And he has also taken the wireless course but he has three weeks to go before he is finally through.'

'Send Theo then.' The number two got up to look at the map. 'Tomas can go into the Franche-Comté later. Do you really think we'll get away with sending the French a woman?'

At his end of the table Major Peters raised his eyebrows.

'Depends on the woman.' Tony Turner closed the file.

The discussion continued until four a.m. Alouette's training and field reports were sifted: 'A tendency to underestimate herself.' 'Quietly intelligent.' 'Expert shot.' 'Survived first tour well and dealt with set-backs.' 'Excellent debriefing.'

'Too eager to go back?' Turner queried.

'Has she matured sufficiently?' asked the number two. 'Or come back with some dashed romantic notions?'

'Now wait a minute.' Turner held up his pipe. 'This girl has survived a dangerous tour. She knows what's out there.

We mustn't fall into the trap of thinking, as some of our respected instructors,' he raised a smile among his listeners, 'too conventionally. We look for subtler characteristics, the commitment, wouldn't you say, gentlemen? The guts.'

Major Peters nodded. 'Are we agreed, then?' he said at last. 'We send Alouette back, with our flying chums at the end of the week if possible, otherwise we will have to wait for the next moon period.'

'How are the wizards in 161 Squadron?' The speaker was referring to one of the two special duties squadrons allocated for pick-ups.

'That is something we must discuss,' said the number two. 'There were no pick-ups by 161 Squadron – or drops by 138 Squadron – in November or December. Can we do anything to help?'

'No,' said the conducting officer. 'Not unless you're in touch with the Almighty. If you are, could you please negotiate a bomber's moon?' The laughter that greeted the sally was stronger than it merited but it helped to relieve tension. Smoke from many cigarettes hung in an acrid layer over the table and the debate continued. So much depended on their deliberations, for the penalties for incorrect decision were so great – from the spectre of unfriendly rival secret services waiting to gobble them up to the knowledge that their miscalculations could result in death.

'Vot vos dot?'

'Dot vos a bompf.'

'All der time der iss bompfs.'

'Dere vos a very fonny joke . . .'

Evelyn had to stop herself laughing out loud. The other passengers might think she was mad. The ITMA programme she had listened to on the hotel radio had been very funny. 'Der newspaper Diplomatische and Damrubbische und Poltische mit Gibberische und Sauerkraut . . .' Harmless, mood-lightening nonsense from supremely silly idiots – and that it was in dubious taste didn't make it less funny.

She was on her way to Paddington to catch a train for a lightning visit to her family in Castle Cary before returning to

Belle-Place with a brief to create and head up a new circuit, Astronomer – before going back to France where the buffoonery of Der newspaper Diplomatische and Damrubbische would not even raise a smile.

Holding her collar up against the cold, she walked through Hyde Park, its elegance now dented by a noisy, smelly piggery near the Albert Memorial, and skirted the allotments sprinkled like brown pocket handkerchiefs around it. Dig, dig for victory, exhorted the posters, pamphlets and newspapers. Plough today. Turn your tennis courts into cabbages and your flower garden into potatoes, carrots and onions. She stopped: despite the bomb damage and the barrage balloons that floated like grey whales over her head, London was fighting back. After a minute she continued on towards the Underground station at High Street Kensington where she boarded a train to Paddington.

She became uneasy when the tube began to move, aware that she was being watched. There was nothing tangible to go on, just the sixth sense that had evolved in France. She contrived to drop her handbag onto the floor of the carriage and looked covertly down the carriage as she retrieved it.

The man watching her was Captain Fuller.

Relieved there was an explanation, she sat upright. The dark, arrogant set of his features and the flopping hair were unforgettable. A quick glance showed her he was in uniform – with a major's crown – holding an attaché case on his knee. He had been promoted.

An attaché case!

She stared at her ticket and told herself that Major Fuller was not likely to be travelling around London with a wireless transmitter. She tried to prise more information out of the diminished reflection permitted by the taped-up windows – but Major Fuller was too far down the carriage.

At this point the train shuddered, slowed and came to a halt. The lights went out. Two seats down from Evelyn a woman screamed and there was a distinct, 'Oh, God, not again,' from the young man sitting opposite. After the light, the blackness of the carriage was thick and frightening.

'Full marks for not acknowledging me,' said a familiar voice beside her, and Evelyn nearly screamed herself.

'Major Fuller,' she said, irritation rising. 'Please don't ever do that again.' She sat down and whispered, 'You know we're not supposed to recognise each other.'

'Quite right.' Jack lowered his voice theatrically. 'There is a strong chance that I'm a double agent.'

If it had not been dark, Evelyn would have stared at Major Fuller. She did not associate jokes with the unsmiling, much-too-pleased-with-himself interviewer she remembered. 'Don't joke,' she said. 'It could be all too true.'

Above them the lights flickered on: a falsely promised deliverance. They went out again. It was becoming uncomfortably hot in the carriage. Evelyn unbuttoned her coat.

'Here, let me,' said Jack and put an arm around the seat to help. Her hair brushed his cheek and he smelt an elusive flowery perfume. French perfume, he imagined, and was consumed with envy. The girl beside him, whom he had so disliked on first meeting, whom he continued to distrust (and yet occasionally to think about), was now a seasoned operator.

'Major Fuller,' her voice came out of the dark. 'You're hurting me.'

Without realising what he was doing, Jack had tightened his fingers on her shoulders. Apologising, he released her. 'You're going back.' He spoke matter-of-factly.

That kind of information was secret and Evelyn knew she shouldn't answer him. In the end she compromised. 'There was a disaster, but now I'm working again.'

'I see,' he said, and she was not sure if it was anger or disapproval she heard in his voice.

It was strange the effect they had on each other: an uncomfortable, gritty rubbing of personalities. Jarred by his tone, she moved further away and arranged her coat over her knees. 'Is my . . . er . . . working unacceptable, Major Fuller?'

'It must be a very tough assignment and— '

'I expect', she flashed back, cutting him off, 'you feel that it is none of your business to comment on it.' Model agents did not lose their tempers or draw attention to themselves but, in this case, Evelyn didn't care. 'Interviewing candidates who go into the field', she continued in a whisper, recognising the quick hot surge of temper which had so often got her into trouble with her father, 'must be so rewarding. And you do it so well.'

Oh dear, she thought. A cheap victory. Glad of the concealing dark, Jack flushed. He was conscious of an irrational disappointment. The girl was no better, or no different, from the rest of her type. Rude, arrogant, patronising. What he had not quite realised was the extent to which he had wanted her to be something else.

'Well,' he said with a laugh that struck a false note. 'You certainly know how to put a chap down. As it happens,' he fabricated, 'I do enjoy interviewing and I'm extremely busy.'

There was a long silence. 'I think I owe you an apology.' Evelyn said. There was another pause. 'I was very rude.'

'Didn't notice,' Jack lied.

It was impossible to see much of Major Fuller's face, but Evelyn felt she must, and could, manage an explanation. 'I am afraid I am very tired.'

'Of course,' he said stiffly.

At this point the lights went on and remained on. The train jerked into motion. Evelyn and Jack found themselves staring at each other, rather flushed and grim. She held out a hand.

'You must think me so ill-mannered,' she said, eyes narrowed in her desire to put things right. 'I am sorry.' After a couple of seconds he took the proffered hand, touched by the courage behind the gesture and more than a little ashamed that he had not taken the opportunity to apologise.

'Let's forget it.' Jack eventually released her hand.

'Good.' Evelyn folded her coat over her knee.

'Well,' he said and got up to return to his seat. He seemed taller and trimmer than when she last met him. She looked up at him, her skin olive in the fractured light. She had rolled her dark hair around her FANY cap, and her eyes were large and curious. For the first time in months Jack felt the first, faint inklings of interest in a woman's body. It was a pity their meeting had not been more successful because it was not likely they would ever see each other again.

'This is my stop,' she said, and reached for her suitcase. 'Goodbye, Major Fuller.'

'Glad you noted my promotion. Goodbye. Good luck.'

He tried not to watch her as she walked down the platform and vanished.

At Paddington Underground station, the smell of grime, makeshift lavatories, sweat and old clothing – a legacy from the Blitz when people slept for months underground – still filtered, heavy and sickening, into the nostrils. Dirt – the thick black soot from the trains – was everywhere: on the floors, in the passages and encrusting the arches. The stench must have been even worse when men, women and children were crammed in together. Evelyn paused and exchanged her suitcase from one hand to the other. To have been down here, night after night, must have seemed like being buried alive. It gave you an uncomfortable precognition of what might happen if you were trapped in a collapsed building. Her gaze rested on a grubby child's shoe lying beside the track. Further up was a woman's cheap cotton stocking. Evelyn shivered a little.

The main-line station was busy. The platforms were crowded with passengers anxious to know if they would get away. Others were meeting trains and were equally anxious to know if they would be on time. Couples kissed each other in corners and on benches, steam plumed from tea urns and sandwiches and solid-looking Bath buns curled up their edges under glass domes. The trains hissed grey smoke from their berths. 'SEARCH YOUR CONSCIENCE. IS YOUR JOURNEY REALLY NECESSARY?' blasted the message from propaganda posters put up by the Railway Executive Committee. It was a very English scene. Sane. Reassuring. Fairly good-humoured. And there were no Gestapo standing watch.

The only reading matter to be had was the Christmas 1941 edition of *Good Housekeeping*, containing a story by Eleanor Farjeon and a depressing article on Christmas catering by the Women's Institute. The recipe for Wartime Christmas Pudding included the word 'sugarless' in bold, challenging type. In the train, Evelyn perused it without enthusiasm.

Shabby and out-of-date – there were neither money nor

materials to replace rolling stock – the train crawled through the countryside towards Somerset at twenty miles an hour, stopping frequently. Evelyn looked out at fields embossed with lines of dark brown earth, at trees clinging to the remnants of their leaves and at roads empty of vehicles. Not a signpost or a station sign remained. They had all been removed and the results were nightmarish.

'Sly Jerry.' The silly ITMA dialogue reverberated in her head. 'Sly Jerry. Don't you mean dry sherry, old man? Don't mind if I do.' With a sigh Evelyn turned back to *Good Housekeeping* and to the delights of fatless, sugarless, eggless Christmas cake. She did not want to think about Jerry, sly or otherwise.

'Good gracious!' Aunt Fanny clutched her hands together when Evelyn appeared in the hall and put down her suitcase. 'Where on earth have you been?'

'Aunt Fanny? How lovely.' Evelyn paused, assaulted by doubt. 'Why are you here?'

'Why, my dear.' Aunt Fanny surged forward to give her a peck on the cheek. 'Didn't you know?' She drew Evelyn into the kitchen and sat her down. 'You look frozen. Here, I'll get some tea.'

Between rattles of the kettle, tea caddy and teapot, Aunt Fanny informed Evelyn she had come to live at Castle Cary for the duration. London was impossible – dirty, chaotic, full of soldiers talking about sex and second fronts. So much nicer the deep peace of the country – lack of central heating, hot water, elegance and a decent cocktail party notwithstanding. Aunt Fanny placed a cup of tea in front of Evelyn. 'I am needed here,' she went on, 'now that your mother . . .'

'Mother?'

Aunt Fanny gave a little smile. 'I think she's gone pleasantly mad, darling. You'll see. Meanwhile, I am having the most frightful trouble with the servants. Your mother's maid has left. Some talk of a factory in Bristol requiring her. As for Cook! I daren't even ask her for a cup of hot water these days. She gives notice each week and her cooking . . .' Aunt Fanny raised her white, manicured hands to the ceiling. 'Her cooking!'

Still bewildered, Evelyn drank her tea and tried to get warm.

In a heavy tweed costume, a tucked and frilled Egyptian linen blouse with pearls, Aunt Fanny had not changed a bit. None the less, it was very odd to see her in the kitchen. Any kitchen. She sat down and faced Evelyn across the wooden table.

'Why haven't you been in touch? You're very naughty, you know. It's caused a lot of trouble with your mother who threatened me with a Victorian decline. I wasn't having any of that.'

Evelyn set the cup in the saucer. 'I couldn't, Aunt Fanny,' she said. 'Please believe me.'

'Hmm.' Her aunt assessed this information. 'I expect it isn't your fault.' All the same, Aunt Fanny looked as though she thought it was. 'Well, your father and Peter are thriving. They should be home soon. That reminds me. Tea.' Aunt Fanny leapt to her feet again. 'This is what I mean. The wretched woman has demanded that she has two afternoons off a week.' She raised her shoulders in an exaggerated gesture of despair. 'At least there is plenty for me to do.'

'Mother?' said Evelyn, and dread began to creep over her. 'You say she's all right?'

'Perfectly.' Aunt Fanny came over to Evelyn and dropped her hands onto Evelyn's shoulders. 'You won't know her. And for that you will have to thank your dear aunt for pulling her together and telling her to take a grip. I agree with that silly ass of a writer: "Aunts are gentlemen." Or perhaps it's aunts aren't gentlemen . . . ?'

With a comforting gurgle from the teapot, Aunt Fanny refilled her cup. Evelyn cupped her hands around the tea. What was her mother going to be like?

The door opened and an unfamiliar woman dressed in a bulky overcoat and big boots stamped her feet on the doormat. 'Brh,' she said. 'I thought I'd never get home.'

'*Mother*!' Evelyn was so astonished she almost dropped the cup. The change in her mother was startling. Her movements were decisive, she looked healthy, alert and even, if that were possible, happy. Eugénie looked round, flung her headscarf aside, ran to her daughter and burst into tears. 'You've come back, my darling.'

Later, catching up with the news in her mother's bedroom

where Eugénie was resting before dinner, Evelyn wanted to know what had happened to her. Eugénie lay back on the embroidered sheets in a double bed that had not been occupied by her husband in years. Evelyn recollected a familiar feeling: love spiked with guilt and worry that she always associated with her mother. 'I've been running the Red Cross in the town. I have to go into Yeovil quite often,' Eugénie announced.

'Running?' Evelyn tried to hide her astonishment. Her mother *running* something.

'Is it so surprising?'

'No, of course not.' Evelyn looked at the familiar interior – chintz curtains from Colefax and Fowler, a pretty French day bed upholstered in striped silk, her mother's silver-backed hairbrushes on the dressing table. (Thanks to Aunt Fanny, a fire burned in the grate.) Her mother had never organised anything in her life. 'I think it's wonderful.'

'So do I.' Her mother closed her eyes. 'I'm loving it. It gives me something quite new to think about and I get away from your father. Aunt Fanny keeps house perfectly well for us all.'

Evelyn was not sure whether to laugh or cry. 'Here,' Evelyn used her free arm to drop a package onto the bed, 'I've brought you a present.'

'A present for me.' Eugénie undid the string with her thin fingers and extracted the contents. 'Chanel perfume,' she said in a slow, puzzled way. 'My favourite.' She held the stopper up to her nose. 'Where have you been, Evelyn?'

'Scotland, Mother.' Surprisingly, perfume was easy to buy in France. 'I bought it from an airman.'

'It's almost as if you've been to France.'

Evelyn got up and put a log on the fire. Outside, it had grown dark and the garden lay under a blanket of cold and damp, waiting for spring – John and the others were waiting for her to return. The fire was hot and she was cheered by the blaze. At least, now, she knew she could leave her mother, reassured that all was well.

* * *

Four kilometres or so from Bertric-Burée in the village of Allemans, Renée Legrand had been listening to her Bakelite radio set.

'Anything interesting?' Monsieur Legrand asked his attractive, adulterous wife. Renée grimaced and shrugged, noticing for the thousandth time how her husband's thick dark hair grew down over his collar and how his hands were beginning to develop age spots.

'Nothing,' she lied, reaching for her coat. 'But I have to go out.'

'Of course, my dear,' said Monsieur Legrand, who understood more than he let on and wished only, after fifteen years of living with Renée, to be left in peace.

Renée got onto her bicycle and rode the six kilometres or so towards Ribérac. At the Café Mas, she dismounted and went inside. Jean-Claude was sitting at a table with a couple of his colleagues. When Renée came up, the men winked. 'Aha,' one of them said.

'All right, all right,' said Jean-Claude.

Renée sat down at the table and asked for a brandy. Jean-Claude lit a cigarette and she gave a discreet nod.

'I've just been listening to a good programme on the radio,' she said, patting her hair under a turban. 'Excellent, it was.'

'How nice,' he remarked, and then, 'Are you busy tonight?'

'Yes, very,' she replied, following their prearranged code. 'But I expect you will be very busy too.'

In this way, the reception committee was alerted that 'Violette' was on her way back to France.

CHAPTER TWO

After she entered the novitiate, Hélène, previously not very interested in food, became obsessed by it. Chicken seething in tarragon butter, pheasant stuffed with truffles, *ficelle piquarde* (pancake stuffed with ham, mushrooms and cheese, served very hot), prunes from Agen, thick dark Périgord honey, sticky, fragrant *tartes aux amandes*, floated through her mind at all times of the day and night like a pornographic fantasy. It had not been a battle she had been expecting to fight.

Each temptation held a purpose, of that Hélène was convinced, and she was pleased when she had routed her greed. Only rationing was likely to encourage its reappearance. Using the crust from the gritty, unpalatable bread, Hélène sopped up the last dregs of soup. Not that her wooden bowl contained much, only some spoonfuls of turnip gruel garnished with shreds of cabbage. The bread was more filling but for those with weak teeth and sore gums, a hazard: a few of the sisters were having trouble chewing.

The Germans were clever. They knew how to occupy a country. Keep a population just above starvation level, and you have a population which devotes its energies entirely to the getting and consuming of food. Only the black marketeer profited and with him came vendettas and violence as the underworld fought for its share. Now there was a new trader on it, the 'BOFS' (*beurre, oeufs, fromage*) who sprang into prominence to deal in these commodities, so necessary to French well-being. In the country it was possible to obtain eggs, bacon and milk. In the cities it was not so easy, and Hélène was well aware of the effect such deprivation would be having on the old, young and ill.

Hélène stared at the piece of soggy bread between her fingers. Sometimes she felt that God retreated and she was left to battle with demons of doubt alone. She knew He was testing her but it was not easy to remain strong and serene when your country was at war and horrible things were being done in the name of patriotism and justice.

The square of linen which served as her napkin was threadbare from decades of use. Hélène wiped her hands on it gently. (Everything in the convent, however old, was treated with loving care. The vow of poverty extended down to the smallest scrap of paper.) Of course, Hélène's craving for Charles and the burn of hurt pride at his rejection had been harder to exorcise than her craving for food but she had set herself to succeed in the religious life she had chosen, and when her doubts massed thickly she reminded herself of that vow. The last drop of soup had gone and she smiled into the bowl at the recollection of herself ten years ago. So earnest, so wounded.

Many of her sisters were still eating, spinning out their gruel as if it was a gourmet dinner. The afternoon would be busy. The patient in bed four needed a blanket bath. Bed six would probably reach a crisis during the night. Bed ten was an especially difficult case. The patient, a young mother, was dying from advanced uterine cancer and needed comfort – as well as the morphine that Hélène could not provide.

She bowed her head as grace was said, rose to her feet and waited with the other sisters to leave the refectory. Sister Berenger, still ill from a troubling anaemia . . . Sister Madeleine, whose rough peasant features contained the gentleness and patience of a true saint. Sister Jeanne of the green fingers . . . It seemed impossible that any of them struggled not to hate, to rebel or to fall into the sin of despair. Hélène would never know if they did or not. Intimacy with another human being was forbidden, leaving the way clear for intimacy with God.

The portress was standing at the entrance to the refectory and indicated with a tug at Sister Hélène's sleeve that she should come to one side.

'You have a visitor,' she said. 'I have taken the liberty of informing Reverend Mother, who has given you permission to receive your guest. I did not wish to disturb your meal.'

Acknowledging this thoughtfulness with a smile, Hélène made her way to a sparsely furnished room set aside for visitors. As she entered, a dark-haired girl rose to her feet and somewhat hesitantly held out her hand. Hélène took it and Evelyn recognised the nun with the distinctive face who had caught her attention at Charles's funeral.

'*Ma soeur*, forgive me for coming. I could not think of anyone else to turn to.'

This was not the first time a relation of a patient had turned up, anxious for advice. Sister Hélène indicated for the girl to sit down and joined her on the bench. Evelyn hastened to explain her presence. A distant cousin of the de Bourgraves, working at Belle-Place . . . Bessy's condition . . . the baby . . . As she listened to Evelyn, Hélène's mind was forced down pathways overgrown from disuse. Family, cousins, a new baby – they were echoes from another life. It puzzled Hélène, as she searched Evelyn's face for a clue, that she could not recollect the particular branch of the family that her visitor said she came from.

'Madame de Bourgrave is very distressed,' Evelyn finished. 'She won't eat. She won't sleep, and she has scarcely spoken for days. Worse, she will not acknowledge the baby in any way.' Evelyn glanced down at her gloved hands. 'Not knowing where to turn, I consulted Gaston and he told me to come to you. Would you be prepared to come and see Madame, Sister?'

Hélène folded her arms into her sleeves and considered. Charity and love dictated that she should do so, but she knew charity would be bought at the price of reopening old wounds.

'What do you imagine, Mademoiselle, that I can achieve where the doctor has failed?'

Evelyn wanted to put her hand on the nun's arm to convey the urgency but the face under the coif did not invite it. 'You are Monsieur de Bourgrave's cousin and I thought someone close to him might be of help. Gaston told me you have a reputation for calming troubled people.'

Hélène smiled suddenly and Evelyn was taken aback by the transformation. 'God bless Gaston. He was always loyal. I shall have to be careful that my head does not swell.' The nun considered Evelyn. The girl seemed deeply concerned. It must be difficult for someone of her age to deal with such a serious matter. 'Of course, Mademoiselle, but I will have to ask permission from Reverend Mother.'

Although she had been out of the convent many times, visiting patients and attending childbirths, she had never returned to Belle-Place. The road to the *château* was as Hélène remembered it. Past the church with its onion-shaped dome, down a dip, along a small valley and then up towards the ridge dominated by Belle-Place from where it overlooked the valley and the square buildings of Lusignac on the further ridge. Nothing had changed. There were fewer trees perhaps, but the same fields were blocked out in patchwork squares, winter rain darkened the earth and stone buildings and carts were still being pulled by horses along the track up to the outhouses.

Gaston opened the door to Hélène, very frail in his black morning coat. He wept as he ushered the two women inside.

'It is good to see you, old friend,' Hélène said, and took his hand. 'Isn't it time you retired and had a rest?'

'*Ma soeur*, never,' he replied and wiped the tears off his cheek without embarrassment.

Hélène laughed and went up the stairs with Evelyn behind her. 'You'll never leave, will you, Gaston?'

Everything had remained the same on the landing: an arrangement of dried flowers still stood on the table. Upstairs a baby was crying. Hélène looked up. 'Is he ill?'

'He doesn't seem to settle very well,' Evelyn explained. 'We've tried everything.'

'Has his mother fed him at all?'

'Dr Mazille tried to make Madame feed him but she doesn't seem interested. Marie has been holding him to her breast at intervals. Madame doesn't even want to touch him.'

'Then we must try again,' said Hélène. Over the years attending confinements she had noticed that mothers who fed their babies tended to develop a special feeling for them. 'It will help the Countess's state of mind.'

Bessy's bedroom was in perfect order. There was a fire in the grate, the curtains had been swept back to let in a watery beam of sun in which motes of dust danced. There were vases of flowers – massed bouquets of hot-house lilies, delicate sprays of winter jasmine and *daphne odora* and even a bunch of narcissi – dotted round the room. Katrine had arranged Bessy's dressing gown over one of the satin-backed chairs.

Bessy lay under the silk coverlet on her bed, her face turned away from the door. She looked unkempt and unwashed, with wild tangled hair.

'She won't let us touch her,' whispered Evelyn to Hélène.

If Bessy noticed the tall, black-clad form approach the bed, she gave no sign. Hélène sat down on the bed and observed Bessy for several minutes. Pale from loss of blood. Shallow breathing. Skin dehydrated. Sores around the mouth. More encouraging, however, there were milk stains on her nightgown which indicated the supply had not yet dried up. Hélène reached over and gently felt for Bessy's pulse. Slow and weak.

'Bessy.'

The hand in hers felt clammy. Hélène laid it down and rolled back the bedclothes to make an examination. 'I've come to help you, Bessy,' she said as she did so.

Bessy heard but did not move. It was all too much effort. Eating, talking, thinking, grieving. She wanted to have nothing to do with any of it. Even breathing demanded strength which she did not possess. Bessy reckoned that if she lay still for long enough, in the end she would die.

'I knew Charles very well,' persisted an unfamiliar voice. The hands felt cool and comforting on her stomach. 'I am his cousin. Perhaps he told you about me?' There was a pause. 'Did you know that when he was very young – six or seven, I think – he had a stammer?'

Bessy moved slightly. The strap on her expensive lace and satin nightgown slipped and one peachy shoulder and swollen, brown-nippled breast were exposed. She's beautiful, thought Hélène, acknowledging it without a tremor. A good wife for Charles. She drew in her breath and reached for Bessy's hand again. ' "Hélène," he used to say, "will you speak to father for me?" Or, "Hélène, be a dear and tell the groom I want the pony saddled." I always did, although I'm sure I spoiled him. But I loved him . . .' Bessy had no idea how much, of course. 'I loved him as you loved him. And if you love someone you are happy to make sacrifices.'

There was still no response from the still figure. Why does this woman come to pester me? thought Bessy. And to preach inanities. She tried to shut out the voice.

'You know, my dear,' Hélène became brisker, 'if you loved Charles you should make an effort. Grief is perfectly natural and you must allow it full rein – for a while. After that, however painful, it is also natural to resume a normal life. Otherwise, I would suspect you wish to punish yourself.'

But I do, continued the monologue in Bessy's aching head. I brought Charles bad luck.

Hélène inspected the bottles on the bedside table. Sleeping pills, aspirin, stomach settler. She turned to Evelyn. 'Is the Countess taking any of these?'

'The sleeping pills, I think.'

'Well, don't let her in future, please.'

Evelyn nodded. 'Very well, Sister.'

'Do you think you could fetch the Countess a hot drink, Mademoiselle? It would do her good.'

Hélène looked around Bessy's room. The connecting door into Charles's was ajar, and she got up and pushed it open. She had never entered this room when Charles was alive and now that he was dead it seemed equally wrong to do so. The room was tidy. The bed cover was arranged without a wrinkle over a single bed with a plain mahogany bedhead. Hélène noticed the crucifix on the bureau and the wedding photograph beside it. The room smelt of expensive lotions and tobacco mixed with leather and tweedy wool. The smell jolted Hélène's carefully reined-in emotions.

When she returned to Bessy she sensed a change in the figure on the bed. Bessy had turned over and was watching her as she approached. The two women looked at each other and tacitly acknowledged that they had something in common.

'Was his stammer very bad?' Bessy asked, greedy for more information. 'He never told me he had one.'

Hélène nodded. 'Sometimes. But by the time he was twelve or thirteen he'd conquered it.'

'We weren't given enough time.'

'No.' Hélène understood what Bessy was saying. 'But you must give thanks for what you did have.'

Bessy wanted to cry out that she did not see why. There was nothing fair or right about Charles's death but the nun's quiet authority stifled the words.

'Now. I want you to drink something and then you must try to feed your baby.' Hélène arranged the pillows behind Bessy's back so that she could sit up. 'What are you going to call him?'

Bessy allowed herself to be propped upright. 'I don't want a baby,' she said at last.

Hélène tucked the top sheet over her. Then she squeezed out the sponge in a bowl of warm water and bathed Bessy's face. She was relying on awakening the maternal instinct. 'You must pull yourself together. Others depend on you. Especially your son. He needs you and you are letting him down.'

When she had dried Bessy's face, Hélène began to comb out the knotted hair. She worked very carefully, bending each lock around her finger until the tawny head was free of tangles.

Evelyn appeared with a tray. 'Bessy, Marie has made this specially for you. Her best *bouillon*.'

'Good.' Hélène took the bowl from Evelyn, dipped a spoon into the liquid and held it up to Bessy's mouth. 'Drink.'

After a pause, Bessy did as she was told. She was too tired to resist and it was comforting to be directed. The first spoonful went down. It tasted warm and savoury. She accepted the second. A tinge of colour came into her face. Spoonful by spoonful, Hélène persisted until the bowl was empty.

'That's better,' said the nun. 'If you neglect the body, the mind suffers also.'

She turned to Evelyn. 'Can you fetch the baby, please?'

'Please, I don't want to see it!' Bessy seemed terrified.

'Why don't you call him Charles?' Hélène set the soup bowl down on the table by the bed.

'I don't want anything to do with it.'

'You are being selfish,' Hélène told her, very gently. 'I am quite sure you don't mean to be.'

Her words stung Bessy. All her life – from the early days in the luxury Long Island house bathed in sun and fresh air, through the dark, terror-lashed time in Vienna, to the brief sweetness of marriage with Charles – she had tried never to be selfish. 'Imagine them all, starving and dying in their thousands.' Bridget, the Irish maid, indoctrinated the young Bessy on the famine in Ireland. 'Hungry and cold, treated like animals, rooting for scraps like pigs. You should think yourself lucky, miss.' Bessy had striven to be serious and high-minded, determined to make life better for others. Now this nun was calling her selfish.

Evelyn returned with a shawled, wailing bundle. Bessy stiffened. Hélène took the baby, laid him on the bed and unwrapped the shawl. The baby's skin was red, blotchy and dry. Working slowly and professionally, she examined his arms, legs, tested the hips and laid two fingers on the frog-like belly. She was well aware that Bessy was pretending not to watch. Then she wrapped the baby up again, drew the sign of the cross on its forehead and held him out to Bessy. Bessy shrugged.

'Very well.' Hélène bent over her, eased down a shoulder strap of Bessy's nightdress and held the baby to a nipple. Bessy sat rigidly. The baby continued to cry. Hélène persisted. 'You will help him if you feed him. See, I think he has a stomach ache from drinking the wrong milk. He needs you very badly.' Hélène supported the baby with one arm, and with her free hand stroked his cheek. Obediently, he turned towards his mother's breast. Hélène talked to him quietly. 'Come on, then, little one.'

The atmosphere in the room grew tense and the baby's cries more desperate. Evelyn found herself holding her breath. Hélène went on talking. Suddenly, the baby found Bessy's nipple and sucked. The noise stopped.

Bessy felt the tug of the baby's mouth and the pricking in each breast as milk began to rise. She squinted down as Hélène continued to hold the baby but her arms remained obstinately at her side. Let them do as they liked, she thought. Her son began to suck in earnest and traces of milk appeared around his mouth. His mouth was hurting Bessy but she welcomed the smart. She could understand pain.

Evelyn gazed at the composition made by the three figures. The nun bending over, holding a baby to a stony figure in the bed, down whose pale face streamed tears for the first time since Charles died.

On the journey back to the convent Sister Hélène sat well back in the passenger seat, while Evelyn drove. The nun seemed exhausted. Evelyn longed to ask some questions but the habit of discretion was becoming second nature to her. It was Hélène who broke the silence.

'Do you have faith, Mademoiselle Liegaux?'

Evelyn tried to answer honestly. 'I have to confess, Sister, that my faith is not as strong as it should be.'

'You will have need of it, Mademoiselle. This war is likely to continue for some years. Our chief weapon must be our faith.'

Evelyn wanted to say that faith was not going to beat the Germans by itself. Hélène must have read her thoughts. 'Prayer is much the best weapon,' she said, and turned her head to look at Evelyn. 'Without it we are lost.'

Evelyn negotiated a difficult bend and decided to take the risk of speaking frankly. '*Ma soeur*, we do need other things too. Men, weapons and medical help.' She swung the wheel to the right. 'Particularly doctors.' Gaston had told Evelyn a little about Sister Hélène and her past. 'Especially if one is working in secret.' She paused. 'Would you be with us?'

Are you with us? Charles. There was something in the way the girl articulated the words that reminded Hélène of Charles's message. A missing piece of jigsaw slotted into the mental picture Hélène had been slowly constructing. *Charles had died while doing resistance work.* 'Tell me more,' she said.

Evelyn obliged. 'Sometimes it isn't possible to reach a doctor or hospital. Or indeed wise. I am sure you understand, Sister. In cases like that, one needs to rely on other sources of help.' She still was not sure how the conversation was going to turn out.

'Which do you require from me? Prayer or medicine?'

Evelyn stopped the car in front of the iron gates of St Euphonie's. The bell was ringing in the chapel and dry, brown leaves whirled about the wheels. 'I hope we can call on you for both, Sister.'

The nun's face gave nothing away. 'You can always come to me for help,' she said, 'providing I have permission.'

'Sister, what if you are not given permission and, furthermore, cannot ask it?' Evelyn had to make this point quite clear.

Hélène reached for the door handle. 'Then I'm sorry but I will not be able to help you.'

'Oh.' Evelyn was disappointed. 'I see.' She remembered her manners. 'Thank you so much for coming, Sister.'

'I will pray for you, Mademoiselle.' Hélène shut the door after she climbed out of the car.

'One thing, Sister,' Evelyn leant over and wound down the window. 'Our conversation. Can it remain private?'

Hélène smiled a wintry smile. 'Who could I possibly talk to about it, Mademoiselle?'

Hélène watched the Hispano draw away. The convent waited to draw her back. She knew every stone of the building, every patch of fern growing from its walls, every pillar in its cloisters. She knew exactly where the sun would hit the paved courtyard at noon and where each herb grew in the kitchen garden. It was her life and she had forged it out of tribulation and sacrifice. She prayed that she was strong enough to keep to it.

Waiting for her in the infirmary was Jean, as underfed and gawky as ever. At Hélène's entrance he sprang to his feet and gabbled at her, 'Sister, I need help. You are the only person I could think of.'

Hélène closed the door and told him to sit down. Jean began to explain. He had been working in the fields – that's why he had not seen what happened – but a neighbour had run to tell him. Apparently, a black Citroën had drawn up in front of the house and two men had arrested his parents and

220

driven away. He didn't know why. Jean confessed to being terrified of going back.

Hélène opened a drawer in the desk and gave him a handkerchief from a stock she kept for patients. 'Calm yourself, Jean.'

He blew his nose and gave a shuddering sigh. She leant over and placed a hand on his shoulder to try to reassure him. Jean looked up expectantly, waiting for her guidance. 'They searched the village,' he told her and blew his nose noisily into the handkerchief. 'I think they were searching for me.' He paused. 'What will they do to my parents?' he asked pitifully.

'Don't allow yourself to think about it.' Hélène was trying to formulate her thoughts. If the Gestapo were watching Bertric-Burée, then Jean must not return. 'Where are your nearest relations, Jean?'

'I have cousins in St Martial-de-Viveyrol.' Jean named a village quite close to the convent.

'Would they take you in?'

'Don't know.'

Hélène looked at the clock on the wall. Half past six. The curfew would be in force and to go out would be dangerous. 'Listen, Jean. I will help you but I must have time to plan. I am going to hide you in the infirmary for the night. Tomorrow you must go to your cousins, try to get new papers perhaps. Or leave the area.'

He shook his head, his fear and distress muddling his understanding. 'I don't want to leave.'

'Well, never mind that for the moment.' Hélène stood up and went over to her log book and flicked through it. The isolation ward at the end of the passage was empty. It would be a simple matter to place a 'No Entry' notice on it, and record a suspected tuberculosis case in the log.

'What will happen, Sister?'

'I don't know, Jean. But I do know you must not panic.' Hélène tapped her fingers on the table top, feeling more alert and decisive than she could remember. 'Listen, we need help in the garden here.' St Euphonie's grew its own vegetables and sold the surplus in Ribérac. It produced a much-needed source of extra income for the convent. 'Sister Aurélie is the head gardener but she has been ill and is not at all strong. I can tell her that I have found someone to help her. Yes, that's it.' Hélène tapped her fingers harder. 'I can tell her that you came to me needing to find work. I suggested that you were employed in the gardens.' She turned with a swish of black serge. 'It might work for a little while until we can decide what is best to do. Of course, I would have to talk to Reverend Mother,' she added, more to herself than to Jean.

Jean wiped his eyes with the handkerchief and held it out to Hélène. She eyed it. 'Keep it,' she said. 'For the moment. Now, you must come with me. As quietly as you can.'

The next morning Hélène requested an interview with Reverend Mother and suggested to her that Jean was taken on as gardener. She omitted to mention – and vowed penance for the sins of omission and disobedience – that she had hidden him for the night. Reverend Mother gave her permission but not without reservation. Jean was taken on and settled so well that he began to advise the pale and exhausted Sister Aurélie in the manner of patriarchal males everywhere. 'So satisfactory, Sister,' Sister Aurélie commented to Hélène. 'The poor boy.' She rubbed cold, transparent hands together and shivered a little. 'I know this is unusual but we must take care of Jean while he is with us. I asked Reverend Mother if he could sleep in the outbuilding down by the south field. Apparently his parents have abandoned him and he doesn't have anywhere to go.' She paused. 'I am sure the sisters are perfectly safe with Jean.'

'Sister Aurélie, you are a saint.' Hélène was amused by Sister Aurélie's insinuation of possible rape. 'You could not have had a better notion.'

A week later, Hélène made a telephone call to the Château Belle-Place, and asked to speak to Mademoiselle Liegaux. It was answered by Bessy.

'Sister Hélène. I am glad you telephoned. I wanted to thank you. As you gather, I am feeling better and I stay up longer each day.'

'I am glad. May I come and see you again soon?'

'Of course.'

'Is it possible to speak to Mademoiselle Liegaux?'

Bessy hesitated. 'Not at the moment. Can I take a message?'

'Yes,' said Hélène. 'Tell her I would very much like to continue our conversation.'

Bessy put down the phone. An odd feeling nagged at her that something was going on which was being kept from her. She pulled herself upright on the pillows and reached for the hand mirror to inspect her face. The sores around her mouth were healing, her hair, which had grown out of its expensive cut, was too long but Katrine had brushed it until it looked reasonably neat. She picked up a lock in her fingers and felt it. It was still too dry but her skin was beginning to pick up colour. The drawn, blank look in her eyes had vanished. She was recovering.

The last few weeks had also vanished into the recesses of her memory. Bessy reckoned she must have gone a little mad after Charles's death. Shocked, grief-stricken, unhinged and exhausted by childbirth, Bessy hated the thought of having been out of control and hated that others had witnessed it. She was determined it would not happen again.

She picked up her mascara box, spat on the brush and began to paint her thick, obstinately fair eyelashes. It was a signal to herself that she could get through the day without crying – Bessy had cried ceaselessly since Sister Hélène had broken through the dam walling her grief.

She got out of bed. There were questions she needed to ask about what was going on in Belle-Place. Slowly, with many pauses, she dressed. Satin underwear, a loosely waisted wool dress and chic little jacket in black barathea which only just fitted across her swollen breasts. (Bessy had been dutifully feeding baby Charles as instructed.) From time to time she heard muffled voices and the sound of splashing from the bathroom. When she was ready, Bessy pushed open the door and looked onto a pleasant domestic scene.

Doing duty as nursemaid, Evelyn was kneeling by the bath, holding the baby in the water. Watching them, very much at his ease, Guy lounged in the wicker bathroom chair. There was a quiet, peaceful atmosphere in the room, punctuated by little cries from the baby who was enjoying his bath.

Bessy held onto the door handle, uncertain whether or not to enter. The sight of her son still stirred up panic and a wish to run away and hide. It was too soon. Bessy did not want to accept the burden of loving him – the knowledge that, as it had with Charles, the love and happiness might be snatched away. She could not face that.

The baby lifted his arms out of the water. His skin still had the mottled look of the newborn and was brushed with downy fluff. The tiny fingers made a stiff fan. At the sight, Bessy's heart lurched. She let go of the door handle and walked into the bathroom. Evelyn, splashed and smiling, lifted the baby out of the water, wrapped him in a towel and offered him to his mother. Bessy accepted the bundle and cradled it awkwardly while she tried to make sense of her feelings.

'This calls for a drink,' said Guy, pulling himself to his feet.

Bessy grimaced, but hugged her son closer.

'By the way,' she said to Evelyn a little later, after struggling to put on the baby's nappy. 'Sister Hélène phoned. She wanted me to tell you that she wished to continue your conversation.'

'Really?' Evelyn was noncommittal. She held out the baby's broderie anglaise nightdress. 'I will get in touch.'

Bessy attempted to wrap her son in a shawl. Then she lifted him up. 'I want to know something Evelyn.'

Evelyn was alerted by Bessy's tone. 'Yes?'

Bessy held the baby to her. 'What do you know about Charles's death?' The blue eyes under the unnaturally black eyelashes had become tense and watchful. 'I want to know.'

'I just helped when Monsieur de Bourgrave was brought in.'

'Please don't lie to me.'

'I'm not.'

'Listen, Evelyn, when you came to Belle-Place, things began to happen. Charles was different. Busier and less open with me. I knew he was up to something and yet he lied to me about it. I am no fool, Evelyn.'

'No, of course not.' Evelyn was not sure how to handle the Countess. Bessy surprised her, however.

224

'Don't you see, I want to help. I want to carry on Charles's work, whatever it was.'

'Remember, you have a baby!'

'Yes. I have a fatherless baby. But that is my business, Evelyn.' Bessy did not want to be sharp but she had to make her point.

Evelyn shook her head.

'For God's sake. Don't wrap me up in cotton wool as Charles always did. Even Sister Hélène is permitted to know more than me.' Evelyn tried to interrupt but failed. 'Aren't I right?'

The baby had fallen asleep. Bessy looked down and traced his cheek with her fingertip. When she looked up at Evelyn her gaze was fierce and very determined. 'Please, Evelyn,' she asked. 'You have been very patient and I have behaved badly. You've been a friend to me and now I may be in a position to help you.'

Evelyn made a decision. 'Very well, Bessy,' she said. 'We will talk about it.'

CHAPTER THREE

'Mama, I'm hungry.'

Mariette sighed and reached for the loaf. She cut the thinnest of slices and spread it with the last of the raspberry jam and gave it to her daughter. Pinched and cold, looking older than her four years, Jeannette took it. '*Merci*, Mama.' Mariette offered baby Jacques the crust to chew but he refused it. She was worried about him. His nose was running and his right eye was gummed together because of an infection. Added to which, he had cried for most of the previous night and she had been forced to take him into her bed.

Jacques had gone to sleep – finally. Mariette had not. She lay with Jacques's breath filtering damply onto her shoulder and her arm turning numb under his weight, trying to think. Where was she going to get some money? Even if she could find employment, who would look after the children? Her mother was too old to be trusted. Perhaps the *château* could do with a bit of help? Perhaps that big bear Jean-Claude could be persuaded to shell out again? On the other hand, perhaps not.

At this point in her reflections the terrors began. Generally they attacked when Mariette was falling asleep. Once they descended on her she found it impossible to get to sleep because they consisted of imagining the worst things that could possibly happen to her children.

Mariette's terrors were an added cruelty to her widowhood, along with shock, grief and resentment. They began when Jacques senior had died of a heart-attack, after only five years of marriage. Mariette often told herself, and almost believed it, that if she had known about Jacques's weak heart, she would never have married him. It would have saved her such trouble and worry. Such loneliness. And an empty bed.

Certainly, if she had imagined that by the age of twenty-two she would be left with two children under four, a run-down cottage and a piece of land that was barely big enough to sustain their needs, she would have laughed and said, 'Not likely, I won't be caught out that way.'

Whenever she thought about Jacques – about his big smoothly muscled body covering hers, his strength and the fun they shared together – she became angry. Angry with him for dying. Angry with Fate for being so unfair. Angry with herself for being taken in and loving a man who was like a tree rotten at the centre.

Jeannette finished the bread and went to play with her brother on the floor. Mariette wrung out the washing in the sink. Thank God the children were quiet. The water was cold and scummy and stung her hands, already sore from digging the vegetable patch. Baby Jacques's nappies were the worst to wash: however hard Mariette laboured over them they remained grubby. She inspected the one on the top of the clean pile, then shrugged before tossing it back into the laundry basket.

'Look after Jacques, will you, Jeannette,' she called, as she let herself out into the back yard. Hostile and inescapable, the cold mounted an assault on her body. It froze her legs and the darned stockings she wore were no protection. She sighed as she pegged out Jeannette's too-short pinafore, her own worn nightdress and her mother's black wool stockings, now rigid from constant washing. Where was she going to find money?

Mariette went round to the wood pile by the front door and stacked some logs into a basket. By now she was shivering in earnest. She picked up the basket and heaved it through the front door. From habit, she glanced up the road.

Mariette was becoming accustomed to the occasionally strange goings on at the end of the garden and tried not to get involved – except for the time when Jean-Claude had made her hide his injured friend back in October. The man, Olivier, said he was a Parisian who had got on the wrong side of the police in Paris. Mariette sometimes speculated as to why Jean-Claude had chosen to help him.

If she was truthful, and Mariette was usually quite honest with herself, she had appreciated the adult company. Children and old women have limited appeal for someone who is dying for a bit of gaiety. So it was with quickening interest she spotted John outside on a bicycle. 'Bonjour,' she called out.

John put on the brakes. 'Bonjour,' he replied, not pleased at being recognised. He had hoped most people would stay indoors on a day as cold as this one, and risked taking the easier route into Ribérac from Lusignac where he was being hidden for the present in a safe house.

Mariette leaned over the gate, which was supported on only one hinge. Behind her, in similar need of repair, a window shutter banged against the wall of the house, sending showers of lime onto the ground. 'Are you well?' she asked.

'Well enough, thank you.'

John had shifted his sleeping quarters at least six times since he had arrived. Of course, he was used to a nomadic existence and the constant disruption did not bother him. Far more of a strain was the relentless undertow of anxiety. He found it impossible to ignore that each time he tuned in his wireless set the Germans were undoubtedly listening – and closing in.

John did his best to combat the insidious nibbling at his confidence. He experimented with deep breathing. At night he recited his favourite roles in a whisper. He composed scurrilous ditties on the subject of the German nation and its habits and fantasised how he would send them, one by one, to Hitler's lair in Berlin. He told himself over and over again that if he was caught transmitting, he would take his lethal pill. None of the stiff upper lip for him. Life, he admonished the pinpricks of fear running up and down his spine, had not been a bowl of cherries and if the curtain ran down, well, no need for epilogues.

'Are you settled in somewhere?' Mariette was not really interested but the question prolonged the conversation.

'Well enough,' he replied evasively, still not sure how much Mariette knew.

She turned to anchor the banging shutter and John recollected how he had once rather fancied her rounded, swaying bottom. Still did.

'Have a glass of Pineau,' she offered.

He hesitated and glanced at his watch. 'All right.' He parked his bicycle and followed her inside.

It was some months since John had limped, exhausted, into this cottage, and he had forgotten how little Mariette possessed. There was nothing decorative – no pictures, no bits of china, no dried flowers, just two chairs, a table, cooking implements and the dresser. At least the fire was blazing, throwing out a band of warmth into which one could squeeze and avoid the draughts. Mariette pushed a chair in his direction.

'Where's your mother?' he enquired. He often wondered how much the old woman gossiped about him to her friends.

Mariette took down a couple of glasses and wiped them. 'Out.' She did not elaborate.

Both the children stared silently at him and John felt guilty for his presence. He felt in his pocket for the chocolate he had been saving for a cold *parachutage*, and offered it to the little girl. Jeannette took it and balanced the slab in the palm of her hand. 'May I, Maman?'

Mariette broke the slab in half and gave the children a piece each. Jacques licked it first, then stuffed his share into his mouth. Jeannette held hers between her finger and thumb and took a tiny bit. Her expression was a mixture of astonishment at this windfall and fear that it might be confiscated. John was pleased he had made the not inconsiderable sacrifice.

Mariette poured the brandy into two glasses and sat down opposite. He raised his glass to her and drank. The stove managed to warm one side of him, the other side remained frozen. He rubbed his hands together. Jeannette picked up her brother. 'I'll put him to sleep, Maman.' Mariette nodded and watched her daughter climb the stairs with Jacques straddled across her child's hips.

'What can I do?' she burst out passionately and without warning. 'How can I make ends meet?'

John was startled. 'Can I help in any way?' He had hardly

spared Mariette a thought since he had left her cottage and now felt remorse for his negligence. Life was evidently difficult for the girl but why she had chosen to confide in him he was not sure. Perhaps sharing a bed, however chaste, entitled you to unburden your troubles.

Mariette's hazel eyes assessed John and located him on her scale of usefulness. 'I'm sorry,' she said at last, making a calculated bid for sympathy. 'I don't know what came over me. Being on my own, you know. And I get so worried.'

'Yes,' he said. 'I know.'

She pulled her chair an inch or so nearer to him and crossed her legs. They were shapely, covered in a fine golden down, with good ankles. Her skirt hitched up and John obtained an uninterrupted view of whiter, softer flesh above her stocking top, touched here and there with bluish veins.

Definitely the Pineau had not been a good idea. Those thighs were infinitely seductive. He drained his glass and stood up. Mariette understood the message at once. 'Don't go yet. Have another drink.' Deliberately, she hitched her skirt a fraction higher.

'I will be late if I do,' he said.

John could feel treacherous muscles between his legs beginning to tighten, and tried hard to think of something else – one of the stickier moments of his career would do nicely.

He had to get out.

It would be so easy to take Mariette to bed. Escapist and comforting. He already knew what she looked like when she slept and how she snuffled occasionally and the habit she had of flinging her arms across his body.

Evelyn was waiting.

He was acutely aware and rather flattered that Mariette was asking him to part her crossed legs, and that no resistance would be offered. He was free to give and take some pleasure – to invite welcome, warmth, release, reassurance.

And danger.

Mariette wondered if she dare push it. John was wavering. Pushed, he might take her upstairs, pull her clothes off, kiss her breasts and allow her to forget her miserable life for a few minutes. Mariette uncrossed her legs. The moment had

230

passed. 'Oh, well, then.' She was sulky. 'You'll be on your way.'

For a moment John thought Mariette was going to cry, and he paused. 'I'm sorry. But I must go,' he said, and went to the door. 'Thank you for the drink.' Mariette did not respond.

The cold fastened around John's face and made him gasp for air. Retrieving his bicycle, he gave a wave through the window to Mariette. She ignored him and stared into the stove, watching its outlines fudge as tears filled her eyes.

She leant forward and threw another log onto the fire. If you had grown used to a man making love to you, you couldn't just forget about sex. Just because you were a widow, your life hadn't finished. Had it? She looked out of the window. '*Merde*,' she swore. The washing was frozen solid and therefore would be twice as difficult to deal with. Mariette reached for her headscarf and tied it under her chin with an angry jerk. As she passed, she glanced into a piece of mirror balanced on the mantelpiece. The scarf did not suit her; it tightened the skin over her cheeks and made her look old and drawn. 'One day, Mariette. One day,' she said aloud.

The promise did not make her feel any better.

'*Bienvenue.*' John spoke into the newspaper which he was pretending to read. He was sitting at the next table to Evelyn. Two girls dressed in overcoats and cork-soled shoes walked past and greeted friends at a table in the corner. Evelyn examined the cup of *mélange national* masquerading as coffee.

'The back entrance is through the door on the right,' she whispered.

'Got it,' he said, after checking it out. 'Did you have a good trip?'

'*Punctuality is of prime importance to an agent. If you are meeting a contact, it is sensible practice to arrive a little early in the area to check for tails and undue enemy presence. On the other hand, do not arrive at the rendezvous too early and hang around. It is asking for trouble – and we don't want trouble, do we, ladies and gentlemen?*'

Evelyn had been punctual. John had not and she had been worried. 'How about picking me up?' she suggested.

John swivelled on his seat to obtain a better view of Evelyn, leant over and asked her if he could use her ashtray. It was a perfect performance, worthy, if he said so himself, of that golden night of triumph – Southend 1934 – when the old ladies with the bags of boiled sweets cheered him after a performance of *Private Lives*.

Evelyn smiled archly. As always, John's brilliant acting left her gasping. Every expression, every gesture was spot on. No one would have suspected that he was anything but a Frenchman enjoying the national pastime of *poursuivre les femmes*.

'Where were you? I was getting anxious.'

'Sorry,' he said. He lowered his voice, and smiled deeply into Evelyn's eyes. She fluttered her lashes back. 'How is the dear old *alma mater*?'

'Cold and butterless. Good wishes from HQ. They wished they could send you a Christmas present. I got a new dress.' She indicated the rather becoming green wool, wide-shouldered and belted at the waist. It matched her eyes. 'Nice.' John twitched his mouth into an appreciative 'O'.

'Anything happened while I've been away?' Evelyn allowed her gaze to drift around the café. The girls in the corner were having fun making loud personal remarks about other customers and giggling. There were four waiters whom Evelyn did not look at long. Waiters were known as likely informers.

John kept his flirtatious smile cemented onto his face while he told Evelyn that Antoine and his wife had been arrested, taken to a house in St Martial-de-Viveyrol for interrogation and transferred to Bordeaux.

'No!' Evelyn put a hand to hide her face. 'When?'

'Watch it,' John reproved Evelyn. Her exclamation had attracted the attention of the couple sitting at the next table. 'It happened just before you got back.'

'The children. What will happen to them?' Evelyn pushed her cup away.

'Look at me, and look as though you're enjoying it,' John ordered. After a second Evelyn obeyed. 'Now listen, darling, you know as well as I do that you're being self-indulgent.' Too upset to answer, Evelyn merely gave a shrug. 'Listen to

232

me, *chérie*.' A warning note crept into John's voice. 'We have to get through this, do you understand?'

She sighed, but for the benefit of any observers, brightened her eyes with false gaiety. John was right. She must not lose her grip before she had begun. 'Of course.' Evelyn touched John's hand with a finger. 'I can't bear to think about Antoine.'

'Well, don't then,' John replied.

'Sorry, I must be tired. This isn't a good start.'

'Uncle "Georges" will put you right.'

'I knew you would.' Evelyn took a mouthful of her rejected coffee. 'Urgh,' she said, and made a face. 'To business. Anyone else taken?'

'As far as I know, Antoine was caught handling forged papers at work. They searched the house and found a second set in the kitchen.'

'I presume they didn't have photos attached otherwise there would have been more arrests.'

'Luckily, no,' replied John. 'Antoine was waiting for the photos to arrive.'

Evelyn assessed this information. Providing Antoine had been careful, the trail would not lead back to implicate any of them. 'Can we get him out?'

John twirled his cup around in the saucer. 'No,' he said. 'Bordeaux would be impossible.'

Evelyn took refuge in briskness. 'We must make sure his contacts cover their traces and, if necessary, go to ground.'

There was a silence.

'Everything all right at the *château*?' asked John.

'Problems. The Countess is ill and Monsieur Maier is very nosy about where I have been. But I think I can deal with it.' She raised her eyes to the door and John saw her stiffen. '*Attention*,' she said softly. '*Doryphores*.'

Two German officers came into the café, wearing standard pattern field-grey army greatcoats with dark blue-green collars. They settled themselves in a corner and ordered coffee.

'Staff officers,' said John, placing the men correctly.

In the old days, the Café Mas had been one of Ribérac's most popular meeting places. It was still busy, only the officers of the German garrison had decided to adopt it and

233

consequently many of the regulars had dropped off. This unlooked-for honour did not exactly please the *patron*, although he did not mind the extra revenue. He looked up from behind the bar where he was polishing glasses and signalled to the waiters. The officers' arrival silenced the noisy girls and one of the prettier of the group applied lipstick to her mouth. A German beckoned her over and, with a giggle, she obeyed.

Evelyn reached into her handbag and left the correct change for her bill on the table.

'*Pay the bill promptly in order that you can leave in a hurry. You do not want the* patron *badgering you if you have to get out.*'

'Listen,' she said. 'I can't go into details. I've come back as chief.'

John's eyebrows ascended as high as she had ever seen them. 'Oh,' he said. 'The King is dead, long live the King.'

'Surprised?' she asked, alert for any sign of disapproval on the freckled features. It mattered to Evelyn how John responded to her news. She valued the unexpected friendship they had formed and she had come to rely on him and to admire the lack of fuss with which he got on with the business. Less easily admissible, Evelyn wanted John to trust her and think well of her. He hesitated only for a second.

'OK by me.' He sent Evelyn one of his comforting smiles and aped Laurence Olivier's tortured vowels. 'The hollow crown, you know, pet. You're welcome to it.'

Evelyn leaned over the table. 'Hollow crown or not, it's done.' Without John's moral and practical support her job would have been twice as difficult and immeasurably lonelier. Luck had been with her, she reckoned. Not all agents got on well with each other. Even if they did, it was far from inevitable that their work methods were complementary. She kept her voice very low. 'You will work for Astronomer and only Astronomer. Not transmitting for any other group, even if they're in a jam.' Evelyn was referring to separate resistance groups who often had neither wireless set nor operator.

'Don't worry, I know.' John looked directly at Evelyn. 'I like my skin.'

'Have you checked the revised skeds I brought with me? Did the crystals survive the journey?'

'Yes and yes,' he replied. 'And don't you dare become too bossy.'

He was laughing at Evelyn, but she didn't mind. 'Step by step,' she warned him, 'and extra cautiously.'

'Quite right.' John put his head on one side. 'Yes, you look very cautious.'

In fact, she looked rather beautiful and he told her so, adding, 'You should be doused. You're positively glowing.'

'How do you fancy my chances at dealing with the Communists?' Evelyn was pleased with the compliment.

'Nil,' he replied. 'Doctrinally speaking, Communists appreciate functional things only, nothing decorative.'

'Thank you.' Evelyn looked back in order to check what the Germans were up to at the corner. The blonde girl was leaning over the shoulder of the better-looking of the two men. All of a sudden she felt daunted. How was she going to manage in such a confused country? Whom could she trust? 'First step is arranging for more weapons. We need dropping zones, and you and I will be going on reconnaissance.'

'In this weather!'

'Thick underwear time,' she retorted in a whisper, thinking of her school days when moral tuition came dressed in a wool liberty bodice. 'It's the very thing.'

She wanted to tell him how important his support was, but the café door opened. She looked up. 'I think you must go.'

From the tone of her voice John knew not to wait to be told a second time. He rose, put some change on the table and sauntered towards the door. In the street, he waited for a troop convoy to pass, crossed the road and stared into a shop window opposite. He could just make out Evelyn in the reflection.

Evelyn checked her change and got to her feet.

'Good morning, Mademoiselle,' said Paul. 'I was hoping I would see you.'

As soon as Evelyn saw Paul come into the café, she knew he would approach her. A dread that he would speak to her, the wishing that he would, a pulse deep in her stomach which she thought belonged only in novels, overcame her momentarily. Then an astringent, cleansing lash of anger. Evelyn reminded herself he was a German officer, responsible for the fate of men like Antoine.

'Good morning,' she said, and struggled into her coat. Paul made to help her. 'Will you stay and join me for coffee?'

'No, thank you,' Evelyn replied flatly.

'Are you sure?' Paul was aware he was taking a risk. The risk of being rebuffed by a French girl who fiercely resented her country being occupied. The risk of becoming caught in an affair that was better left alone. But Paul also knew that something existed between them. 'Are you quite sure?'

Evelyn began to pull on a pair of tan leather gloves. She shook her head. Paul observed her ugly bitten nails and a storm unleashed in him – tenderness, curiosity, intense attraction, fired by a determination not to let go. Evelyn's hands disappeared into the gloves. 'What a shame, I wished to ask you something.'

They stared at each other and then Evelyn picked up the newspaper from the table. On the centre page John would have taped his latest message from home base. Decoded.

'What do you want to ask me, Major?'

The *patron* placed three cups on the bar and from them issued the delicious smell of real coffee. For a second she closed her eyes.

'I was wondering, Mademoiselle, if you would like to attend a concert with me? Some of the members of the Berlin orchestra are on tour and will be travelling around the area in the middle of February. I would like to take you.'

A waiter carried the tray of cups over to the German officers. He set it down in front of them and the smell of coffee flooded the room, stronger now, tantalising and hypnotic.

'It will be a good programme.' Paul wanted an answer.

'Von Hoch.' One of the Germans waved at Paul from the table. 'Coffee.'

Evelyn shook her head, her longing for a cup of real coffee muddling with other feelings to do with Major von Hoch.

'I know what you are thinking. You are thinking, "I wish

this man would go away and stop pestering me".' His smiled warmed her, charming and oddly sympathetic.

My God, thought Evelyn. If this man seeks me out and I can't deny I want him to then I am useless. She tried to summon back the anger of a few minutes ago.

Paul misread her hesitation. 'I understand your reluctance,' he said. 'Our introduction was unconventional, for which I apologise. Of course, the situation is not easy, but . . .'

'I will think about it,' Evelyn said, deciding it was best to leave the café as quickly as possible.

'Of course,' said Paul. 'I will telephone you at the *château*.'

The school house at Ribérac, the Palais de Justice and the Hôtel de Ville – the latter a whimsical two-towered *château* with a balcony and mansard roof which faced up the street towards the Place Nationale – had been commandeered by the Germans. As headquarters went, the Hôtel de Ville was suitably impressive and the sort of building that appealed to the German administrators.

'Monsieur?' Paul stopped in the vestibule. One of the French telephonists at the switchboard was struggling with a problem. 'I can't understand the ranks. Some people ask for Major and Lieutenant so and so, and others ask for *Sturmbannführer* and *Haupsturmführer*. What's the difference?'

Paul explained that the Germany army had ranks which corresponded to the French army's. The ss also had its own ranks and these were the ones with the odd-sounding names.

'Oh, I see,' he said. 'So they're not in the army.'

'No,' said Paul. 'Not at all.'

As he had told Paul, Major Blumberg had been shipped back to Berlin. Blumberg, reflected Paul grimly, had done the Ribérac garrison a disservice in more ways than one. His replacement was ss Sturmbannführer Fleischer from the sd, a friend of its leader, the ruthless ex-naval officer Reinhard Heydrich.

Accompanied by two adjutants of cowed demeanour and his interpreter, a grey-suited, wrinkled German-French *patissier* called 'Billi', Dietrich Fleischer moved in to set up a centre for sd operations in the area. When introduced to Fleischer

Paul had been struck by the haste with which Fleischer informed him that he practised as a lawyer in Berlin, numbering among his clients some of the highest ranking members of the Party.

Paul discovered Sturmbannführer Fleischer installed in the room which opened onto the balcony. The room was well proportioned and contained a fine chandelier, a fireplace with a marble surround, a bronze statue of Eros and a rosewood table that would serve as a desk. A man on the make – for such he concluded Fleischer was – would be unable to resist the grandeur and indeed, as it turned out, Fleischer had ousted two lower-ranking officers to take possession of the room.

'Ah, von Hoch,' said Fleischer when Paul came into the room. He was stowing papers in a drawer. Paul noticed the Nazi Party membership book which lay open on the desk.

Fleischer placed the book in a top drawer and locked it. 'Just a little precaution.' Then he picked up a paper from a pile on the desk. He seemed ill at ease and to be searching for something to say. 'I see the operations led by my organisation in Russia are going well.'

Paul made no comment. The gossip trickling in from Russia and Poland in particular, cited the brutality displayed by the *Einsatzgruppen* (ss Special Units which included members of the sd). The *Einsatzgruppen* travelled behind the army to deal with the civilian population. Paul had also gathered that the behaviour of the *Einsatzgruppen* resulted in a group of generals protesting to the German High Command. Not strongly enough, it seemed. The *Einsatzgruppen* continued to work unhindered. So far their presence in France had not been overt. Fleischer, however, was known to be a crony of Heydrich's. Who knew what the two men had discussed over cognac on their night-club outings?

'Yes,' said Fleischer. 'The Jewish problem will soon be dealt with. I gather Finland— ' Fleischer stopped. It was not a good idea to broadcast that Finland was now rid of Jews.

'How interesting,' Paul replied. 'You have the latest reports, I take it?'

The look Fleischer threw him was not friendly. 'Naturally.

We in the *Sicherheitdienst* are kept up to date.' His tone alerted Paul. It was possible Fleischer knew of Paul's real work. He needed to take care.

Fleischer recited from memory. 'The SD follows wherever possible behind the advancing troops and fulfils duties similar to those in the Reich, maintaining the security of political life.'

'That is a very wide directive,' Paul commented. He walked over to a chair and sat down. Fleischer observed Paul's limp. Bad eyesight had prevented his becoming an active soldier and he hated being reminded that he had never fought on a battlefield. Nor was Fleischer pleased at being dispatched to a town like Ribérac. He would have preferred the larger – and more civilised – arena of Paris or Bordeaux. But others had got there first, a problem that was not new to Fleischer.

From boyhood, it seemed, richer, better-connected and always more popular contenders had beaten Fleischer to what he wanted. He never understood why, merely grew cunning in order to compensate. A cunning matched by an intense yet fundamentally childish desire not to be outdone, fuelled by a resentment of the injustices done to him. Thus, he was quite accustomed to placing his own advancement ahead of his principles.

'Tell me, Sturmbannführer,' Paul asked, 'did you tell me the other evening, that you hold a degree in philosophy?'

'Correct,' lied Fleischer.

'And also you are a lawyer?'

'Yes.'

'A theoretical question: should one obey orders even if one considers they are dubious?'

Paul noticed that Fleischer's feet and hands were small for one of his size. He had a sudden vision of a grubby soul lurking inside the man's big frame, and imagined – he had no evidence, only insight – that Fleischer's career had thrived on lies and distortions. Until now Paul had been inclined to dismiss him, but he realised that if he did he would be making a mistake.

The gold filling in Fleischer's front tooth looked dull. *'Befehle sind Befehle,'* Fleischer said slowly. 'Orders are orders. There is no debate.'

'I see,' said Paul. 'Would you be kind enough to give me your brief as to your work in Ribérac?'

Fleischer did not appreciate Paul's informal manner. It indicated that von Hoch was not taking him seriously. 'When I was instructed by ss Obergruppenführer Heydrich,' Fleischer inflected the words carefully, 'the Obergruppenführer indicated that the measures to consolidate the occupation in this part of France are to be carried out under the leadership of the senior officer of the sp. In this case,' he paused for effect and enunciated the word with a good deal of satisfaction, 'myself. I will work in conjunction with the Gestapo.'

His words decided Paul. He got up to leave, resolved to lock up his private files in the safe in his office. He was not – and von Bentivegni's warning was still fresh in his mind – going to hand information over to a man like Fleischer. If questioned as to their whereabouts, he would pretend they had been lost in an administrative snarl up. These days, lost files were a standing joke.

Fleischer went over to the sideboard. 'Nice piece of furniture,' he commented, running a hand over it. On a tray was arranged a loaf of white bread, butter and dark honey. Fleischer cut himself a piece, buttered it, covered it with honey and returned to his desk. 'It is a wonderful thing, is it not, Major von Hoch, to be living at such a glorious point in German history and to be serving the Führer?' He bit into the bread and a drop of honey escaped down his chin. He wiped it with a handkerchief.

'Yes,' Paul replied curtly. Fleischer reminded him of a child at a nursery tea and, for the first time, he was glad that he was no longer an active soldier. If Fleischer represented the new Germany, then – Paul found it difficult to formulate the thought – she was not worth fighting for.

'Don't be so fatalistic,' he heard his father say. 'There is more than one battlefront.'

For his part, Fleischer was wondering if he would have to put up with this unresponsive signals officer, handsome though he was. Perhaps a spell in the Eastern territories would dispel his arrogance?

CHAPTER FOUR

DRT TO BDQ . . . ASTRONOMER SHAPING UP. STOP. REQUIRE
MONEY. STOP. SEND TWO H ONE. STOP. TWO H TWO. STOP. TWO
H FIVE. STOP . . .

'Blimey,' said John when he read this part of Evelyn's message. Can they spare all those H containers for us?'

'I jolly well hope so. But there is a chance we won't get them.'

'They're not the ones who need to sleep with revolvers under their pillows.'

'We can but try. Carry on, Georges.'

. . . PROPOSE DZ SEVEN FIVE ZERO FOUR VERTEILLAC TWO TWO
FIVE ZERO APPLE. STOP. BBC AU CLAIR DE LA LUNE. WHERE IS
MY THIRD MAN? STOP. ALOUETTE

BDQ TO DRT . . . YOUR THREE TWO ACKNOWLEDGED. STOP.
REQUESTS NOTED. STOP. AGENT COMING FIRST. STOP. GOODS
LATER. STAND BY FOR APPLE PICK UP. BBC AU CLAIR DE LA LUNE.
GOOD LUCK. STOP.

DRT TO BDQ . . . THANK YOU. STOP. ALOUETTE

CHAPTER FIVE

14 Rauchstrasse
Berlin
14 February 1942

Darling Paul,

I miss you so much. It's quite impossible to put it into words. Of course you know I'm no good at that sort of thing anyway so you will have to imagine that I'm writing the most beautiful prose. It's very late at night, and I have just returned from dinner at the Italian embassy. (The ambassador is a sweetie.) The moonlight shone on the lake there and it reminded me of the time we went boating at Silberbirchen late one night.

Life is *very* uncomfortable. I have got a new job which pays a pittance (310 marks after deductions *and* my boss keeps me late every night.) But you can't say I'm not doing my bit. I was kept busy over the New Year organising a clothing collection for our men in Russia. A *Volksopfer* – the people's sacrifice. I sacrificed my mink. I hope you approve. Actually, I'm rather pleased with myself at the moment. I suggested to Cristel Cranz (do you remember when we watched her win the gold medal at the Winter Olympics?) that she donate her skis. Guess what? She did.

I went to see a private showing of *Der Gasmann*. Reichsmarshall Göring was sitting in front of me and he laughed himself almost sick. I didn't think it was terribly funny. Some of us went on to a nightclub afterwards. Very *lässigkeit und lottem*. (You don't mind if I'm becoming a sleazy do you, darling? It's certainly great fun.) Swing is all the rage – I love 'Sweet Sue'. But one has to be a little careful.

The powers that be don't like swing. It's supposed to be dreadfully decadent.

Yesterday Siegfried Gehrbrandt took me out to dinner and proposed over the brandy. I refused him, of course. He said that I was the sort of woman who grew more beautiful as I got older. I think he might have spared me that.

When are you coming back? I can't bear it much longer. Let me know.

Always,
    Ingrid

Ribérac
20 February '42

Dear Ingrid,

Thank you for your letter. I am glad you are well and enjoying yourself, despite the new job. Berlin is certainly a world away from Ribérac. There is no swinging here I'm afraid. I am kept very busy of course.

Ingrid, I will get to the point. I cannot marry you. I am very serious about this. Please understand me. I am deeply sorry to hurt you, and I mind very much that I allowed myself to be led by your good nature and generosity.

Thank you for everything.

Love,
    Paul

23 February

Darling, darling Paul,

If you give me up, I can't live. I promise you that. I couldn't tell you this before.

Ever,
    Ingrid

What had she done?

Mariette wrapped her arms over her breasts and stared up into the darkness. Beside her, white-fleshed and hard-

243

muscled, lay a stranger: Corporal Werner Schwarz. He was snoring slightly, but not unpleasantly. Mariette squinted sideways. Corporal Schwarz's uniform was scattered all over the floor where he had pulled it off in flattering haste before devouring her. That part of the evening had been extremely satisfactory. No less abandoned were Mariette's clothes which lay twined in his. Thin print dress, darned cardigan and newspaper-lined shoes. Mariette had been glad when they were both naked – she knew her figure was good – and she could forget that her clothes were shabby and unflattering.

The night was long and she half expected Jacques to cry. He was so hungry these days. Mariette remembered the night he was conceived – her husband had been a little drunk – and the night he was born. At the end of an exhausting labour Jacques had put him into her arms and she had lain back, truly happy.

Through the wall, Mariette heard Jacques cry out. She tensed and pushed back the sheet, ready to get up, but then he seemed to settle. Mariette relaxed. She thought of Jeannette, huddled no doubt into one side of the bed, her finger in her mouth and an arm round a maize cob which did duty as a doll. Jacques would be lying bundled up beside her. Mariette's love for them welled up, strong and undeniable. She turned onto her side towards Werner.

How did she find herself lying with wet thighs beside a German soldier?

Her eyes roamed up and down the unfamiliar body. He was not very old. That would account for the impatient fumbling haste. Mariette put out a finger and stroked the German's cheek. Perhaps he was missing his girlfriend or wife? Gertrude or Heidi. She might ask him.

It had been a simple accident. The butcher's shop at Ribérac was in the rue Gambetta. It was run by an old goat with a bulging stomach and scanty moustache. He often slipped an extra bone or two into Mariette's bag in return for her allowing him to pinch her bottom and press the occasional wet kiss on her mouth. But queues for food were getting longer and the women in them keener at spotting anyone receiving favours. Today Mariette had spent the best part of two hours queuing for a bit of loin, only to end up with a meagre portion of bone and gristle only fit for soup. Miserable and cold, she ignored the butcher's leer and stepped back into the street.

Disgusting old man, she thought, and hovered at the street corner, wondering if she dare go into the café opposite to scrounge a drink off someone. As she stepped into the road, a motorcycle driving round the corner swerved to avoid a pothole in the road, skidded, and felled Mariette. She lay stunned while the sky heaved overhead.

'Fraülein. Wie geht es lhnen?'

Gradually, she understood that someone was speaking to her in German. When she did not reply, the voice switched into heavily accented French. 'Are you hurt?' Mariette struggled into a sitting position. Nothing worse could happen to her now. She made an effort to pick up her scattered shopping. 'I'm sorry,' said the voice. 'Let me help you.'

He picked up the small parcel of bones and a loaf of bread which had rolled into the gutter. Mariette dabbed at the cut on her knee with a handkerchief. 'Oh no.' She saw the state of her coat. It was filthy and the hem had been torn. She struggled upright, beginning to sob, her hands clasping the torn wool in a gesture of despair. The coat would be almost impossible to replace.

'If you don't mind the motorcycle, I'll take you home,' said the German. 'Please. It's the least I can do.'

Mariette allowed herself to be led towards the machine and helped onto it. Placing her hands on the firm waist underneath a grey wool tunic, she ignored the stares of her acquaintances still queuing outside the butcher's. Mariette felt a slap of air on her cheeks as the motorcycle roared forward and knew that by tomorrow most people in Ribérac would know that she had accepted a lift from a German. She hunched her shoulders against the cold and against them.

Werner Schwarz had been a walk-over. Within two minutes of entering the cottage he was offering to bring food over for the family. After that Mariette only needed to drop a hint and he agreed to come for the evening meal. The children stared out of the window at his big gleaming motorcycle, astonished and a little fearful. Werner took them outside and lifted them onto the saddle where they shrieked with laughter. In the evening he brought a ham, a huge bag of glossy coffee beans, butter and cheese.

Mariette ran her hands over the parcels. When would they eat the food? How long could she make it last? Five or six meals if she was clever. Would it be best to use the butter for cooking or to eat it on bread? Good decisions.

Of course, the smells and texture of the food were part of the seduction. Each mouthful of ham spiked with sweet-sour pickle was a prelude to his mouth on her breast. Each sip of dark, aromatic coffee as comforting and heady as the scent of a well-tended masculine body, the full soft fat of the cheese as yielding as her own.

What on earth was she going to do now?

Paul was checking through Major Blumberg's papers in preparation for handing them over to Fleischer who had demanded to see them. He had report number 21, VTM25 in front of him. Vertrauemann 25 was generally reliable according to Blumberg's notes. A butcher in the rue Gambetta, he was privy to a lot of local gossip. The reports were painstaking; transparent reflections of a small mind. Even the paper he wrote on, the squared paper that the French used, seemed impregnated with his pettiness.

'Monsieur *le docteur* was observed driving towards Verteillac on the evening of 21 February. He told his wife that he was going to attend a labour, but I cannot verify this. Madame Blanquefort was overheard saying: "Damn the verdigris . . ."'

Here the butcher had appended a note: 'A slang word for Germans.'

How contemptible this man is, thought Paul. How myopic and mean. Nevertheless, it could not be denied that Blumberg, and now Fleischer, depended a great deal on his malicious snippets of gossip. Paul felt depressed. He gathered up the files and dropped them into the OUT basket.

How was he going to work with Fleischer? Paul anticipated not only a clash between their respective organisations, but also a clash of wills between themselves. Fleischer was a menacing presence but he was a fact of life.

Paul had sent a coded report back to *Abwehr* headquarters in the Tirpitzufer, detailing the developments at Ribérac. The report mentioned that Ribérac's population (normally 10,000) had been swollen by refugees from Alsace, Strasbourg and the north and supplies and accommodation were stretched. The population appeared acquiescent, however, and there had been no serious incidents since the one in November in which a sergeant had been murdered.

Unless something shocked them into resistance, such as the shooting of forty-eight hostages in Nantes in October 1941 – a retaliation for the assassination of a German colonel. Paul was convinced that the shooting had triggered a wave of resistance activity. He spread a map of the area over his desk. The red demarcation line ran through Bazas, Langon, Sauveterre de Guyenne, Montpon, Ribérac, La Rochebeaucourt, La Rochefoucauld. Where, among these forests, lanes, villages and towns, would they take action?

Obvious targets were German personnel. Others included railways. Reports in from the Angoulême depot indicated that goods wagons, the special *wagons de grande capacité*, intended for Germany had developed a peculiar habit of getting lost up sidings. Food and equipment that left France in good condition arrived damaged and often inedible in Germany. Paul was aware that the *cheminots* often tossed rotten vegetables into a fresh consignment, or even poured acid over them. Better still was the simple trick of switching the way-bills stuck onto the sides of the trucks so that food earmarked for Germany was sent somewhere in France.

He called through the door of the office. 'Oberleutnant, could you phone Mademoiselle Liegaux at the Château Belle-Place and tell her I will pick her up at seven o'clock tonight.'

'Yes, sir.'

He had planned the coming evening carefully. It had taken several phone calls and much persistence to persuade Mademoiselle Liegaux to accompany him to the concert.

The lieutenant came into his office. 'More reports, sir, just in from the listening stations in Paris. Apparently there are two illicit wireless transmitters working in this area. The stations at Augsburg and Bordeaux are trying to pinpoint them.

One of them has transmitted a couple of times this week already. We stand a good chance of catching him.'

An hour later, Evelyn wheeled her bicycle around to the back yard of the farmhouse. At her approach, geese in the field behind set up an indignant noise. Evelyn hid the bicycle behind a piece of machinery, picked her way through the yard covered in droppings and feathers, and knocked at the door of the house. It was opened by an old lady dressed in a pinafore which had lost all its colour. When she saw Evelyn, she removed the cigarette hanging from her mouth and beckoned her inside. Evelyn took a deep breath before entering.

The room was filthy and in it hung the sweet, sickening stench of tomcat. Dust and grime lay in piles in the corners and the windows were opaque with grease. Evelyn let her breath out cautiously. She knew from previous visits that it would take a minute for her stomach to settle.

The farmer was sitting by a brown Bakelite radio, the dial already tuned to the BBC frequency. Evelyn was offered the second chair, which she accepted. The farmer's wife stood behind them.

At the suggestion of Georges Bégue, a wireless operator operating in France who was being hounded by radio detection vans and Vichy police, a novel system of 'personal messages' which was now well established had set up with the BBC. These messages functioned as signals: an agent listened to the radio for his prearranged phrase – 'le scarabe d'or marché', 'le bébé s'appelle Napoleon', and then moved into action. The scheme saved wireless transmission time and reduced the danger for wireless operators.

'It's time,' said her host, and poured out a glass of Pineau. Evelyn refused and asked if she might be allowed to switch on the radio. The farmer consented. Evelyn turned it on and static buzzed around the room.

'The jamming must be bad today,' said Evelyn, feeling obliged to apologise for the BBC.

'Bloody Boches.' The farmer stroked his unshaven cheek with his finger. Years of dirt had encrusted into numerous runnels under the skin. Evelyn turned back to the wireless. She had grown fond of both him and his wife. Elderly and poor they might be, but they had never refused her entry and never once indicated that they knew what would happen to them if they were caught listening in to the BBC.

She leant over and placed her ear to the front of the radio. It was smooth and cold. The jamming screeched, grew worse, and miraculously died down. The bell-like tones of the BBC announcer came through. *'Voici quelques messages personnels.'* Evelyn held up her hand. *'Le scarabe d'or ne marche pas sur la route . . . Angèle m'a donné sa main . . .'* The couple looked at her, intent and expectant. Evelyn shook her head. Nothing so far. *'Le bébé Poisson est adorable . . .'* Please, she prayed. Please not tonight.

'Au clair de la lune . . .

Evelyn sat up. The signal had come. If the phrase was repeated on the seven o'clock news that evening, the pick-up was on. Unless the weather closed in, a Lysander was due to take off from RAF Tangmere and fly towards the chosen landing ground, where Evelyn and her team would be waiting. Where she must be waiting.

Pressing Evelyn's hand uncomfortably tight in his own, the farmer begged her to be careful. He and his wife had the tact not to ask any questions. Evelyn thanked them and said goodbye as quickly as possible.

Taking in lungfuls of fresh air, she coasted on the bicycle downhill towards Ribérac. Procedure: Alert the reception committee. Ensure everyone has correct post-curfew papers. Requisition two extra bicycles and the van. Torches. Where were they? Had Jean-Claude managed to get hold of an extra battery? Depute Bessy to listen to the seven o'clock news.

Why tonight of all nights?

CHAPTER SIX

At half past seven that same evening – the seven o'clock news verified that the pick-up was going ahead – Evelyn watched from Bessy's bedroom window as a staff car pulled into the drive.

'He's here,' she said. She bit absently at her nails and tore a piece of cuticle.

Bessy was resting on the day bed. 'Evie, do change your mind. Say you're ill or something.' Bessy pleated her dressing gown sash nervously. 'It's too dangerous. Especially tonight.' She switched to English. 'You've made your finger bleed.'

Evelyn dropped her hand. She dabbed at the savaged nail with a handkerchief and the linen became spotted with red. She stared at the stains for a moment and then sat down at the dressing table. A powder puff lay in a cut-glass bowl and she powdered her nose for the second time in ten minutes. 'Don't panic me, Bessy. I've got to get through this.'

'I don't see why. I'll tell Gaston to ask von Hoch to go away.'

'He telephoned four times. In the end . . .' Evelyn applied more lipstick to her bottom lip. 'I had to give in.' She pressed a hand to her stomach. 'I just hope I don't have to eat too much.' She gave a taut smile.

Bessy swung her legs onto the floor and went over to the window. 'Gaston's letting him in,' she reported.

'How do I look?' Evelyn had borrowed a black *crépe* evening suit, hoping that in black she would appear dull and older than her years.

'Very nice. Much too nice, even in that suit.' Bessy left the window and came over to where Evelyn was sitting. Placing her hands on Evelyn's shoulders she looked at her reflection in the mirror. 'You're being very brave,' she said softly.

'Don't.' Evelyn fiddled with a hairbrush. 'It'll be fine – as long as I get back in time. If I'm sufficiently boring he'll lose interest.' She squinted down at her borrowed stockings to see if the seams were straight. She picked up her handbag. 'Wish me luck.'

Bessy brushed Evelyn's shoulders with a clothes brush. 'Of course.'

Paul had dispensed with his driver for the evening. He drove fast towards Ribérac. 'I've been looking forward to this evening.'

'Monsieur.'

He steered the car around a tight corner. 'The moon is bright tonight.'

Evelyn's gardenia perfume filled the car. It had been some time since Paul had smelt such a luxurious feminine fragrance. Evelyn was sitting very still on the leather seat, gazing out of the window.

The moon was holding. No rain and only light cloud. Minimal wind. Providing the ground wasn't too soft, conditions were perfect. She shifted and felt the silk of her stockings against her legs and the roughness of her bitten nails in her palms. It had to go well tonight. Not only was she due to complete her team of trained SOE agents with the arrival of a sabotage expert but also it was the first operation she had organised as circuit leader. If this was a success they could begin to plan *parachutage* operations bringing in the weapons and equipment they needed so badly.

'Would you prefer to be silent?' Paul broke into her thoughts.

'I'm sorry, Monsieur.'

Someone took good care of Major von Hoch's uniform. His boots were immaculate and his leather belt oiled and supple. A devoted batman, perhaps. Evelyn suspected Paul was the sort of man who received loyal service. Under the peaked hat his fair hair was brushed and carefully cut.

'If you've made contact with a German officer,' an officer back in London commented, 'perhaps it could be made to work to our advantage. I will speak to the bosses.'

'You mean I could work as a spy?'

'Consider. There is a *cordon sanitaire* – or *insanitaire* if you prefer – around France. As a result, we are desperately short of information, particularly detail from within the German army. But I won't give orders. SOE is not an espionage organisation. As you know, it operates on a military basis. We are not obliged to do anything except carry out our own objectives. Remember, if you pursue this contact you will be in extreme danger. You must get out at once if there is the slightest hint that your cover has been blown.'

Cruising in Paul's car, panic stiffened Evelyn. She clutched the top of her handbag. Then her training reasserted itself. She repeated a comforting nostrum: most people can face most things.

Paul concentrated on driving. 'You're looking at me as if I were a combination of Bluebeard and the Marquis de Sade,' he said lightly. 'I promise you I'm neither.'

'I'm sorry. I did not mean to.'

Paul made a further effort to enliven the conversation. 'I'm afraid the Berlin Philharmonic is not playing this evening. They are in Paris. However, the substitute is very good.'

The tiny auditorium in the Ribérac theatre was full to overflowing. As she settled into her seat, Evelyn was careful not to look round; she had already recognised a couple of faces, notably Monsieur and Madame Devereux. Paul leant over.

'I would have liked to buy you a box of chocolates, but sadly there aren't any.'

'Don't worry Monsieur. I prefer to eat chocolates in the morning.'

'Do you?' said Paul, fascinated by this unexpected revelation.

For the first time Evelyn managed to smile. 'Yes. I can eat more of them then.'

Paul balanced his cap on his crossed knee. 'I shall think of you tomorrow morning, eating pralines and fresh cream truffles for breakfast.'

'Ginger, actually. Ginger and caramels.'

At that Paul raised an eyebrow. 'You have a decidedly individual taste,' he commented.

Paul had predicted correctly. The orchestra was extremely

good and played Haydn and Mozart in the first half of the programme with a lightness of touch that left the audience momentarily silent with appreciation before they erupted into applause. Evelyn joined in wholeheartedly. The music had acted as an opiate, dulling her anxiety over the pick-up and this unwanted meeting. For a short time she escaped the claustrophobic atmosphere of the theatre and the dangerous implications of the man sitting beside her.

Paul clapped enthusiastically and turned to Evelyn. 'I hope you like Wagner,' he said. 'He makes up the second half.'

But Evelyn could not concentrate on the Wagner and longed for the concert to end. Her mind returned obsessively to the pick-up and fretted over the dinner ahead.

'Did you enjoy the Wagner?' Paul enquired over the table at the black-market restaurant near Allemans.

She knew that Hitler favoured Wagner's music. 'Not really,' she said. 'Am I speaking treason?'

'Almost.' Paul offered her the menu.

'Do you like his music?'

'We have a saying in Germany which goes: *Still sprich durch die Blüme.* Hush, speak through flowers. In other words, it is sometimes best to camouflage your opinions. Let us speak of Wagner through the flowers.' He glanced round the room. 'I think we are in a room full of black marketeers,' he attempted a joke. 'Plenty of *avoirdupois.*'

'And Germans,' she reminded him in a low voice.

He hesitated. 'Of course, and Germans.'

The dining room was in the wing of a converted manor house. Panelled in wood and painted light grey, it was furnished with grey and gold curtains and lit by candlelight. A fire burned at one end of the room. The men wore tailored suits. The women wore outfits from Grès or plain, exquisitely cut dresses worn with patterned jackets and heavy, flashing jewellery. Evelyn was pretty sure that her fellow diners included a couple of representatives from the Duffours gang – a band of underworld operators in Gestapo pay. Her eyes widened for a split second when she recognised Jean-Claude ensconced at a table by the fire. Jean-Claude looked straight through her.

Evelyn could not remember what she ate. The conversation was strained and awkward, punctuated by tense silences.

'Is your family in the wine business, Mademoiselle Liegaux?'

She braced herself for his inevitable questions. 'No, we are farmers.' She felt she had better enlarge. 'We are distant cousins of the de Bourgraves.'

The wine Paul chose was good, but Evelyn repeatedly refused his offer to refill her glass.

'Perhaps you will prefer the Sauterne?' he said when their *tarte aux pruneaux* was placed in front of them.

She sipped at it. 'The noble rot,' she remarked. 'It's very good.'

'I thought since you're in the business you would appreciate it.' It appeared an innocuous remark but it flashed through her mind that he was suspicious of her.

When will this end? she thought and put down her glass.

'Where do you come from in Germany, Major von Hoch?'

Paul's description of the house and estate got them through coffee. He told her about shooting parties, summer picnics, Sunday hikes in the Black Forest and the constant shifts to find money to repair the *Schloss*. 'I might have to turn to the palette and brush after the war. We are running out of paintings to sell.'

He toyed with the coffee cup. Evelyn's nerves were jangling. 'Did you always want to be a soldier?'

'Yes. But I was wounded a few years ago, so I'm no longer in the front line.'

'What sort of work do you do in Ribérac?'

'I'm a signals officer,' he lied.

'Sending messages. That sort of thing?'

'Yes. Nowadays an army relies almost entirely on signals.'

'I imagine you're in charge?'

He pushed his cup to one side and assessed the innocent-seeming face across the table. 'Look,' he said. 'You're not really interested. I think it's time I took you home.'

'Yes.' Evelyn felt intense relief mixed with disgust at herself. 'I am a little tired.'

He glanced down at the basket of uneaten bread. 'I should

take some home for the children in my billet,' he said. 'They are always hungry.'

'Why don't you?' Evelyn produced a clean handkerchief from her handbag and spread it on the table. 'Here.'

Paul smiled conspiratorially. He handed her some slices and watched as she wrapped them in the handkerchief and tied it with a knot.

She gave him the bundle. 'I hope they enjoy it.'

'I'm sure they will.' Paul got to his feet, leaving his Sauterne unfinished. Evelyn followed suit, casting a quick look at Jean-Claude who was talking to his companion.

Several pairs of eyes observed them leave the dining room and pass under the draped brocade curtain in the doorway.

Back in the car, Paul made no attempt to talk. They drove in silence through the puddles of shadow. The moon glanced intermittently onto his face, turning his hair to bleached silk. Watching Paul unobtrusively, Evelyn made a discovery. Hating was easy. Hate was an emotion that allowed an agent to strip the enemy of his human face. But she had made a fatal miscalculation. She had put at risk Astronomer and its members for a concert and a black-market dinner – to discover that she could not hate this enemy.

Paul drove up to the front door of Belle-Place and halted the car. 'I'm sorry, Mademoiselle Liegaux,' he said. 'Perhaps this evening was a mistake.'

'Major . . .'

'My name is Paul.'

'Thank you all the same.'

Evelyn held out her hand and Paul took it and turned it over to look at her bitten nails. 'Have you always bitten your nails?'

'Yes,' she said. 'Since I was a child. I've tried everything, including gall and iodine.'

He laughed. 'How unpleasant.' He returned her hand. 'Well, good night, Mademoiselle. I hope you sleep well.'

He waited until she had gone into the house before driving away, thankful that the episode was over and that now he could put Evelyn Liegaux out of his mind.

* * *

255

Evelyn ascended the staircase two at a time. In her room she paused to check the shutters were closed and switched on the lamp by the bed. Her clothes were ready, folded up in the top drawer of the *armoire*. A blue jersey of the type French fishermen wore, men's corduroy trousers, a *canadienne* with fur-lined collar, two pairs of thick socks and black beret edged in brown leather.

In her hurry she tossed the black evening suit on the bed, then thought better of it and hung it up. Her room must look as tidy as possible. She dressed as fast as she could and extracted a pair of leather boots from the wardrobe. Then she put her torch, hip flask and a packet of cigarettes into her pocket, switched off the light and, with her boots in her hand, trod lightly down the passage. It was eleven thirty. The pick-up was scheduled for half past midnight.

Bessy had made sure that the lock on the kitchen door was well oiled and had also arranged for Evelyn to have a spare key. Evelyn let herself out and relocked the door. She padded through the wine cellar and the secret passage to the arch in the wall where she retrieved her bicycle from the outhouse and a Sten gun from under a pile of sacks. She wheeled the bicycle down the path to the field, once thick with maize, now ploughed and heavy going underfoot. Once she was on the road she made good time.

As agreed, Jean-Claude was waiting in the van by Mariette's cottage. 'Good,' he said as she dropped, panting, into the passenger seat. They drove in silence over the demarcation line. Jean-Claude's big hands confidently manoeuvred the vehicle along the road. 'You dined well, Violette, I take it?' Jean-Claude was the first to break the silence. 'A handsome young officer for company.'

'Couldn't get out of it,' said Evelyn. 'What were you doing?'

Jean-Claude's mouth stretched into a smile, as if he was enjoying a joke at her expense. He tapped the side of his nose. 'None of your business.' The paralysing notion that Jean-Claude was a double agent sent a jolt of fear through her: it was not impossible. With an effort Evelyn dismissed the notion.

The other members of the reception committee had already

arrived at the landing strip when they got there. John, Pierre Coutances (recruited by Evelyn a couple of weeks previously) and two boys from Villetoureix whom Jean-Claude swore were reliable. They were huddled in a group, sharing a bottle of wine and eating local sausage. The chosen landing area seemed mysterious in the moonlight and a sprinkling of cloud that had appeared from the east threw stippled patches onto the grass. The road ran alongside the field and leading off it was a lane that led into a wood. His face blackened with charcoal, John ran over to Evelyn. 'We've got a problem.' He gestured towards the far end of the field.

'*Merde! Les vaches!*' Jean-Claude swore loudly. 'We must get rid of them.'

The cows, who had been grazing peacefully, were surprised by the sight of several black figures running towards them with outstretched arms. They swerved and dodged but eventually allowed themselves to be herded towards the copse at the north end of the field.

'All right,' Evelyn panted. 'It's time. Could the look-outs go to their places. One by the gate, the other on the lane. Olivier, Jean-Claude and I will take up positions. Pierre, you watch the road.'

'Synchronise time?' John tapped his watch.

Evelyn squinted at her own. 'It is now midnight. It should be here within half an hour.'

'Let's have another drink,' said John. 'Go to it with the red wine swilling in our veins.'

'Fool,' said Evelyn affectionately.

'A wise fool, though.' John tipped the bottle up and drank and then passed it over to Evelyn. He had on the shabby grey suit of the other day, collar turned up against the cold. He stamped his feet. 'My feet are always flaming wet.'

'Remember.' Evelyn pitched her voice so the others could hear. 'If the Boches arrive, run. No taking them on unless absolutely necessary.' She knew perfectly well that Pierre, at least, wouldn't mind having a pot-shot. 'There's no way we'd win but we might stand a chance of escaping. Is that understood?'

'Agreed,' said Pierre. A tall emaciated man, dressed in a

worn corduroy suit with large pockets, Pierre lived on an isolated farm towards Verteillac where he existed entirely self-sufficiently. He appeared light on his feet and Evelyn suspected that he supplemented his living by poaching. She wet her finger and held it up. 'Down wind is this way.'

They made their way over the wet grass. John took up a position a hundred and fifty yards downwind of Evelyn, Jean-Claude fifty yards to the right of John, making an inverted L shape. If all went well, the plane would drop down at the first torch, taxi to the second, turn at the third and taxi back to the first where Evelyn would be waiting. From there it would be ready for immediate take-off. Silently she went over the Morse for the letter K.

How was the pilot doing, she wondered, negotiating his way through cloud, wind eddies and flak? Had he briefed himself thoroughly before take-off? She hoped he had studied the map and memorised the features – towns, rivers, forests – which would tell him he was on the right route.

All ears strained for the engine note.

Down the road there was a loud snap. A twig or branch breaking. It came from the direction in which Pierre was posted. Evelyn whipped round. Nothing. Nothing but shadows and night sounds.

There *was* someone in the undergrowth. She heard the snap again. Then silence. What was Pierre doing? Evelyn was debating leaving her position to investigate when she heard the muffled hum of a plane.

Jean-Claude's voice floated through the darkness. 'Those bloody animals!'

Still uneasy, Evelyn turned to see what was the matter. The cows had wandered back onto the landing strip. She pocketed her torch and ran towards them. 'Shoo,' she hissed, arms stuck out like a scarecrow. 'Shoo.' The cows shied and ducked and to her relief, lumbered back towards the copse. Evelyn sprinted back to her post.

She was only just in time. The Lysander flew into sight, silhouetted in the moonlight like a woodcut from a child's book of fairy tales, its wing struts and wheel casings clearly visible. Her throat tightened as she stared up at it. 'You beautiful thing,' she whispered. For a moment she thought of the immense effort that had been made on their behalf and the diligence of the people involved in this operation: the FANY secretaries and coding clerks, teleprinter and wireless operators, the holding station staff, the aircraft mechanics, the girls in the shed who packed the equipment, the weather men who sat up all hours, the dispatching officer and the plotters in the ops room, the cook who organised the agents' last meal on English soil.

The Lysander circled once. Evelyn pulled the torch out of her jacket pocket and signalled the letter K repeatedly. 'You lovely thing, you,' she almost shouted up into the cold, moonlight sky. 'We're down here.'

CHAPTER SEVEN

The pilot signalled back the letter K and switched on his headlights. He circled for a second time to make sure he had the landing strip lined up and started to make his descent.

The plane touched down at the correct point of the inverted L made by torches, bounced once and then coasted. The engines roared as the pilot put them into reverse and a blast of air almost knocked Evelyn off her feet. The Lysander taxied back to her and stopped only a few yards away. The cockpit opened and the pilot emerged with a revolver in his hand.

'*Bonjewer*.' His accent was terrible.

'*Bonjour*,' Evelyn shouted over the still-racing engines, feeling quite tearful. 'You made it.'

'Nice easy landing strip,' said the pilot, who sported a handlebar moustache.

Evelyn wanted to reach up and hug him. 'You've got two bods?' she asked, handing him up a bottle of champagne and some scent.

'Correct.'

The first 'bod', dressed in stone-coloured trenchcoat and felt hat, scrambled down the ladder holding a primed revolver as prescribed by the drill. The second handed down the luggage. Evelyn passed up to the pilot a couple of coded reports which were too long to send by wireless. 'Good luck,' she said. 'And thank you.'

The pilot grinned and pulled the ends of his moustache. 'All part of the service, ma'am. I'll go anywhere for a pretty face.'

The second bod jumped to the ground. John hustled them over to the edge of the field. It was not quite the warm welcome that she and John had received when they arrived in France, Evelyn thought, but it would have to do. The pilot pulled the cockpit hood back into place. Evelyn gave the thumbs-up signal and the plane taxied forward. The entire process had taken seven minutes.

Hot, fuel-laden wind from the engines bathed Evelyn's face and their noise made the earth vibrate. She shoved her hands into her trouser pockets and watched the Lysander take off. For a moment it seemed to hang between the tree tops and the moon. Then the pilot waggled the wings in farewell, banked to the left and the plane disappeared into the night sky.

Exhilarated with their success, Evelyn ran to the gate to greet the incoming agents. The words of welcome died on her lips.

Facing her was Major Fuller.

Jean-Claude turned up the collar of his jacket, swung the strap of his gun over his shoulder so it hung down over his back and lit a cigarette. 'Nice one,' he remarked with satisfaction. He cupped his hands to hide the glowing tip. Evelyn and Jack avoided each other's eyes. 'You'd better tell the others to move off,' she said to Jean-Claude.

Sensing the tension, John stamped his wet feet for the hundredth time. 'Jolly nice to see you chaps but it's after my bedtime. We'd better get going.'

'Yes, welcome,' Evelyn finally managed. 'We're going to take you to a temporary safe house. It means riding a bike but it's not far. From now on, no talking, please, and no smoking. I'll lead the way and you must follow twenty yards behind. If you hear me cough, hide.'

'No Boches around?' Jack spoke for the first time.

It was understandable that Fuller should be cautious but his question irritated Evelyn. 'I think you can trust us to know what we are doing.'

He glanced up. 'Well, let's get going then.'

Jean-Claude brushed the footprints away by the gate. Evelyn checked the torches and the luggage, and helped fasten the suitcases onto the bicycles. Major Fuller had evidently brought a wireless set. The two look-outs were already cycling away down the road back to their homes. Pierre emerged silently from the shadows, his gun swinging from a leather thong around his neck.

'Did you hear anything before the pick-up?' Evelyn asked him. 'I thought I heard someone in the trees near you.'

Pierre frowned and said, 'We'd better investigate.'

The resistants looked at each other, each thinking the same thought. 'Quickly,' Evelyn whispered.

'You go on ahead,' said Jean-Claude and snapped off the safety catch of his gun.

'We must go now.' Evelyn was worried. 'I'm afraid your bicycles have no lights.'

She led the silent procession down the shadow-stippled road, swerving now and again to avoid the biggest ruts. The very last person she had expected to see was Jack Fuller. The initial shock was receding and she began to be curious as to why he had given up his job at headquarters. She turned left off the road and led the party up a dirt track which petered out when it came to a small beamed farmhouse.

Evelyn dismounted. 'Put the bicycles in the henhouse over there, please,' she said in a low voice, placing hers behind a stack of wooden crates.

The farmer, a staunch anti-Nazi, was keeping watch for them. As the group filed cautiously round the back of the building and up through an excellently maintained kitchen garden, he opened the door. 'Ça va?'

'Ça va, Monsieur Vaux.' Evelyn stepped out of the shadows. 'We have brought the two men.'

'Please come in.' The old man gestured for them to enter. Evelyn knew that this farm had been in the same family for years. The land had not been parcelled up by succeeding generations and before the war had flourished, with yields well above average. The German levy on food, however, had seen to it that profits collapsed. Consequently, Monsieur Vaux was a ready recruit, prepared even to take the severe risks of keeping a safe house. He led them down a whitewashed passage cluttered with outdoor garments, walking sticks and boots, into the kitchen.

An oil lamp cast a yellow tinge over the whitewashed walls and from the heavy beams hung hams and bunches of drying herbs and delphiniums. The room was dominated by a huge oak dresser which displayed to advantage a fine Limoges dinner service. A stove at one end of the kitchen sent out a substantial heat. The table in the centre was laid with a gingham cloth on which were bowls, bread and wine in plain bottles.

The new agents settled into the chairs which the farmer pulled out for them. 'This is Theo,' said Jack, 'and I'm Tomas.' They accepted bowls of soup which the farmer's wife was ladling out from an industrial-sized china tureen. Evelyn checked outside the back door and in the pantry that led off the kitchen. Then she allowed herself to sit down. The farmer ate with them while his wife stood behind his chair and darted forward every so often to refill the bowls.

Jack wiped soup from his mouth. 'This is very good, Madame,' he addressed the farmer's wife. 'You are an excellent cook.' The farmer's wife seemed pleased with the compliment. He held out his bowl for a second helping. 'I felt too queasy to eat before we left.' So he is human after all – Evelyn cheered up at the thought. 'Theo here ate for both of us,' he added.

Evelyn studied Theo across the table. Young and fair-skinned, he talked quickly with a lot of hand movements and appeared avid and very earnest.

John helped himself to more bread. 'What's the news?'

Steam spiralled up from the replenished tureen. The farmer's wife put plates of home-made pâté, sausage and *boudin noir* on the table with a bowl of home-made gherkin pickle.

'Hitler gave General Brauchitsch his marching orders in Russia. He's now assumed personal command of the entire German army.' Jack spoke first.

'Really?' Evelyn sat upright.

'The Russians launched a counter-offensive and Brauchitsch failed to deliver the victory that Hitler demanded. The army's short of equipment and exhausted. They must be freezing to death out there.'

'Any other news?' John speared a gherkin on his knife.

'Hong Kong has fallen to the Japs.'

'My God,' said Evelyn. There was a grim silence.

'The poor buggers.' John bit a pickle and winced at its tartness. 'I don't fancy facing those Nips.' He finished the pickle and washed it down with a gulp of wine. 'What's on in London?' He made an attempt to clear the sombre atmosphere.

'Americans,' said Jack. 'They're arriving in droves.'

'Over there, over there,
Send the word, send the word over there,
The Yanks are coming, the Yanks are coming
Drum, drum, drumming everywhere . . .'

John sang the words in his light tenor voice and the effect on his audience was strangely moving.

He shattered the mood by blowing a raspberry.

Evelyn laughed and poured herself a glass of wine. Turning her attention to Jack, she said, 'What are your orders?'

'Theo is your sabotage expert. I'm in transit. My training was beefed up at the last minute. They need somebody down south fast. Can you hide me until I've made the contacts?'

'Of course.' Evelyn did not relish the idea of hiding Jack. It was a problem she had not anticipated. At least he was going to move on soon. She reckoned he was probably heading for the Toulouse area. The Germans had commandeered a big powder-making factory near the town and the resistance might well be planning to blow it up. 'What are the others up to?' she asked.

The heat in the room was stifling. Jack unwound the cravat from his neck and took off his jersey. Then he emptied his pockets. Map. A deadly looking knife with a serrated edge and a tiny compass which could be attached to a collar.

'Goodness.' Evelyn eyed the objects. 'The Org has been busy.'

'It certainly has. There are boffins working day and night developing tricks like these.' He held up his pipe and unscrewed the stem to show her the minute cavity underneath the bowl.

'I'm afraid you can't go around with that knife,' Evelyn said calmly. 'It would give you away immediately. I shouldn't think there's one like it in the whole of France.'

Scrubbed of make-up, Evelyn's face in the lamplight was almost boyish. Her eyes were clear; she seemed at ease and in control. Another person entirely from the gauche, defensive Miss St John of their first meeting when he interviewed her.

'Please hide it,' she said quietly.

Jack looked up but said nothing.

Madame Vaux, who seemed fatigued, urged them to eat her special apple cake. Knowing the effort that had gone into its making, Evelyn accepted a piece. The light from the lamp shed its clandestine glow on the faces of the small band sitting at the farmhouse table, their backs to the surrounding gloom. Evelyn would remember this scene: the oil burning against the darkness; the disparate collection of people drawn together by their hatred of the Nazis.

There was a scuffling outside the kitchen window. A man's muffled cry and a thud which sounded like a fist on flesh. Evelyn and John leapt up and made a grab for their guns. John ran to the window and Evelyn slipped behind the door, fitting a magazine into her Sten.

Monsieur and Madame Vaux shrank back against the dresser and the farmer put a protective arm around his wife. 'Is it the Boches?' she stuttered.

John pulled the black-out back half an inch. He could see nothing. Theo and Jack were throwing their belongings into their rucksacks.

'Could be,' whispered Evelyn. 'But they tend to use cars. It's more likely to be someone spying on us. Where the hell's Jean-Claude?' She raised the safety catch on the Sten with a soft click just as the first bars of 'Je tire ma révérence' were whistled outside. Evelyn lowered the Sten. 'It's Jean-Claude.'

'Where've you been?' Evelyn asked when he appeared in the doorway.

'Come with me,' he ordered. 'Quickly.'

She followed him into the pantry. 'What's happened?'

Jean-Claude felt in his pocket for his cigarettes. Shadowed by stubble, the big square face loomed down at her. 'We've nabbed a songster. He was spying on us at the pick-up. Pierre caught him. I think I've seen him kissing German arses at the Café de Maisons in Verteillac. Pierre is guarding him.' He pressed his face closer to Evelyn's. 'You are going to have to deal with him.'

Evelyn knew Jean-Claude was testing her.

'Bring him in, then,' she said.

When she returned to the kitchen she noticed that Madame Vaux had taken down a picture from the wall and was sliding it behind the dresser. Her husband told her not to be so foolish, but she paid no attention. 'If anything happens, I want it to be safe,' she said obstinately, 'for our son.'

'Please go upstairs,' Evelyn asked them both. Monsieur Vaux ushered his wife towards the staircase. After a minute their footsteps could be heard on the wooden floorboards upstairs.

The kitchen door opened and Jean-Claude and Pierre pushed a man into the room ahead of them. His wrists were bound behind his back with cord and he was dressed in a loud striped suit with baggy trousers and a wide tie. He looked like a *maquereau*; the sort of pimp with whom John was familiar from his time in Marseille so long ago. Blood dripped sluggishly from his nose and onto the acid blue of his shirt. Jean-Claude prodded him forward with his gun.

The man seemed surprised at the sight of Evelyn, and put out his tongue to lick the blood which had congealed on his upper lip. Evelyn swallowed.

Justice en gros. Rough justice.

'What were you doing?' she asked the man. He was around twenty-five years old and, on closer inspection, very shabby. He did not answer but spat blood-flecked spittle onto the floor. Jean-Claude laid his gun on the table, Pierre kept his trained on the target.

'He saw the whole pick-up,' said Pierre.

'Why?' she asked the sullen figure. 'Was it for money?'

The man raised his head and looked straight at Evelyn. 'What makes you think you have the right to ask me these questions?' He shifted and winced as the rough cord cut into his wrists.

Jean-Claude gave a derisive laugh. A thought gelled in Evelyn's mind: This man is a thug and I'm glad we are on the same side – and understood that she was making her way

266

through a labyrinth without a guide and with no knowledge of what lay at the end.

'You've got no right to try me,' the man repeated stubbornly. 'Commies.'

Justice en gros. What road had led Evelyn to this farmhouse in France, to preside over the fate of a shabby stranger for whom she could find nothing but pity?

Unconsciously it seemed, the French had ranged themselves at one end of the table, the English at the other. The earlier camaraderie was gone.

'Do you deny you were spying on us?' asked Evelyn.

The man did not look at her. 'No,' he replied in a flat voice. 'You were dead easy to follow.'

'Give him a cigarette,' said John from the window.

Jack took one out of his pocket, lit it and stuck it between the man's caked lips. He whispered to Evelyn, 'Do you want me to handle this?'

'No.' She shot him a look. Previously so reassuring, the light from the lamp made the faces appear pallid and strained.

'Look,' Evelyn said. 'I will ask you once more. Were you spying for the Boches?'

The man shrugged. His jacket was fraying at the cuffs and the buttons were loose. 'It won't make any difference what I say.'

'Were the Germans paying you?'

Jean-Claude took the cigarette from the informer's mouth. 'Speak up.' He twisted the tied hands up the man's back. 'Talk, you bastard.'

The bloodied face contorted in pain and fear. Then it went blank. 'All right. The Germans pay me.' Jean-Claude's grip tightened. 'France is rotten, riddled with Communists and Jews.'

'How did you know about us?'

The man shrugged his shoulders. 'I was in Villetoureix when I saw your friends set off after curfew.' His lips cracked in a humourless smile. 'Fools.'

'Kill him,' said Jean-Claude. 'Why waste time?'

'Wait a minute,' John said. 'You can't just do that.'

'Oh, yes we can.'

267

The knot that had been forming in Evelyn's stomach tightened. 'Olivier is right, that's not our job.'

'For Christ's sake, spare me the moralising and get on with it.' Jean-Claude's angry voice jerked her back to the business in hand. 'It's kill or be killed.'

Evelyn took a deep breath. 'We'll take a vote.'

'I vote for death,' said Jean-Claude instantly. 'This man is guilty by his own admission. He deserves all he gets.'

'Is there any alternative?' said John, and turned away. Pierre merely drew his hand across his throat.

'I think,' the excitement had drained out of Theo's face, 'I should not intervene.'

'Shoot him,' said Jack. 'You can't take the risk of letting him go. I'm sorry.'

'Your vote, Violette,' said Jean-Claude. Evelyn ignored him and stared at the wall where the picture had hung. Madame Vaux would have to whitewash the patch it had left, she thought. The others were waiting. Kill or be killed. She made herself look straight into the eyes of the informer as she spoke: 'We have no choice. He'd run straight to the Boches. Take him outside.'

The man gave a snuffling cry. John took the cigarette he was smoking and placed it in the man's mouth. 'Easy,' he said.

It did not take long. Pierre led the informer out of the room and Jean-Claude followed. Within a few minutes, a shot sounded.

'Well, that's that,' said Jean-Claude when he returned. He picked up the wine bottle, filled a glass for himself and then passed the bottle to Evelyn. She pushed it aside and ran out of the room.

Outside it was very cold. Evelyn gulped mouthfuls of fresh air. She took a few steps from the house, then she leant over and was violently sick.

CHAPTER EIGHT

In January 1942 Rommel retook Agebadia in North Africa and the British withdrew from the Malay Peninsula to Singapore. By February Singapore had surrendered to the Japanese and in March they completed their conquest of the West Indies. In May the Russian opened the Kharknov offensive, the Germans counter-attacked, and were victorious. Rommel launched a large-scale Axis offensive at the Gazala line. Two Czech nationalists assassinated ss Obergruppenführer Reinhard Heydrich, chief of German secret services. The British mounted a thousand-bomber raid on Cologne. In early June the battle of Midway began and on the seventeenth the British withdrew from Libya leaving Tobruk isolated.

Meanwhile, France struggled with its divisions. In the occupied zone it was forbidden to listen to the BBC or to read newspapers expressing anti-Nazi views. You needed a permit to travel, ration cards to buy food, special passes to cross the demarcation line. Food, fuel and clothing dwindled as the German occupiers commandeered large stocks for themselves.

In the more rural unoccupied zone the population fared little better. Working through the puppet government at Vichy, the Germans ensured that they creamed off a large percentage of French produce for their own people. Farmers and small-holders suffered. Encouraged by the German security forces, the Vichy police hunted down 'terrorists' and 'subversives' and co-operated in draconian anti-Jewish policies.

Resistance grew, slowly, throughout the country. Underground journals circulated. Anti-Nazi posters appeared on walls overnight. *Passeurs* organised movement over the demarcation line. A flourishing black market traded in food, medicine and clothes.

In London F-section was informed of the work of the

Gaullist agent 'Rex', whose brief to co-ordinate resistance groups of all political persuasions was yielding results. There was cautious optimism at the news that SOE agents had been instrumental in destroying the biggest dry dock in France at St Nazaire. In June the American equivalent of SOE, the OSS, was set up by 'Wild Bill' Donovan – and a partnership was formed that injected fresh enthusiasm and American vitality into their work. After the setbacks of October 1941 when important F-section agents had been arrested and the circuit Autogiro had collapsed, new circuits were emerging. Among them Chestnut, Prosper, Monkeypuzzle, Detective, Prunus, Scientist and Pimento.

At Château Belle-Place the Astronomer circuit was taking shape. Recruiting was painfully slow, for security reasons. Suitable fields were marked as dropping grounds, barns, out-buildings and woods as arms caches. Transport was organised, *boîtes aux lettres* set up and safe houses arranged.

It was exhausting, dangerous work requiring dogged persistence, tact and rigid secrecy. The Astronomer team spent long hours in cafés and houses. Ostensibly passing the time of day, they were alert for the clues that indicated the speaker might be safe to approach. They chose members who moved around because of their work: taxi drivers, insurance agents and people such as *croquetiers* – pelt collectors – who needed to visit homes regularly. They employed people with influence: the local priest, lawyers, midwives, policemen, doctors and landowners.

Evelyn knew what she wanted. Security above everything. There was to be no repetition of the Merrygoround disaster. Her circuit was to be built from cells consisting of five or six members. Each cell elected a leader who reported to Evelyn. None of the cells would ever contact each other. Each agreed on separate weapons dumps, dropping grounds and forms of transport.

Jack Fuller remained with the circuit. Theo went south in his place to Toulouse. The reason: a violent and unexpected personality clash between John and Theo. 'He irritates me, Violette,' said Theo. 'He's a security risk in my opinion. Far too casual.' Reluctantly, Evelyn arranged for Jack to remain.

John teased her unmercifully. 'You promised me, you know— '

'Promised what?'

'Never to become too bossy. And look at you, a natural autocrat.' He adjusted his face into mournful folds. 'And I thought you were such a nice girl, too.'

Smiling, Evelyn looked up from the accounts she kept on a piece of folded paper hidden in the floorboards. Despite the bravado, John looked worn and anxious and she tried to cheer him. 'I thought you would appreciate the challenge of a powerful woman.'

'Certainly, *mein Führer*.'

She returned to the accounts which always failed to tally. Each penny she spent on travel expenses, oiling contacts, paying forgers, required accounting for to home base . . .

'Listen, Evelyn,' said Bessy. 'Can't we recruit Guy?'

Evelyn sighed. 'No, I don't think so.'

'Why ever not? You've made Sister Hélène a sleeper. Why not my brother?'

'There would be too many of us under the same roof.' Evelyn had anticipated Bessy's question. 'What happens if either one of you is taken?' Bessy picked up the baby's toys from the floor of the Blue Salon.

'You've changed, Evie. This work's made you harder.'

'Wiser, Bessy. Please understand I couldn't rely on his silence if you were taken by the Gestapo.'

Bessy winced.

Security was not easy to enforce among the housewives, schoolteachers, civil servants and farm workers who were approached and recruited. How could one prevent gossip at a Sunday meal or in a lover's bed, hints being dropped between business partners, friends or spouses? Evelyn feared leakages through fear and envy but most of all through the corrosive effect of constant anxiety. But she also knew that trust, the trust she and Charles had worked with, had to be there.

On 21 June 1942 Tobruk fell to Rommel.

CHAPTER NINE

Mariette sat in the waiting room of the *mairie*. The summons conveyed by Werner had ordered her to come in for questioning at nine o'clock on 10 June.

She was frightened, and her fear had paralysed her ability to think, and left her blundering up a mental *cul-de-sac*.

Mariette placed a hand on her bulging stomach. The baby was giving her trouble today. Perhaps she had eaten something bad? More likely it was nerves. It was lying right down in her pelvis in a way that neither Jeannette nor Jacques had ever done.

A German baby.

Jeannette was very excited about the idea of having a brother or a sister; even Jacques pointed at her stomach and articulated, *'Bébé'*. Mariette was neither excited nor pleased. She hated it.

She had begged Werner to be careful from the first time he visited the cottage way back in January. He had assured her with promises – and this is where it had landed her. Pregnant and the butt of local gossip. With a bit of luck, no one will guess who the father is, thought Mariette. She always insisted that he hide his motorcycle – his precious, pampered motorcycle – on the other side of the demarcation line.

She shifted on the bench and reluctantly faced facts. Sooner or later someone would be bound to find out, she supposed. Mariette persuaded herself that she did not care what the townspeople thought of her: give them two kids and a house to run on nothing and they'd soon be clamouring for a bit of comfort. Werner had been generous. He'd amused the children, brought them food they hadn't seen in years and kept her bed warm. Where was the sin in that, for God's sake?

Having a baby, though, weakened your defences, stripped a layer off the surface. It left you weepy and longing for comfort. But at the root of her depression lay the terror of being left on her own and that she didn't want to have any more secrets.

If only she hadn't got pregnant. A baby in return for a lump of ham and a wedge of cheese. More work. More worry. More stretching of her paltry income. Werner Schwarz promised to give Mariette money for the child but she did not intend to rely on his promises. Why should she? One day he'd be off home, back to his faithful Gertrude or Heidi. Then what?

I've grown used to Werner, she thought, easing a swollen foot out of its shoe. He was kind and a generous lover. True, he spent too much time polishing that dratted motorcycle and he often bored her with his attempts to convert her to the worship of Adolf Hitler and his Nazi Party but Mariette ignored all that nonsense. What she liked was Werner telling her about his life in Germany and of his home near Hanover.

Drink would make him talkative and then he would describe the forests of his homeland, full of beech, linden, silver birch, elm and ash. He told her how the foresters kept *Kindergarten* for the young trees and how beeches were felled in November and oaks early in the new year. He told her about the animals that roamed wild in the woods and regaled her with stories that he had been told as a child, stories that had been passed down by generations of foresters. He told her, too, about the hiking trips he took with his brothers on which they had huge picnics of pumpernickel, cheese and beer. Mariette would watch Jeannette's attentive little face and Werner's big, bony hands as they arranged and rearranged the things on the table as he talked and a shutter would open onto another world.

'We eat good breakfasts at home,' he said, the morning after they had shared a bottle of Pineau and sat up late. Jeannette sat on his knee. 'Boiled eggs, tomatoes, ham, sausages, cheese. We eat it off wooden boards.'

She glanced up at the clock on the wall of the waiting room. Nine thirty. She had been kept waiting for half an hour. Why she had been asked to come, Mariette had no idea, and she cursed the baby once again for making her mind so thick and sluggish.

A man and a woman entered the room. Through the open door, Mariette caught sight of the corridor outside packed with clerks and soldiers. The couple sat down on a bench beside Mariette and whispered to each other. The woman had evidently been crying and the man had his arm round her, trying to comfort her. Mariette could see that they were nervous. She watched the woman twisting her handkerchief round and round her fingers. Round and round.

She glanced down at her lap. How she hated this baby. Hated and resented it. A corporal (Mariette recognised the same number of stripes on the sleeve as on Werner's model army tunic) called her name and beckoned to her. She got up, leaving the worried couple staring after her, and was shown into the office of Major von Hoch. The door closed behind her. Mariette hovered uncertainly. The room was more informal than she had expected. There were books on a shelf, a vase of roses, which were shedding their petals on a table, photographs of a substantial house with battlements by a river and the enticing aroma of coffee.

Paul was collating reports on resistance activity drawn up by the garrison's intelligence officer with the help of information from *Abwehr* listening-in posts. They confirmed an illegal wireless transmitter operating in the Ribérac area. He got to his feet and came towards her. 'Come in.'

He was an authoritarian-looking figure in his tunic and breeches. He wore long riding boots and a leather belt, and his peaked cap lay on the chair he indicated. Mariette picked it up and placed it on the edge of the desk. Paul poured a cup of coffee from a jug which stood on his desk. 'Would you like a cup, Madame?' Mariette accepted with alacrity and hoped her hand would not shake.

'Cigarette?'

'Can I keep it for later?' she asked. The strong coffee made her feel faint but it was delicious.

Paul handed her the packet of cigarettes. 'Keep it, we have plenty.'

I'll bet you do, thought Mariette, and tried to look grateful.

Paul returned behind his desk and sat down. For a moment he said nothing; he was learning to understand the value of silence. He scribbled an amendment in the margin of a report. If there was an illegal wireless set operating in the area the listening-in stations would need to pinpoint it by the process called triangulation – a system which, in this case, would involve the stations at Paris, Bordeaux and Augsburg.

Meanwhile, the Château Belle-Place had already been earmarked as a likely site for illegal wireless transmission, and Corporal Schwarz's confession that he was sleeping with a French girl who sometimes went up to the *château* gave Paul the toehold that he required to investigate the activity at Belle-Place without causing alarm.

At last he spoke. 'Your baby, Madame. When is it due?'

Mariette's mouth pursed in unconscious distaste. 'September, I think. I'm not quite sure.'

Paul looked over at Major Blumberg's calendar depicting an idealised winter scene in the Bavarian alps. 'I see. It is now June. Do you have everything you need?'

Mariette stiffened. 'That's my business,' she said. 'Why, are you offering anything?'

'Perhaps.' Paul made a quick note. 'Have you ever been employed at the Château Belle-Place?'

'On and off. I sometimes help out.' Mariette was baffled.

'How well do you know the household?'

'My mother worked there for some years and the cook is a friend of mine.'

'Do you know Mademoiselle Liegaux?'

'No.' Mariette fixed her gaze on the jug of coffee. 'I think she's some relation of the Count although nobody had ever heard of her before she arrived.'

'I see.' Paul sifted the implications that slithered into his mind. He changed tack. 'Madame Maisson,' he said gently. 'You can be quite open with me. I am not recording this interview. Corporal Schwarz has told me about your friendship.' Mariette eased her seriously strained cotton dress. 'He works for me, you know,' Paul continued, 'and, to a certain extent, I am responsible for him. He's very young.'

Paul's manner disarmed Mariette. 'He's old enough to do what men like doing.'

He looked at her stomach and at her puffy ankles. 'Yes, indeed.' He poured some more coffee into her cup and as he was handing it back said, 'Your baby, Madame, is German. How do you think your fellow countrymen will feel about that?'

Mariette reached for a cigarette out of the packet he had given her. She rolled it between her fingers. 'It's none of their business.'

'Of course, but they will want to make it their business. It doesn't take much to start gossip in this town, as I'm sure you know.'

Mariette smiled artfully. 'It needn't be his, you know.'

'My dear Madame, it doesn't matter who the father of your baby is once it becomes known that you have been entertaining a German in your home.'

She flicked ash into the saucer where it soaked into a slop of coffee, and quickly took another drag. 'What do you want, Monsieur?' She had heard what some of the men were promising to do to women who slept with Germans once the war was over. Paul opened a drawer in the desk and took out a roll of notes. He placed it in front of Mariette.

'It's quite simple. I want information.' Paul did not believe in outright blackmail and reckoned shrewdly that paid information was more reliable.

Mariette couldn't take her eyes off the francs. A big fat roll of them sitting on the desktop. There must be thousands in that roll. 'What sort of information?' she asked, mesmerised.

'Nothing too difficult.' Paul almost felt sorry for the girl. 'Find a way to go up to the *château* regularly. Find out who visits it and why. What does the Countess do? Who are her friends?'

He watched a variety of expressions pass over her face. Fear. Cunning. Self-interest. She seemed riveted by the money and he pushed it closer to her. 'Have you a good doctor?'

'They cost money.'

'We could see to it that you are looked after.'

The francs were right in front of her. She could take them by merely stretching out a hand.

'Do you need time to think about it?' he asked.

She looked up. 'You want me to spy for you. In return you pay me?'

'The money in return for information and your silence on the subject. Both. Is that clear?' Paul paused. 'And all you have to do is tell Corporal Schwarz what you know. I give you my word that no one else will know of our arrangement.'

She considered. Good. A new dress. A lipstick, maybe. A shawl for the baby. She knew perfectly well that to say yes made her an informer. When she was a child, Father André told her the story of Judas and how he betrayed Jesus. At the time, it had meant nothing. Mariette stubbed out her cigarette defiantly. Judas did not have two fatherless children, a lazy mother and a war to contend with.

'All right,' she said, thinking that maybe she would get away with betraying very little, and put out her hand.

'Good,' said Paul and handed her the notes. 'If anyone asks why you were here,' he helped Mariette to her feet, 'just say we were examining your papers.'

Mariette took a long time getting home. The morning bus had left by the time she emerged from the *mairie* and with a groan she began the walk back. At the crossroads by the river she was fortunate enough to cadge a lift from a farmer with a horse-driven cart full of vegetables. It bumped and jolted her up the hill to Bertric-Burée.

The weather had been very warm but now it was becoming uncomfortably hot. Mariette dismounted, sank down onto the grass verge, already turning brown from the sun, and massaged her throbbing ankles. Bees buzzed around a clump of wild sweet pea and the cicadas made their ceaseless, drowsy noise. The bell sounded at St Euphonie's. Mariette watched a nun mount the rise and pedal hard towards her on a bicycle. As the nun approached, Mariette was treated to a glimpse of a much-darned black stocking, and was slightly surprised to see so much of a nun exposed to view.

'It's Mariette Maisson, isn't it?' Sister Hélène braked. 'I saw your mother today at the clinic.'

'Yes,' said Mariette in a low voice. She didn't want to have to talk to anyone at the moment. Hélène took in the swollen stomach; so it was true then. She laid her bicycle on the verge and knelt down by the pregnant girl. 'My dear,' she said. 'Are you in trouble? Can I help?'

Mariette put her hand in her pockets and felt the roll of francs. 'No,' she said rudely, guilty and ashamed in the face of such kindness. 'I'm fine.'

Hélène looked down at Mariette. The girl was so young, so wounded and so at the mercy of events that it hurt her to see it. She remembered herself at the same age, her feelings of isolation and insecurity, and saw them reflected in the sulky face on the verge. And Mariette was in trouble, however hard she denied it. 'If you come up to the convent I can give you a salve for those mouth sores of yours.' Hélène tipped Mariette's chin up gently and examined the ulcers at the corner of her mouth. 'Are you eating enough vegetables?' Mariette nodded. Hélène noticed that the girl was in danger of splitting her dress. 'I have a store of clothes which I keep for patients. Maybe you would like to come and choose something?' She added hastily as Mariette directed a disconcertingly intense pair of eyes on her, 'They are only old clothes, I'm afraid.'

In fact, Mariette had been indulging in a little daydream of buying a scarlet dress on the black market. 'If you like,' she said to Hélène.

Mariette levered herself upright with the help of the nun's proffered arm and picked up her basket, her stomach jutted out, large and full. Hélène noted the characteristic pregnancy marks on the girl's cheeks, the distended belly button underneath the thin cotton dress and the full, pale mouth. She was completely unprepared for the violent twinge of jealousy she experienced.

Shocked at herself, Hélène retrieved her bicycle. 'My dear,' she said, neglecting to choose her words with her usual care, 'who is the father? Can he help?'

Mariette shrugged, but appeared a little less sullen. 'No . . . thank you.'

'Promise me that you will come and see me if you need

anything,' said Hélène, getting onto her bicycle, and Mariette wondered why the sister was taking her predicament so seriously. Reluctantly, she relinquished all thoughts of the scarlet dress for the time being.

'Yes, *ma soeur*, thank you,' she called out after Hélène.

Mariette started to trudge home. Any thoughts of the devil's bargain she had struck with Paul were firmly pigeon-holed in the don't-think-about-it category. It was a category she had often found useful. Instead, she thought about the money.

The niggle in her back that had been bothering her earlier returned – a fist hitting sharply on her spine. To her relief, as she rounded a corner and the cottage came into view, it subsided.

A troop convoy passed her on the road, sending a cloud of dust into her face. The soldiers called out something, in German. Mariette didn't imagine it was complimentary. She gestured back.

Once in her own kitchen Mariette dropped the basket and eased herself into a wooden chair and a more serious pain squeezed the small of her back. As she suspected, her mother was in a bad mood at being left alone for so long. 'Where've you been? Drinking in the Café Mas, I'll bet.'

Mariette screwed up her face. 'Never you mind. Have the children had their meal?'

'Of course.' Her mother banged the saucepans down on the stove as a way of making her protest felt. 'Fine time to leave me to cope with everything with my visit to the clinic this morning . . . Fine time to get yourself in the straw,' she added under her breath. 'Of all the stupid things . . .'

Mariette looked at the black-clad back with dislike. She had heard it all before, many, many times. 'Can't you stop making such a noise?' she said. 'It's going straight through my head.'

Her mother banged down another pot and Mariette groaned. The older woman turned. 'Are you all right? You look a bit odd to me.'

Mariette had thrown herself back in the chair and arched her back. As the spasm took a grip the two women caught each other's eyes. 'Oh, God,' said Mariette.

'Get upstairs,' said her mother, and started to fill the kettle from the bucket.

Much later, Mariette opened her eyes and saw that Jeannette was standing by the bed with Jacques in her arms. They were staring at their mother with tear stains on their cheeks. Mariette made an enormous effort to smile. 'Hello,' she said. 'I'm fine. Don't worry. Now you go downstairs and play. I'll be all right.'

Mariette watched them leave the room before she closed her eyes. The moments of relief between the contractions grew shorter and she imagined she was floating up by the ceiling, looking down at the sweating, restless figure on the bed. She supposed she could be dead. The idea quite appealed to her. If she was dead she would never have to worry about anything again. Death meant peace. Then she remembered she had a roll of francs to spend.

When she opened her eyes next, her mother was bending over her with a wet cloth, which she placed on Mariette's forehead. 'Easy now,' she said, pushing back the damp hair from Mariette's face. 'It won't be long.'

'It's much too early,' said Mariette.

'I know.'

It had grown dark and the oil lamp was turned down very low in the corner. It was a kind, soft light. The mother hovered over her daughter, the two women united by childbirth in a way they seldom were every day.

'Listen, Mother,' said Mariette during a lull in the contractions. 'It won't live and that's a good thing.'

'We'll see,' said the older woman.

Mariette was right. The baby was too premature to survive. Her mother put the child into her arms. He was tiny and bluish, with thin, stick-like arms and a preternaturally wise expression on his face. Despite everything, Mariette loved him on sight. The baby tried to cry but the effort was too great. Instead he gave a mewing sound. His minute hands clawed the air for a moment and then he lay still. She stroked his face with her finger and waited to feel relief. None came.

Her mother took the baby from Mariette, wrapped it in a

small piece of sheeting, and laid it on the chest of drawers. 'I'll bury it in the morning,' she said. 'Try to sleep.' She turned off the lamp and left Mariette in darkness.

Mariette lay listening to her mother moving around downstairs. She stared into the darkness. Her hands explored her empty, jelly-like stomach. Only a short while ago, he had been in there, she told herself. Her face screwed up with the effort not to cry. I can't let him go, she thought.

She raised herself up on the pillows and eased her legs over the side of the bed. The cotton wadding between them made it difficult to move, but with difficulty she was able to scoop up the limp, awkward bundle. She got back into bed, uncovered the face of her dead son and held him until she fell asleep. When she awoke the next morning, the baby had gone.

The children were outside in the lane and she could hear the rhythmic thuds of digging in the garden.

After a while there was silence.

Mariette found herself grasping the edge of the sheet while tears pushed their way down her face.

CHAPTER TEN

It was hot and thunder flies were out in force. Jack Pickford sat under a chestnut tree at one end of a field, assaulted by humidity and the sickly smell of cow parsley. Evelyn was stretched out beside him with a piece of grass between her lips. Her eyes were closed. They had left Brossac, where they had been recruiting, and were due to return to home territory cross-country. In keeping with their cover as representatives of a pharmaceutical firm, Jack was in a suit and Evelyn was dressed in a borrowed tan linen skirt with a loose, short-sleeved jacket. Her arms were brown and she wore a painted wooden bracelet to match her earrings. Tiny drops of moisture beaded her upper lip and sprinkled down her neck, and her hair had worked loose from its combs. She looked very peaceful.

'Are you OK?' Jack asked.

He sounded tired and dispirited. Evelyn lazily opened one eye and then shut it again. She sympathised. After months of heightened tension back home, training and preparing to go in, the day-to-day plod which was an intrinsic part of being in the field could be depressing. The six months since he had arrived had alternated between bouts of frantic activity and long periods of lying low and doing very little. Holed up in cheap hotels and safe houses, constantly on the move, the main relief an occasional conversation in a bar, fatigue and loneliness could hover, vulture-like, over one's spirits. Yesterday she and Jack had cycled forty kilometres and her palms had blistered badly. Today they must have clocked-up thirty-five. They spent one night in a cheap hotel where they dined off indifferent food and a second in a safe house close to Guîtres, where they slept on a wooden floor wrapped in musty blankets. 'Surely', people asked them everywhere they went, 'the Allies will invade in 1943?' Who was to know?

Evelyn flexed her right knee; it was twingeing and she was worried that she had strained it. If she couldn't ride a bicycle, they were in trouble. She made an effort to block out everything but the warmth of the sun on her face and the smells of high summer.

'I really should come with you,' Evelyn argued when they were planning the trip. 'It's difficult when you're not French to get under the skin of the people. It's what's left unsaid that's almost impossible for a foreigner to gauge. Do you know what I mean?' She picked her way carefully around Jack's ego. 'I think we should break the rule about being seen together for once.' To her surprise, Jack had not disagreed.

Evelyn pulled up another piece of grass to suck. The fleshy bit at the end of the stalk flattened between her teeth and the taste evoked the times she had lain in the grass at home and planned to escape from her father and the monotony of the farm.

Jack rummaged in his saddle-bag for a piece of sausage he had saved. He unwrapped it, cut off a slice and offered it to Evelyn. She ate sleepily. The last few days had gone well. Jack was proving a good colleague. Where she had imagined he might be curt and bad-tempered, he had been patient and equable. Where she had anticipated taciturnity and humourlessness there was neither. Instead, although he was rough and unsentimental when necessary, he displayed a wry humour and on occasion he was unexpectedly thoughtful. Evelyn knew he was making an effort to smooth away the memory of their previous encounters.

'Do you think French attitudes to the occupation are changing?' When they met, Jack would often ask Evelyn's opinion of the people about whom – he was only just beginning to realise – he knew very little.

'Hard to say, but I think they may be, yes.'

'It's the fence-sitters I find hard to understand. They know what occupation means by now.'

Evelyn gave him one of her smiles. 'I don't think I can

283

judge, Jack. Families are put at risk and the politics are so complicated.'

She sat up and pulled a bit of paper and a pencil out of her pocket. 'Operation Michelin. We must start to plan it.' She began to sketch out a map with quick, light strokes. 'Here's the road leading up from Ribérac. So.' Leaning on her knees she drew the factory situated on the steepest bit of the hill above the town, overlooking it, and a track running east-west along the top of a cliff situated behind the factory buildings.

Jack said, 'Right. What about our contact?'

'Our contact inside tells us that the factory supplies tyres and spare parts for German army vehicles. The owner has also been persuaded to set up a section to manufacture tyre treads for the Panzer tanks. Apparently, the Germans are planning to transport plant from factories in the Ruhr.'

'The objective, then, is to wait until the new plant is in place and then blow the factory. Do we know when it's due to arrive?'

'Some time during the next few weeks.'

'Can we approach the owner for information?'

'No. Apparently he is happy to co-operate with the Germans.'

'What about threatening him?'

'I think not.' Evelyn considered. 'We can't ignore the possibility he might inform on us.'

Jack studied Evelyn's map. 'We need to infiltrate the workforce with some of our men. Afterwards, they can disappear.' He lit a cigarette. 'That should shield the workers from reprisals. Any candidates?'

'You've heard about the *réfractaires*?' Evelyn retrieved the map, lit one end with Jack's lighter and watched it burn.

'Yes, local gossip is full of them.' Jack was referring to the men who lived rough in the countryside in order to avoid being called up to work as factory labour in Germany.

'Jean-Claude is in touch with a couple. They might be prepared to help.'

Evelyn lay down again. Jack wrapped up the remains of the sausage and put it into his pocket. 'Good idea.' He flopped backwards onto the grass, undid the buttons of his shirt and wiped the sweat off his forehead with a hand. 'Briefing will have to be faultless.' He squinted at Evelyn lying relaxed in a patch of sun, oblivious of him and a longing to be normal for five minutes swept over him. Just to be close and intimate with another person. He did not like to disturb her peace, but Jack had a need to talk. 'Do you ever wish you had never taken on this work?'

'No,' Evelyn murmured. She was going over the plan for Operation Michelin in her head and she did not give Jack's question her full attention.

Jack rolled over on the grass towards Evelyn. Surprised, she opened her eyes. 'You were so nervous at that first interview,' he told her. 'I was sorry afterwards I'd been so unpleasant.'

'I'm afraid I didn't take an immediate liking to you,' Evelyn said, eyes still closed, sweeping her hand through the grass. 'Still, I made up for it that time in the Underground.'

'Yes, I remember. You were damn rude to a senior officer.' Jack flashed her a grin and rolled even closer.

Evelyn sat up. 'Phew. It's too hot.' She brushed at the grass in her hair and looked down at the figure lying on his stomach beside her. 'I've often wondered why you decided to come into the field.'

Jack propped his chin on his arms and scrutinised worker ants filing in and out of an ants' nest. 'Someone I knew died.'

He seemed a much lonelier and less confident figure than the one she knew. Evelyn's sympathy stirred. 'I'm sorry.'

'I was wrong about you.' Jack reached up and trapped one of Evelyn's hands. 'You're much tougher than I imagined.' He looked at the blistered palm. 'Inside, that is.'

Uncomfortable, Evelyn withdrew her hand. 'Your friend that died. Was he or she special?'

'Very,' he replied curtly and dropped his chin onto his forearms. He did not like the mental picture he had of Daniel lying pell-mell with all the other bodies in a rotting ship on the ocean bed. *Bones stripped clean.* 'Very,' he said again.

This was a new side of Jack and Evelyn was silent for a moment. 'Why don't you light a candle in the church at

285

Bertric-Burée?' It was a lame attempt at comfort but it was better than nothing, and she felt she owed it to him to try.

'I could.' Jack managed a grin. 'Don't worry about it. I'm fine.'

With an effort he sat up. 'There's an ant on your neck.' He leant over to brush it off and, as he did so, Evelyn's brassière strap slipped from under her sleeve down a brown arm. Both of them looked at it and Jack swallowed. Then he reached out and gently tucked it back under her sleeve. They stared at each other until Jack dropped his hand.

Evelyn hid her embarrassment. 'Operation Michelin,' she said quickly. 'We must set the date.'

Jack turned away and did up his shirt. 'I hope we're going to have enough time to brief and train the men.'

Evelyn stood up and began to pack her bicycle basket. 'I just hope it's worth it.'

'What do you mean?'

'I'm worried about the risk to life.'

Jack tied his briefcase onto the back of his bicycle with a piece of cord. 'All we can do is try our best to minimise it. We must do our job, Violette.'

Her old irritation flared up, unjustly she knew, and she was sorry for it. She leant on her bicycle while he finished and tried to suppress it. It was up to her to make their partnership work. 'Is that parachute cord?' she asked suddenly.

'Yuh. I had nothing else.'

'You must get rid of it. The Germans look for that sort of thing. Jean-Claude told me.'

Jack swung his leg over his bicycle and set off over the grass. 'Sure,' he agreed. But his voice held a decided edge.

'*Bonjour*.' Guy called out of his studio window at Belle-Place.

'*Bonjour*.' Evelyn waved.

For a few seconds, Guy watched her as she disappeared round the back of the house, and then he returned to his painting. She was very interesting, this reserved young woman. More interesting, he was prepared to bet, than she let on.

He had just returned from a two-week painting trip in

Beynac. ('And a good thing too,' Bessy confided to Evelyn. 'Guy's been driving me mad with his schemes for doing up the place.') He had collared Evelyn the previous evening in the hall and asked her if she would pose for him. 'You demand to be captured on canvas,' he told her. 'A green-eyed nymph. Untouched, of course.' Provoking, amusing, inquisitive and insistent, it was impossible to be angry with Guy.

If he was going to put her on the spot, then she was going to retaliate in kind. 'Are you going to join up, Guy?' she asked quietly. 'After all, America's in the war now.'

Guy looked at Evelyn as if he had not heard right. 'You don't imagine I'm going to fight, do you? My dear earnest Mademoiselle, I like my skin and I'd like to preserve it intact, if at all possible. Besides,' Guy pushed one of his recent Dordogne landscapes in front of Evelyn, 'you wouldn't want me to risk damaging my hands, would you? I might get frostbite or even a bullet in them.'

Hypnotised by his cheek, Evelyn looked at the painting. It was of a castle perched on a breathtakingly high rock-face above the sleepy, shiny Dordogne, underneath an intense blue sky. Guy had caught the light and drama of the scene so well that she almost cried out. 'It's good,' he said, and she had to agree.

Guy was in the room Bessy allocated him for a studio. Despite the warm weather the room, with its thick stone walls, was chilly and he rubbed his hands together to restore the circulation. Why Charles's first wife had chosen ice-blue curtains and white paint for a room that never saw the sun, he could not comprehend. Guy spent a couple of satisfying minutes mentally refurbishing the room in soft pinks and yellows, adding one of his own paintings – a summer scene – over the fireplace.

Evelyn definitely intrigued him. That was why he asked her to sit for him. He anticipated the satisfaction of working in the warm olive skin tones and dark browns of her hair. He picked up a pencil and started a preliminary sketch. He was hoping to catch Evelyn in a reflective mood so that he could highlight the mix of shyness and determination in her expression.

Sex was a fascinating business and Guy was something of an authority on the subject – not so much on the crude mechanics as on the mystique that one could weave around the act. Undoubtedly, the secret of successful seduction lay in the planning. First plant the idea in a woman's mind – the more unwilling and surprised the better. Allow the notion to germinate – this could take twenty-four hours, alternatively, it had been known to take a year. If she was young, curiosity often did the trick. If she was older, nagging doubts about her vanishing sex appeal might well prove persuasive. Time and time again, Guy had waited for a woman with the patience born of experience and the capitulation, orchestrated to perfection, was always thoroughly satisfactory to both parties. Of course, the problem then was to prevent any complications arising from his grateful victim falling in love with him.

The pencil point travelled along the outline of Evelyn's mouth and stopped. Guy couldn't deny that Mademoiselle Liegaux was not exactly responsive to him and that piqued him. Not that he overwhelmingly desired her – his taste ran to the more glamorous and buxom – but her indifference posed a challenge. Guy was also a trifle suspicious. Considering she was the secretary to the *château*'s wine business, she was away a great deal. Guy drained the wine in the glass by his elbow. Women repaid study – some more than others, of course. He picked up his brush again, thought for a moment, and gave in to an amusing and malicious impulse.

When he had finished the room felt even chillier and he wanted his lunch. He stood and assessed the drawing and, with a shrug, took down the canvas and stacked it against the wall.

There was no one in the dining room downstairs, and the table was not laid. Intending to forage, Guy made his way downstairs.

The kitchen was a large whitewashed room with a larder, a wash room and a drying room leading off it. Guy had only visited it a couple of times. He poured himself some of Marie's home-made lemonade and, glass in hand, explored the rooms. The layout appeared to be original, as was a stone bowl set into the wall and the fireplace. He had discovered the larder

288

and was pondering the merits of rabbit pâté when voices alerted him. Clutching a bottle of wine, he wandered back into the kitchen.

When she saw him Marie gave a little shriek. 'Monsieur.'

'You don't mind, I hope?' Guy was at his most charming. 'I wanted lunch.'

'Oh, I will see to it at once,' said Marie. 'Madame de Bourgrave said that no one would be in today. Please wait a minute. I will bring it to you in the dining room.'

'Don't bother,' said Guy. 'I enjoy slumming it sometimes.' He turned to Marie's companion. 'Do we know each other?'

The girl looked up from the eggs she was transferring from her basket into the egg rack. 'Mariette Maisson,' she said quickly. 'I live near here.'

'Really.' Guy searched for a corkscrew and glasses in the drawer. 'Now why haven't I seen you before?'

'I don't know, Monsieur, I come up here quite a lot.' Mariette lifted the egg rack onto the sideboard. She was dressed in a bright red cotton dress and white thick soled shoes and her full skirt swirled as she turned.

Guy's attention pricked. He pushed a glass of wine towards her. 'How nice to have someone as pretty as you in the *château*.' She quivered visibly at the compliment – as Guy had suspected she might. He accepted the plate of ham and endive salad that Marie put in front of him and invited Mariette to keep him company. After a quick look at the scandalised Marie, Mariette did as she was told.

'I am Guy Maier. I'm working on the late Count's library,' Guy explained through mouthfuls.

'Yes, I know,' she said. 'Marie told me about you.' Mariette drank the wine. 'Are you foreign, Monsieur?'

Guy frowned. 'If you mean my accent is a little strange, I was brought up in Canada but I am French.'

Mariette finished her wine while she digested the information. Guy was aware that the girl was staring at him with barely concealed interest. As he did not want any more awkward questions, Guy went into the attack. 'I'm a painter you know. Now tell me, where are the best views around here?

I've walked around quite a lot, but there may be some places I've missed.'

The girl blinked at him and he saw that she had nice hazel eyes, surrounded by thick brown eyelashes. 'Would you like to model for me?'

'Monsieur!' Mariette dropped her gaze to the table.

Guy glanced up from the ham speared onto his fork. 'I'm not asking you to take your clothes off,' he said matter-of-factly, fully aware of the implications of this suggestion. 'You can if you wish, of course.'

This one is easy prey, he thought to himself. Mariette made the mistake of allowing Guy to refill her wine glass. Nothing was said, but a message was sent and received across the table. Muzzy and elated, Mariette abandoned any loyalties she might have had towards Werner Schwarz (he hadn't been to see her for . . . well, since before the baby) and she wanted this man so badly it almost hurt. She was captivated by the assurance that his well-cut clothes exuded, the ease and arrogance of his manner, the suggestion of a life she thought was beyond her grasp.

'Yes, I'll model for you,' she replied.

Guy laid down his knife and fork. 'The role appeals to you, then? Well, let's not waste time. You can try it out after lunch.'

A little later, Guy led Mariette (who was struggling with a sense that none of this was happening) towards one of the fields that lay above the *château*. In a daze, Mariette followed him, her dress brushing through the undergrowth in a scarlet swirl.

The grass in the hidden dip that Guy found feathered above them in a lazy response to the breeze. It sent restless shadows onto their bodies. Late poppies burned in the dry green and gold and the blue flax winked at the sky. Except for the sunburn on his neck and arms, Guy's skin was white and very smooth. He smelt of fresh sweat and cologne and, as he lay on top of her, she fell in love with his body's freshness and cleanness.

'Where have you been hiding all this time?' Guy was regretting what he was doing. On closer inspection, Mariette did not attract him. Her body was pleasant enough but slack and unhealthy and she had a faintly peppery odour. He willed himself to continue.

Not long afterwards, Mariette lay beside him on the grass, her chin resting on her arms and her long eyelashes closed. The sun dried the sweat on her back and warmed her bare buttocks.

It had happened. A man, better than she had ever imagined, had come to change her life. Mariette stretched out her legs and her toes tangled lazily in the grass, the stems brushing the soles of her feet. A golden haze drifted behind her closed eyes, and for the first time in years she felt her longings quieten and her body become peaceful.

Wanting to touch him again, she stretched out a hand to Guy, but he rolled away, sat up and began to pull on his trousers. He got dressed quickly and bent to pull a reluctant Mariette to her feet. 'Time to get going,' he said briskly, and looked at his watch.

She obeyed him – and a doubt squirmed into her mind. 'When do you want us to meet again?' she asked. 'It's easy to arrange. My mother can always look after the children for an hour or so.' She pulled her dress over her head.

Guy avoided the naked appeal in Mariette's eyes. 'Some time, perhaps.' He sounded casual. 'I'm very busy.'

His dismissive tone killed her happiness and she knew he had made a fool of her. She bent to do up her shabby cork sandals, her red dress pooling on the ground. 'This didn't mean anything to you, then?'

'My dear girl. How could it?'

Mariette looked straight at Guy and his eyes shifted away. 'You're a bastard!' she said suddenly.

Guy was taken aback by Mariette's response and liked her better for it. 'Well done.' He smiled patronisingly. 'You never know, we might get to know each other better after all.'

Mariette flicked him an unfathomable look. 'No, thank you, Monsieur.' She reckoned that if she was quick she could get away from this man before she burst into tears of rage and disappointment. So she picked up her basket, turned and walked away without another word.

Guy shaded his eyes against the sun and watched Mariette's

progress across the field, the scarlet of her dress matching the poppies. It made quite a nice composition, he thought: 'Peasant Girl Leaving her Lover'. Then he straightened his jacket and whistling an aria from *Don Giovanni*, made his way back to the *château*.

In Berlin on the same afternoon, Ingrid sat down to write to Paul.

'Yesterday was awful, I had a letter from Aunt Hilda in Cologne. She lost her home in a bombing raid and on top of that Trudi her dachshund was killed. She's in a terrible state and I'm arranging for her to go home to Silberbirchen. Judging from your letters – I wish you'd write more often, Paul – it sounds much more peaceful in France.'

Thank God, Paul was in the comparative safety of France. Only last week Manfred von Essen had gone down in his plane. 'Putzi' Hollonsernin had been killed on the Eastern Front, and in today's paper there was an announcement that Hans Burkhardt and Gunther von Lupke had died *für Führer und Vaterland*.

'When are you coming home, Paul? You must be able to get some leave soon. I want to talk to you about something I've heard . . .'

The phone rang in the hall. Ingrid put down her pen and went to answer it.

'Is that the very beautiful Ingrid Sturmbakker?'

'Siegfried.' Ingrid tucked the receiver under her chin and pulled a chair towards her with her foot. 'Why are you phoning?'

Gehrbrandt was unusually direct. 'I thought you would like to know that your beloved hero will be coming back to Berlin. Recalled for questioning.'

'Questioning?' Ingrid sank into the chair. 'Why?'

'His father has been arrested for possible subversion. And Paul has been ordered by Admiral Canaris to return to Berlin for obvious reasons.'

'How do you know?' Ingrid felt the blood draining from her hands and feet.

Gehrbrandt hesitated. He had just returned from a meeting

292

in the Tirpitzufer where he and his new boss in the SD, SS Brigadeführer Schellenberg, had confronted *Abwehr* chiefs. The SD accused the *Abwehr* of incompetence, an accusation based on the *Abwehr* having failed to discover the correct number of Russian divisions ranged against German and treason. The SD it appeared, had picked up hints from their underground contacts that the *Abwehr* was rife with anti-Nazism. Greatly to Gehrbrandt's satisfaction, one of the names under suspicion was Paul von Hoch's.

'Answer me, Siegfried. How do you know?' Ingrid sounded panicked.

Gehrbrandt relaxed a little further into his armchair. 'I'll tell you if you come to the cinema tonight. I have tickets for *Die Grosse Liebe*.' He enjoyed the pause at the other end of the line. He knew Ingrid wanted to see the film, which starred the popular Swedish actress Zarah Leander. 'Come on, Ingrid. Dinner afterwards.'

'All right.' Ingrid was too anxious to expend the energy on saying no. 'Will you come and collect me?'

She put down the receiver, returned to the bedroom and sat down rather shakily on the camp bed. Why on earth had Graf von Hoch been so foolish? How like him to put his family at risk. Ingrid began to take out her hairpins and thought savagely: Graf von Hoch should have learnt to keep his mouth shut like everyone else.

The camp bed creaked underneath her. At least, Ingrid often reflected, it was a bed of sorts. These days not everyone had one. She pulled up her skirt, released the stockings and began to roll them carefully down her legs one at a time. Paul was coming back! But under what threat? Ingrid needed to think about it.

If Ingrid was absolutely truthful with herself – which she was not always – she had grown used to Paul's absence. In fact, she sometimes thought that it was something of a relief. With Paul, Ingrid needed to deploy all her energies to make herself beautiful and desirable. She needed wit, cunning and determination. Just now, those qualities were all used up in the exhausting, unpredictable business of everyday life and she had none left over.

Of course she never hinted as much in her letters. She never told him how frightened she was when the Allied bombers turned the sky into a spitting, blazing hell. Nor of her panic when she tried to find her way to work along a street which was no longer there.

The flat in the Rauchstrasse with its rose-silk lampshades had gone, disintegrating like a huge pink peony crumpling in the sun. With a roar and a hiss the fire had taken hold, the entire apartment block vanished and with it most of Ingrid's possessions. Along with much of Berlin, her home was reduced to drifts of ash and rubble, the remnants of a burnt-out past.

A friend who had abandoned Berlin for the country had offered her the use of this flat and Ingrid accepted and was proud of herself for making do. Unlike her friend, she held on to her job at the foreign ministry and resisted her parents' entreaties to go home to Silberbirchen, feeling that it would be cowardly to leave.

She bent over the mirror and ran her fingers through her hair. Ingrid did not want Paul to see her with grimy hair, laddered stockings and unpressed clothes. She did not want him to see her sallow skin and hollow eyes. She did not want him to see her when she was less than perfect. Pushing back her hair from her temples, Ingrid studied her face for wrinkles. For a moment she imagined she detected the beginning of a crow's foot in the corner of her right eye and bent closer to the mirror. Her fingers stroked her cheeks, pale from fractured sleep and indifferent food. Enough. She let her hair fall back and turned away from the dissatisfying image in the glass.

Thinking about Paul was not a good idea. Ingrid sighed. She knew she should take his advice: forget him and marry Siegfried.

A crack snaked diagonally up the wall. One of the window panes had shattered in the explosion when a bomb fell in the next street. But there was hot water. Ingrid went into the bathroom and turned on the tap. The water was discoloured and came in a trickle, and she was too tired to stop herself from thinking, uselessly, of the deep, jasmine-scented baths she used to take for granted. She shook the towel free of the dust that slicked over everything these days, put it on the chair and got into the bath. If her face was ageing, her body was still good, the skin white and her breasts round and soft. Leni Soltmann had told Ingrid about exercises that made your ankles thinner and, obedient to Leni's instructions, she lifted her leg out of the water and twirled her foot.

After a moment, Ingrid dropped her leg back into the water. She put her wet hands up to her face and began to cry.

CHAPTER ELEVEN

Two men let themselves into Henri's bicycle shop. Ten minutes later two more slipped in through the side entrance as another sauntered along the street, stopping to look through the shop window at the bicycles inside, and decided to enter. Lastly, Evelyn wheeled her bicycle along the street and disappeared up an alley beside the shop. It was twelve noon on 20 July 1942.

In the room above the shop the men were already talking and smoking when Evelyn got there – John, Pierre, Jean-Claude and the two new recruits for Operation Michelin, the brothers Nicolas and Martin Richard. The latter came from near Vauxains where they and their father struggled to farm land parcelled into tiny fields on a small acreage between the woods and the main road.

Dressed in baggy trousers and black jackets, they had very short hair and sunburnt necks. Nicolas, the younger, cracked jokes and puffed furiously at cigarettes. His older brother, Martin, appeared more taciturn and thoughtful.

The men were making inroads into a bottle of *marc* and Evelyn sat down at the table around which they were sitting. She half-heartedly told them to stop drinking until after the briefing and her request was greeted with derision. John informed Evelyn that if she wished to join a temperance society that was her affair. Then he relented. 'Pressures of office, darling. I understand.'

She grinned up at him from the message she was drafting. 'And not much evidence of the red carpet treatment either,' she said and wondered what the Frenchman thought of the incomprehensible English. She held out the message to John.

He read it and then burnt it with a match. 'Got it.'

'We'll see you later, then.'

'No, Violette, I'm not missing the big bang.'

'Olivier.' Evelyn was not sure whether John was serious or not. 'You know you can't.'

'You need all the people you can get.' That was true. 'I'll make a bargain with you, chief, I won't go into the factory. I'll act as cover.' He stuffed his hands into the pockets of his worn jacket. 'I need a change, darling. All work and no play is making me a dull boy.' The lines that ran between John's nose and chin were more pronounced these days and the fair skin, under the orange freckles, was loose and pallid. Evelyn knew John was tired. Tired from hours of coding and decoding, from the nerve-fraying job of transmitting, from the business of transporting the set from safe house to safe house every few days. From loneliness.

There was a quiet knock at the door and a voice gave the password: '*Après moi le déluge.*' Pierre moved behind the door and took his revolver from his pocket.

Covered in grey-white dust from the road, Jack entered and pulled off his beret. He opened a carpenter's bag and extracted a dismantled Sten. 'I'll get on, if you don't mind.' He held up the barrel and spoke to the men. 'Calibre: 9 millimetre. *Voilà. Ici se trouve le refroidisseur. Ici le cran de sureté et puis le bouton de tire coup par coup.*' His audience gathered round, except for Pierre who would use his own gun. Evelyn allowed herself to drift. Rigorous and a good teacher, Jack was utterly absorbed in his task. Was he as single-minded as the persona he projected? As she thought, Jack looked up and caught her eye.

'Plastic explosive', she heard him say, 'is relatively inert. It won't explode if struck by a rifle or a bullet. To do so, it requires a detonator.' He held up a pencil detonator. 'The detonator is colour-coded. When it is in place you must press this ridge here – don't forget. It releases acid which controls the spring. Then clear out.'

The atmosphere was thick with cigarette smoke and Evelyn wished she could open the window. She checked her watch. 'Fifteen more minutes,' she told the men.

Jack continued. 'Violette and I have already cut the explosive into blocks and wrapped them in sacking. Each man will

297

carry one block.' He took a piece of paper out of his pocket and for the umpteenth time drew on it a plan of the factory and its surroundings. 'This is the factory lay-out.' He jabbed his finger down on the paper. 'We are aiming to destroy this section in particular. I will lay the explosive. Pierre, I want you to put the generator out of action . . . here. Our contact in the factory informs us that although there is a constant guard outside, the factory itself is not well protected. We have managed to obtain a duplicate key to the generating room and the door to the assembly area is only fastened by padlock. The rest of you will provide cover from the outside. Jean-Claude and Martin will be providing a diversion if necessary. They'll be stationed here, on the east side where the wall has collapsed a little.'

Evelyn took up from there. 'There are four guards on duty for a period of four hours each. Their reliefs spend their off-duty hours in the guard room. Here.' She held up Jack's map. 'It's ten yards or so from the main gate. It has a window facing the approach road. They change over at eight, twelve and four o'clock. The factory itself is surrounded by a brick wall approximately three metres high, and the guards patrol it in pairs. It's too high to scale in the time, so we'll have to take advantage of the short period when the front gates are unguarded. We'll be springing the break in just before the midnight changeover.' She paused and the men remained silent. 'There's one weak spot – access is a problem. The obvious approaches are so heavily wooded we couldn't get the van within two kilometres.'

Pierre pushed himself upright from the wall. 'We use the cliff,' he said impassively. 'I know a path down it. It's danger-ous, but the Boches won't have found it, that's for sure. There's a track within a few metres of the top.'

'I'm not scrambling down any cliff.' Martin Richard evidently did not like the idea.

Nicolas squared up to his brother. 'Getting too old, are we?'

Martin's eyebrows drew together. 'Why you little— '

'Shut up,' Evelyn advised Nicolas. His cockiness deflated, he subsided into silence.

Jack was dismantling the Sten. 'All I ask is that we don't give the Boches a bit of easy target practice.'

John shuddered in an exaggerated way. Jean-Claude was leaning against a wall smoking. He made no comment.

'It's the best idea we could come up with,' said Evelyn. 'The Boches will assume we've used the road. The cliff path should give us a ten-minute lead or so.'

Suddenly the hot, sleepy room was full of movement and talk. Jack held up his hand for silence and repeated the briefing until everyone was quite clear as to their part.

'And what about me?' John fixed Evelyn with an uncharacteristically hard stare.

'You win.' Evelyn slipped her arm through his. 'You can provide cover with me. We certainly need an extra man.'

'Good.' John's smile under jaded eyes was particularly sweet and affectionate.

'In return, I want you to drop a letter into the convent to warn our contact there it is possible we may be needing supplies. The password is "Have you a refill for a petrol lighter?" '

The men slipped out of the house in ones and twos into the hot afternoon. The scorching weather had been settled in for over a week now. The days dawned in a wreath of chiffon mist which disappeared as the sun burned it away. In the afternoons, dry air rolled down the valley in hot, dusty waves. It shrivelled vegetables growing in allotments and turned the wrought-iron work in Ribérac so hot you could not touch it. Downing bottle after bottle of wine, the men in the fields became flushed with alcohol and black-clad women slipped sideways on their chairs as they dozed outside their doors.

After the meeting Jean-Claude drove to Renée Legrand's cottage where he changed the number plate from a stock he had hidden there. Renée let him in and together they went upstairs. Renée lay back naked on the heavy liven sheet given to her many years ago by her mother-in-law and watched Jean-Claude's buttocks with a mixture of amusement and affection. A photo of the deceased Madame Legrand gazed down sternly on their white fleshy bodies.

'You must be up to something,' Renée murmured at last. 'I can always tell.'

Jean-Claude raised his head. The hairs on his chest were shiny with sweat, and the big shoulders sheened with damp. 'None of your business, my girl.'

Renée wriggled underneath him. 'Why do you do it, *mon cher ami*? What's in it for you?'

Jean-Claude traced a prominent blue vein across her breast. 'It might not have occurred to you, my dear, but one day the Nazis will have gone. Then I wish to live with a clear conscience.'

'You mean,' Renée slapped his finger away, 'you want to make quite sure you're seen to be on the winning side so that you can be Mr Big round here when the war is over.'

'I can't stand women who try to be clever,' he said lazily. 'It doesn't suit you, Renée.'

The woman laughed good-naturedly and performed one of her little muscular tricks which always got Jean-Claude going.

'Don't, he said. 'I need my strength.'

She disengaged herself and reached for a glass of water. 'Have you noticed that none of the fat cats stir themselves to get rid of the Nazis? It's always the ordinary people.' She lay down again and pulled him over her. 'One of these days you are going to get caught,' she said seriously. 'Please be careful.'

Jean-Claude said, 'I'll shoot myself before they take me.' and placed his hand on her round, full bottom. Renée was quiet.

As the sun went down, the air cooled rapidly, promising more mist. Evelyn and Jack worked hard throughout the afternoon distributing guns and making contact with the look-outs posted inside the factory. They reported normal activity. The German plant was in place but not yet operational.

Two incidents occurred during the late afternoon. First, a German soldier demanded a lift from the van ferrying guns. It would have been madness to refuse him. The soldier sat in the back with his legs hanging over the tailboard and leant for support against the boxes in which the Stens were hidden. He was quiet and seemed preoccupied and glad of the rest.

Each time he shifted against the boxes, Evelyn had to close her eyes.

John had a close shave too. He was transmitting up at La Cavalière, a remote farmhouse set well back from the road. To his horror, a detachment of armed soldiers filed along the road towards the house just as he was finishing the transmission. He tapped in the final letter of the group with his right hand and reached for his Colt with his left, praying that the aerial – hidden under the wall creeper outside the window – was completely out of sight.

Madame Séguis, the owner of the farm, rose bravely to the occasion. She rushed into the garden and berated the officer in charge for trespassing on her property. They were disturbing her bees and the honey would be ruined. Such was her presence that the German officer apologised, promising never to cross her land again. Sweating like a pig, John listened in some awe to Madame Séguis's performance. Afterwards the two shared a glass of brandy and the fraught Madame Séguis burst into tears and John tried to distract her by telling her that her performance was worthy of Sarah Bernhardt in her prime. It was not far from the truth.

After distributing the guns, Evelyn cycled back to Belle-Place, exhausted. She ran a bath in Bessy's bathroom. Every muscle was aching from a combination of tension and exertion and her hair was thick with white, gritty dust. She shook bits of gravel into the water and they sank to the bottom.

Evelyn was completely submerged when Bessy came in, shut the door and sat down in the wicker chair by the window. Evelyn sat up and slicked back her hair so that it streamed in a wet sheet down her back. She grabbed a flannel to wipe the soap from her eyes. In a blue linen dress, Bessy looked cool and neat. She had taken to pulling her hair back from her face and the effect was to accentuate the peachy skin and strong features. Bessy had recovered her health and strength and her energy and inventiveness seemed boundless. Her capacity for organisation was unrivalled in Evelyn's experience. Everything – from the baby's nappies and the number of eggs used in the kitchen to wine labels and business letters – was ruthlessly marshalled, inventoried and managed. It was

Bessy's idea to put small red lights into the charcoal burners on the van in order to give the impression that they were using charcoal instead of petrol which had been secretly stockpiled. It was Bessy who was keeping the *château's* wine business running and who had procured a pile of dark sweaters, black trousers and black berets for use by the circuit members on night operations.

'I'd love a cigarette,' Evelyn said in English. Bessy felt in her pocket and opened an almost empty packet. 'God knows where we will get the next lot from. Monsieur in my favourite *tabac* told me he could no longer sell me any under the counter as the men came first.' She flicked the packet with her finger. 'I'll have to find another source.'

'I'll get you some from the next *parachutage*.' Evelyn soaped between her toes. 'Hasn't Guy got any?'

'He says he needs them all himself.' Bessy blew a stream of smoke up to the ceiling and leant over the bath to give Evelyn a puff. 'You know, Evie, I still think we should get Guy to work for us.'

'Bessy, we agreed!' Evelyn sounded sharper than she intended. Bessy reached for a china saucer off the window ledge which she used as an ashtray. She looked thoughtful. 'Don't you like him?'

'Of course I like him,' Evelyn said, standing up and reaching for a towel. 'You know the reasons.'

'Then it's not Guy who's making you lose so much weight.' Bessy contemplated Evelyn's hip bones jutting through the reddened skin.

'No, Detective Pinkerton.' Evelyn wrapped her towel around her and stepped out of the bath. Bessy's accuracy was a little unnerving.

Evelyn had not seen Paul von Hoch since the night of the concert, but the more time elapsed, the more obsessively she thought about him. Her appetite had gone, too, but this she attributed to the strain of her work. She wrapped a second towel round her head.

'Sorry,' said Bessy. 'I didn't mean to pry. Here let me help.' She towelled Evelyn's increasingly sharp shoulder blades. 'Don't get too thin, honey.' She reached for the powder puff and dusted talcum powder over the white back. 'It's just . . . I'm very fond of Guy. Of course, I know he's got his faults.' She patted Evelyn's shoulder with the powder puff. 'Drink and women. And his vanity.'

Evelyn pulled on her knickers and fastened her brassière. 'You make him sound very simple.'

'Most of us are,' said Bessy, 'See you later.'

At eight o'clock both women were ready. Bessy was dressed in a Schiaparelli dinner gown trimmed with sequins, her hair braided into a coronet around her head. She wore bright red lipstick, diamonds in her ears and black high-heeled shoes.

'You'll do,' Evelyn said appreciatively as she packed dark trousers and a black jersey into her rucksack. She had borrowed a dress in midnight blue from Bessy's seemingly endless wardrobe, which she matched with a pair of blue satin shoes. Bessy brushed Evelyn's hair back from her forehead.

'Bessy, do you think I'm pretty?' Evelyn asked the question reluctantly, but she wanted to know.

Bessy took it seriously. 'You are lovely, Evie.' As she spoke she anchored the heavy, dark hair with a pair of diamond-studded combs.

'Bessy!' Evelyn expostulated at her generosity. 'Are they heirlooms?'

'Sort of,' said Bessy. 'But there's nobody left to notice if they go missing.'

It was time to move. 'Torch.' Evelyn checked off the list on her fingers. 'Knife. Map. Charcoal.' She put them into separate rucksack pockets. 'Spare detonators and gun.' These last she hid carefully under the clothes.

'Papers.' Bessy checked their permits.

Evelyn tightened the drawstring on the rucksack, leant over the window sill to check there was no one outside and dropped it with a soft thud into the courtyard below. In the half-light it was barely visible under the wall.

The women turned to each other, both of them paler than usual. On impulse, Evelyn went over to Bessy and hugged her. 'Thank you,' she said. 'Thank you for everything.'

Bessy held Evelyn close for a moment. An intense bitterness

for Charles's death made it difficult for her to speak. 'We must go,' she said.

The two of them descended the stairs and said good night to Gaston, who closed the door behind them. Bessy started the engine of the car and backed up towards the spot where Evelyn's rucksack had fallen. Evelyn retrieved it and stowed it in the back under a rug. She got in beside Bessy.

'*Merde*,' she encouraged. Bessy let out the clutch and the car rolled under the stone arch and down the drive.

Bessy had arranged dinner with her friends the de Livorines as an alibi. It was, as usual, excellent. The de Livorines lived in a manor house on the outskirts of Ribérac in a style which the war had only marginally diminished. Charles used to tease them about their *nouveau* origins. The de Livorines had lived in the area only since the Revolution, whereas the de Bourgraves had been at Belle-Place a hundred years longer.

Dinner was served in the stone hall overlooked by an unfortunate reconstruction of a minstrels' gallery. The de Livorines were charming, cultivated people, anxious to press the best food and wine on Charles's widow and, naturally, they quite understood when Bessy indicated that she was still a little under the weather and needed to retire early.

By eleven o'clock, Bessy was driving through Allemans towards Bertric-Burée. The Hispano turned right up a single track road and then right again onto a much smaller track which could barely accommodate the huge car. The track wound through dense wood to a pond that lay behind a cliff face. It was covered in green scum and was fed by a desultory stream that ran in through a gash in the earth filled with slaty outcrops of rock and tangled tree roots. Evelyn had been there only once before and had disliked the sinister atmosphere. The damp undergrowth by the pond was ochreous brown and the roots of the trees, which pressed right up to the water's edge, could be seen, partly submerged. Trees which had died and fallen into the semi-stagnant water gave off the stench of rotting vegetation.

Bessy drove past the pond, flicking her headlights on from time to time. The track narrowed even further, and she slowed the car to a walking pace. At the point where an oak tree had sent its roots right across the track, she stopped and backed the car so that it faced the way they had come. Evelyn opened her door and got out. She picked up the smell of leaf humus mingled with sharper injections of fox. A wind rustled the top of the trees but the air trapped underneath the canopy was still, damp and uncomfortably warm.

Evelyn took off her satin shoes – even the faintest trace of mud or leaf mould was a potential clue – and put on rope-soled espadrilles. Bessy opened the rucksack and passed Evelyn the clothes inside it. Evelyn took off her evening dress and put on the trousers and the jersey. Then she dabbed at her face with the stick of charcoal and rubbed it quickly into her forehead and cheeks. Last came the beret which she pulled well down. Having assembled the Sten and checked the pencil fuses, she got back into the car to wait.

St John, Evelyn. Born 21 May 1919. Father British. Mother French. Code Name: Alouette. Field Name: Violette. Cover Name: Evelyn Liegaux. Parachuted into the Périgord October 1941. Operated as courier for Merrygoround. Her circuit destroyed, she formed Astronomer and ran it as chef du réseau . . .

At half past eleven, Bessy raised a finger and hissed. There was the sound of a vehicle approaching. 'Someone's coming.' Evelyn let herself out of the car and slipped behind it, holding the Sten ready. Bessy pushed the rug over the rucksack and closed the door gently as Evelyn lifted her head cautiously to look through the back windscreen. The vehicle came into sight and stopped fifty metres from the Hispano. The softly whistled phrase '*Au clair de la lune . . .*' issued from the open driver's window. 'It's them.' Evelyn pursed her lips and whistled in reply, '. . . *Mon ami Pierrot.*'

Shadowy figures jumped down from Jean-Claude's van and pushed it back into the bushes so that it was completely hidden by low branches and undergrowth. One by one the men materialised: shadows with blackened faces, holding weapons which shone dully in the moonlight. Pierre. John. Jean-Claude. Nicolas. Martin. Bringing up the rear, Jack greeted her with a curt nod.

Guns held at the ready, the group fanned out. Evelyn grasped Bessy's hand briefly through the window before heading into the seemingly impenetrable wood between Pierre and John. Bessy gave a thumbs-up to their retreating backs and rolled up the window. She settled herself for the long, anxious wait.

Before they reached the cliff edge, Pierre told the group to drop onto their stomachs. They squirmed forward out of the tree cover into an open stretch three metres wide lit by moonlight. The factory below appeared bigger than in daylight and the thud of the sentries' boots in the yard was clearly audible to the group spreadeagled on the cliff top.

'Move sideways,' Pierre instructed them calmly. 'Don't try to go straight down. The path's too narrow and steep.' As agreed, he went down first, moving slowly but confidently. Sliding occasionally, Evelyn followed and, carrying parcels of explosive strapped to their waists, the men fell in line behind her.

'For Christ's sake,' she heard John mutter under his breath as a stone plummeted down the cliff. Its noise seemed deafening.

They panted with the effort of keeping a steady foothold on the scree, Evelyn's breathing sounded noisily in her ears. Sweat ran down her back and under the waistband of her trousers. As she descended she grabbed hold of exposed roots offering precarious support. Gradually, the tortuous descent levelled and Evelyn was able to jump down onto a scrubby patch of grass that fringed the base of the cliff. A thick beech hedge formed a barrier between them and the factory wall.

'All here?' she asked, as the last man jumped from the rock face and the group assembled in the shadow of the hedge.

Within the minute the six men and one woman were through a gap in the hedge and making their way to their stations, two of them zigzagging around the back of the factory to the west wall, the rest filing in the opposite direction towards the main gates.

CHAPTER TWELVE

Jack crouched down at the south-east corner of the compound and waited for Pierre to join him. The two men merged into the shadow thrown by the wall. Behind them, Evelyn, John and Nicolas dashed one at a time towards the sentries' hut, dodging behind a pile of tyres for refuge half-way across the open space. Reaching their objective, they flattened themselves against its blind wall. Nicolas was trembling and John touched him reassuringly on the shoulder. 'Calm down,' he mouthed, and tried to forget that his own guts felt as if they were dissolving.

Eleven fifty-six . . . four minutes to change-over time.

Pierre and Jack at the factory wall were the first to hear the four sentries preparing to end their shift.

'Main building clear?'

'All correct,' came the answer.

'Generator?'

'Clear.'

'Final circuit and then a drink.'

I wanted to do this, thought Jack, trying to calm his breathing, and wondered for a split second what Daniel would have made of this calculated flirtation with death.

The senior guard unlocked the wrought-iron gates, let himself and his colleagues out and padlocked them behind him with a rattle of chains. They split and disappeared in opposite directions around the wall to make a final inspection. One pair, chatting desultorily as they rounded the corner, came within a metre of Jack and Pierre crouching motionless in the shadows.

As soon as they were at a safe distance, the two *résistants* sprinted towards the main gates. Pierre caught hold of the chain and steadied the gates while Jack scaled them monkey fashion. From her vantage point behind the hut, Evelyn watched the dark shape shinning up the ironwork. 'Go on,' she willed it. Jack was already half-way up. Any minute now the relief detachment would emerge from the hut.

'*Achtung*!' A shout rang out. It came from one of the guards who had stepped outside the hut to urinate. He spotted Jack trapped on the gate like an insect on a fly paper. Reaching for the gun slung over his shoulder he let off a round of bullets which spattered the gate. His aim was wild and he missed Jack, who for an instant had frozen. Whether it was the scream of bullets hitting metal or Pierre's urgent, 'Get down!' which galvanised him into action, Jack did not wait to find out. He let go and dropped the two metres to the ground. With a thud, he landed beside Pierre. Both men fell to their knees and let off a round of bullets, catching the sentry in the chest. He staggered and fell.

'Go back,' Evelyn ordered John and Nicolas. 'I've got to deal with the telephone.'

On the opposite wall, Martin and Jean-Claude heard the commotion and began diversionary fire, to which the guards on the perimeter inspection retaliated. Evelyn slid round the wall of the hut as three guards charged down the wooden steps, one of them with his feet only half into his boots. John shot him from behind a pile of empty petrol drums and he died instantly. His companions were dispatched equally quickly as Jack and Pierre picked them off.

Evelyn leapt up the steps and into the hut. Inside – a mess of coffee cups, cards, papers and rumpled camp bed – the telephone was ringing. Evelyn yanked the cord out of the wall but whoever was at the other end would certainly know by now that something was wrong.

She jumped down the steps, stopped to pull a gun from the hand of one of the dead soldiers, bent double and zigzagged towards the cover of the petrol drums.

John and Nicolas had reached the south-east corner and ducked into the shadows. At that moment a pair from the first detachment of sentries rounded the far corner at a run. Nicolas, beside himself with fear, let out an audible whimper, and for a split second the four men were face to face. John aimed his Sten. A burst of gunfire and both sentries sprawled forward, their guns clattering to the ground. Pierre, whose quick action had saved their lives, stepped from the inadequate protection of a sapling at the north-east corner of the compound and beckoned them on.

Of all bloody times to have an hysterical adolescent on my hands . . . thought John. 'Follow me,' he whispered. 'Don't run in a straight line.' He reached into the shadows and pulled the cowering Nicolas towards him by his jacket. 'Bloody get going,' he ordered, and jabbed the barrel of his gun into the boy's stomach. 'Otherwise I'll have to shoot you.' He had played the seedy mobster several times in repertory and managed, even to his own ears, to sound convincing.

With a sharp intake of breath, Nicolas did what he was told. The two men ran full tilt past the dead sentries, round the north-east corner and headed for the gap in the hedge. The sound of vehicles approaching at speed came from the direction of the main road.

To the clatter of Jean-Claude's and Martin's retreating fire, the group, Evelyn with them, fought their way through the thick, tangled branches which threatened to drag the guns out of their hands.

'Jesu!' Nicolas threw himself fruitlessly at the cliff face. Pierre pulled him back.

'This way, you fool.'

Evelyn scrambled after Pierre and searched for a foothold on the rock. John and Jack offered cover until Evelyn had gained enough purchase and then turned to start their own ascent. A final salvo from Jean-Claude and Martin and they too were making for the cliff face.

'Scatter at the top.'

Without warning, Nicolas swivelled round on the path and let off a round of bullets at the ground below.

'You stupid— ' Jack jerked down the barrel of Nicolas's gun. 'You've given away our position!'

As he said the words, a detachment of soldiers were racing around to the back of the compound, shouting to others to follow. A burst of gunfire exploded on the cliff face.

Evelyn stretched up to grasp a dangling root just out of

reach. 'Go on, Violette.' Jack pushed her from behind, giving her the few extra centimetres she needed. She lunged at the root and heaved herself up, the soles of her espadrilles ripping as her feet scrabbled for a foothold.

Pierre stopped, levered his back against the rockface and aimed at the soldiers below. The hedge obscured his sights and he was forced to wait until the first soldier emerged into his line of fire. Pausing only long enough to see the man fling away his gun with the force of the impact, as a bullet lodged in his stomach, Pierre set off again. His knowledge of the path and poacher's agility meant that he was some way ahead of the others.

A second soldier swerved past the body of his companion, dropped to his knees and shot uncertainly into the dark. Evelyn tucked her foot behind a firm outcrop of rock, steadied her aim and returned fire. As she did so a volley of bullets hit the rockface and ricocheted off at all angles. She ducked. *'All I ask is that we don't give the Boches a bit of easy target practice.'* Jack had been proved right. Then she took aim once again, fired, and the German soldier, a small figure several metres below, clutched his arm and fell sideways.

'Good girl.' Jack had caught up. In reply, Evelyn placed a finger on her lips and pointed downwards. A contingent of about six soldiers milled at the foot of the cliff. The man Evelyn had wounded shouted at his colleagues.

'They haven't found the path,' she whispered.

More booted feet pounded towards the cliff, and they started to climb again. The sound of men was accompanied by a crescendo of barking, as dogs, released from their chains, hurled themselves through the beech hedge. *'Peste.* The dogs will be onto our scent.' Pierre's voice came from above.

The Alsatians bayed and dropped their noses. With a clatter of paws against rock, the leader detected their scent and sprang up the path. There was a sharp command from its trainer as he hacked his way through the hedge. 'Away, Stukka, get 'em.'

There was no time to deal with fear. Like hunted animals, the imperative was to get up the cliff and away. Fingers and faces were ripped and scratched. Clothes tore on jagged stones. Lungs sucked in great draughts of warm air and blew them out inefficiently. A fusillade of bullets interrupted the shouting below and all the time there echoed the baying of the pursuing dogs.

Anxious to make up for his cowardice, Nicolas turned, took aim and fired in the direction of the dogs. There was a howling whine and a moment's unnerving silence. Then a second dog took up the cry.

Another burst of gunfire. Nicolas groaned, tottered and fell forward. His gun plummeted down the cliff, bouncing off rocks and starting a cascade of scree. With one arm Jack grabbed at the youth to prevent him sliding back down the path. Then he felt for his pulse. 'He's dead,' he said aloud.

Pierre, who had slithered down to help, hoisted the body over his shoulder. 'Can't leave him for the Boches. They'd get his family.' Sure-footed as ever, he resumed the climb.

They were not out of range yet. Bullets raked across the cliff face within centimetres of the scrambling, breathless group, and shouts and the scuttering of pebbles indicated that the soldiers were well on their way up the cliff path behind the dogs.

John had continued to climb when Nicolas fell. There was nothing he could do to help the boy. His head down, he could hear Evelyn up ahead. Suddenly he gave a cry of pain as his weak ankle wrenched and twisted on a loose piece of rock that gave way under him.

'What is it?' Evelyn scrambled down to him.

'It's my ankle. The bad one. Don't worry. *Go on.*' John spoke through waves of sickening pain. He swayed, grabbed at the cliff face and breathed deeply in an effort not to faint. The noise of the dogs swirled through the fuzz in his head.

'Get up, Olivier.' Evelyn shook John and slapped him hard across the face. 'Open your eyes. We'll help you.'

John did his best to return from the dark, weightless place into which he was floating. Arms were being hooked under his shoulders and the smell of warm wool as bodies pressed against his pushed up his nostrils.

'Nearly there,' Evelyn gasped. She pulled herself over the top. When she and Jack had manhandled John up onto the cliff edge he lay retching with pain. Pierre emerged from under the cliff with Nicolas's body and disappeared without a word into the trees.

'Leave me!' John was almost incoherent.

Jack said, 'Don't waste your breath.'

Shooting intensified below. The cacophony of shouts and barking grew more distinct and Evelyn could make out the rasp of boot studs against rock.

'Leave me,' John repeated faintly. 'You know the rules.'

'Listen.' Evelyn brought her face close to his, but she kept her gun trained on the cliff edge. She knew perfectly well it was against the rules but she was not leaving John to the Nazis. The stubbornness that had seen her through training and the nurturing of Astronomer asserted itself. 'I'm not leaving you.'

'Keep down!' Jack had an acute mental picture of being picked off at the top of the cliff.

Evelyn put an arm around John. 'Try. Please.'

'Of course I'll bloody try.'

They crawled towards the cover of the trees. Evelyn reached it first and collapsed face down, heaving long breaths of dry leaf mould.

They were far from sanctuary. 'Get up!' Evelyn tugged at John's hand.

'I'll stay with him,' said Jack. 'You go. You're the chief.'

Evelyn glanced back towards the cliff edge and then through the wood to where Bessy would be waiting. 'OK.' Bending down in a swift movement, she cupped John's white face in her hands. 'Don't you dare give up.'

Jack put an arm round John's waist and hooked his right arm round his own neck. Then he pulled the injured wireless operator upright. Evelyn swung her Sten over her shoulder. 'Go to St Euphonie's,' she told them. 'Ask for the infirmary sister and use the password.'

Then she was running as hard as she could away from the two men, pounding over the springy mass of leaves, brambles, fallen branches and mossed roots.

As soon as she saw Evelyn, Bessy started up the engine. She was trembling so hard it took her two attempts and she had to struggle to get the car into first gear. 'Come on, Bessy,' she urged herself. The Hispano was moving forward as Evelyn drew level, pulled open the door and fell inside. Bessy put down the accelerator and they began to bump down the track. 'Boches!' Evelyn was panting so hard she could only manage the one word. It was quite sufficient.

Bessy pressed her foot down harder. 'The others?'

'Pierre got away,' Evelyn managed to get out. 'Jean-Claude and Martin I don't know. The other two . . .' She rubbed the sweat drops out of her eyes. The other two.

'Tell me later.' Bessy concentrated on steering the car, neck so tense that the tendons stood out.

Using side lights only, she drove as fast as she dared back past the stagnant pool and along the track. Her eyes were now attuned to night light, but she was forced to swerve violently once or twice to avoid driving off the track altogether.

Evelyn dismantled the Sten and put the pieces into the rucksack. She pulled off her beret and jersey and wriggled with difficulty out of her trousers. Taking a pot of cold cream from Bessy's bag she rubbed it into her black sweat-streaked face and wiped it off with a handkerchief which she stuffed into a pocket of the rucksack. Then she squirmed into her evening dress, kicking off her espadrilles and wriggling her feet back into the high heels. She packed the trousers, jersey and dusty espadrilles into the rucksack and hid the Sten among the folds.

At the turning onto the single track road, Bessy slowed right down. Evelyn opened the car door and dropped down onto the verge. Two days previously, she had made a hiding place here from an old drainage pipe lying in the ditch. Into this she stuffed the rucksack, and picking up the branches she had left for the purpose she threw them over the opening.

'Go through the cover story,' she said to Bessy when she got back into the car. She pulled at the strands of hair that had worked loose and patted them back into place. 'I've lost a comb.'

'Never mind. We can't go back to look for it now,' said Bessie grimly. She went over their alibi. 'We were dining with

313

the de Livorines and left reasonably early. On the way home, the Hispano broke down and we have only just got it started again.'

Evelyn's handbag was in the glove compartment. Evelyn retrieved it and searched for her lipstick. Using a hand against the dashboard to steady herself, she smeared it over her lips. 'One, two, three,' she incanted, and took her time to rub the top and bottom lips together.

'What?' Bessy slowed the car down for a corner.

'It's a technique for calming the nerves.' Evelyn dropped the lipstick back into her handbag and shut it, then pulled at the bodice of her dress and adjusted a twisted sleeve. 'I shouldn't have got you involved in all this, Bessy.'

Bessy switched on the car headlights. 'I chose it, remember?' she replied.

The powerful headlights of the Hispano seemed to narrow the world down to a beam of yellow light whispering between a hedge on their right and an open field to their left. Evelyn thought of baby Charles lying pale and open-mouthed in sleep in his crib and knew that Charles would never have forgiven her.

'Four,' said Bessy. She turned to look at Evelyn. 'Keep counting. There's a patrol blocking the road.' She braked and the car came to a halt in front of a couple of soldiers from the *Feldgendarmerie* pointing businesslike weapons in their direction. Bessy gave a quick glance at Evelyn, wound down the window and smiled sweetly at the approaching men. 'Evelyn, there's some charcoal on your chin.'

Evelyn opened her handbag, got out her mirror and fussed at her face. She continued to do so while the Germans asked Bessy what she was doing out after curfew and why.

'*Il faut retourner à Ribérac, Madame*. At once, *schnell*.' The German officer's French was bad but good enough to make it quite clear that, whatever the reason the ladies were abroad at this time, all vehicles had to go to Ribérac for an immediate check. He confiscated their identity cards, took the number of the Hispano and walked back to his jeep. There the two women watched as he made a radio call. His companion, meanwhile, mounted an armed guard over them. When the

Feldwebel returned he spoke to Bessy through the driver's window, ordering them to report to the *mairie* where they were expected. Their identity cards would be returned tomorrow.

Ever afterwards Evelyn remembered that strange drive to Ribérac. Operation Michelin had been a catastrophe. One of her team was dead. In all probability the circuit was burned and there was a good chance that Jack and John had been taken. Anaesthetised by the events of the last few hours, Evelyn felt nothing.

The courtyard of the *mairie* was alive with men and vehicles arriving and departing. Orders were being shouted, doors slammed, trucks being revved and over it the intimidating sound of several pairs of heavy boots running at speed. As they drove in, a troop carrier full of soldiers accelerated past them.

Inside, the women were told to sit and wait on a bench in a room blazing with electric light. They sat and listened to the activity in the corridor, to terse conversations being conducted in undertones and the insistent ringing of telephones.

They sat in silence. 'The baby,' Bessy said at last, as if she had only just absorbed the implications of their predicament.

Evelyn took her hand. 'Don't panic, Bessy. We'll be fine.'

Bessy returned the pressure of Evelyn's fingers. 'I was thinking about my childhood at Great Neck, and about Bridget, my nursemaid. Vienna, where I saw what could happen in the world. And here . . . My father often talked about his great-grandfather who sat it out with General Washington at Valley Forge when most of the men died of cold and dysentery. I come from a family of fighters and rebels, Evie, but God knows, if it's at the price of your husband or son—'

'Bessy, not here. Later. Concentrate on the cover story.' Evelyn watched the door, expecting it to open at any minute.

Concentrate instead on night interrogation at Wanborough.

'Get up.' The encounter with cold air as blankets are ripped away from your body. Torches blazing cruelly into your sleep-sodden face. Hustled in the dark through the stone-flagged kitchen. 'Don't talk.' Down to the cellars with their stone pillars and deathly chill.

315

'Who are you?' Shadows lunging at you across the floor. Faceless shapes with upraised hands. The paralysing sting as they hit you. 'Talk.' The menace of the night outside the leaded windows above your head. A groan that you don't recognise as your own as they push you into the tiny game larder. Door slams. The long, aching, white-with-cold wait until they let you out and Jim or Ned or Robin apologises for having to do such things.

Paul looked up as a corporal showed the women into his office. Evelyn stood beside the Countess, her evening bag tucked under one arm, her hair falling onto her shoulders and her eyes brilliant with some emotion. Paul pushed his hands into his tunic pockets, stabbed by a sudden anger. If he had held any illusions about Evelyn Liegaux, he had been misled. She was no innocent.

It looked as though she was something far more complicated. Paul knew that to work in the resistance – if indeed she was a *résistante* – required special qualities, not the courage of the open battlefield but a less flamboyant and more profound commitment. But, if this was true, she also possessed something that stirred him even more than her courage: a cause for which she was prepared to risk her life. He envied that.

'Good evening, Madame de Bourgrave, Mademoiselle Liegaux,' said Paul. 'Will you kindly tell me what you were doing out so late?' Bessy started to relate the cover story fluently and convincingly. Her voice was quite steady and Evelyn blessed her.

'I see,' said Paul, injecting just enough scepticism into his tone to demonstrate that the interview would not be plain sailing. 'You understand that I will have to check your story. Would you be so kind as to give me the telephone number of your host?'

Bessy searched her bag and read out the number from her address book. 'Mademoiselle Liegaux was your companion?'

'Yes.'

Paul used reasonably gentle interrogation tactics. 'What time did you arrive? What time did you sit down to supper?

316

What were you given to eat? Whom did you sit next to at the dining table? When did you leave . . . ?'

'About eleven o'clock.'

'Are you aware there is a curfew?'

'Perhaps,' said Bessy. 'We felt it would be impolite to leave earlier.'

Paul's gaze fixed on Evelyn. 'What caused the car to break down?'

She shrugged. 'Major, I am no car mechanic. It could have been the fuel pump – it has caused problems before. The Hispano is an old car.'

'What did you do after failing to get it started?'

'We sat inside. There was little else we could do. We were both tired and fell asleep. When Madame la comtesse woke up she tried to start the engine again and it did.'

'Can you show me where you were?' Paul pointed to the map he had spread out on his desk. Careful not to appear too expert, Evelyn turned the map this way and that, as if puzzled by it. Eventually, she put her finger down on one of the roads leading from Ribérac. 'I'm not very good at this sort of thing.'

'I have to agree with you, Mademoiselle. That is not the road you were stopped on.' He changed tack. 'How elegant you both look. I regret I was not present at your dinner. But I wonder why you needed this.'

He opened the top drawer of his desk and produced Evelyn's beret. 'We searched your car.'

'It must be one of my husband's berets,' Bessy improvised. She held out her hand to retrieve it.

'Possibly.' Paul retained the beret. 'But it has been worn quite recently. It is damp with sweat.'

'I think . . .' Bessy put a hand up to her forehead. 'I think I need to sit down . . . I haven't been all that well.'

'Madame!' Evelyn put her arm around Bessy. 'Here, lean on me.' She looked up at Paul. 'Couldn't you let us go? We have nothing to tell you, and the Countess is not in good health.'

Paul rang the bell on his desk and the corporal reappeared in the doorway. 'Show Madame la comtesse back to the waiting room and bring her a cup of coffee.'

317

I tried, said the look Bessy threw Evelyn. Paul watched Bessy's retreating back until the door closed and then turned to face Evelyn. For a second time, he reached inside his drawer. 'This was inside the beret,' he said, and threw a diamond-studded comb onto the desk.

Evelyn stared at it for what seemed like a very long time. In the electric light the stones flashed hard white. Then she picked up the comb and pushed it into her hair. 'Thank you,' she said quietly. 'I thought I had lost it.'

'Evelyn,' Paul began, 'I think – '

The telephone prevented Paul from finishing. It did not matter, Evelyn knew what he was going to say.

'Von Hoch.' These days, Fleischer did not bother to apologise if he interrupted Paul. 'You can send the detainee in to me if you please.' Angry at the interference, Paul replaced the receiver.

'I am afraid you are wanted by Sturmbannführer Fleischer,' he said to Evelyn. 'I must warn you . . .' He hesitated while he selected the right words. 'I must warn you to be careful.'

Evelyn tucked her handbag firmly under her arm and smoothed down the skirt of her dress. 'Thank you, but I have nothing to hide.' She could not help asking, 'Will you be present at the interview?'

Paul shook his head. He came round the desk and put out his hand and touched her on the elbow. She stepped aside. It was more than she could bear. 'You must come with me,' he said.

'Sit down.'

Evelyn recognised Sturmbannführer Fleischer as the man with whom Guy had been talking in the café on the day she collected him. He looked cross and liverish, with dark brown smudges under his eyes and a bilious tinge to his skin. Indeed, Fleischer had been over-indulging in food and wine and was suffering as a consequence. He poured himself a cup of peppermint *tisane* and Evelyn checked the room and estimated her chances if she jumped out of the window. Her eyes widened when she saw the porcelain figures on a side table under the photograph of Adolf Hitler.

'I collect them.' Fleischer followed her gaze. He swirled the *tisane* around the Sèvres cup and crumbled a brioche. 'I am very fond of porcelain.'

Indeed he was. To her certain knowledge, Evelyn was looking at the best examples of French eighteenth-century figurine sculpture – shepherds caressing pink-cheeked shepherdesses, patched beauties flirting with cicisbeos, laughing children playing games of skittles. How many homes had been ransacked for these?'

'Beautiful, aren't they?' Fleischer sipped the scalding tea and waited for it to relieve his indigestion. 'Now. You must answer some questions.'

At Beaulieu Evelyn had memorised enemy uniform, the variety of styles and marking for each rank – collar patches, *Waffenfarben*, gold braiding, the runic flashes. The effect was to make the German army and Nazi security forces take on a sort of glamour, a gruesome fashion parade of shoulder flashes, coloured wrist stripes and emblems, peaked caps heavy with insignia. The reality which faced her was infinitely more banal: a dyspeptic, middle-aged man running to fat, who looked more like an insurance salesman than an officer of the SD. A pair of bloodshot blue eyes met hers. 'You'll take coffee.' Fleischer poured it from a pot on his desk and pushed a cup and saucer towards Evelyn. 'Your car broke down when you were returning from dinner with friends. Am I right?'

Remember the chameleon, said John's voice in her head. Blend. Evelyn gave her story as briefly as she dared. Fleischer's cup chinked against its saucer and he crumbled the brioche into ever smaller fragments. 'What is your job?'

Evelyn told him that she acted as secretary to the Belle-Place wine business.

'Who runs the business now the Count is dead?'

'Madame de Bourgrave.' As she had been taught, Evelyn offered no more information than was strictly necessary.

'Do you like your employer?'

'Yes,' she shrugged, 'but we are not intimate.' So that's his ploy, she thought. She took a mouthful of coffee. It made her head spin. Her trained faculties warned her to be watchful: the interview was going too smoothly. She sensed impending

319

danger. Clang, went a clock in the corner. Clang. Two o'clock. Fleischer sipped his infusion quickly, as if every mouthful contained the stiffening he needed.

Suddenly, he leapt to his feet and threw the contents of Evelyn's cup into her face. She gasped with shock and pain, as its flarepath travelled over her breast, down her stomach and soaked into the top of her stockings. 'Monsieur!'

'Now, give me your reasons for being out after curfew!' Fleischer requested. He rang the bell and gave an order to the soldiers that appeared in the room. 'Tie her hands.'

Evelyn let out a sob. 'Please, please, what have I done?' Fleischer was hoping that his rapid change of tactics would disorientate her so she would let him think that.

The soldiers were efficient and tied her hands to give maximum discomfort. Evelyn arched her spine against the wooden chair back to take the strain. Fleischer took a cigarette from a silver box engraved with a swastika, lit it and passed it to one of the soldiers. 'You know, Mademoiselle, I agree with your friend. He told me you were very pretty when we picked him up earlier this evening. He also told me you were working for him in the resistance.'

'Interrogation methods: they will try and deceive you into believing that someone has talked. It is designed to make you feel angry and hopeless . . .'

On the other hand, how could she tell what had happened to the others? Had any of them talked? Jean-Claude. Surely it would take longer than a couple of hours for him to break? Unless, God forbid, he was in with them. And what about Martin? Was he the weak link? Am I the weak link?

Don't panic. One. Two. Three. Four. Concentrate on my own story. Forget about the others. Evelyn opened her eyes.

Fleischer sauntered over to the side table and picked up a china shepherdess. His eyes followed his forefinger as it ran down the hooped skirt. Then he looked up and nodded at one of the soldiers.

The burning tip of a cigarette was positioned a fraction above Evelyn's cheek. 'Your terrorist friends, Miss Liegaux. Do tell me about them.'

The coffee was turning cold and damp against her skin and

the material of her evening dress moulded to her scalded body. She raised her head carefully and her vision filled with a vapid porcelain face out of which stared impossibly blue eyes. Fleischer was intimidatingly close. He nodded a second time and the cigarette began to move. It travelled down her jawline, dropping fragments of burning ash onto her uncovered neck. It rounded her breast. 'Go on,' urged Fleischer. The cigarette hovered. 'Please don't force me to damage you, Mademoiselle Liegaux.'

Evelyn bit her lips, fighting the fear and disgust. Fleischer replaced the figurine with its companions. His little talks with a fellow officer experienced in interrogation had been useful. (When he first arrived in Ribérac, he had been privately concerned that he wouldn't have the stomach for such an interview. He needn't have worried.) 'Show Mademoiselle what I mean, corporal.'

The soldier holding the cigarette was barely more than a teenager. He obeyed his senior officer and pushed the burning tip of the cigarette into the side of Evelyn's left breast. His nicotine-stained teeth were level with her eyes. The smell of charred silk flowered into the room and a scorched circle reproduced itself behind Evelyn's closed eyelids. She began to sweat, great drops that ran from her temples down the side of her face and neck and into the smouldering dress, and thought, I *must* trust myself.

'Where were you tonight? The truth, this time.'

The corporal relit the cigarette and pointed it at her neck. A lock of hair hissed and shrivelled. The acrid smell curled under Evelyn's nostrils as scorched twists fell into her lap.

'I think you were doing something you had no business to be.' Tears of pain stood in Evelyn's eyes. Deliberately she sobbed again. 'Please. I don't know what you are talking about.'

'All right.' Fleischer gave a signal and the rope around her wrists was liberated. He lit a second cigarette, leant over and stuck it between Evelyn's lips. 'I'm so sorry I had to take extreme measures, Mademoiselle.' She inhaled gratefully, pleased that her hand did not shake as she took the cigarette from her mouth. She was damned if she would give Fleischer the pleasure of watching her rub her breast.

He sat down at his desk and his expression was that of the boy who has come top of his form. It wasn't conviction that spurred on men like the brioche-nibbling Fleischer. She watched him dip a piece into his tea. Men like this were frightened of being rated weaker than their peers. Fear, the fear that every child recognised from the playground, perpetuated barbarity.

She wiped her face. 'Please, have you finished with me, Monsieur?'

'Sturmbannführer, if you please.' He leant back fussily in his chair. 'And no, I have not received a satisfactory answer yet.' He wiped crumbs from the corner of his mouth.

With a weary sigh, Evelyn repeated her story.

'Dear, dear, I thought you had absorbed my lesson.'

'Do you think I'm lying?' Evelyn's tone trailed a nicely judged balance of bewilderment and resentment.

'Mademoiselle, I do not believe in coincidences. There is cause and there is effect. There has been plenty of each tonight.' His eyes slid over to the figurines as he raised a finger. Once more her arms were pulled behind her and she felt the rope lacerate the tender skin at her wrists. Evelyn braced herself. The corporal bent down to pick up the cigarette which she had dropped and held it over her unwounded breast.

'I'll make it easier for you,' said Fleischer. 'You give me the cause and I'll provide the effect.'

'I've told you –' Evelyn jerked out her story for the third time. Her throat was dry and tight and she could not swallow very easily. 'The Countess and I . . .'

The door opened. Calm, but pale with anger, Paul stood in the doorway. 'That's enough, Fleischer. I was questioning this woman, not you.'

CHAPTER THIRTEEN

In a gesture designed to taunt Paul, Fleischer allowed the soldier to hold the lighted cigarette over Evelyn for a fraction longer. Then he gave the order to desist. The corporal untied Evelyn's wrists and the blood began to flow painfully back into her fingers.

'I will take over, if you please.' Paul limped into the room. 'There is a problem downstairs, Sturmbannführer, which requires your attention.'

Fleischer considered. Von Hoch evidently had an interest in this girl, and he was curious to know why. He reviewed the possibilities. Was it sex he was after? Fleischer reckoned von Hoch might well be the type to permit himself a little indulgence away from home. Or was it – and here Fleischer's instincts sent him conflicting messages – that von Hoch thought the girl possessed information that he wished to extract for his own use?

'You are needed urgently, Sturmbannführer.' Paul was adamant.

Obviously von Hoch was determined to stand his ground. Fleischer did not yet feel in a position to challenge the *Abwehr* openly. That tussle was to come, and head office in Berlin had instructed him to take it quietly for the time being. He replaced the cup in the saucer.

'Consider yourself lucky, Mademoiselle, to have the gallant major defending you.' Fleischer intended to convey menace in this remark but the effect was of malice.

Paul remained impassive. Fleischer's gaze raked over the tall figure with an expression similar to the one with which he regarded his china figurines. In recent months the annoying von Hoch had lost some of his playboy swagger and gloss: he seemed older and more reserved. Fleischer dropped his

323

files into the desk drawer, locked it and, with a scrape of chair leg across the floor, got to his feet. He picked up his cap. 'We will discuss this matter later, von Hoch,' he said, and signalled for the corporal to follow him out of the room.

The airless, sweat-laden atmosphere was stifling. Paul drew back the curtains and pulled open the tall windows. It was four o'clock. Ribérac lay below, its roofs just discernible under the lightening sky. There was a bitter taste in his mouth from too many cups of coffee and too many cigarettes. The main overhead bulb was off, leaving the desk lamp burning, and the light changed from electric yellow to the spectral white of predawn. Evelyn felt a draught from the fading night's chill cool her neck. She huddled in the chair. Her wrists were smarting and angry red weals criss-crossed over the blue veins. Paul poured a glass of water from the jug on the sideboard.

He knelt beside Evelyn and gave her the water and she took it gratefully. Then, very gently and unselfconsciously, he brushed aside the charred silk around her burn and examined the red, puckered flesh underneath. Evelyn flinched. 'It's blistered, I'm afraid. You must keep it covered.' He extracted a clean handkerchief from his pocket and brushed traces of ash from her lap. 'You should get it seen to as soon as possible. I'm sorry I don't have anything here to soothe it.'

She did not want Paul to see her crying so Evelyn put up a hand and covered her eyes but it was no use. Tears of shock and relief trickled through her fingers. Paul adjusted the neckline of her dress to make her comfortable and prised her hand from her face, careful not to touch her wrists. Then with his handkerchief he mopped her running nose and wet cheeks, and wiped at the coffee stains.

'I'm afraid you will be in shock for a little while,' he told her.

The lump at the back of her throat prevented her from replying. Paul searched for a dry patch on the handkerchief and reapplied it to her face. All trace of the awkwardness and constraint that had dogged their last meeting had vanished and Evelyn closed her eyes. She knew without a doubt that

Paul had intervened to stop Fleischer because he loved her. Paul cupped her cheek in his hand and she reopened them.

'Better? Not going to faint?'

She shook her head. Paul sat back on his heels. 'You look less pale.'

Evelyn looked down at the front of her ruined dress. 'Is questioning always like this?' she asked. 'I'd heard gossip, but . . .'

The question discomfited him, and she was sorry. 'Every country employs interrogation techniques.' Paul hesitated and then said carefully, 'But not every German behaves like Fleischer.'

'There are others like him?' Evelyn was careful not to appear too well informed.

'There are others.' Paul glanced at Hitler's eyes boring down into the room from the overlarge photograph on the wall. Whichever way he looked, the stare seemed inescapable.

'Can't it be stopped?'

Paul smiled with a hint of bitterness. 'Not easily.' He got to his feet and picked up Fleischer's cigarette box. Then he extracted one, lit it and gave it to Evelyn. He watched while she smoked it. Every now and then she would remove a speck of tobacco from her lips and her hair fell forward over her cheeks. He wanted to brush it back and feel its soft weight in his hands.

'What are we going to do?' he asked after a moment.

Evelyn felt an enormous weariness wash over her spirit. She knew she could not trust Paul. She must not trust him and there was nothing she could do but keep up the masquerade – the subterfuge and enormity of the dangerous *mascarade* she had elected to join – and not yield to the temptation to lay her head on Fleischer's desk and say to Paul that, yes, she would tell him everything.

'What are we going to do?' Paul was waiting for an answer. He calculated that Fleischer would return at any minute.

'I'm frightened.' Evelyn tried to sound like the fictional Evelyn Liegaux. It was the truth – she *was* frightened, thinking of what had happened to Jack and the others, of the repercussions of Operation Michelin. And of what would happen if Paul was forced to hand her back to Fleischer.

'Don't be.' Paul leant against the side of the desk and Evelyn could look at him unobserved for a couple of seconds. Obviously his leg was aching for he rubbed it.

She struggled to her feet. 'Thank you for taking care of me, Monsieur.' He turned and looked at her with an unreadable expression in his eyes. 'Are you going to let me go?' she asked.

Paul stubbed out his cigarette; he appeared to be making a decision. 'Yes. Yes. I am.'

She remained quite still. Only the tiniest movement of her shoulders indicating her relief.

He limped over to her and took both her hands in his. His long, brown fingers strayed over her bitten cuticles and tracked the tendons running from finger to wrist. 'I wish I knew more about you,' he said. 'Really knew.'

Was he playing with her? A cat dandling a dying mouse in its paws? Was he teasing her for some private enjoyment, before the *coup de grâce*? Was he – God forbid – a Fleischer, only more subtle?

'Please understand, Evelyn.' Paul stroked her wrists. 'It doesn't matter to me who you are.'

He was very close and his closeness blotted out the suspicions. It was an incongruous place, this Nazi lair, she thought, to discover happiness. Adolf Hitler presiding, plundered figurines on the table, the swastikaed cigarette box and the litter of ash on the floor. Where might they have been? In a hotel room in Paris, perhaps, overlooking grey roofs tipped with soft yellow sun. Drinking *café au lait* in a bar by the river. Or, taut-eyed and aching from dancing all night, returning in the fresh exhilaration of an English morning . . . 'Mother,' she would say, dragging an elegantly rumpled Paul into the drawing room at Castle Cary. 'This is Paul. I love him.' And Eugénie would pat the sofa where she always sat after breakfast and beg Paul to come and talk to her . . .

Evelyn looked at him, angry at her own innocence. Things did not happen like that – but for this minute, the small disobedient minute that she allowed herself, it did not matter, only Paul mattered. Paul looked down at the burnt breast and scarred wrists, and turned away to stop himself from kissing her.

'I've been summoned back to Berlin. I won't be seeing you again.'

'No!' Despite herself, Evelyn's exclamation revealed more than she intended and she tried to cover it up. 'Will you be returning?' she asked politely. In response, Paul put his hand under her chin and made her meet his eyes.

'If after the war is over, I come back for you, what then?'

Evelyn wondered how much more she could stand. 'No,' she said, forcing the words out. 'Please don't come back for me. I . . . I may not be here.'

Paul released Evelyn and said what Fleischer's telephone call had prevented him from saying earlier. 'Why? Did you leave home to work in the resistance?'

'What did they do to you?' Bessy was driving erratically through Ribérac on their way back to Belle-Place. 'How did you persuade them to let us go? And where on earth did you find the hair comb?'

Evelyn put up a hand and felt her hair. She had almost forgotten about the comb. 'It was found in the car.'

'I was so frantic when he produced your beret. He didn't get anything out of you, did he?' Bessy swerved at a crossroads to avoid an early-morning cyclist.

'No. Of course not,' said Evelyn wearily.

'But how did you explain the beret, Evie? You were so long. What were they doing to you?'

Evelyn held up her wrists. 'This.'

Bessy took one horrified look and was silent. The car began to climb up the hill towards Bertric-Burée. Daylight had arrived. The men were already out in the fields and lines of flower-sprinkled mown hay stretched out behind them. Washing was already hanging in the garden of one cottage and a woman hoeing rows of beans in another. The world was embarking on a new day and if she kept quiet, Evelyn calculated, then perhaps the tight knot inside her chest might begin to unravel. At the turning to the village, Bessy brought the car to a halt.

'What else happened, Evie? How did you persuade them to give you back the beret?'

Evelyn opened the glove compartment, searched for Bessy's cigarettes and parried. 'You're not trying to suggest something, are you?'

Bessy slumped back in the seat. 'Yes . . . I mean, no. I don't know what I think. You were two hours in there.' She shrugged. 'It's the worry and the relief. I didn't know what was going on and I kept thinking of the baby. What would happen to him if I was taken?'

Never trust anyone. Evelyn passed Bessy the cigarette packet. They sat in silence for a moment. 'The question is,' said Evelyn at last, 'will I be putting you in danger when I disappear?'

Bessy was puzzled. 'What do you mean?' Evelyn opened the car door and swung her silk-clad legs outside. 'Have some fresh air.' Bessy joined her on the dew-slicked verge.

'If an agent is picked up by the Boches and questioned . . .' Evelyn checked the road to see if anyone was coming '. . . then there's nothing for it but to get out. You're burned.' She plucked at the burn mark on her dress. 'But if I do disappear, it's bound to confirm the Boches' suspicions about Belle-Place and draw them down on you.'

The two women leant against the bodywork of the Hispano and smoked their cigarettes. A dawn breeze had got up, which whipped the hair back from their faces. The scent of wild thyme mixed with the pungent tobacco. Bessy's plait had worked loose from its hairpins and her mascara was smudged into a grey thumbprint under her eyes. She looked desperately tired.

'Don't go, Evie,' Bessy almost begged. 'I don't think I could stand it on my own. Anyway, I can't imagine Belle-Place without you.'

Evelyn put her arm around Bessy, and Bessy relaxed a little. 'Don't mind me,' she said. 'You must do what you think best. She dropped her head onto Evelyn's shoulder for a moment.

Evelyn stared over the dishevelled tawny head towards a clump of walnut trees and the sun-filled horizon.

'Did you leave home to work in the resistance?'

The programmed lie, 'I don't know what you mean,' was triggered automatically in response to Paul's question. And he hadn't believed her.

Muddled with exhaustion, uncertain of Paul, loving him. She was sure only of one thing: wherever she went he would come with her, like night following day, like the heartbeat pumping the life round her body.

CHAPTER FOURTEEN

For a few seconds John and Jack watched as Evelyn turned and started to run – tripping now and then on roots and brambles – back to the waiting car. 'The pond,' urged Jack. They hesitated no longer. The two men set off at a stumbling, lopsided pace. There was no chance of reaching the van in time, which they wordlessly acknowledged in the split second that Jack made his decision.

The continuing sound of shooting from under the cliff indicated that Jean-Claude and Martin were still alive and putting up considerable resistance, but the dogs must have been gaining on them.

Leaning heavily on Jack, John made a gargantuan effort to ignore the pain which was now shooting up his leg. Jack used his spare arm, in which he held the Sten, to hack at the tangled undergrowth. Frequently he had to let go of John so that he could slide through the cramped space beneath a fallen tree trunk or use both arms to fight with the tentacles of bramble which ensnared them. Both men pulled off their telltale berets to prevent them being caught up in the branches and stuffed them in their pockets. The sound of men and dogs breasting the cliff top – a shouting of orders and a volley of shots – and Jack and John caught sight of the dully glinting pond.

For a moment Jack considered wading upstream along the narrow gorge but on rapid investigation he realised it was practically impassable, certainly for someone in John's condition. They plunged into the water up to their waists, guns held above their heads, boots sliding on the muddy sediment of the pond bed and kicking up stinking flotsam. At one point John tripped on a submerged root and dropped his gun. For a moment, unable to get his footing, he flailed, gulping mouthfuls of the brackish water. Grabbing him by his collar, Jack pulled John upright. 'My gun's gone,' he said despairingly.

After the warmth of the night, the water was surprisingly cold. Jack pointed towards a place where the pond was overhung with a thick tangle of branches and ivy. The two men made towards it, trying to keep their splashing as noiseless as possible. The trees muffled the noise of their pursuers, and the noise of the dogs came from all directions but both men realised that once on the cliff top the search party would have split up and fanned out. It was impossible to tell how close they were or in which direction they were heading.

Up to their chests in water they reached their hiding place and dipped their heads under for a moment in order to slip under the protective overhang. Jack wedged his Sten between two branches while John reached up to pull the canopy lower over their heads. The smell of decomposing vegetation and semi-stagnant water was overpowering.

'Now start praying,' whispered Jack.

'I'm an atheist.'

'Well, pray anyway.'

A sound of cracking branches close by – and the men submerged themselves even further until all that was left above water were the tops of their heads. With a loud yelping, the Alsatians arrived at the water's edge at the exact spot where the two agents had waded in a few minutes earlier. They were closely followed by a number of men. Through a gap in their camouflage Jack counted six soldiers and three dogs. He moved imperceptibly nearer to where his gun was lodged. John remained motionless: the cold mud poultice bathing his ankle was beginning to numb the pain. The dogs barked, and circled like starlings, beating decreasing circles as the scent grew fainter and colder and bewildered, one of them splashed about in the water until its trainer whistled it back. Jack could see that the men were confused. One gave an order and the posse split, heading off in opposite directions along the bank.

Torchbeams swept the bank, the surface of the pond and the encircling trees in wide arcs, crossing and recrossing each other. The dogs continued to bark in counterpoint to the staccato commands of their trainers. Jumpy in the unfamiliar terrain, the men hacked their way through the heavy undergrowth, feet splashing through patches of marsh, loosing off occasional volleys into the moonlit wood.

A lone Alsatian pattered within metres of their hiding place. Jack and John sucked in a lungful of air and ducked under. The dog was followed by a soldier who stabbed with his gun at the tangle of marshy grass and tree roots at the water's edge.

Every second was a lifetime to the two agents. As his lungs strained, John began to see red in front and the blood pounded in his ears. When he could stay under no longer he surfaced as slowly as possible, letting out a silent explosion of breath. At the same moment Jack emerged. Both took deep breaths and went under for a second time. A minute went by and the two men were forced to resurface.

A succession of muffled shouts indicated that the Germans had finished searching the pond and were heading off into the wood. Jack and John waited until the noise of men crashing through undergrowth faded into the distance. Even then they could not move. There was a chance that the search party had left snoopers; it was impossible to tell in the half-light. Thus they remained, silent and unmoving, until dawn filtered through the canopy above them.

The early service in which she gave thanks for the new day comforted Sister Hélène. She had spent a difficult night, turning from side to side on the straw mattress. Jean had told her yesterday that the Germans were stepping up the house-to-house searches in the Ribérac area. Apparently they were looking for an enemy wireless transmitter.

Hélène was not sure, nor would she ever ask, but she had a good idea who was involved. Naturally, her contact with Evelyn was limited; indeed, they had agreed that they would not meet again and any instructions would be sent via a cut-out.

Hélène waited each day for the message that would tell her she was needed. Not unnaturally, the waiting jangled her nerves a little, and during the vulnerable hours of night activated her conscience. *I should inform Reverend Mother*. She had not done so yet.

It was still dark as Hélène left the chapel and made her way across the courtyard at St Euphonie's to the infirmary. She held the keys in one hand.

'Sister?'

A shadowy figure detached itself from the wall. Hélène started and had to put a hand over her mouth to stifle a cry.

'Where can I find the sister in charge of the infirmary? I have an emergency patient.'

'I am in charge of the infirmary.'

The man let out a long breath. 'Would you by any chance have a refill for a petrol lighter?' The voice, a man's, was hoarse and uncertain.

He was soaking wet. She took in the mud-covered clothes and the stench of stagnant water which clung to them. Then she saw that a second figure was propped against the infirmary wall.

'No,' she said calmly. 'We don't use lighters in the convent. You had better come in.' She unlocked the surgery door and held it open for the two agents to go inside. She followed them in and locked the door behind her.

Checking that the shutters were fully closed before she did so, she turned on a small lamp in one corner of the room.

'Are you able to help us?' the first man asked. His dark hair was plastered with filth.

The other sank onto the wooden bench. 'I think I'm going to faint,' he announced. 'Exit stage left.'

Hélène moved over to him and tipped John's head forward over his knees. 'Were you followed, do you know?' she asked Jack over John's head.

'I don't think so, but there are search parties out for us.'

Hélène reflected for a minute or so. 'You are safe for a few hours but you can't stay in here. Please take your boots off.' She bent down to untie John's laces. 'Can you help him up?'

Jack held out a hand and John grasped it. 'Come on, old man, one more push.'

Hélène picked up a black leather bag that she had kept in readiness for the past year and led them out of the surgery and down a flagstone passage. Leading off it were nail-studded wooden doors recessed into stone arches. The men's sodden socks left wet footprints on the stone flags as they followed the nun along the cold, silent corridor. At the end, Hélène produced a key and unlocked the last door on the left. Pushing it open she said, 'Enter, if you please.'

Behind the door was a small bare room, just big enough to hold two iron beds, a diminutive table, on which stood a jug and bowl, and a wooden chair. The only relief for its starkness was a statuette of the Virgin standing on a shelf in one corner. Clean threadbare towels' lay folded on the end of the beds. These were pushed against the walls and cotton coverlets were tucked under the mattresses with geometric precision.

'This is the isolation room,' Hélène told the men.

'God help them!' Jack spoke without thinking.

Hélène looked at Jack. 'He does,' she said. 'Now listen.' She pulled back the coverlets, helped John to sit down on the chair and bent to examine his foot. 'If anyone asks, you are suspected TB cases and I, Sister Hélène, am in charge of you. A little coughing wouldn't go amiss. The main ward is next door, but, please, you must not leave this room. The window overlooks the garden. You know to keep the shutters closed, of course. It's an easy drop to the ground below if you need to escape, and there is a gate set into the garden wall opposite which leads out to the fields.'

Jack eased his shoulders, aching from the strain of supporting John for so long. 'What's the time, Sister? My watch has stopped.'

'Five thirty-five. Now, I will attend to this ankle and then you must get some sleep. I will arrange for you to be taken out of the convent later this morning.'

While she talked Hélène was placing bandages and ointments on the table and rolling up her sleeves. Dizzy with exhaustion and pain, John slumped back on the chair and allowed her to undress him. She reminded him of those implacable black-robed nun-saints he had read about in childhood; St Catherine or St Theresa. Stern, self-flagellatory mystics and healers who ventured into plague-ridden cities and lazar houses. This one, with her patrician face and bony,

334

expert fingers, was exactly in that mould. She could not avoid hurting him as she pulled off his dripping socks and rubbed an arnica ointment into his swollen ankle. When she looked up after securing the bandage with a small knot he was paper white.

Hélène got up from her knees, helped him into bed and tucked the coverlet around him. 'In the morning your contact leaves here with a load of vegetables for selling in local villages. He keeps his cart in the shed opposite the infirmary. It is recognisable by the earthenware pot standing outside it. When the time comes I will take you back to the surgery and you must pretend to be outpatients. Then you can make your way to the shed where your contact will be waiting to hide you.' She finished attending to John and looked up. 'I should warn you that this is the first time we have tried this operation.'

'Where will he take us?' Jack longed for a strong drink and a cigarette.

'He will drive you towards Belle-Place, which is his next stop, and let you out by the woods below the *château*. After that, you are on your own.' She picked up John's jacket and trousers. 'Give me your clothes, please,' she said to Jack. She turned her back as Jack, too tired for self-consciousness, undressed quickly and in his underpants handed her his soaking garments. 'Go to sleep now.' She closed the door, locked it, and hung up the notice which said: 'No Entry'.

John lay with his eyes open staring at the statuette of the Virgin. In his half-conscious state she became the Goddess of Fortune. 'Well, old lady,' he addressed her, 'we do meet in some unexpected places.' He fell into a feverish doze, punctuated by shouts, barking and gunfire as he relived the night's events. He could see himself clambering out of the pond onto the bank, then Jack half pushing, half pulling him out of the woods and over field after dusty field. The sky paling from violet to the faintest mauve. The stench of their clothes and his feet slipping inside his mud-filled boots. Pain jarring up his leg. Time after time Jack encouraging him onwards. The surge of relief as the stone walls of St Euphonie's came into view.

Before John fell properly asleep he heard Jack say quite clearly in English, 'God, I want a cigarette.'

Sister Hélène should have been exhausted. She had just completed a fortnight on night duty on top of which she had also put in long hours during the day because her deputy had fallen ill. On leaving the two agents she had hidden their wet clothes in a locked cupboard. In the pocket of the smaller jacket she found a blurred photograph of a pretty young woman with cat-like eyes. This she slipped under her belt. Then she had gone to the sluice and filled a bucket of water to wash the men's footprints from the flagstones. That done – Hélène had been nervous at the sounds of the patients awaking in the wards on either side – she went to her cupboard of second-hand clothes and looked out some suitable replacements for them.

Returning to the surgery, Hélène tried to marshal her thoughts. Fatigue made her light-headed and her mind felt wooden, lethargic and useless. At this, of all times, she chided herself, when she had to think calmly and clearly if these men were to survive.

The clock struck nine. Surprised at the lateness of the hour, Hélène checked the time against the watch pinned to her chest. The men had been sleeping for three and a half hours and Jean was due in thirty minutes.

Forcing herself not to hurry, Hélène folded the new clothes into a basket, covered them with a piece of sheeting and carried it down the corridor to the isolation room. She unlocked the door and let herself in. Both men were asleep. The younger one was sprawled on his back with a lock of hair flopping over his forehead. The other one was huddled into a foetal position. Even in sleep he looked drawn and tense and he was muttering words she could not make out. The air smelt of sweat and stagnant water and Hélène was tempted to open the window.

'Monsieur.' Hélène shook Jack by the shoulder. 'It's time for you to leave.'

Instantly awake, John sat bolt upright. 'What is it?' he said, and reached for his gun in a reflex action.

'Take it easy.' Jack soothed him. 'Thank you, Sister.'

John heaved his legs over the side of the bed and yelped as his torn and stiffened muscles made contact with the floor. Hélène knelt and checked the swelling. 'It will be a little easier when you have walked a bit and loosened it. All the same, you should rest it when you can, otherwise it will take a long time to heal.'

'Thank you, Sister.' He began to shiver. Hélène rose to her feet and placed a hand on his forehead. 'You've probably taken a chill. I'm afraid I haven't got any spare medicine.' John shivered harder and felt the beginnings of a headache massing behind his eyes.

Pulling on unfamiliar clothes with muscles that had lost all elasticity was a clumsy and painful process. Neither man made the effort to talk as Hélène, again on her knees, struggled to help John fit a sock over his puffy foot. It was twenty past nine before she led them back to the surgery, gave them their damp boots to put on and allowed them out into the courtyard.

'Your contact should be here already and waiting for you. Just make your way slowly towards the shed I told you about. Good luck and hurry.' As they were going she pressed the photograph of Minou into John's hand and said, 'I found it in your pocket.' He did not have time to thank her.

The men did as she had instructed. Careful not to watch them crossing the courtyard, Hélène bent down to pick up a scrap of paper lying on the ground and, obedient to the vow of poverty, examined it to see if it could be used for anything.

'Sister.'

Reluctantly, Hélène straightened up. Reverend Mother did not usually visit this part of the convent in the early morning. Yet more unusual was for her to summon a sister in person. Reverend Mother was framed between two stone pillars in the cloister, like a figure from a medieval Book of Hours. One hand was raised imperiously and all that was needed to complete the picture was the gilding of a halo behind her head.

'Yes, Reverend Mother?'

Once again distrust of Hélène battled with the obligation for charity in Reverend Mother's expression. 'Sister, I have received a telephone call. I wish you to come to my office. Some German officials are on their way here to question us.'

Obediently, Hélène took off her cuffs and placed them in her pocket. Then she followed the remote figure of her superior along the edge of the cloister, a grinning devil's face leering back at her from a stone corbel. Hélène averted her eyes. 'Have you used me, Lucifer?' she wondered with a sudden lurch of doubt.

She had never liked Reverend Mother's room. It was plain, comfortless and full of uncomfortable memories. Inside its restricting walls, Hélène had accepted some bitter medicine: when as a short-skirted postulant, Reverend Mother cast doubt on her vocation, and when some years later, she summoned Hélène, now professed and black-veiled, to kneel in front of her desk to tell her that her life in God was flawed by obstinacy and pride. She must push herself harder. Always harder.

This morning, Reverend Mother appeared uncharacteristically irresolute. She stood behind her desk and allowed her rosary to slip back and forth through her fingers. 'Do you have any idea why the Germans should wish to question our infirmary sister?'

'No, Reverend Mother.' Ever since Evelyn had recruited her, Hélène had imagined that telling the first direct lie would be the most difficult thing she would have to encounter. She had been wrong. It was remarkably easy.

'Then we will pray, Sister.' Reverend Mother hitched up her habit and used the edge of the desk to lever herself onto the floor in front of the crucifix with its figure of the tortured Christ. Hélène knelt beside her, back ramrod straight, her habit flowing out over her feet.

'Blessed Lord,' Reverend Mother chose her words carefully, 'You know our imperfections— ' A loud knocking interrupted her intercession. Reverend Mother paused for a second. 'Let not pride and false duty stand in the way of true obedience. Amen.'

Impatient at the delay, Fleischer and his companion pushed past the flustered portress into the room. The nuns rose to their feet and folded their hands inside their sleeves, their faces polite triangles under their coifs.

'Good morning,' said Fleischer. The presence of holiness had no effect on him but he thought it would be expedient to begin, at least, in a conciliatory manner. 'I am sorry to disturb you, but this is urgent business.' Fleischer assumed full command and the young *Haupsturmführer* took his tone from his superior officer. He stared rudely at the nuns and took out a notebook in which he began to write. Without asking permission, Fleischer picked up Reverend Mother's paperknife from the desk. 'We are looking for terrorists who are thought to be in the area.'

Under her sleeves, Hélène's fingers tightened around one another.

'We believe at least one or two of them were wounded.' He paused. 'Have you treated anybody for gunshot wounds?' Fleischer balanced the knife on the tip of one finger. 'Have you, ladies?' As he talked, the expensive gold filling in his front tooth flashed discreetly.

Hélène glanced at Reverend Mother who nodded permission for Hélène to speak. Hélène answered, 'I am the infirmary sister. No one has been treated for gunshot wounds in my surgery.'

'Think carefully. If I am not satisfied with your answers I can take you in for questioning.' Like all bullies, Fleischer insisted on being treated with respect and he was beginning to feel irritated. Hélène pronounced the German title perfectly, and glanced down at the watch pinned to her breast. It read nine fifty. If Jean had carried out the plan as they had arranged, the two men should be hidden in the cart by now.

'Are you late for something, Sister?' Fleischer noted her surreptitious look. It took her a moment to recover.

'Morning surgery starts at nine thirty. There will be patients waiting for attention.'

'You will take us to see the log.' Fleischer made it clear that surgery would have to wait.

Hélène bent her head to avoid letting the German witness her angry flush. She could tell that Reverend Mother was equally annoyed. This was the first time the Nazis had stepped inside her domain – indeed, that the war had encroached any further into her convent, as far as Reverend Mother was aware, than in the form of malnourished babies and cases of aggravated tuberculosis. 'Monsieur,' Reverend Mother addressed Fleischer, coldly but reasonably, 'I think you can assume that, as nuns dedicated to the service of Our Lord, we are sworn to speak nothing but the truth.'

With a clatter, the paperknife dropped back onto the polished desk top where it swung round in circles. Fleischer scrutinised the women and calculated the odds against the old bellwethers being genuine. Hélène remained outwardly impassive but inside experienced a new anger: I will fight these people, so help me God. 'Please come this way, gentlemen,' she said.

The sun was up and making inroads into the mist that layered over the valley floor. It was going to be another boiling day. Hélène and Reverend Mother led the men through the cloister towards the stone arch that led into the courtyard. They passed several nuns, all of whom folded their hands into their sleeves and pressed back politely into the wall. Such was the rigour of their religious training that not one of them expressed surprise or anxiety at the sight of Reverend Mother in the company of a Nazi officer.

Several patients were gathered around the infirmary door when they arrived. A baby was crying and its mother was walking it up and down. 'Take her inside and sit down on the bench. I'm just coming,' Hélène told the young woman, and laid a cool finger on the baby's hot face.

'You won't be long, will you, Sister?' asked the mother, little more than a girl herself. She began to cough.

Fleischer took a step back. 'What's wrong with her?' he asked in German.

'Probably tuberculosis. It is exacerbated by malnutrition as a result of meagre rations.' Hélène's German was excellent and Fleischer blinked.

Out of the corner of her eye, Hélène saw Jean lead the horse and cart out of the shed across the courtyard towards the back entrance to the convent.

Each wedged into one of the big wicker panniers, Jack and

John lay under a heap of vegetables. The smell of earthy carrots, courgettes and the spice of freshly picked tomatoes picked at their noses. It was uncomfortably hot and airless and the slightest movement made dirt trickle into their ears or down their backs. Crooked under him, John's ankle sent silent screams through his leg.

The cart slithered a little over the cobbles and voices speaking in German filtered into the agents' hiding place. John forgot about his ankle. 'Stop him, I want to question him,' said a voice.

'Wait a minute, Jean.' Sister Hélène sounded cool and measured. The boy brought the cart to a halt.

'How often does he come here?' Fleischer walked over to the cart.

'One moment!' Wishing to regain control of the situation, Reverend Mother interjected at this point. 'The boy works in our garden, Monsieur. He makes vegetable deliveries quite frequently. The surplus from our garden is delivered to our customers in surrounding villages. I am sure potatoes and suchlike do not interest you, gentlemen, so let us continue.'

Fleischer was not going to allow himself to be outmanoeuvred by a nun. He leant over the side of the cart and ran his fingers over the potatoes. Dirt curdled under his fingernails. Suddenly, he drove his hand down hard towards the centre of the heap. Hélène put a hand to her face and swayed.

'Sister!' Reverend Mother was unsympathetic. 'Are you unwell?'

Sister Hélène clasped her forehead and gave a weak, martyred smile. 'The sun,' she explained. 'And I am very tired from night duty.'

'Come, gentlemen.' An increasingly alarmed Reverend Mother indicated that Fleischer should pass into the infirmary. 'The log you wish to see is kept in the surgery. I think we should continue. The sister is not well.' With a flurry of her veil Reverend Mother turned her back on the Germans and headed for the infirmary,

Fleischer extracted his hand from the potatoes and shook the dirt of his fingers while the *Haupsturmführer* leant over and helped himself to a peach from the pannier next to the one in which John was hiding. An instinct told Fleischer that something was not quite right. Something lay underneath the nuns' smooth assurances but he could not put his finger on it. He watched Jean pull on the reins. The cart moved forward. The local population must be made to understand that he was not a man to be fooled with. Picking the dirt from under his fingernails he addressed Hélène. 'Your German is excellent. Where did you learn it?'

'If the Boches can help themselves, then you certainly can, Messieurs. Please take as much fruit as you like.' Jean held out a brown arm to help Jack and then John off the cart. 'You must be hungry.' He had grown during the months he had been working at the convent. In his earth-stained overalls and beret low over his eyes he looked maturer than his years.

'Thanks.' Jack took a couple of peaches and a large tomato and put them in his pockets. 'You've been kind.'

Jean had dropped them on the Lusignac road below Belle-Place. John's wireless was hidden in a hut on the perimeter of the *château*'s lands, close to a neighbouring house called La Bachellerie. He had used it several times for transmitting. Anticipating the walk ahead, John shivered despite the hot sun.

'Be a good chap,' he asked Jack, 'and do your deaf leading the blind bit. The sked's due in half an hour.'

Jack linked his arm through John's and they began the short, but for John tortured, walk up the wooded track towards La Bachellerie. The air was clear and shimmering with heat. Dried grass rippled in the occasional eddies of a light breeze and they passed trees heavy with red and black plums. All John wanted was to lie in the sun and forget about the past few hours. He could look at the photograph of Minou and remember the time in Marseille. He could plan what he would do when he went back home . . . The effort to keep going made him dizzy; buzzing circles bounced around his skull and the sun had developed a curious trick of changing its position in the sky. 'This is worse than training school,' he panted.

Jack decided to keep talking. 'At least in France there's

cheap wine, sun and the prospect of a pretty little *poulette* now and again. There was not so much as a pub at Arisaig, if you remember.'

'Too well.' John pulled himself forward another painful step. 'Mind you don't get clap, my boy.'

'I like the women round here,' said Jack, thinking of green eyes and dark hair. 'Blonde, raven-headed, Titian.' John glanced up at his companion and felt envious. Jack was young and strong, qualities he felt were slipping away from him.

Once used by farm workers during harvest and fruit-picking but now abandoned for a larger one in the north field, the hut they were heading for had the advantage of electric power. They passed round the back of La Bachellerie, a substantial farmhouse, and set off over the maize field towards the hut, which they could see on the horizon. When they were within a hundred or so metres, they stopped.

'Check for the thread on the door,' John told Jack.

The latter went ahead, sliding cautiously around the windowless wall and squinting at the wooden door latch. An unbroken thread ran from handle to lock. He gave John the thumbs up.

Inside lay abandoned rusting machinery and tools – a scythe, a fork and a wicker basket with a gaping hole. The wireless transmitter was hidden under a floorboard over which John had dragged a pile of sacks. Jack pushed them aside and retrieved the set. 'Are there guns in here too?'

'Yup. A Sten and a Colt.'

'How many rounds?'

John shrugged. 'One seven-round box for the Colt. Thirty-two round box for the Sten.' He was concentrating on setting up his set.

In the past, especially when working in the dark, John had sometimes allowed fantasy to creep in and imagined that the simple routines held some sort of poetry. The brightly glowing bulbs lighting the dark, the urgent, erratic tapping, the whooshing and hissing in his ears, the secrecy and tension, and he in the middle of it doing his bit. Now, he was just tired, feverish and in pain.

'Quiet!' Jack pointed the assembled Sten out of the window.

'There's someone coming.' He tensed in a firing stance and then relaxed. 'It's Violette.'

She was running at full tilt – unwisely – through the maize towards the hut. The door swung open, letting in a stream of sunlight. 'Thank God. You're both safe. Here.' Pale and breathless, she retrieved a scrap of paper from her pocket and scribbled down a message.

OPERATION MICHELIN ABORTED. ONE DEATH. ONE CASUALTY. ASTRONOMER AT RISK. WILL REGROUP. ALOUETTE.

John pulled his code book out of the box and began to transcribe.

'If there's any trouble, get out of the back window and head cross-country to Verteillac,' Evelyn said. She picked up John's Colt, ready to use it if necessary.

Jack went outside to take up the watch. The sun was very hot and a butterfly darted across his vision, a brilliant blue hovering spot. Sweat gathered at the corner of his eyes. He thought of cucumber sandwiches and tea on the lawns of his Oxford college. Dear old infuriating England. Frumpy, puritan and sane. Jack scanned the horizon. So far, all clear.

The Morse key was becoming slippery with the sweat from John's finger tips. He was unusually clumsy and he had to think twice before taking even the simplest of actions. Like she had so often before, Evelyn laid her hand on his shoulder and squeezed it. John adjusted the headset, listened to the waterfall in his ears and glanced up with a grimace. 'Here we go.' It was 10.25 a.m.

At that moment in the German listening station in Paris, a spot glowed on one of the cathode screens monitoring the radio frequencies. One of the operatives picked up a telephone. '*Achtung*,' he said. '*Drei vier sechs fünf KiloHerz*.'

There was a rustle of anticipation in the room. Telephones rang at the stations at Brest, Nuremberg and Augsburg. Their monitoring equipment immediately homed in on the lone wireless. A lighted beam sprang instantly onto their screens from which a precise direction was obtained.

At 10.27 a.m. the three listening stations relayed their findings to the central operations room where they materialised as threads on the large wall map. They crossed to form a triangle with Ribérac in the Périgord at its centre.

The operations room telephoned Ribérac headquarters at 10.34 a.m. The signals officer, Major von Hoch – who was half expecting a call from Paris – was informed. He gave orders that three detector vans with false French number plates should position themselves at the three points of the triangle.

The vans drove off at speed, the men inside tuning their radios to 3465 KiloHerz. The enemy transmitter went quiet, presumably waiting for its home station to respond.

Paul waited beside the signals clerk at the *mairie*. It was 10.40 a.m.

At 10.42 a.m. a stream of Morse poured onto the airwaves. The home station had begun transmitting to its clandestine operator. The men inside the vans used the dots and dashes to pinpoint the position of the lone wireless, all the time drawing nearer to their target. The first van turned into the wooded track that led towards La Bachellerie.

Home station had a long message to send. John found himself scrawling numbers continuously for well over ten minutes. Evelyn kept watch at the window. She was deeply uneasy. Outside Jack wiped his face on his sleeve. As the German detector van came into sight, he tensed. 'Boches! Get out.' Evelyn cocked the Colt and John looked up. He had almost finished. Home station sent its signing-off configuration and waited for John to tell them their signal had been intelligible.

John wrote down the last letter and lifted his hand to the Morse key. REPEAT LAST GROUP, he signalled. Home station obliged. QSL, he tapped, relieved: I acknowledge receipt. AR: over and out. This procedure took only thirty seconds. It was enough.

The German detector van accelerated up the road and braked, followed closely by a second. The back doors were flung open and heavily armed soldiers jumped down. They divided, half turning their attention on the farmhouse, the others heading through the maize towards the hut.

'Abort, for God's sake,' hissed Jack. He tore down the aerial at the window. John ripped off his earphones, threw the code book, message and pencil into the attaché case. Evelyn disengaged the power supply and frantically coiled up the wire. John thrust the whole lot at her.

'Get going.' His voice was quite calm. He knew his damaged ankle would take him nowhere. He heard the crack of falling maize stalks. 'What are you waiting for?'

'Give me the wireless,' said Jack through the window. He grabbed it from Evelyn and disappeared.

Evelyn hovered. 'For Christ's sake get going.'

She shook her head. 'Go on,' John shouted at her.

Evelyn came to her senses, gave John one last, agonised look, threw him the Colt and made for the door. Then she was gone, running like the wind after Jack.

The seconds that followed expanded for John. It seemed like an age that he took to pick up the Colt, though it was only a matter of seconds. Then he posted himself by the window in a position ready to shoot.

Evelyn heard the first shots when she was about three hundred metres away. Instinctively, she leapt into an irrigation ditch from where, out of the corner of her eye, she could see Jack, a distant figure running hard under the cover of a hedge. It was barely a minute before the shooting ceased. Evelyn emerged – she had to keep running. A wire fence blocked her path and she dropped to the ground and started to wriggle under it. The earth was hard and her mouth filled with dust. Her dress caught on the wire and for a moment she fought an impulse just to lie there and wait for the Germans to find her. 'Don't let me down, duckie,' said John's voice in her head. 'The show goes on even if you're weeping blood.' Tears streaking the dirt on her cheeks, she wrenched herself free, got to her feet and started to run.

John had almost exhausted his first round of ammunition by the time the first German soldier burst into the hut. He swung round and caught him on the shoulder.

'Buggers,' he said aloud, but the word was lost in the renewed onslaught of fire. John jerked and at once the world began to whiten around the edge of his vision and the hut to fill with blurred grey shapes.

'Minou,' he whispered, surprised that he minded he was dying. He thought he had come to terms with death long ago. The desire to remain alive was tenacious and his finger tightened on the trigger, only to find that no strength remained. 'Buggers,' he repeated.

PART THREE

February 1943–June 1943

John's death diminished the time that was left. Perhaps it was the more superficial aspects – the jokes, the camaraderie, the shared sense of purpose. It killed, I suppose, the optimism – which should not have existed.

His end had been lonely and violent; but we gave him a comrades' funeral in the Bois de Jovelle. All of us were there: Pierre, Jean-Claude, Martin – still grieving for the death of his brother – Bessy and Jack, who fired a salute over the wreath of flowers that stood in for John's body. I chose red and white carnations as I knew John had liked them. 'Nice flowers with a bit of theatre,' he would have said. I tried to remember the words of the funeral service but all that came to mind was 'dust to dust'. Instead I adlibbed. 'Dear Lord, please accept the soul of a good man who died fighting tyranny. Let him rest in peace.' And then I thought of the collaborator we had shot who lay in his secret grave. Someone was grieving for him, too.

The SD launched reprisals following our attack on the tyre factory. They took six men at random from the Ribérac area and shot them. The responsibility for their deaths fell on us more heavily because we knew they had died for a failure.

After hearing of the killings Bessy turned to me and said, 'I hate these people so much, Evelyn.' I remember the look on her face to this day.

An age ago, back in training school, I would have agreed with her. I hated the Nazis who drove through the Maginot Line as if it was a row of skittles making France appear ridiculous or lacking in resolution to the rest of the world. I hated them for the division they brought to France, Frenchman hating Frenchman. I hated them more after learning what was happening in the occupied countries.

But I had learnt that to return depravity with hatred is too simple a response. It is merely a reflex. My experience with the men and women of France who risked their lives again and again taught me that. John's selfless acceptance of his fate taught me that. Above all, falling in love with a German taught me that.

Nothing is simple. Neither love, nor trust, nor hate, nor evil.

It is no use fighting if it is at the cost of our humanity. It is no use surviving if, by the end, we are powerless to love.

CHAPTER ONE

The tram was going to Kurfürstendamm. It hissed down the Unter den Linden towards the Brandenburg Gate, *Berlin raucht Juno* – Berlin smokes Juno cigarettes – painted on one side.

Ingrid watched it idly from one of the tables in Kranzler's café. A copy of *Das Reich*, dated 20 February 1943, lay folded on the table in front of her. The tram moved on and she transferred her attention back to the newspaper. The editorial proclaimed: 'The bourgeois era with its false and misleading notion of humanness is over . . .'

The editorial unsettled Ingrid and once again she looked up and stared out of the large paned window onto the street. It was bitter weather outside and flakes of snow fell now and again from a crystalline grey sky. So, she thought, along with coal, leather shoes, potatoes and green vegetables, plentiful cigarettes and her favourite magazine *Die Neue Linie* (which had taken to publishing depressing sections on '*Strickerei und Stoff*', or home-knitted fashion, and which was to close), humanness was a thing of the past. It was, after all, total war. Now it was the bombs – fifty-pounders, hundred-pounders, incendiaries, accurate, deadly, sent hurtling down by the Allied bombers – which consumed the lives of all Berliners.

Ingrid had learnt to cope with the bombing, more or less, the moments of pure terror and the devastation. She was resigned to the shifting of familiar topography and to the peculiar sense that the world was sliding into a bomb crater.

Sometimes she felt guilty that she was able to close her eyes to the Jews having disappeared from Berlin, melted from public office, hospitals, universities and schools, their names chipped off memorials and their synagogues closed down. She felt she had no option but to ignore it and to join in the complicity of her friends who changed the subject when veiled references to prison camps were dropped into conversation.

Ingrid needed to live, and the business was becoming laborious enough without being hampered by an intrusive conscience.

A waitress with a big bow in her hair brought over a cup of hot chocolate which Ingrid sipped slowly to make it last. Christmas had been a dispiriting affair this year, despite the authorities' promises of extra rations. The train journey to Silberbirchen had been long, cold and dreary, and Ingrid had been forced to stand in an unheated corridor for most of the way with no food. She had been luckier than most. The train had pulled into one station where Red Cross sisters were handing out coffee to a service train and one of them kindly offered Ingrid a cup. She drank it on the platform while watching the soldiers climb back into their train.

At Silberbirchen Ingrid's parents had been tactless enough to ask her when Paul was going to marry her. The question dominated her visit, and her attempts to answer it came out to the dissatisfaction of both parties. Ingrid had returned to Berlin in a more determined mood.

Paul had gone home to spend Christmas with his parents and to see his father, who had recently been released from prison. The family had Admiral Canaris to thank for that.

At the thought of him, the line of her lips softened and her blue eyes looked expectant: she was so glad to have him back. He was joining her at Kranzler's and they were to spend the afternoon together. He was ten minutes late – but at least the chocolate was good. The café was crowded with smart socialites, matrons and soldiers on leave. A couple of officers were drinking chocolate and eating *Stollen* with their fur-decked wives. Ingrid felt rather acid as she contemplated the glossy pelts; she had sacrificed her mink for the men on the Russian front. She could have done with it now, she thought, looking down with distaste at her worsted flannel skirt. Still, the atmosphere was warm, pleasantly smoky and chocolate-scented, and in it you could almost forget to grumble about the war. People wanted to enjoy themselves and to ignore the news of the German retreat announced at Stalingrad on

1 February. Mother Russia had finally exacted revenge – the only country to do so since Hitler had commenced his seemingly unstoppable career as the War Lord of Europe.

It was the first serious set-back for Germany and Goebbels's measures announced in the interests of 'Total War' were clear enough. No more horse riding in the Tiergarten (Goebbels considered the practice an affront to working people), luxury restaurants such as Zum Alten Schweden, the Neva Grill, Peltzer's and Horcher's were to close, confectioners, chocolatiers, beauty parlours, couturiers and hairdressers were also the target of the puritan *Gauleiter* of Berlin. Press reports on sporting events were to be curtailed and from 1 March all periodicals not relevant to the war effort were to close. Rest in peace *Die Neue Linie*! Ingrid would miss its smart frivolity, its absorption in nothing more important than *haute couture*, and the whiff of sophistication it granted its increasingly shabby readers.

Ingrid sighed. Her world was changing very much for the worse. Her tongue explored a tooth that required attention, and she sighed again at the jumpy little ache her tongue provoked. These days it was unwise to develop toothache because dental materials were running short and she had deliberately not applied oil of cloves because it was so pungent. Instead she had dabbed on the last of her perfume because she wanted to smell delicious for Paul.

He had changed. The old courtesy was still there, the flashes of heart-stopping charm, the ease of manner. But he had grown more distant. A frightening experience in France perhaps? Something horrible he couldn't bring himself to talk about? Ingrid did not want to pry. And the truth was – scared she would not know how to deal with it – she did not want to find out. Anyway, her role was not to ask such questions; it was to divert Paul and offer soothing, unquestioning support.

Ingrid's thoughts drifted back and forth until she was distracted by the excellently cut tweed costume of the woman at the neighbouring table and Paul had sat down next to her before she noticed him. He kissed her cheek.

'As elegant as ever, Ingrid. How do you do it?' Pleased, she flashed him her most seductive smile and patted her hair under the absurd hat tilted over her face. He contemplated the picture she made. 'What were you thinking about so hard?' he asked gently.

He was aware that her blue eyes were a shade less pleading these days. Nevertheless, the quick slanting glance betrayed a nervousness. 'I was thinking about you.'

He regretted his question. 'You're not alone,' he said lightly, to deflect what he recognised as the opening salvo in one of Ingrid's campaigns. He signalled to the waitress. 'Judging by the papers piling up on the desk at the Tirpitzufer, others are thinking of me. As a work horse.'

'Yes,' she said, 'but they don't love you.'

Despite himself, Paul was touched by the simple dignity of her declaration. With something of his old swagger, he lifted one of her hands to his lips and kissed it. 'You are too good for me, Ingrid,' he said, and meant it.

Outside in the street, elegant 'swing' boys picked their way through the crowds. One of them bumped into a prostitute with slashed-red lips. He shouted abuse at her. Paul watched as, frightened, the prostitute scurried away down a side street.

'Paul!' Ingrid called him back from his daydream, as ever trying to deduce what he was thinking.

Paul pulled himself together. 'Can you remember your reactions when you first visited England? Or that time you went to America with your parents?'

'Goodness!' Out of habit, Ingrid looked round to see if anyone could overhear what they were saying. 'That was ages ago. The main thing I remember about England was the freezing houses.'

'Practical Ingrid.' Paul smiled. 'Anything else?'

'The food wàs awful.'

'And?' He waited. Ingrid tried hard to think of something interesting to say. 'I'll tell you what I remember, Ingrid. It's how relaxed the people were. Nobody cared what my political views were.'

'Yes,' she countered, doubtfully.

He leant over the table. 'Do you know what has happened to Carl von Ossietzky?'

Ingrid was bewildered at the change of subject. She brushed

a finger across her mouth to signal Paul to be quiet. Carl von Ossietzky was the former editor of *Weltbühne*, a notoriously free-thinking journal. 'No, I don't,' she said, under her breath. 'Does it matter?'

'I've just found out he's dying in a Gestapo hospital.' Since Paul had been back in Berlin he had uncovered sinister information about the fate of political dissidents and read confidential *Abwehr* reports detailing ss plans to deal with the 'Jewish problem'.

'I see.' Ingrid didn't, but she didn't want Paul to realise that. A hint of impatience slid into her voice; she had planned on discussing important subjects this afternoon.

'Do you?' said Paul, watching her carefully. Ingrid did not have access to the sort of intelligence he had, of course, but she appeared so incurious.

The blue eyes widened in sudden hurt and Paul was sorry he had brought up such a sensitive subject. A watery February sun flooded her face under the hat and he saw properly, for the first time, how worn she was.

'Sorry, darling,' he said.

Ingrid fingered the tablecloth and spoke with a touch of asperity. 'I know you think I'm ordinary but I'm clever enough to know we have to get on with life.'

Paul had always admired her pragmatism, for he saw that that was what gave Ingrid her strength. But for himself, he was different and he had always known it.

The last few months in Berlin had seen Paul becoming increasingly depressed. Subjected to sp questioning and a desk-bound job, working in a city operating on fear and rumour, his frustration and guilt were growing. '*Can't they be stopped?*' Evelyn's question was one he often asked himself, and his conscience worried at him. Far, far easier to fight and die on some freezing battlefield on the Eastern Front like his friend, Heinrich Breker. A clean, uncomplicated business. He had a sudden image of Evelyn clutching at her burnt dress, the skin under her eyes smudged violet with fatigue, her cheeks drained of colour. Memories – the feel of satin skin, long thin feet in scrubby leather shoes, gardenia perfume, dark eye-lashes around startlingly green eyes which had been

357

both apprehensive and tender, and a puzzling smile – assaulted him at odd moments . . . and hurt. The warm, damp beret had clinched that Evelyn was working for the resistance but it did nothing to dispel Paul's sheer physical need to hold Evelyn and feel her response. Opposite, Ingrid busied herself with the powder puff and shut the compact with a snap. Paul looked at her freshly powdered face: he had left Evelyn behind in France and the slow, exquisite delight, the prerogative of lovers, of he and Evelyn discovering one another.

Paul knew that he should have debriefed Fleischer when he left, as well as informing him of his suspicions, not least concerning Belle-Place. Mistrusting – even hating – a man, should not stop you doing your duty, argued the logical part of his brain. But Fleischer was a criminal working for a criminal organisation, and he had to align those facts with his conscience.

Paul reached over, took one of Ingrid's hands and turned it over so that the palm lay upwards. He traced a pattern on the cushion of her thumb with his finger. Her hand curled round it in response and she raised it to her cheek.

'Ingrid. I must talk to you seriously about Silberbirchen. You realise that if the Russians beat us and invade Poland and eastern Germany, Silberbirchen lies in their path?'

Ingrid dropped his hand and gasped. The idea of Silberbirchen in Russian hands was almost as painful for Paul as it was for Ingrid. She thought frantically. 'What can we do?'

'You must hide everything of value. I will go with you to Silberbirchen to help if you like.'

A little dart, with triumph engraved on its shaft, lodged in her breast, and Ingrid hung on to the sensation greedily. She got to her feet and held out her arm to Paul. 'Thank you, darling,' she said and smiled to herself as she pulled on her black suede gloves.

They returned to Berlin two weeks later and spent the night in Ingrid's borrowed flat on two mattresses laid side by side on the floor. The visit had been tiring and difficult. The Sturm-bakkers were no longer young and it was hard for them to

358

absorb the unpleasant facts that Paul repeatedly reiterated. In the end, however, they had been persuaded, and ten days of planning and organising the disembowelling of Silberbirchen began.

Paul supervised the taking down and packing up of the most valuable paintings. There were portraits dating from the Napoleonic era, landscapes and jewel-encrusted miniatures which had to be wrapped in sacking, loaded onto carts and taken to the railway station for the first leg of their journey to Paul's family home. Books were lifted down from their library shelves, stacked into tea chests and placed in the cellars with the family documents. The silver – salvers, candlesticks, monogrammed knives, forks and spoons, stud boxes, cigarette cases and a valuable collection of christening mugs – was packed into trunks and stacked in the ice-house in the woods. Frau Sturmbakker's jewels were sewn into money belts ready to grab at the least sign of trouble.

Only the linen and china remained in the cupboards; lace bordered tablecloths, fine linen sheets, pin-tucked muslin nightclothes. So too did the Sèvres dinner services, *jardinières*, perfume bowls and examples of early Wedgwood jasperware. These were too difficult to deal with and there was so little time.

Heavy shoes, rucksacks filled with provisions, money and maps lay ready in the stable. The dog cart was oiled and repaired and the trap rewheeled. Each member of the family chose a winter and a summer travelling outfit and kept it ready in their rooms. Thousands of marks were transferred discreetly into a Swiss bank account.

Paul and Ingrid dined early and went to bed. Lying beside him, Ingrid smelt very feminine, a mixture of face powder and warm female flesh. Wafts of her perfume drifted under his nose as Paul's lips travelled across her shoulders, and the fragrance aroused a desire in him so sharp for Evelyn, he was forced to bite his lip.

Would it have been like this with her? Did her skin taste the same? Would she have closed her eyes and raised her face like Ingrid?

Paul kissed Ingrid's white shoulders again. Longing for

Evelyn drew him into that bleak inner landscape he remembered walking in as a child but never with such utter loneliness. In an effort to keep faith with what he did have with Ingrid, Paul shut his eyes and pulled her closer.

After she had fallen asleep, Paul lay awake. His father was safe, thanks to Admiral Canaris who had pulled the right strings. Thinner but no less defiant, Graf von Hoch had been extracted from the Flossenburg prison and packed off to Koblenz. Paul had faced questioning by the SD during the six weeks his father was imprisoned but the Admiral had spoken up for him too.

'I can't do it a second time,' he warned Paul. 'You are now on Gestapo files.'

'Look, Papa,' Paul in his turn warned his father, 'it wouldn't end with you. They would take Mother and Otto as well.'

'Think carefully, Paul. Honour or compromise?'

His father was mistaken. It wasn't as simple as that. It was the sort of statement which reminded him of the black and white of his childhood beliefs.

Paul turned over. He didn't feel well. Propping himself up on his elbow, he pushed back the blanket and reached for a cigarette. It tasted acrid and the smoke burned the back of his throat and made him feel hotter than he was. It was probably nothing. A cold, perhaps.

Tomorrow he would be told about his next posting. Paul suspected he would be sent to the Russian front. The Admiral had made it clear that he was worried by the stranglehold exerted by the SS in Russia, and wanted reliable reports as to what was going on.

Paul stubbed out the cigarette. No point in speculating. Wherever it was, he was sure of one thing, he did not want it to be anywhere in France.

The next thing he knew Ingrid was shaking him. 'For goodness sake, what's the matter? Are you having a nightmare?'

Paul turned his head with difficulty. 'Have I been talking in my sleep?'

'You certainly have.' She swung her legs out of bed. Paul watched her and waited to feel better. The sheets felt damp and lumpy, and lime dust from the bombed building next door filtered through the stuffy atmosphere. The sun was already up and a slanting ray thrust in through the curtains, white and brassy. 'Let's move into a hotel,' he said suddenly.

Ingrid laughed as she fastened her blouse. The last fortnight had seen her grow more sure of their relationship. By becoming involved in her family affairs, Paul slotted more securely into the warp and weft of her life where she so badly wanted him. 'Fine.' Not surprisingly she approved of the idea. 'You choose one.' She disappeared into the kitchen and came back with a cup of coffee. 'But don't expect better service.'

The pain in Paul's back became apparent when he was getting dressed. Then it struck him hard under the shoulder blades. He sat down on the mattress. Something *was* wrong, but he said nothing to Ingrid.

The pain accompanied him to the Tirpitzufer, hovered in his back for a while, moved to his chest and mounted an assault on his head. Paul's grasp of enemy activity in France loosened and he found himself fumbling for words. Von Bentivegni stared at Paul in some surprise. 'You don't look well.' Paul regarded his mentor with a glassy look and repressed the overwhelming desire to close his eyes and to slump back into the chair. 'You know our friends in the SD want to have another word with you soon,' said von Bentivegni. 'Are you prepared?'

Paul sat up. 'I don't know why they want to see me again.'

'Of course you do.' Von Bentivegni crossed one polished boot over the other and his monocle enlarged one eye to savage proportions. 'They've got their hooks into us, Paul, and you know it.' He pressed the monocle deeper into his eye socket. 'Now Paul, take care. This is likely to be the beginning of an open campaign against us. The Führer is not pleased with the Admiral.'

'The Führer is not pleased.' Sturmbannführer Siegfried Gehrbrandt – newly promoted – echoed von Bentivegni. They were sitting in Gehrbrandt's office in the SD headquarters in Wilhelmstrasse, where Paul had been summoned that afternoon.

'With me?' Paul asked flippantly. He had drunk a lot of

brandy to get rid of the headache and it was making him reckless.

'With the *Abwehr*,' said Gehrbrandt. 'However, I imagine you have nothing to worry about, von Hoch. Or do you?'

'Of course not.'

'The *Abwehr* let the Führer down badly over the question of how many divisions the Russians could put into the field. He always trusted the Admiral.'

In the corner of the room, a blonde-plaited clerk sat taking down a record of their conversation. Paul glanced at her blank face and was reminded of his secretary Fräulein Mitter. 'Yes,' he said, 'but it was unlikely to have made any difference in the end.'

'What do you mean?' Gehrbrandt scented his chance to bring down a charge of treason. He leant forward over his desk. 'Do you mean the German people are incapable of victory?'

How thoroughly he had changed from a boring, importunate young man into a zealot – a jackbooted copy of Hitler's Aryan prototype.

'Gehrbrandt. It is obvious you are no soldier.' It was an unwise remark and Gehrbrandt flushed with chagrin. 'To keep such a front open is a huge task at the best of times. Unreliable supplies – I gather one division had women's brassières delivered to it instead of boots – no roads to speak of, a different railway gauge and the Arctic winter. Add to that a bottomless well of Russian troops for Stalin to use as cannon fodder, and we have problems.'

'Are you criticising the Führer's judgement?'

'Merely laying the facts before him, Gehrbrandt.'

'What about the Dieppe incident?' Gehrbrandt threw in a reference to the inadequate intelligence supplied by the *Abwehr* to Hitler in August 1942.

'Look,' said Paul, who reckoned he had about ten minutes before he fainted and he was damned if he was going to give Gehrbrandt the pleasure of seeing him collapse, 'the Allied raid on Dieppe was launched by the British to appease Stalin. They knew perfectly well it wasn't going to succeed. So did we and we can learn from their folly. The enemy used new

362

guerrilla tactics in their advance party and they are bound to have obtained information on our coastal fortifications. We should work from there.'

Gehrbrandt returned to the subject of Russia. 'Did you know Admiral Canaris informed the Führer that in his opinion the invasion of Russia was a mistake?'

'Did he now?' The Admiral had struck Paul on occasion as over-cautious. Although in this case perhaps the timing had been wrong, Paul silently applauded his leader's courage. Gehrbrandt came round the desk, shifted the miniature Nazi flag that did service as a paperweight and leant back against the desk in front of Paul.

'Herr Major. There are those who think that all is not well in the *Abwehr*. There are suspicions – more than suspicions – that there may be traitors in the organisation. Do you know anything about this?'

Paul's contempt for Gehrbrandt kept him silent. 'Ah, you *do* know something?' Gehrbrandt's head darted forward.

'No, of course I don't.'

'May I remind you, von Hoch, you do have certain responsibilities – and, of course, your family to think of.'

Paul rose to his feet. 'If that was meant to be a veiled threat, Gehrbrandt, it was less than subtle.'

'I haven't finished the interview yet,' Gehrbrandt warned Paul.

'But I have. I don't know anything about traitors, Gehrbrandt. Nor should you concern yourself with my responsibilities.'

Gehrbrandt had been wanting to needle Paul over Ingrid for a long time. 'As an officer and a gentleman, you should be aware— '

Paul did not allow him to finish. 'Spare me the innuendo, Gehrbrandt. Ingrid is a grown woman and she is at liberty to make her own choices. Do you understand?' He put on his gloves and picked up his cap. Gehrbrandt came close and thrust his face into Paul's. 'If you discover traitors in the *Abwehr*, it would be wise to let me know their names, von Hoch.'

Paul stepped back, fever shuddering through him. 'If I did,

I promise you would be the first person to hear.' He adjusted his gloves. 'By the way, Ingrid asked me to send her regards.'

Gehrbrandt stiffened and turned his back. On his way out of the room, Paul thought he heard a stifled giggle from the clerk.

When he returned to the flat, he received a scolding from Ingrid for having gone out when he felt ill. 'Don't,' he begged. 'Just leave me.'

It was so unlike him that Ingrid was silenced. She felt his forehead and reached for the phone. Her movements danced along the line of Paul's vision. Then he fainted.

CHAPTER TWO

'So,' said Fleischer with distaste. 'You slept with a French girl. Is she Aryan?'

His question flustered Werner as it had not occurred to him to ask Mariette if she was Jewish and he realised he had been deficient in his duty. 'Yes. Yes, I'm sure she is.'

'You realise that under the relevant sections of the 1942 decrees you would be committing a major crime?'

'Sturmbannführer,' interjected Werner desperately. 'I am sure Madame Maisson is not a Jew.' He was regretting the impulse that had prompted him to request an interview with Fleischer.

They were in Fleischer's office at the *mairie* in Ribérac. Hitler's photograph now had a large Nazi flag draped under it, and there had been several additions to the china collection. Otherwise the room was the same as on the day of Evelyn's interrogations. Fleischer was enjoying himself – as he did frequently these days – especially since unoccupied France had fallen like a ripe plum the previous November and he was anticipating promotion. He had grown much plumper and less seedy-looking. His uniform was immaculate and the highly polished boots almost managed to hide that his feet were too small for his height. Fleischer opened a file and pulled a plate of *tarte aux amandes* towards him. Since Christmas the weather had been very cold indeed, and a blast of bitter air streamed in through the open window. 'Shut the window,' he ordered his aide.

Outside in the street a couple of women were shouting to each other and their conversation was truncated as the window closed. Fleischer opened the file, scrutinised the *tarte* and decided to hold out. He glanced up at Werner. 'Are you nervous about something, corporal? You seem very awkward.' Fleischer's hand edged towards the plate and then folded across the file. 'Why have you come to me? Did you think I would enjoy hearing about your amatory adventures?' He inflected the word 'amatory' as if he was discussing the latrine arrangements.

The colour in Werner's face deepened. 'No, Sturmbannführer. I merely thought I could be of use to you. The girl works at the Château Belle-Place and I thought— '

'Oh. Now why do you think I would want to know about the *château*?'

'Major von Hoch, sir, wanted to keep an eye . . . if you see what I mean, sir.'

Fleischer's interest was aroused but he hid it. After the promising leads he thought he had obtained the night of the failed terrorist attack on the factory and the shooting dead of a clandestine radio operator, he had congratulated himself on smashing the underground cell known to be operating in the area. Recently, however, reports were coming in of a new transmitter starting up. 'If Major von Hoch was keeping an eye on the *château*, I'm sure he would have told me,' he said. The thought of Paul von Hoch being onto something he had missed galled Fleischer, and it piqued him into extra vigilance.

Too late, Werner realised that he had exposed Major von Hoch in an incriminating light and felt more muddled than ever. 'Perhaps it's in the files, sir?'

'Perhaps,' commented Fleischer, his curiosity threatening to cancel out his appetite. 'I will look into it. Meanwhile,' Fleischer had spent too much time plotting his own advancement not to recognise the signs in someone else, 'where do you come from, corporal?' Werner told him.

'Aha, a forester. Large family?'

'Yes.'

'I see.' Fleischer saw very well. 'We would rather like a promotion, wouldn't we? Or a citation, a mention in dispatches to send back to your family who can then boast about you to the village. The local hero. Am I right?'

Werner blinked nervously. That was precisely what he wanted. Like many of his fellow soldiers, he considered it his duty to carry out the Führer's wishes – indeed, he was proud to do so. But it was very difficult to make your mark as a member of the occupying force – much easier by far to win glory in combat on one of the front lines. Werner, however, was irretrievably in France, running around like a glorified errand boy. Having puzzled at the problem, he had concluded that by offering to obtain information from Mariette he would be put in line for promotion. 'That would be nice, yes, sir.'

'Was this your own idea?' Fleischer flicked up a questioning eyebrow.

Although Werner respected the accretion of power that Sturmbannführer Fleischer wore these days like flashy insignia, he distrusted him. Now all he wanted was to get away. The whole idea had been a mistake, and he felt out of his depth. And, far from encouraging him, the portrait of his Führer on the wall was an intimidating presence. 'Sir, perhaps . . .'

'You will bring this girl in for questioning.'

Werner had been anticipating a few pleasant trips to Mariette's cottage, not a demand from Fleischer to bring Mariette in for interrogation. 'Sir, must I?'

'Why not? You told me about her. Or were you planning to keep it a little secret between us two?'

'Sir, if I bring her in, she won't trust me.'

The almond cake did look extraordinarily good and Fleischer could resist it no longer. He picked up a piece. 'Trust, Schwarz? What on earth are you talking about? Trust has nothing to do with it.' A spray of crumbs spattered onto the papers on Fleischer's desk. He chewed and the almond cake disappeared.

Werner swallowed. 'Yes, sir.'

'What's the matter?' Mariette asked Werner several hours later. 'Didn't you like it?' Her tone was modulated with a hint of martyrdom. 'Are you worried about something? Or have you gone off me?'

Werner sat on the edge of Mariette's bed and bent to lace up his boots. 'It was fine,' he said. 'It always is.'

Mariette lay back and ran her hand over her stomach. At least that was hard and flat again. 'Do you want some coffee?'

Seeing that Werner had brought the coffee beans, she felt obliged to offer.

'*Ja*. If you please.'

'It's nice to see you.' Mariette sounded rather sarcastic. 'I thought you had given me up. The last time must have been before Christmas.'

'Well . . .' Werner seemed uneasy and embarrassed. 'I have been busy.' He straightened up. 'But I often think about you, and about . . . you know.'

'Oh,' she said. 'You mean the baby.' Mariette rolled out of bed, stood up and reached for her wrapper. 'That was over months ago. It was a good thing,' she added, and tried to pretend that she meant it.

Werner started on his tunic buttons. 'I do like you, you know, Mariette.'

She giggled at that, and a ripple of something like affection went through her. It seemed a long time since Mariette had felt anything but apathy – a long time since Guy Myers had used her and then told her to go away. A long time since Werner had first rolled up on his pampered motorcycle and lifted the children onto the saddle. Even Werner's temporary absence had not bothered her. She had learnt not to expect too much. Even so, she reached over and touched Werner's mouth with her finger, enjoying his clean-cut boyish blondness. Werner was not Guy Myers, but he was nice. Comforting and somehow safe. She knew where she was with him. 'Right, soldier boy. Coffee's coming. But you'll have to hurry. My mother and the children will be back soon.'

While Mariette busied herself in the kitchen, Werner wrestled with the remainder of the fastenings and stared out of the window. He had never imagined that he would miss his forests so much. He enjoyed the Périgord countryside, but he wanted to be back in his forest. He missed the scents of leaf mould and pine. He missed walking through the trees, counting the beeches and chestnuts and watching for chamois, elk, martens and hares. In short, he was homesick.

Sighing, he pulled the quilted cotton coverlet over the sheets, patted ineffectually at the bolster and went downstairs.

Mariette always made good coffee. Werner sat facing her across the table and drank it slowly while he worked out the next move. Mariette's cotton wrapper had fallen open across her thighs, and when she leant forward Werner caught a glimpse of the v between her breasts. He looked away, hating what he was going to have to do.

When he told Mariette that Fleischer wanted to see her, Mariette did not like it either. The relaxed, almost trusting expression fled and she threw Werner a look of utter bewilderment. 'I thought all that had come to an end when the other man left.' It had been such a relief when Paul had gone and she did not have to tell Werner about the goings on at Belle-Place. Not that Mariette had ever found out anything she thought really interesting. 'Have you got me into trouble?'

'Please don't ask questions,' Werner said. 'Just come with me to Ribérac.'

She pushed away her coffee and stood up. 'What have you done, Werner?' Her voice rose in pitch.

'Mariette, I wouldn't do anything to harm you. How could you think such a thing?'

'You tell me.'

'It's no use, you've got to come. Otherwise they will pick you up. Please believe me.'

She could see he was very serious, and after a minute Mariette went upstairs and got dressed. He helped her put on her coat, to which Mariette submitted without a word. Without a word she allowed him to help her onto the motorcycle.

Once she would have enjoyed the thrill of roaring down the road, clinging to the broad back of her lover. It would have been an exciting, giddy diversion. Instead, the cold wind drove ice into her heart where it crystallised into dread.

When they reached the *mairie*, Werner handed her down, guilty and unable to look her in the face. 'I'll wait for you,' he whispered.

Mariette did not reply. He tried to squeeze her hand but she pulled away, and he was left with the feel of her frozen skin, surprised by how much he minded her contempt.

* * *

369

The *écrevisses* he had eaten the previous evening had disagreed with Fleischer and the effect had been violent and unpleasant. Consequently he was in a vile temper. Nevertheless, Fleischer could not permit himself to stay in bed; he did not like to think of what might go on behind his back. He sipped at a glass of peppermint tea and wondered if the shellfish had been deliberately doctored and whether he should call the restaurant's chef in for questioning. The announcement of Mariette's arrival did nothing to lighten his mood. Another French slut.

When she was ushered in, he did not ask Mariette to sit down but launched straight into his attack. 'Your children. How old are they? Where is their father?'

Mariette felt so angry with Werner that she forgot to be intimidated by the uniform with the notorious ss flashes. She stared Fleischer straight in the eye and answered his questions without hesitation. 'Yes,' he interjected a couple of times. Then he changed tack. 'What a shame you have no husband to support you.' He observed with a shudder the darned socks and the goose pimples running up her arm under her cheap coat. Surely Schwarz – in Fleischer's view a good-looking young man with silky bronze skin and thick bright gold hair – could have done better. Still, at least she was evidently not Jewish.

'You want to know why you are here,' Fleischer snapped as his stomach twinged warningly. 'I will get to the point. I want some intelligence – information, you know – and you appear to be the person to provide me with it.'

The girl's mouth drew into a sullen pout. 'I don't know anything,' she said quickly.

Fleischer observed her cynically and pushed a packet of cigarettes towards her over the top of the desk. 'Go on,' he invited, and watched her light up. 'You work at the Château Belle-Place. I have reason to think that certain terrorists are using it as their base. I want you to ask a few questions, keep your eyes open for anything unusual going on, that sort of thing. I'm sure you know what I mean. Corporal Schwarz will relay the information to me.'

'I haven't been up there for months,' Mariette said defensively. 'Since . . .' she broke off. She was not going to tell this man that she had not been up to Belle-Place since the episode with Guy.

'You will arrange to return to work there, Madame, and you will report back via your friend, Corporal Schwarz.'

No banknotes this time, she thought. No offers of medical help. She shook her head. 'I don't want to do it.'

Fleischer did not have the energy to embark on long-winded methods of persuasion and, anyway, the girl was not worth the effort. In a case like this a simple demonstration would do the trick. 'Come with me,' he ordered.

His thick, breeched figure preceded Mariette down the stairs. At the bottom he stopped, belched discreetly into his hand and indicated she should descend a flight of stairs to the cellar. Half-way down, Mariette grew frightened. It seemed a long way to the bottom. The walls ran with damp and there was an obnoxious smell seeping up the staircase, an unfamiliar sickening odour. Fleischer prodded Mariette along a stone passage off to the right which opened into a room lit by a bare electric light. Under it sat a couple of guards playing cards and drinking out of tin mugs. The smell was so bad here that Mariette almost retched.

'Foul, isn't it?' said Fleischer, belching audibly. He took his handkerchief out of his pocket, held it to his face and beckoned to one of the guards who had jumped to their feet on seeing him. 'Show us cell three.'

Almost faint from the smell and the sense that something terrible was about to happen, Mariette searched frantically in her coat pocket for her handkerchief. The guard selected a key from his hoop and fitted it into a door set into the stone which had a 3 chalked on it.

'I hope this will be instructive, Madame,' Fleischer said through the handkerchief, and Mariette wanted to laugh hysterically at the absurd picture he made.

As the guard opened the door, Mariette felt Fleischer's hand in the small of her back. She stepped forward into the open doorway. The thing that lay on the straw mattress inside the cell didn't seem human any longer. At the sound of the door opening, it raised its head and Mariette was unable to look away. From the place where the mouth should have been issued a word. It might have been 'please', she couldn't tell. As her eyes adjusted to the gloom she made out a hand raised towards them and, by its shape and smallness, knew that it belonged to a woman.

'This one has four children.' Fleischer's voice was muffled through the handkerchief.

The guard closed the door and moved on to the next cell. 'Please, no!' whispered Mariette.

Ignoring her, Fleischer stepped aside so that Mariette obtained an uninterrupted view of the inmate of cell number 4. She backed away, stumbled against the guard and gave a sob. Fleischer ordered her brusquely to follow him back upstairs.

In the office, she stared at the lustred china figurines as Fleischer gave orders for a fresh pot of peppermint tea. 'Now, down to business. Are you going to do what I asked?'

Mariette's shock made it difficult to reply, and she could only stare at him. Fleischer unscrewed the top of his fountain pen. 'My dear Madame, you don't want to end up downstairs, do you?' He could have been referring to the kitchens from the matter-of-factness of his tone, and Mariette wondered if this man was mad.

'Why are those people down there?' she asked at last through dry lips. 'What have they done?'

'Various things. They made friends unwisely. Some refused to be obliging . . .'

Mariette's protest was stifled before it was voiced and her anger at what she had seen dissolved into panic. Why me? she thought. What have I done?

Across the desk Fleischer guessed something of her thoughts. 'Well?' he said impatiently. 'Hurry up.'

Mariette was forced to close her eyes on a picture of Jacques and Jeannette crying out for her as a uniformed Werner beat her face to a pulp. 'Monsieur,' she said, shaking. 'There is someone at the *château* who is a little suspicious.' Mariette began hesitantly, but gradually warmed to her theme. Fleischer relaxed back into his chair. 'His name is Guy Maier . . .' That will sort him out, she thought.

Twenty minutes later when she walked back into the street holding a packet of cigarettes, Werner crossed over the road towards her. He had been waiting by his motorcycle, occupying a long thirty minutes by polishing it unnecessarily bright. 'Was it all right, Mariette?'

Mariette did not answer him. She was sobbing too hard – with fright and with shame. She was also sobbing because her life was such a mess and she could not see what was right or wrong any more.

'Mariette.' Werner grabbed at her hand. 'Please look at me.'

She clutched Fleischer's cigarettes to her chest. 'Just go away.'

Werner chafed her hand between his. 'I'm so sorry,' he said. 'So very, very sorry. Please believe me. I would never have done this if I'd thought.' He rubbed harder at the hand, crushing the knuckles, but she took no notice. 'I can't say this very well, Mariette, but I care too much for you to wish you any harm.'

Recovering enough to be surprised, she looked up at the corporal. Tears smeared down her cheeks and filled her eyes. 'Go away,' she said. 'Leave me in peace.'

'Can't I come and see you again? Please.'

Mariette paused. No more butter, no more cheese or coffee or ham, no more comfortable chats over glasses of beer, no more stories of the forest, no one beside her in bed, only that terrible, belching man harrying her for information.

No.

She pocketed the cigarettes and wiped her nose with the back of her hand. 'Why not?' she informed Werner in a hard voice. 'I might as well be hung for a sheep as a lamb.'

Marie told Mariette that she would be pleased if Mariette wanted to take on extra work at the *château*. It was becoming so difficult to get help these days. 'The men are being sent away to Germany – or they're in hiding. And nobody else has much time to help out, what with queuing for rations and everything.' Marie tapped the kitchen table with the knife she was sharpening. 'Even Mademoiselle Liegaux has gone home to Tours. It quite upset the Countess. I found her crying over it once.'

Mariette carefully washed a bunch of early spinach in the sink. 'Why did she go?'

'I don't know,' said Marie. 'Her family wanted her back at home. She left in September, I think it was. The Countess hasn't been able to replace her so she's doing all the work herself.'

The spinach was dirty and required a vigorous wash. Mariette wrapped it in a clean linen cloth and took it outside to the stable courtyard to shake it dry. She stood enjoying the struggling spring sunshine, wondering if she should tell Werner that Mademoiselle Liegaux had left her job at the *château* when a black-robed figure wheeled a bicycle through the stone arch. The spinach water dripped through the tea-cloth onto Mariette's feet as she watched Sister Hélène being ushered in through the front door by Gaston. Now that the fright of her interview with Fleischer had worn off, Mariette faced the prospect of spying for him with resignation, even boredom. What on earth did he want to know about a pampered widow, and a handful of elderly retainers? There was Guy, of course, but Mariette reckoned she'd catered for him already. She returned to the kitchen.

Bessy was reading in the Blue Salon when Hélène was announced. She was reclining on the sofa with her tawny hair drawn back into a roll, twisting and untwisting the pearls at her throat as she digested the papers on her lap. When Gaston opened the door, she slid the papers under a cushion and got up to greet her guest.

'You seem well, Sister,' Bessy said, after scrutinising Hélène in her direct way. Although Hélène had come to represent strength for Bessy, there had always been the suggestion of an unresolved inner struggle in the nun. On the occasions they had met, Bessy always noticed a certain rigidity in the way Hélène held herself – that and her guarded answers to questions about the family had alerted Bessy.

'I think you might be interested in these.' Bessy retrieved

her reading matter from its hiding place and gave the papers to Hélène. She rang for Gaston. 'Tea?'

Hélène smiled. 'Such an English habit. But I'd enjoy keeping you company. Reverend Mother has permitted me to come and enquire after you but I can see it was unnecessary. How is the baby?'

'Not a baby any more,' Bessy replied with regret, 'and almost talking.'

Bessy was hoping to discuss Charles's teething problems but Hélène was diverted by the contents of the pamphlet. '. . . that children, that women, fathers and mothers be separated from one another and dispatched to an unknown destination, it has been reserved for our time to see such a spectacle . . .' The document was signed by Monsignor Jules-Gérard Saliège, archbishop of Toulouse.

'Where did you get this?'

'Well,' Bessy said, dropping her voice, 'it's being secretly distributed from parish to parish by cyclists.' She held up her hands in a gesture of warning. 'Please keep your voice down.'

Hélène turned the paper over. 'I am very glad,' she said. 'I have felt guilty sometimes that the Church has failed to speak out. I've been praying that our leaders would do so in the end.'

'Hm.' Bessy poured a cup of tea from the tray that Gaston had set down on the side table. 'I'm afraid, *thé à l'anglais* is all I have.' She handed a cup to Hélène. 'You know that since the Germans invaded Vichy France last December they have issued a compulsory work order for all able-bodied men?'

'I hear talk in the infirmary,' Hélène replied, 'but everybody is so confused and frightened these days one can't be sure of anything.'

'Gaston told me that hundreds of young men have gone into hiding. They face execution if caught.'

Hélène drank her tea and tried to enjoy it. 'I heard that the Germans evacuated the entire old port of Marseille. Simply turned all the inhabitants out.'

'Yes, I heard that too.'

There was a pause. Bessy twisted the pearls at her throat and changed the subject. 'How is your work at the clinic?'

'Yes.' Hélène leant forward on her seat. 'That brings me to the point of the visit. St Euphonie's needs money to buy drugs. Many are unobtainable but we can get morphine and aspirin on the black market.' As she spoke she assessed Bessy's pearls: milky, lustrous, large as aniseed balls. The Countess followed the line of the nun's gaze and her big eyes widened as she understood.

'I see,' she said. 'Yes, well, I have been meaning to sell some of my jewellery to raise money for the hospital in Ribérac. Marie's mother was treated there recently.'

Hélène smiled encouragingly.

With only the tiniest of hesitations, Bessy undid the clasp at her neck, and the pearls slid snaky soft into the palm of her hand. She was conscious of the contrast between the severe black lines of the nun's habit and her own beautifully made, albeit worn, navy blue serge skirt and lambswool jumper. She pressed the necklace into Hélène's hands.

'They are very beautiful.' Hélène examined them carefully.

'Yes, Sister, they are. Charles gave them to me.' Bessy felt absurdly tearful at the thought of their fate. 'But I'd rather they bought drugs. And I'm sure you would too.'

Bessy had not realised that Hélène was capable of grinning. The broad smile transformed the chilly features and made the nun seem ten years younger. Hélène examined the clasp. 'Two good diamonds. They alone must be very valuable.'

Bessy almost laughed. 'How very worldly you are, Sister. Perhaps you don't need help to sell them on the black market?'

'Certainly not. I have my agents.' Hélène spread the necklace between her hands. 'One should never trust appearances, my dear.'

Bessy leant back against the blue brocade of the sofa. 'You know, I remember being rather jealous of you once, when Charles told me what friends you had been in childhood.'

'There was absolutely no need.' Hélène thought how very typical it was of Charles to describe them as friends.

'I think he loved you very much,' Bessy said earnestly.

'I have no past life, you know, other than my life in God.'

Rebuffed, Bessy gathered up the papers on the sofa. 'Dear

me,' she said a shade acerbically, 'I do so think it is better to talk about these things.'

'Perhaps.'

To defuse the tension that the mention of Charles had engendered, Bessy changed the subject. 'Will you be coming again, Sister?'

'I don't think so.' Hélène held out her hand to say goodbye.

'I hope you are able to get the drugs you need.' Bessy accompanied the nun to the door of the Blue Salon and instructed Gaston to fetch Sister Hélène's bicycle. The room felt very empty when she returned and she watched Hélène from the window exchanging a few words with Gaston before mounting her bicycle and riding off down the drive. Feeling lonely, Bessy glanced at her watch. Charles had been taken out for a walk by Marie, and she thought Guy was painting in his studio. These days he did little else apart from his forays into the town where she suspected he spent his time drinking. 'Don't fuss, twin,' he snapped when she scolded him about it. Bessy took the hint.

She straightened the blotter on her desk and looked up at the portrait of Charles that hung above it. It was a large, boldly executed oil that she had never liked. Nevertheless, it was a daily reminder of how much she missed him. She sighed and turned away. She missed Evelyn too, and wondered where she was. In a safe house? Living rough in the woods with the *réfractaires*?

A week after the tyre factory raid, Evelyn had walked out of Belle-Place with her suitcase, declaring that she was going home to her family after staging an argument with Bessy in the hallway the day before. Bessy had also let it be known to as many people as possible how disappointed she was by this behaviour, how she had relied on Evelyn to help with the running of the *château* and its wine business and how ungrateful the girl was to abandon her, knowing full well how this snippet of gossip would spread around the neighbourhood.

Since July, Bessy had only seen Evelyn three or four times at snatched meetings in safe houses. There was no passing of intelligence, they merely wanted to reassure each other that all was well. Bessy would not have been human if she had

377

not felt some relief that someone who had the potential to destroy them was no longer living under her roof but she missed Evelyn, her presence at meals, her bad jokes, the shared interest in clothes, her enthusiasms for food and books and the inestimable comfort of her female companionship. There was another bond: Evelyn had been there when Charles died and Bessy could never forget that.

When the war ended . . . when? . . . Bessy planned to take a vacation in America. Show off baby Charles to her family. Eat as much as she liked – damp, dark devil's food cake with fudge icing, squaw bread and salt cod stew, waffles drowning in maple syrup, Virginia ham with turnips and gravy. She imagined walking down Fifth Avenue and looking into shop windows stuffed with goods: silk stockings, pure wool dresses, leather shoes. She could buy books. Luxuriate in the optimism and energy that had disappeared from France. When the war was over.

To shake off her depression, she went in search of her brother.

'Ough.' Bessy shivered as she came into the room which smelt strongly of linseed oil and turpentine. 'How on earth do you manage to work in here when it's so cold?' She pushed aside a stack of tubes and leant back against the table.

'Careful,' he said, not bothering to look up. 'Supplies are getting short.'

Guy was working hard at a picture and obviously did not welcome the interruption. Bessy glanced around the studio. It was a mess of canvases, filthy rags, tubes of paint and empty bottles. It continually surprised her that the fastidious Guy could work in these surroundings. 'Disgusting,' she commented.

'Go away, sis.'

'Guy.' Bessy decided to broach a subject that had been on her mind. 'Isn't it time you did something?'

'I'm doing plenty.'

'Be serious!' Bessy spoke more sharply than she intended.

At this Guy looked up from his work. 'Oh, Lord.' He predicted, 'Another lecture.' He looked up at his twin with raised eyebrows. 'I know you too well, Bessy.'

His sister fiddled with a brush on the table. 'All right, but I've got to say this. I really mean it, Guy.' Out of habit she put up a hand to touch her pearls and felt a bare throat. 'When we were children we used to promise that we would always tell one another the truth. We said we'd never fudge an issue if it involved the other.'

Guy put down his brush slowly and with great precision. 'If you mean you wanted me to tell you when I thought your boyfriends were awful, then yes.'

She shook her head with impatience. 'Don't be flippant.'

'Then don't go on.' He sounded good-humoured, but Bessy recognised of old the edge that had crept into his voice. She knew it indicated that a tussle lay ahead and sometimes she had retreated worsted. But today she was driven by her old daemon: a pricking conscience. 'Guy, you must join up. It's your duty.'

'Duty, shit,' replied her brother. 'Mind your own business.' He picked up his canvas and looked at it. 'What do you think of this?'

At first Bessy did not pay it any attention but then something about the painting caught her attention and she looked more closely. Two figures in a field. Shaded by a chestnut tree with a hot blue sky above. Between the couple there was a surface intimacy, because the man was embracing the woman. There was an underlying tension, however, in the eyes of the woman, who was twisting away in the man's grasp. The woman was Evelyn.

Bessy made no comment except, 'It's very good.'

'Of course it is.' Guy was matter of fact. He tapped the edge of the canvas with one blue-stained finger. 'This is what matters, not going out to die uncomfortably on some goddamned battlefield.' He squinted at the tree on the canvas. 'I haven't got that bit quite right.'

Bessy had not realised until now how much Guy's attitude repulsed her. It was so easy and agreeable at first, but on reflection totally specious. She struggled to put her objections into words. 'You must be prepared to do more than paint. Your principles must tell you that.'

'Oh, don't be so simple,' said Guy unkindly. 'There are no

379

grey areas for you, are there, Bessy? Stupid people think like that and you're not stupid. By the way,' he said, noticing her bare neck, 'where are your pearls?'

'You're wrong.' Bessy cut across him with a passionate outburst. 'Utterly wrong. Don't you see what's happening in France? We must try to stop it.'

Guy was searching through a stack of canvases. 'You shouldn't believe everything you hear,' he said, finding the one he wanted. 'People exaggerate.'

'Don't you care at all, Guy?' she asked in a low voice.

He folded his arms across his chest and leant back against the table. 'I look at it this way' – Bessy had the disturbing impression that she was listening to a stranger – 'I have a duty to myself to survive. I am far too valuable to waste. I'm safe at Belle-Place for the moment, I'm excited by my work and you like having me around. I'm not prepared to put my neck voluntarily into a noose. Besides, I don't fancy trekking over the Pyrenees.'

Before she stopped to think Bessy said, 'Then Evelyn was right to . . .'

'Yes,' Guy's voice resembled a whiplash. 'And what was little Mademoiselle Liegaux right about?'

Bessy cursed her slip. She had been about to say Evelyn was right not to recruit Guy. 'Nothing,' she said coldly, and thought to herself, I hate this war even more than I thought. It's driving Guy and me apart.

Nettled by the allusion to Evelyn, Guy picked up the canvas he had looked out, placed it on the table and swivelled it towards his sister. 'Here, look at this. Who's this beauty?'

'Evelyn!' she answered with a gasp. The portrait was subtle and deliberately provocative. It depicted a young woman with ivory skin and green eyes. Yet it had a flaw. Guy had painted in the mouth with cunning, mixing deceit and slyness, triumphant female predatoriness and contempt. The effect was monstrous. 'It's wicked,' Bessy pronounced, and looked away, adding in a low voice, 'And you're cruel to have done such a thing.'

Guy teased. 'It's an artistic impression, Bessy, that's all. Don't take it so damn seriously.'

She was silent at that. Guy swung the portrait down off the table and turned it face in to the wall. Then he reached for a bottle of wine on the mantelpiece and poured himself a glass. 'Where is she, by the way?' he asked casually.

Bessy made for the door. 'I'm beginning to understand something. Evelyn had the temerity not to fall over herself at the sight of your male beauty. Is that it?'

Guy drank a mouthful of claret. 'Could be,' he said. 'I wasn't that interested in her. Not enough to make an effort, anyway. She was just a pretty subject to paint.'

'Leave her be, Guy. You don't understand.'

'Ah,' he said, quick as a flash. 'There is something unusual about the girl. I thought there might be.'

Bessy looked down at her hands. 'Concentrate on your painting, Guy, since that is what you want, and don't poke your nose into other people's business.'

Guy was checked by this uncharacteristic snub from Bessy. His smile disappeared and he poured himself some more wine. 'Do you mean, sister, that I shouldn't become involved in your childish little muddles? Oh yes, I know more than you think I do. And you with a young son to protect.'

Guy had hit her where he knew it would hurt most. Bessy paused with one hand on the door handle. 'I love you, Guy, and I suppose I always shall, but there are some things we had better not discuss.'

He laughed rudely. 'Go away and stop being pompous.'

Sick at heart, she jerked open the door. 'You should join up, Guy.'

Left alone, Guy emptied a third glass and enjoyed the burning path the wine made on its way down to his stomach. All the same, he was frowning as he drank. Bessy's attack had not left him entirely unmoved; he had a deep-rooted respect for his sister. For a brief moment he toyed with the idea of doing as she suggested – he even saw a chance to achieve fame as a war artist – until the idea struck him as too funny. Guy Myers and uniform were anathema to each other and he knew perfectly well that he would never have the energy or the conviction to fight.

He stretched out a foot and poked the back of Evelyn's

portrait. 'Stupid girl.' The conversation with Bessy had anchored some floating suspicions. Guy was sure that Mademoiselle Liegaux had been up to something while she was at Belle-Place – and that Bessy knew about it. He was also practically sure that she had not gone 'home' to Tours or anywhere else for that matter. Only a week ago, he had been walking up the road to Lusignac when a car passed him. A passenger in the back seat had looked remarkably like Evelyn. At the time Guy had not paid much attention but now the sighting began to make more sense.

It piqued him that something was being kept from him and he made up his mind to question Bessy later. He analysed the portrait thoughtfully and an idea took shape. Picking up the canvas, he carried it out of the studio and down the passage to Evelyn's old bedroom.

It was extremely neat and smelt empty as unoccupied rooms often do. Guy crossed over to the empty fireplace and propped the portrait up against it. Then he stood back to admire the effect. The girl's skin tones gleamed in the darkening afternoon light; her painted face and strange mouth dominated the room. Guy contemplated it with some satisfaction and then left the room, closing the door after him.

CHAPTER THREE

Since Evelyn abandoned Belle-Place as her headquarters, she had been constantly on the move. A bed shared here with a child, another in the corner of a barn, two nights in a seedy hotel in Chalais, another in a brothel in Périgueux, and an uncomfortable week over Christmas and New Year stuffed into a tiny but freezing attic.

The German invasion of the Vichy zone in November 1942 – taken, they said, in response to the Allied invasion of North Africa – had increased the circuit's difficulties. The demarcation line still existed in fact if not in theory and travel was still as hedged around with obstacles. German soldiers and security forces were now everywhere.

Dressed in a grey divided skirt, a blouse and a grey jacket, carrying only a spare set of underclothes and spare socks in her luggage, Evelyn moved on every three days. After she left Belle-Place, she made Jack cut her hair, which he did with reluctance. They were in a room above a bar in Lusignac. Jack fetched a bucket of water, wet Evelyn's hair and clubbed it off with a pair of scissors.

'Samson's revenge,' he said, and held up the four inches for Evelyn to inspect.

Then he helped her to apply red dye from a bottle, wiping the drips from around her hairline. Afterwards they examined their handiwork in a small pocket mirror. Still stained with smudges of red dye, Evelyn suddenly appeared very Italian. A Veronese beauty with newly exposed neck and jawline, whose name, according to her forged identity card, was now Marie Vertvertier. Jack whistled and said, '*Bella*,' a compliment which Evelyn accepted with little grace.

By May the dye had almost grown out, and Evelyn's hair was long again, luckily undamaged by the fierce chemicals.

Her underclothes were now down to one vest, shrunk beyond recognition by constant washing and hasty drying over fires, and one pair of socks which she was forced to rinse and dry overnight, often putting them on still wet.

No more silk-swagged beds or silver-backed hairbrushes laid out on the dressing table. No more companionable meals eaten with Bessy and the luxury of late-night conversations by the fire in the Blue Salon. Evelyn had been spoilt and she knew it. Yet landing up in the care of Madame Gérine was an excellent alternative. Madame Gérine ran the farm in her husband's absence as well as her own poultry business. She administered to seven children, the youngest being only ten, and still had time to take in needlework to supplement the family income. *Mère* Gérine was a formidable woman who did not appear at all daunted either by her domestic burdens or by the German occupiers.

'I am so bored with those *salauds*, the Boches,' she would announce, particularly if another restriction or deprivation had come into force. 'Bored to the depths of my soul, may the good Lord forgive me.' She was a mountainous lady, given to roaring laughs and sudden explosions of temper, whose husband had been deported to Germany in 1940 where he worked in the armaments industry. Her house was immaculate and Gérine hospitality was a local talking point. Madame Gérine adored cooking, rose to the challenge of rationing and produced superb meals to which she invited a succession of friends, thus forcing Evelyn to take refuge upstairs. She was one of the sanest people Evelyn had met in a long time, and her stay in the isolated farmhouse was an oasis of good humour and normality. Despite the danger involved in harbouring a 'terrorist', Madame Gérine invited Evelyn to stay with her for as long as it took to get rid of the vermin from France. Evelyn accepted the offer for as long as she dared.

Madame Gérine went out of her way during her busy day to make sure that Evelyn was comfortable. Easing into a smotheringly soft duck-down bed each night, in the company of a collection of national dolls of particularly garish appearance, and with a parting sign of the cross made over her by Madame Gérine, Evelyn could only be grateful.

'*Je suis votre ange de la résistance,*' Madame Gérine would say, leaning over the bed, spreading her fat arms like wings. Then she would shake with laughter at her wit. Evelyn reckoned it was the truth. With their courage and willingness, women like Madame Gérine were the linchpins of a resistance that was growing and growing . . .

Where there was once caution born of fear or indifference, now there were voluntary offers of help from all sides, as well as open expressions of hostility to the Nazis. Above all, there was a swelling tally of *réfractaires* and Evelyn sent several messages back to home station with details of the growth of an underground army . . .

Evelyn stood up on the bicycle pedals as her least favourite hill came into view and began the ascent. She was on her way to meet Jack at his safe house in Chapdeuil.

In principle their objectives were clear: to recruit and to train the recruits as thoroughly as possible. (Evelyn still blamed herself for Nicolas's death: for letting the boy go into Operation Michelin with barely any training.) Between them they had organised two successful container drops, one in October last year, and the second in March. The supplies had been brought in by Halifaxes and arrived precisely on targets Blackberry and Quince (Quince being sited outrageously close to a Panzer division on exercise). The drops had increased their standing with their teams. Evelyn now possessed a respectable supply of Stens, Lee-Enfield rifles, Mills grenades, plastic explosive, detonators, field dressings and money. She also had access to '*conforts*': powdered coffee, tea, cigarettes, chocolate and unmarked cigarettes which, enjoying the pleasure they gave, she distributed among the *réseau* members.

The first drop had also brought with it a new wireless set – a Type 3 Mark II. London promised to send over a new operator as soon as they could train one. Until then, Jack was operating the set. Evelyn was apprehensive until he explained he had completed the special training course.

'Why?' Evelyn was curious why a sabotage specialist should have taken wireless training.

'Obvious.' Jack smiled rather engagingly. 'It makes you less dependent. We should all be able to send messages, don't you think?' He spread his hands in a John-like gesture. 'What would you have done without me?'

If she had not been saddened by a sudden aching reminder that John was dead, Evelyn would have laughed.

She began to pant as she neared the crest of the hill and her calf muscles began their daily protest at the treatment they received. It was an amazing piece of good luck that Jack could step into John's place.

'No breast-beating, duckies, if you please . . . Well, just a little then, but not too much.' In the first few days after John's death, Evelyn had been flattened by 'if onlys' and kept hearing his voice in her ear.

'You're tired,' Jack said brusquely when Evelyn tried to explain how guilty she felt about John's death. 'Olivier understood the risks, and he was sensible enough to get himself killed. That way they couldn't beat any information out of him. There's a good chance the Boches will never know who he was.'

Practical and astringent, the words helped to pull Evelyn's thoughts into order. She was pleasantly surprised that Jack understood how best to help her.

By now, she was panting in earnest. The trees along the verge had brilliant acid-green leaves. An eddy of wind caught her face and cooled her. Her divided skirt flapped over her thighs as she crested the hill and began to coast down the road towards the village of Verteillac. Lussac manor came into view on her left and she braked to turn up the path that led up to it.

Later in date than Belle-Place, the manor was enclosed by a stone wall and had a double flight of steps leading up to the front door. Evelyn enjoyed looking at the house as she dismounted and, pushing her bicycle, walked slowly past the front gate.

Ten yards further up the road she came to a barn. She stopped, pretended to adjust the chain on her bicycle and pulled a piece of paper out from under a loose coping stone. Keeping the paper concealed in her hand, she pedalled along an unmade track until she rounded the corner. Here she halted in order to read the message.

'Report in Boche HQ states that Mariette Maisson, who works intermittently at Belle-Place, has been questioned by Fleischer. She is known to have a German lover. Jean-Claude.'

'Bloody hell.' Evelyn tore the message into minute fragments and stuffed them under a thick bank of hedgerow. Then she turned the bicycle around.

A hour later she arrived blown and panting at the village of Chapdeuil, having successfully negotiated her way over the old line. Dominated by a thirteenth-century *donjon* and its ancient *pigeonnier* the village had once thrived. Now the stone cottages were flaking with neglect and an air of general malaise hung over the streets.

At Labelle's, a large, square, three-storeyed stone house, Evelyn wheeled her bicycle across the back yard and hid it behind a rotting henhouse. When she was sure it was safe to do so, she whistled the opening bars of 'Je tire ma révérencé', and a dark head appeared in the upper window.

A fire burned in the kitchen and Evelyn settled in front of it with a mug of *bouillon* from a pot on the stove. Even though it was May, the afternoon was cool. Jack had been up early helping the family in the fields before they went off to market with the week's crop and was dressed in muddy overalls. He was also unshaven.

'So,' he commented after Evelyn gave him the latest piece of information from Jean-Claude. 'You were right to leave Belle-Place.' He pushed back his hair and left a smear of dirt on his forehead.

'I must inform Bessy,' she told him, reaching over or impulse to brush it off.

Jack nodded.

Evelyn picked up her mug and drank some of the soup. 'Are you going to come and meet the boys living in the woods? I reckon I'll need to be there for about three or four days.' Jack and she had decided that they should use the *réfractaires* in operations. Evelyn opted to train a group living in the woods by the lake of Jemaye, and Jack would join her, whenever possible, to train them in basic sabotage techniques.

'The maquis lot? Of course. I'll come with you and return when my sked's due.'

The fire made Evelyn feel drowsy after her exercise and a silence fell. It was very pleasant to sit and say nothing, enjoying a moment of peace. Jack stood in front of her, warming his backside and rubbing at his eyes. 'If I stay here much longer I'll turn into a complete drunkard.'

She smiled sleepily. 'Drinking in the fields again?'

'It's a point of honour to get through a litre before lunch.' Jack was plainly in awe of this feat of consumption. 'I have to keep my end up,' he explained.

'Have some *bouillon*, maybe it'll sober you up.' The fire spat an ember at her feet and she rubbed it out with her toe. The kitchen smelt of the dried hams and herbs hanging from the ceiling. It was a pleasantly cluttered room with a peaceful, unhurried atmosphere. Reluctantly Evelyn stirred herself.

'Are you pleased with your new set of identity papers?' A contact of Evelyn's had discovered a brilliant forger in Bourdeilles who was willing to work for them. His first task had been to make Jack some fresh papers.

'Thiery, Jacques.' Jack recited the information and pushed back his hair. 'Born 10 September 1910, in the 8th arrondissement of Paris. Son of Tomas Thiery, architect, and Marie Mortier, spinster without profession. My family moves to Australia when I am still a toddler, but I come back to France for holidays and for military training at Centre Mobilisateur d'Infanterie at Reuilly . . .'

Evelyn drained her mug. 'Help,' she said. 'I can't take all that in.'

Jack removed the mug from her hands and set it on the table. Then he placed his hands on the armrests of her chair and leant over her. He was suddenly deadly serious. 'But you have to. Your life depends on you remembering these details.'

Trapped by him, Evelyn wondered what was coming.

'I'm in Paris,' he continued after a pause, 'blowing a legacy from my father when war breaks out. I am taken prisoner in the rearguard actions. However, owing to a heart complaint, the Boche repatriate me, so I continue my interrupted career as an insurance agent . . .'

Their faces were inches apart. Jack peered into hers and tried to understand what lay beneath her startled expression.

Then he dropped his hands and stepped back. Feeling self-conscious and oddly deflated, Evelyn bent over and rubbed her bare legs which were beginning to mottle in the heat of the fire.

'Is everything all right?' he asked from above her.

Evelyn tensed. 'Of course,' she replied quickly.

'You're fretting about something, Violette, I can tell. Want to talk about it?'

Jack's sympathy touched Evelyn on a raw nerve. She got up abruptly and went to the window as if to check the back garden. 'No, there's nothing wrong,' she said.

He came up behind her and placed his hands on her shoulders. 'Sure?'

She swallowed and did not dare to make a reply. If only she could tell someone, even Jack.

Composing her features she swung round. 'Don't you have a sked due?'

He nodded. 'Yup.' Jack picked up a pad and pencil from the table. 'My advice to you is to forget him.'

'Jack, I tell you, *nothing* is wrong with me.'

Jack shoved his hands into his pockets and regarded her. 'I've been anxious a couple of times myself,' he remarked drily. 'If you say you're OK, then so be it. But for God's sake, don't take any risks, Violette.'

It would have been unfair to snap at Jack for stating the obvious. Evelyn's real anger was aimed at herself. 'No, of course I won't,' she said, and followed him out of the room.

They negotiated the yard and made for the larger of the two barns which made up the outbuildings. The barn was fitted with a pair of double doors – a feature of the area – and was centuries old. Inside, there was a complicated system of internal beams stretching across the ceiling, perfect for string-ing out the aerial. At one point it had been partitioned by a stone wall but this had crumbled and the farmer had stacked layers of withies up against it, thus creating a curious patchwork effect. The wall closest to the road was disintegrating, which made it easy to mount watch through the gaps from inside. Jack eyed the hay piled two metres high in bales at one end.

'I've always dreamt of making love to a girl in a haybarn,' he said lightly.

Once upon a time Evelyn would have flushed with embarrassment at such a provocative remark. Now she just grinned and teased Jack back. 'A milkmaid, perhaps, or a beautiful willing Tess of the d'Urbervilles?'

Jack had climbed up the hay bales, pulled an attaché case out of a covered hole in the top, and was extracting the aerial lead which he began to drape along the beams. 'Not fussy,' he said, 'as long as they're dark with green eyes.'

'Get on with it, Tomas.' Evelyn pointed at her watch. Jack felt in the hay for the Sten which was hidden there, lay on his stomach and handed it down. Evelyn took up a post by the hole in the wall.

Jack opened the case and plugged in the TX and RX plugs. Then he opened the spares box, arranged the mains and battery leads, plugged them in, connected the battery terminals and snapped the correct lead into the electric power point that hung from the central beam of the barn. After that he loaded his Colt pistol and arranged a couple of grenades beside him on the straw. He selected the correct crystal and began to tune up the receiver.

Evelyn, listening to the familiar noises of the radio being prepared for transmission, kept her eyes on the road. Once or twice she glanced over her shoulder at Jack who was now concentrating on tuning the transmitter and matching the aerial. The characteristic waterfall hissed in the earphones and he responded by easing the tune-send-receive knob to transmission. After flexing his fingers, he sent out the call sign.

The irregular bleep of the Morse was clearly audible to Evelyn. At least that part of the circuit was operational, despite the setbacks. Jack was not as good at wireless transmission as John, who rarely made a mistake and was naturally precise. It was something that neither Jack or Evelyn wanted to discuss.

An unidentifiable sound made her tighten her grip on the skeleton butt of the Sten. Evelyn swept her eyes professionally over the road outside and into the fields beyond. Nothing at eye level. Nothing at waist level. Nothing at ground level. She settled down to wait.

Twenty minutes later, Jack took off the earphones. 'Some joker thought up a long one today,' he announced, and began to pack up the wireless. 'Hold the crystal for me, would you.' He handed down the small Bakelite box containing the quartz crystal before pulling in the aerial and coiling it up. Evelyn studied the object in her hand; so very small – not more than two inches square – and so very incriminating. 'Where do you hide the crystals?'

'Never you mind.' Jack jumped down in a flurry of straw. 'We can use the house until dark. You look cold.'

They spread the code book out on the kitchen table and began work on deciphering. Evelyn made coffee and they drank it while decoding the message. It was a companionable interlude. 'I can't get this one,' said Jack. 'Listen.'

'IMPERATIVE RADIO TRANSLATER AT . . .'

'They mean transmitter,' said Evelyn, overwhelmed by sleepiness. The letters on Jack's pad began to jump and blur, and her eyelids flickered with the effort of keeping them open.

'Actor,' said Jack. '*Actor*? Who's he?'

'Don't know.' Evelyn's head went down onto her arms and she was asleep.

She woke when someone stroked her cheek. Dazed, she turned towards the hand. 'Evelyn?' enquired Jack, and she had to think hard as to whom the familiar voice belonged. 'It's time to go.'

She rose to a sitting position, a red patch on her cheek from the pressure of her arm. For one heart-stopping moment she had imagined that the voice belonged to someone else. 'Why did you let me fall asleep?' she demanded. 'I've wasted time.'

'Because you needed it, that's why.' Jack stacked the bits of paper he had been writing on. 'Anyway,' he said lightly, 'you weren't being much help.'

'Have you done it?'

'Most of it. I'm not the best decoder in the world.'

Evelyn held out her hand and he put a piece of paper into it. The message was clear.

IMPERATIVE RADIO TRANSMITTER 73 3 ST AULAYE FIVE ZERO TWO FOUR PUT OUT OF ACTION. STOP. TOP BRASS INTERESTED. STOP. LET US KNOW SOONEST PLANS. STOP. CONFIRM DZ 75 7 LEGUILLAC FIVE ZERO TWO ONE CHERRY BBC TANTE JOSEPHINE ECRIT UNE LETTRE. STOP. ANY REQUESTS. STOP.

'God, a really big one.' Evelyn dropped the message onto the table. The two agents looked at each other.

Jack said, 'They want us to blow up a socking great wireless station.'

For a moment Evelyn relived the events at the tyre factory: the noise of the shooting, the darkness, the scrambling, stumbling fear, the dead men – and for one shameful moment she wanted to run away and leave the responsibility of leading the circuit to someone else. 'Right,' she said, and tried to sound professional, if not enthusiastic, 'we must do some planning.'

Jack threw the scraps of paper onto the fire and watched them burn. 'Have you got the map?'

Michelin number 75, fold 3, map reference 502240 revealed the village of St Aulaye, eighteen kilometres or so west and south of Ribérac. They knew it slightly. Evelyn looked up. 'We'll have to arrange a recce date.'

'Yup.' Jack checked the time. 'You'd better get going.'

She pulled his cigarettes towards her and lit one. 'We need more men. Apart from Jean-Claude, Pierre, me and you, I reckon we'll need three extra men. Sleepers can provide back up, of course. I hope that I can get some of those *réfractaires* trained in time.' Jack noticed that Evelyn's newly grown hair feathered over her collar as she moved. 'I'd rather not involve too many people.'

'Are you starting to see double agents in trees?'

'Almost.' Evelyn gave a wry smile. 'Anyway, I'd rather see them in a tree than in my circuit.' It was one of her bad jokes and fell very flat.

Jack pulled her to her feet. 'Go away,' he ordered. 'You need a good night's sleep.'

Evelyn tied her thin cotton headscarf under her chin. 'Since you keep on about it, I will.'

He noticed also how her hipbones stood out through her grey skirt. 'Are you eating properly?' he asked.

Evelyn did not answer. 'Got enough money?' she said. Jack nodded. He watched her in silence as she buttoned her jacket, her face pale and her green eyes preoccupied.

'Evelyn.'

'Yes.'

'Don't do anything silly, will you?'

'I don't know about you but I'm saving up all my silliness till I get home,' she said, and let herself out of the room by the back door.

He watched it close softly after her and felt an unaccustomed loneliness. The door reopened and Evelyn put her head round. 'My sleeping bag. I'll be needing it in the woods. Can you arrange to get it to me? I daren't put it on the bicycle.'

'Oh . . . right,' Jack said, conscious that he was disappointed. 'Yes, I'll do that.'

'Tomas.'

'Yes?'

'Thank you.'

'It's nothing.'

'See you in a couple of days, then,' and Evelyn disappeared.

The farmhouse kitchen with its hissing fire and piles of china stacked on the dresser seemed very empty.

CHAPTER FOUR

The track through the trees wound to the left and dropped towards the river Rissonne which, at this point, was not much more than a trickle. Evelyn pushed onwards, wobbling slightly on her new bicycle – bought on the black market at enormous cost to His Majesty's Government. Definitely a wartime model, its handlebars were made of wood rather than chromium and it was lacking in the finer detail of pre-war bicycles. Still it was an excellent machine and justified the name 'Corsair' painted onto its bodywork. Evelyn already felt attached to it.

Jack and Pierre were waiting at the crossroads. Jack leaning on his bicycle – a less exciting affair than Evelyn's – 'borrowed' from the local tax inspector and quickly camouflaged with a pot of paint.

'Have some bread,' said Pierre, after they had greeted one another. He produced the end of a big loaf from his pocket and hacked off a slice.

It had rained hard during the last few weeks, soaking summer rains which drenched the trees and puddled on the sodden ground. Evelyn's patched shoes leaked.

'Any news?' Pierre asked.

'The 158th Division at Limoges has moved out. The 10th ss Division is still in Angoulême, and the garrisons are in place at Périgueux and Bergerac. Apparently,' Evelyn paused to chew her bread, 'most of them are just boys scooped up from places like Silesia.'

'Bastards.' Jack broke off more bread.

'The sd have set up a headquarters in Périgueux in the Credit Lyonnais. You've heard about the *milice*, Pierre?'

'Who hasn't?' Pierre sounded bitter. The *milice* had been formed as a supplementary French police force to cover what had been previously Vichy France and which was now under German rule. In less than six months it had become a byword for brutality. People made bitter jokes that the *milice* sickened even the Gestapo.

Jack shielded his eyes against a watery sun. 'Shall we go?' he asked, watching Evelyn out of the corner of his eye. She looked better than when he had last seen her, less exhausted and strained. He bent over to pump up a soft tyre, knowing he could no longer ignore his feelings.

The last thing Jack had wanted was to fall in love. Particularly with a girl like Evelyn. Love was a dangerous encumbrance for an agent: it made you vulnerable and liable to take risks. Nevertheless, obstinate, infuriating and inescapable, the knowledge that he *had* so far forgotten himself to fall in love with her was ever-present. Not that Jack intended to do anything about it: loving Evelyn was something he had to put up with, as one puts up with the inconveniences of short sight or left-handedness and learns to live with them. He finished pumping up the tyre. At least she had no idea.

Once over the river the three of them threaded their way down the tracks that led between the thick forest, dotted here and there by uninviting, muddy *étangs*. Evelyn's eyes watered with the effort, for Pierre set a good pace and the mud was slippery and difficult to negotiate. Jack cycled up ahead, his dark head bent over the handlebars. A branch whipped at Evelyn's bare leg and left a sliver of blood. She brushed it away and resolved that in future she was going to wear trousers. She smiled to herself on imagining Aunt Fanny's shriek of horror at this unfeminine behaviour. It's too late, Aunt Fanny, she thought.

After ten minutes' hard going, Pierre dismounted and told them to hide their bicycles. Then they went ahead on foot. The ground under their feet was layered with oak and beech leaves and scattered pine needles. It was a good place to be, quiet and unvisited, and Evelyn stole a breath of pure enjoyment.

Her mood changed abruptly as the stench hit all three at the same moment. 'What's the smell?' she asked Pierre.

Pierre shrugged. 'I'm afraid it's the camp.' He cupped his hands and gave a long whistle.

'My God,' said Jack. 'The average Boche could smell them at five hundred yards.'

Evelyn swallowed apprehensively. She reckoned she'd toughened up a lot in recent months but she wasn't sure how she was going to stomach living among this smell of decaying meat, inadequate sanitation and unwashed bodies.

Pierre stopped when the top of a head accompanied by the muzzle of a gun appeared over the top of a fallen tree. On recognising Pierre, the rest of the body appeared and vaulted over onto the path. '*Salut*,' said the *maquisard*, and held out his hand to Pierre. 'We are delighted to see you.'

'*Bonjour, mon vieux*,' said Pierre. 'This is Tomas and this is Violette.'

'*Bonjour*.' The man shook Evelyn's hand. 'I am Frisé, nicknamed so because, as you see, I'm going bald.' Evelyn took an immediate liking to him.

'*Bonjour*. We're pleased to meet you. London sends its greetings.'

'London?' Frisé was delighted by this information. 'London knows about me?'

In the interests of productive diplomacy Evelyn decided to embroider the truth. 'Of course. You are an important part of the plan.'

'Wonderful.' Frisé's pallid, unshaven face, crowned by strands of greasy fair hair, stretched into a smile. Dressed in wide grey trousers wet at the turn-ups and a disintegrating leather blouson jacket, he was a slight, down-and-out figure who badly needed a bath. 'Come with me. The others are still sleeping. It rained last night and kept us awake.'

They followed him for another two hundred metres, the smell growing worse. They emerged into a clearing, fringed by oaks. Blinking in the full light they saw in the centre of the clearing a natural hollow over which was erected a rough and ready awning made from branches. Under it was a mattress of branches and leaves on which lay five or so bodies, apparently asleep.

The remains of a fire smouldered fitfully outside the shelter, surrounded by discarded tins and food, including a half-eaten loaf and some rancid butter wrapped in greasy newspaper. Everything was covered with a layer of mud.

'Up!' Frisé shouted at his companions. 'Get up, you pigs!'

Slipping and sliding in the mud at the entrance to the shelter, the sleepers stumbled to their feet. 'This is Albert,' Frisé told the visitors as a big, raw-looking youth stumbled from under the canopy, hauling up his trousers. 'And this is Toni.' The *maquisards* mumbled a greeting.

Toni smelt strongly of drink and his cheap double-breasted suit was almost beyond redemption. He had a fresh scar on his chin and did not look as though he had been over-endowed with brains. Both men were obviously hung over. Somewhat daunted, Evelyn glanced at Jack and with a twitch of his mouth he implied that he understood what she was thinking.

'I gather you have a weapons cache,' he said to Frisé. 'Can I take a look?'

'Yes, Pierre brought in a couple of rifles and four Colts.' Frisé pointed to the trees where an outcrop of rock had split to form a natural hiding place. Jack went over to take a look. When he returned he looked angrier than Evelyn had ever seen him. He leant over and whispered into Evelyn's ear, 'The fools have let the stuff go rusty.'

'Shush,' she said. 'We can talk about it later.'

'When I think of how that pilot risked his neck getting it here.'

She laid a restraining hand on his arm. 'Calm down. It probably isn't their fault.'

Jack looked round at the dismal camp. 'Will you survive?'

She could not resist pinching his arm. 'With these charmers? Better than you.'

The rain returned during the night and trickled through the inadequate covering above the communal bed. It soaked into Evelyn's sleeping bag and she began to think that death was preferable to life in the wet. Nauseated from the smell and from the effort of trying to eat the half-cooked meat which the *maquisards* had served for the evening meal, she was also cold, damp and miserable.

She gazed up at the inadequate roof and thought about her bedroom in Belle-Place, remembering how the moonlight shone through the unshuttered windows onto the polished floor and how welcome Marie's stone hot-water bottle had been. Gallantly, the *maquisards* insisted that Evelyn sleep at the end of the improvised bed so that she was not trapped among their heaving tossing forms, but it did nothing to prevent her being soaked. Abandoning all pretence of sleep, Evelyn tried to light a cigarette and failed because the tobacco was too damp. Toni lay beside her, his foot crooked uncomfortably under her leg, and every so often, he muttered in his sleep, intimate, fretful, discomfited sounds. She lay down again and mentally gritted her teeth.

The next morning, her underwear plastered to her skin and her skirt flapping damply around her legs, Evelyn laid aside tact and issued some requests. Sanitary arrangements were the first priority, and within an hour two pits were dug under the trees and penalties agreed for those who did not use them. The kitchen arrangements were moved away from the sleeping area and a water rota established.

'Even if you can't undress, you can wash the uncovered bits,' she teased the indignant men when they protested.

On the second day, Evelyn held a conference of war over a midday meal of bread, sausage, '*confort*' chocolate and brandy from Toni's capacious hip flask. They smoked English cigarettes and thrashed out a training plan while Evelyn assessed her material. Although they concealed it with bravado, it was obvious that, if they were truthful, they found nothing ennobling about shivering in an insanitary hideout with no prospect of the end of the war in sight. Nevertheless, Frisé, the eldest at twenty-two, was dying to 'have a go at the Boches'; Albert, his cousin, was a year younger and equally battle-hungry in a less vocal way. Marc, Toni and Maurice were only nineteen – strutting, feisty little bantams aching to bloody their spurs.

Sceptical at first of taking orders from Evelyn, and a little wary of the English connection ('Does General de Gaulle know about this?' asked Frisé, whose allegiance apparently lay with the General), Evelyn had to work hard to establish herself – after all, she remarked later to Jack, she was barely older than them – and to bring them round to her proposals.

After the uncertainties of the past few months, it was a challenge she found herself enjoying and she respected their unquenched spirit. These boys had spent the best part of a winter on the run – anything, they said, not to be shipped off to Germany – living in wretched conditions. Cold, permanently damp, undernourished, bored, untrained and unbloodied, they were, nevertheless, the nucleus of a secret and untested army.

'Where do you get your food?' Evelyn wanted to sort out practicalities. Frisé grinned. 'Someone like Pierre gets hold of forged coupons and then sends his daughter off to different shops. Otherwise we rely on friends to send in supplies.'

'I stole a whole load of wine from the Boches the other day.' Toni spoke with a self-satisfied smile and tossed back his dirty hair.

'What about cigarettes?'

'We raid the *tabacs*.' Frisé's tone indicated that Evelyn was näive to raise such a question. He added, 'It's acceptable.'

Evelyn braced herself. 'Look, this must stop. You belong to an army now. We will be supplying you with Stens, grenades, and rifles. In return you must behave like soldiers, not looters.'

During the lively debate that followed, fast and full of local idiom, a lot of wine and brandy was passed round in dirty bottles. The rain stopped for the first time in days and the sun struggled through the trees. The wet undergrowth began to steam in the warmth. The food and drink was making them drowsy. A ring dove sounded and a jay sent out its rusty screech. Suddenly the camp seemed less alien, even friendly.

Evelyn forced herself to concentrate. 'You must learn to strip, clean, and assemble your guns until you can do it in the dark,' she told them. 'You must do this at different times. If you were all cleaning your weapons at the same time and there was an ambush— '

'Have another drink,' advised Toni.

The men were happier once a routine had been established and the camp was much cleaner and more comfortable than before. Frisé acted as leader and developed a habit of staying close to Evelyn. She broached with him first the idea of using three of them for an operation that was being planned.

Frisé appeared pleased.

'Tomas will train you in the use of explosives and take you through the plan when it's been completed. In a couple of days I'm going out on reconnaissance and I'll be formulating the detailed plan after that.'

'When will it be taking place, this operation?' Frisé shifted from one foot to the other, eager and excited.

'I think we can be ready in three weeks or so.'

On the third day, Jack arrived, looking to Evelyn remarkably rested and groomed. 'I've had a bath,' he teased her unfeelingly, and slipped an arm round her shoulders.

'Don't come too close,' she warned. 'I smell.'

'I can bear it.' He handed Evelyn the latest message from London written on a piece of cigarette paper. 'Are they happy?' she asked before she looked at it.

'Home station want us to get on with it as soon as possible.'

'PROCEED SOONEST OPERATION BAKELITE,' Evelyn read.

'The navy probably want to get a convoy down to the Med,' said Jack. 'They'll need the wireless stations at Bordeaux and St Aulaye put out of action.'

'The earliest we can do it is three weeks,' said Evelyn.

'Well, Operation Bakelite will have to be June, then.'

When she left the *maquis* camp with Jack the following day, the men shouted affectionate goodbyes.

'Tell everyone the Maquis Jemaye is flourishing.' They had adopted the name of an *étang* nearby. She had been accepted.

Evelyn left the camp on Monday. On Friday Jack, Jean-Claude and she squeezed into the front of Jean-Claude's van and headed for St Aulaye.

'It's madness, if you want my opinion,' Jean-Claude declared. 'Things are not getting any better.' He turned off the main road from Ribérac onto a smaller road which ran up behind the radio station. 'I should know. I hear about it most

400

days at the headquarters. Gestapo. SD. Now the *milice*. They're swarming all over the place.'

'Hey.' Evelyn was sitting between the two men. She had never felt particularly drawn to Jean-Claude – had even doubted him – but she was concerned by his gloomy tone. 'You mustn't think about it, my friend. It does no good.' She tapped him on the knee. 'I often wonder how you get away with what you do.'

Jean-Claude smiled cynically. 'People have set ideas about policemen. They expect them to be what they say they are. I say I am an ardent supporter of Hitler's Germany and I'm believed.' He squinted at Evelyn. 'Do you ever regret coming to work for us?'

She thought of many things. 'No,' she said definitely. 'No, I don't.'

Jean-Claude negotiated a bend in the road. 'For you two it is an adventure,' he remarked. 'For us it is our lives and our families.'

'We can die, too,' Jack interjected quietly.

'True, my friend.' He eased the van over a pothole, and parked it behind a couple of convenient bushes twenty metres or so further down from the entrance to the field. He pulled on the handbrake and turned to the two agents.

A few minutes later, the three of them were lying flat on their stomachs looking down at the St Aulaye station from the south. Jack monitored the traffic in and out of the main gate and along the main road.

'Two ten-tonners carrying relief troops. One army staff car with two officers. One van with French number plates delivering vegetables,' he noted.

Meanwhile, Evelyn sketched a plan of the station. Set back from the Coutras-Ribérac road about 1½ kilometres from the centre of the village, it was surrounded by a high double wire fence. An unmade track ran south-east from the back of the compound and emerged opposite the field in which they were lying.

Jean-Claude consulted the map. 'I estimate it would take twenty minutes or so for reinforcements to arrive from Ribérac.'

401

'How many masts?' Evelyn asked.

'Six.' Jack counted them and Evelyn annotated her map.

Jack adjusted the sights on the binoculars. 'If we blow up the central pylon holding up the main mast, there is a good chance it will bring down the rest. There are one . . . two . . . three . . . four cables anchoring it. I should say that if we place a pound of explosive on each cable then the mast should fall, the others with it.'

Evelyn had longer sight than Jack. 'The cables are divided into three hawsers anchored by rings into concrete blocks.'

'How high are the blocks?'

Evelyn looked hard. 'That's the joke,' she said at last. 'They look about three metres high.'

'How in flaming hell do we get up those?' Jack swore.

'We'll have to practise our acrobatics.' Evelyn fiddled with the sketch. A blockhouse lay to the west of the masts. A smaller building housing the sentries who patrolled the perimeter every fifteen minutes was situated closer to the wire over by the main entrance. Next to it was a five-metre-high wooden look-out post with a searchlight.

Jack's eyes narrowed as he calculated the amount of explosive needed.

'How do we get in?' asked Jean-Claude.

'We can't use the approach road. I think we should go in from the back and cut the wire. We'll need to plan diversionary tactics to give cover if we're spotted. Tomas and one other will lay the explosive. That should take, what . . .' Evelyn glanced at Jack for confirmation, 'five, ten minutes at the most. Then we retreat into the woods, making our escape cross-country.' Evelyn scribbled down more measurements as she spoke.

'Come on,' said Jack. 'We've been here long enough.'

'I'll go ahead to check it's clear.' Jean-Claude began to walk up the field.

They watched him climb over the gate and jump down, lightly for such a big man. Evelyn made the final touches to her sketch, folded it up and hid it in the hem of her skirt. Jack wrapped his binoculars in his handkerchief and put them in his pocket.

'Come on then, my darling.' He exaggerated the 'darling'.

Hand in hand, as if they were lovers out for a stroll, they walked back up the field, and Jack surprised Evelyn by lifting her over the gate. She was crouched down, brushing mud from her shoes when the sound of speeding vehicles coming up the lane from the main road jerked her upright. Those vehicles meant business.

Jack didn't waste time. He grabbed Evelyn and pulled her across the road and up into the wood on the other side.

Evelyn had taken the precaution of studying the map. 'Follow the stream. It leads up into the forest,' she hissed at him and, putting her head down, she ran as hard as she could.

Two army lorries spun to a halt in the road and within seconds bullets whined into the trees after them, pattering like heavy rain. She and Jack put on speed, leaping over the undergrowth and dodging branches that tried to whip into their faces and ran up through the tongue of trees until it broadened out. They dropped into a dry stream bed running at right angles to their previous direction and followed it – a ploy they had learnt at training school. After two hundred metres or so, they scrambled out of the gully and headed up again into the middle of the forest. Gradually the sound of gunfire grew fainter.

'I hope Jean-Claude made it,' Evelyn panted.

In his Ribérac office, Fleischer placed a finger on the map and marked St Aulaye. 'Two men and one woman did you say?' He looked up at Obersturmführer Mundt for confirmation. The *Obersturmführer* had only recently arrived from Berlin and was eager to make an impression.

'Yes, sir. They were spotted by sentries doing a tour of the area. They used binoculars and were keeping under cover. Unfortunately, they did not obtain exact descriptions. A posse went after them but lost them in the woods.'

'I see. Is there any idea who these people might be?'

'No, sir.' The *Obersturmführer* was nervous and conscious of his inexperience. His fellow officers had warned him that the *Sturmbannführer* could be both vicious and unfair.

Fleischer poured himself a cup of coffee but did not offer any to Mundt. 'Well,' he said quietly, 'you must track them down.' He pulled the map closer. 'Let's think. If I was running away, where would I go?'

'What did you say, sir?'

Mundt was beginning to irritate Fleischer. 'Keep away from the table with the porcelain on it,' he said. 'Use your wits, if you have any. Where might they have gone?'

The map appeared irredeemably blotched with green to Mundt. 'There seems to be an awful lot of forest, sir,' he said desperately.

'Oh, get out.' Fleischer drank his coffee. 'Ring St Aulaye. Tell them I will be organising night searches on likely houses and hotels in . . .' He wrote a list on his pad. 'Montpon. La Rochebeaucourt, Chalais. St Barthelmy, Échourgnac and Aubeterre.'

'Hotels, sir?'

Fleischer lost his temper. 'Do you have no brain at all? These terrorists probably have excellent papers and pockets full of money. They don't want to spend a night in the woods, even if it is nearly June. You are a fool, Mundt. Get out.'

Fleischer drained his cup, wandered over to the side table and picked up his current favourite piece of china. Painted in the famous *gros bleu* and *rose pompadour* and gilded with rich gold leaf, it was an early example of Sèvres biscuitware. It formed part of a group: a lady, her gallant and small boy playing skittles at their feet. The owner, who had lived in a small *château* near Bordeaux before his Jewish ancestry had been pointed out to him, had been very reluctant to yield it up with his other possessions. Fleischer could never resist touching the figurine: he ran his finger gently down the painted breeched thigh.

After a couple of minutes spent thus in pleasant contemplation, Fleischer made a telephone call and talked to his colleagues in the sp headquarters in Périgueux. He suggested that the Périgueux branch bring in some of their suspects for questioning to see if they could pick up any information that would help him, and he would do the same. When he had finished the conversation, he recalled Mundt to his office.

'Get me Corporal Schwarz, will you. I wish to see him.'

'How long till curfew?' Evelyn was exhausted.

Jack continued to plod along the track. 'Another two hours, I would say.'

They were trekking across the ridge above the village of St Barthelmy, having walked cross-country thirteen kilometres or so from the radio station. Both were fit and used to exercise but even so they were flagging. Evelyn knew of a safe house in the village, and they agreed to take a chance to see if they could spend the night there. She took out her handkerchief, spat on it and rubbed at her face. Her skirt had torn in a couple of places and she attempted to arrange it so the tears were hidden.

She mourned the imminent demise of her faithful grey skirt. 'God knows where I'm going to get another one. How do I look?'

'Like something out of *Vogue*.'

Evelyn helped to brush away the dirt and leaves from Jack's dark hair. 'Thanks, *camarade*.'

Jack gave a short, grim laugh. 'Don't mention it.'

'We'll go round the back of the house, and I'd better go first and speak to Monsieur Chapuy.'

Without warning, Jack pulled Evelyn towards him and rested his cheek against hers. His body felt warm and comforting and for a few seconds she leant against him, enjoying the feeling of security.

'Let's go, then,' he said and released her.

Ten minutes later, they slid through a convenient gap in the wooden fence into the field at the back of Monsieur Chapuy's farm. Evelyn led Jack along a path of flattened earth through an immaculately tended vegetable garden, scattering stray hens and ducks. Jack waited behind the henhouse until Evelyn had alerted the farmer.

Monsieur Chapuy did not seem put out by his unexpected guests – or even very surprised. 'My wife is away,' he told them, reaching up for the glasses on the shelf. 'But she has left a mountain of stew for me to eat, and I would be glad of the help in eating it.' He poured Evelyn and Jack a glass of *marc*. 'She's gone to visit the tax inspector's wife in Montpon. I tell her that it's unwise to be too friendly with a tax inspector. They know too much.' Monsieur Chapuy laughed heartily at his own joke and refilled their empty glasses.

Madame Chapuy might have been friends with a tax inspector's wife, but she made excellent stew. Her elderflower champagne was also delicious. When she had finished, Evelyn sagged back in the chair, and allowed herself to drift. The kitchen was like so many she had slipped in and out of during the year. Cluttered, easy, full of the good smells of food and herbs. She resolved one day to have one like it.

Afterwards, Monsieur Chapuy showed them to the spare room at the top of the house. It overlooked the main street and was obviously Madame Chapuy's especial pride. The curtains and bedspreads were made from a shiny pink satin and ruched at every opportunity. There were stuffed satin cushions on the bed and plaster cartouches of the Virgin and the Saints arranged on the wall. Embossed wallpaper paid tribute to a gloomy species of ivy. Evelyn eyed the bed.

'I'll sleep on the floor,' said Jack with only a hint of resignation.

'Thanks.' Past caring that he was there to watch her undress, Evelyn removed her skirt and shoes. She had a blister on her ankle and touched it experimentally, hoping it was not going to give trouble. Then she crawled between the highly starched sheets and let every muscle go slack. She caught a flash of bare legs as Jack got out of his trousers, and fell asleep instantly.

She awoke into a cool grey light. For some reason she was sure Paul was in the room, and her heart beat appreciably faster. Suddenly, she knew she would try – she must try – to find Paul after the war was over.

Strengthened by the thought, she half opened her eyes and for a second she imagined that the figure watching out of the window *was* Paul. The figure moved. It wore no trousers and Evelyn remembered where she was. She sat up with a start. 'What is it?'

Jack lifted a finger to warn her to be quiet and beckoned with his other hand. Evelyn threw back the sheets and tiptoed to the window. Jack pressed his mouth against her ear. 'Mantrap,' he breathed.

The light was patchy and uneven, and it was cold with the pre-dawn chill. She recoiled at what she saw outside the window. The street was filled with German soldiers. Underneath the window of the opposite house a truck was parked and another was rolling down the road. The driver had cut the engine and was using the brakes very gently so that it did not make a sound. Evelyn's toes dug into the bare wooden floor. She ducked and crawled back to the bed, pulled on her skirt and shoes and smoothed the crumpled blankets and sheets. Then she shoved the blanket Jack had used under the bed.

'What are they doing now?' she whispered when she rejoined him at the window.

Jack handed her his Colt and pulled on his trousers. As he did so, the back of the second truck was opened from inside and twenty or more soldiers jumped silently onto the road. Evelyn stared. 'They haven't got any boots on.'

'We'd better get out.' Jack took a cautious second look. 'Too late.'

The grey-socked ghosts ran along the length of the street, and set up machine-gun posts at each end. Other ghosts took up a position around the large house opposite the Chapuys'.

'They've got the wrong house,' said Evelyn, and shivered. There was something horrible about the silence. 'You're right. We've got to try to get out.'

But before they could make a move, a car drove through the machine-gun post at one end of the street and halted in front of the staked-out house. Two men got out of the back. One of the bootless soldiers went over to confer with him before melting back to his post.

The two men walked towards the house and knocked loudly on the door. When it opened, a light shone on the metal plaques around their necks. '*Feldgendarmerie*,' said Jack.

They left the window and tiptoed down the staircase past Monsieur Chapuy's bedroom into the kitchen, where they eased back the bolts on the back door and slid out into the yard. As they left the cover of the house they saw a light flash on in the one opposite. Vignetted in an uncurtained window on the second floor was an elderly man sitting upright in bed, gazing at the two *Feldgendarmerie* officers. The terrified man's open mouth was visible from where they stood.

Evelyn and Jack filed down the earth path, past the bean stakes, onions and carrots, a clump of cornflowers and the irises towards the fence. As they stepped warily past the henhouse, one of the occupants set up an agitated clucking inside. The two agents froze.

Monsieur Chapuy's big double-doored barn served as cover while they checked that the Germans had not thrown a dragnet around the fields.

'Looks clear.'

There was another flurry from the henhouse and Jack flicked the safety catch off the Sten as Evelyn squeezed through the fence. It was a steep haul up to the ridge, but they did it in record time. At the top, they looked back. It was just possible to make out the *Feldgendarmerie* emerging from the house. They were crossing the street to Monsieur Chapuy's. Lights began to flash on in the house, including the bedroom they had so recently vacated. Feeling goosebumps run up her arms, Evelyn folded them across her chest and prayed for Monsieur Chapuy.

Five minutes later the *Feldgendarmerie* departed, their car racing over the cobbles and out of the village.

'That's odd,' Evelyn commented. 'Why haven't the rest of them gone?' Then she understood. 'The Boches without the boots,' she said. 'They're still there. They've set a trap for someone.' She tripped over a clump of fern and grabbed at Jack's arm for support. 'Please, let Monsieur Chapuy be safe.'

'We'll stay here until dawn,' said Jack. 'We can't use the roads and it'll be too difficult to get through the woods until there's more light.'

'Yes,' she said, feeling cold and very jumpy. 'Yes.'

Jack took off his sweater and threw it over a log. 'Here, sit on this,' he suggested. Evelyn did as she was told, and settled down for the wait.

Later, when she awoke from a restless doze, she discovered Jack had slumped across her shoulder. Squinting down at her watch, she saw it was five o'clock and shook him awake.

The sky had turned creamy white with a high cloud, but hinted of sun, proper sun, to come. Down in the village, having failed to flush out any agents, the Germans were forming up. A sergeant counted them, and his order for them to fall into parties of three for a smoke was clearly audible. When their cigarettes were finished the men donned their boots, formed up and a grey rectangle marched out of St Barthelmy and left it to sleep in the early-morning peace.

Evelyn groaned with the discomfort of her stiff muscles and damp clothes. 'Jack, we have to get on with plans for the St Aulaye operation.'

CHAPTER FIVE

'*Couillon!*' The cyclist swerved, righted himself and continued up the road.

Evelyn picked herself up from the verge and examined her hand. The cyclist had come up so suddenly from behind she had not heard his approach. Leaping aside as he yelled, she had fallen awkwardly and grazed her hand.

'*Couillon* to you!' she shouted after the retreating back and licked her bleeding hand. Then she sat down opposite the gates of St Euphonie's and struggled to tie a handkerchief over the wound. It was Paul's handkerchief, now stained and grimy.

Evelyn was on her way to Belle-Place. It was the first opportunity she had had to warn Bessy about Mariette – she regretted that so much time had elapsed since she received Jean-Claude's message. She was also desperate for a hot bath and some fresh clothes. Exhausted after their narrow escape the previous night, every movement was an effort.

A nun let herself out of the gates and came over to her. It was Sister Hélène. She reached into her habit and drew out a leather roll containing the first-aid kit she always carried. 'You'd better let me take a look.' She added under her breath. 'I'm glad I've met you. I've been wanting to make contact.'

Evelyn proffered her hand. 'Trouble?'

Hélène inspected the damage and tested Evelyn's fingers. 'Does this hurt? No. Good.' She dabbed at the graze and applied some salve from a tiny glass pot labelled 'calendula'. 'A black car has been seen driving past the gates twice a day for the last couple of days. Of course, it may be a coincidence. The Nazis have not visited us since that occasion last July.' She was referring to Fleischer's visit on the morning after the tyre-factory raid.

410

Evelyn watched the nun wind Paul's handkerchief across her hand and tie it. The makeshift bandage stretched tightly across her palm – a symbol, she suddenly thought, of the recent clampdown.

'Thank you, Sister,' she said audibly for the benefit of passers-by. 'That is a lot more comfortable. How lucky for me you were around,' and whispered, 'Thank you. I will warn whoever is necessary. Goodbye,' she added in a louder voice.

Hélène tucked her scissors and the salve back into the leather roll, adjusted her sleeves and watched Evelyn until she had disappeared round the next corner. The girl looked very tired and thin but in the circumstances this was understandable. She was evidently in need of good food, rest and, Hélène imagined, the comfort of unburdening herself to someone she could trust.

Since the war started, Hélène had seen it so often before. Patients who came to her surgery and said, 'Heal my sickness', when what they really wanted was for her to exorcise the grief, guilt and hatred festering in them, and Hélène would sit and listen, often for hours at a time, prompting skilfully now and again. The art of listening was one which the war had taught her. Reverend Mother had been wrong; they were all of them inextricably caught up in the Nazi occupation of their country. Whether for good or ill was for God alone to judge.

Hélène looked around to see if she was being observed. Secrecy had become a reflex – stained, if you like, on to her soul – and sometimes she was aghast at her capacity to sustain the clandestine. It took skill to preserve secrets in a community where she was bound over to expose her most humble thought.

The road was empty now, except for a cluster of thrushes pecking at snails under the hedgerow. With a jarring plunge into the past, Hélène acknowledged that she had always had these abilities: her silent suffering over Charles, her stubborn refusal to cry out after he rejected her – 'Help me!' – the secrets which she had kept from Reverend Mother since the day she entered St Euphonie's. She was a perfect candidate for the clandestine life – and those were not the qualities that shaped an obedient nun. Hélène paused before moving on. Was she employing that stubbornness to prevent God from breaking down the barriers to her soul?

It was dusk when Evelyn emerged from the wine cellar at Belle-Place and let herself in at the kitchen door. Taking off her shoes she slipped up the back stairs. Unable to enter the *château* until after dark, she had used the time to grab a few hours' sleep, wrapped in some sacks she had found in the cellar.

As she let herself into the room, Bessy looked up from the dressing table where she had been staring into the mirror, and dropped her hairbrush when she saw who it was. 'Good God! Evie, you gave me a fright. Is there any trouble?'

'There has been a bit.' Evelyn advanced into the room. 'I hope you don't mind, Bessy. There's something I want to talk to you about. I also need some new clothes.' She held up the hem of her torn skirt.

The two women kissed each other and Bessy hugged Evelyn hard. 'Ugh. You smell dreadful.'

Evelyn managed a laugh. 'So would you if you'd just spent four days and nights sleeping in a wood. Can I take a bath?'

'Don't hesitate for a moment, Evie,' Bessy encouraged hastily. 'Draw it at once and use the soap. My one and only tablet.'

'I couldn't possibly do that to you, Bessy.' Evelyn was already stripping off her clothes and making for the bathroom. Bessy picked up and inspected the clothes Evelyn had left behind and dropped them gingerly into the back of her wardrobe. Then she began to look for suitable replacements.

'You'd better have my blue serge,' she called out. 'It's very hard-wearing.' As she already had it on, Bessy changed into a green worsted skirt and joined Evelyn in the bathroom. 'Here,' she said, opening the wall cabinet, 'wash your hair with this.'

Evelyn sniffed at the open bottle and was transported back to a time when creams, scents and bath unguents were a part of her life. Pampering smells, devoted to the feminine business of conjuring beauty and spinning illusions. A wave of homesickness flooded her, painful images of people and places she never imagined she would recall with nostalgia. What were they all doing back on the farm? Struggling with the pigs and calves, probably. Or gathering for tea round the fire. Drinking sherry with neighbours on Sunday morning, all those betweeded, ruddy-faced men and women – straightforward, mildly philanthropic, country-loving people from whom she had wanted to escape.

'Hey,' said Bessy. 'Where are you now?'

Evelyn was standing in her underwear gazing into space as the bath filled up. 'Sorry.' Evelyn returned to the present and focused on her friend's face. 'How are you, Bessy?'

The other shrugged. 'It's so lonely sometimes,' she explained. 'It's difficult not to brood when you're doing nothing. You imagine things . . . horrible things. I feel rather like a butterfly pinned inside a glass case. You know, under scrutiny and unable to move.'

'Is Belle-Place under surveillance? Have you noticed anything unusual?'

'No, nothing like that.' Fear sometimes paralysed Bessy, the fear of what would happen to baby Charles, to her and to Belle-Place if the Nazis discovered her involvement in the resistance. Most of the time she could control herself but the strain told.

'Bessy,' Evelyn stretched out a soapy hand to her friend, 'I do understand, and I wish there was something I could do.' She added judiciously. 'You have Guy, of course.'

Bessy dropped into the bathroom chair. 'Guy?' she repeated in a strange voice. 'Not really.'

'Did he believe the story about me going home?' Evelyn slid down into the hot water and sighed with pleasure.

'I think so.'

'Bessy.' Evelyn soaped a long leg. 'I don't want to worry you but I've heard that Mariette Maisson . . . do you know her?'

'Yes,' said Bessy slowly. 'She helps Marie.'

'Well, we think she's spying for the Nazis. She was seen going into Boche headquarters and – ' Evelyn's head disap-

413

peared under the suds and rose again, 'she's got a German lover.'

'Good God!' Bessy was quiet and then said, 'The little tramp.'

Evelyn attempted to rinse the soap from her hair. 'Don't sack her, it might arouse suspicion. You'll just have to be vigilant. I won't be able to come here again so the danger will be minimal, Bessy, don't worry.'

Bessy appeared both sad and weary. She came and knelt beside the bath. 'Here, let me.' She took the tooth mug from Evelyn's hand and rinsed her hair of the remains of the shampoo. 'Do you think we will ever, ever get through this war?'

'Hey.' Evelyn grabbed Bessy's hand with slippery fingers. 'Don't give up. We just have to believe that we will. All of us.'

Bessy leant back on her calves. 'Yes,' she said reflectively, her head on one side. 'You're right,' and getting to her feet with a sigh, 'Look, I'm going downstairs to get you something to eat. I'll also find out more about Mariette. When she comes and so on.'

'Do be discreet,' Evelyn replaced the precious bar of soap in its dish. 'Bessy,' she looked up, 'I understand. I really do.'

'Of course you do.' Embarrassed by her lapse, Bessy was at her most brisk. 'There's no need to say anything.'

Evelyn soaked in the bath until the skin on her fingers resembled a prune and then reluctantly got out, towelled herself dry and dabbed powder all over her body. Her skin sang from the scrubbing she had given it and felt new and clean. Bessy's satin wrapper was on the bed; she took it and sat down to attend to her hair.

As she brushed it dry Evelyn studied herself. Her face must have grown thinner. Certainly her eyes seemed larger, gleaming dark and emerald green, flecked with satiny black specks. She gazed at them. Did they reveal the shadowland underneath?

Evelyn pulled a face at such an idea and lifted the lid off the face-powder bowl. Arranged – as always – with exemplary neatness, Evelyn took pleasure in looking at Bessy's beautiful things; lipsticks, a block of mascara, scent bottles and a pale blue swansdown powder puff. She powdered her face in front of the mirror, applied a jasmine scent to her neck and wrists and ran her nose along her arm enjoying being clean again. When she looked up, Bessy's wedding photograph, which had been removed to the mantelpiece, caught her eyes and she felt a painful little tug at her heart for Bessy's loss.

When Bessy returned, however, bearing soup and fruit on a tray, Evelyn was dozing on the day bed. At Bessy's entrance, she shot to her feet and felt for her Colt.

'You won't get far in a dressing gown,' Bessy commented drily and Evelyn fell back onto the cushions. 'Here, eat this and tell me what's been happening.'

Evelyn told Bessy as much as she could and asked her if she could use her old bedroom for the night, at least until dawn, when she would slip away before the household woke up.

'You won't be hearing from us for some time. There's . . .' Evelyn hesitated. It would be dangerous, especially now, to burden Bessy with extraneous information. '. . . something going on.'

'I thought there might be.'

Jack and Evelyn had agreed it would be sensible and strategic to go and hide further south after the operation and lie up for a while. 'We will have to leave this area completely afterwards,' Evelyn told Bessy. 'One day I will come back to see you. I promise. I owe you such a lot and I . . .' She finished rather incoherently. 'I couldn't have got through without you.'

Tears made Bessy's eyes seem bluer than ever. She brushed them away impatiently. 'Go on, Evie, it's not over yet.'

As Evelyn walked down the corridor to her room, a shadow loomed up on the wall and she darted instinctively into a doorway. Then she realised it was probably a reflection of a cloud coasting across the moon. Evelyn paused at the entrance to the bedroom before pushing open the door an inch.

Nothing had changed. The hairbrushes lay on the dressing table and the bed was made up just as she had left it. Evelyn folded Bessy's clothes over the chair, hid her revolver under a cushion and placed her money and a packet of cigarettes on the dressing table. Under the window, the gardens sloped away to the ha-ha and the roofs of the pepperpot towers shone in the moonlight – beautiful, unearthly and remote from what was going on in France. Looking down at it, Evelyn suddenly remembered it was her birthday tomorrow – 21 May. She would be twenty-four.

A girl had died during the past year, may she rest in peace, that restless, impetuous and awkward creature. How important her social *faux pas* had seemed back in England – and how easy it had been to reduce her to emotional rubble. How simple her pleasures then – like hunting – and how simple her pleasures would be in the future . . . To wake up each morning free from anxiety, to face the day without a plan in her head, to know she had got through.

Evelyn turned her head and something caught her eye over by the fireplace. She swung round and her hand flew up to her mouth. After a moment, she crossed over to the fireplace and bent down to look at the picture propped up against the empty grate. When she stood upright again she was shaking from shock.

Why had he done it? Even in the bad light, it was obvious the portrait was offensive, a canny, clever, sleight of hand to make her look duplicitous, even evil.

She did not notice the door opening very slowly but she heard the laugh. She whirled round.

'So,' a soft voice stated from the doorway. 'You came back for a visit. How nice.'

'Guy!'

Guy nudged the door shut with his foot and advanced into the room. 'I watched you darting in and out of doorways just now. Rather strange behaviour, I thought.'

'I was in the area and came to see how Bessy was. She asked me to stay for the night.'

Guy had been drinking and his words were slurred. 'Really, Mademoiselle Liegaux. You should be a better liar than that by now.'

'Will you please go. I wish to go to bed,' Evelyn wrenched open the door and gestured into the corridor.

'I think,' said Guy, with the ponderousness of the half drunk, 'I think you're a little tense. One who likes play-acting and using people.'

'You're not making sense, Guy.' She changed tack, and made her voice soft and conciliatory. 'Why don't you go to bed?'

Guy smiled. 'See what I mean? Play-acting.' Since his accusation was entirely accurate, she said nothing.

'Shut the door,' he ordered.

He dropped down onto the bed, and looked up at her. Made by a first-class tailor, his dark olive green suit set off his colouring. Guy knew how to dress. 'Just who are you?' he demanded, and leant back on the silk coverlet.

'You seem to have made your own mind up about that.' Evelyn pointed at the portrait.

'I thought you'd like it. I'm thinking of exhibiting it in New York after the war. Come on, Evelyn, you haven't given me a straight answer.'

'I'm a cousin of the family's, you know that.'

'Rubbish, Mademoiselle Liegaux. I think you're a good deal more interesting than that. Were you Charles's mistress?'

'No.' Evelyn was outraged for Bessy. 'How like you to think of something like that.'

'Sex, my dear girl.' Guy held up a wagging finger. 'It goes on a lot more than you think. But I believe you. I do. You're probably as pure as the Madonna. I'm much more interested in what else you've been up to.'

'Guy, please.' An intimation of what she might be forced to do to neutralise Guy took root. At all costs, she had to avoid a scene which drew attention to her presence in Belle-Place. 'This is so silly. Why don't we talk tomorrow?'

'Come here.' When she remained where she was, Guy repeated the command. 'Come here, I tell you.'

There were not many options open to her: Evelyn did as she was told and sat down beside him. Guy reached out and caught her in a hard grip and she almost cried out. Close to, his teeth seemed impossibly white. Good, strong, American, nurtured teeth, which she knew would taste of tobacco and brandy. 'You're hiding something,' he told her, slurring his words a little. 'You don't feel right to me, you never have.'

The habit of noticing details, now so engrained in Evelyn, did not desert her. As she tried to work out what to do next, she registered the monogrammed handkerchief drooping from his breast pocket and the expensive Cartier cufflinks. But the fact that the knot in her wrapper belt had come loose had not been lost on Guy either. Lazily, he pulled it undone. 'Girls like you need teaching,' he said. 'They need to be taught to appreciate the right kind of man.'

'Do they?' Evelyn said provocatively. 'And are you going to teach me, Guy?' Her exposed skin shrank at his touch and she willed herself to remain quite still.

'Of course,' he replied, and ran a hand up her stomach and across her breasts. 'I hope you're a fast learner.' Evelyn's breast goosefleshed as he ran a finger over the nipples. 'Is that all you're going to offer me? I am afraid you do have a lot to learn.'

Obediently, Evelyn slipped off the satin wrapper. Guy reached up and unhooked her brassière. 'Made in Paris, I think,' he said, dangling it from a finger. 'It must be Bessy's. Tut. You girls should make a rule. Never share underwear.'

'Do cheap gibes come with the lessons?' Evelyn managed a smile, as Guy placed his hands on either side of her waist and pulled down her knickers.

'You must learn to take a joke, Evelyn.' Guy stood up and ran his hand down her flank. 'Get in.'

After a minute, he joined her in bed, hot from brandy and lust. He kissed her on the lips and then on her shoulders and breasts.

Evelyn discarded the counting technique as useless in this particular situation and tried not to go rigid. *This is the oldest trick in the book and it doesn't cost that much.*

'Come on, Evelyn. Relax.' Guy rolled her over so that she was lying face downwards and brushed his fingers over her thighs and up her back, sometimes using long strokes, sometimes short. His hand lingered on her buttocks and returned to her thighs.

'A work of art.' His voice came from a long way above her,

slithering through the darkness created by her tightly shut eyes. Evelyn might have laughed at Guy's allusion if she had not been so close to tears. He turned her over onto her back again, put his hands between them and pushed her legs apart. His lips on her mouth were wet. She felt his fingers catch in her pubic hair and bit her lip.

After a few minutes, Evelyn realised she could bear it; she even experienced the faintest, the most fleeting, echo of a response. She cried out at the crucial moment because Guy hurt her. He stopped and scrutinised Evelyn with bloodshot eyes.

'You *are* a virgin,' he said. 'That makes it all the more exciting.'

Guy's orgasm was long and noisy, after which he lay on top of her, breathing quickly. Sweat larded their stomachs and trickled off Guy's back. 'Did you like it?' he enquired.

Evelyn would have given almost anything to have been able to tell him that she hated it, but that was a pleasure she had to deny herself. 'Mostly,' she lied as he traced a line from her chin to her breast with one finger.

'A virgin.' Guy disengaged himself. 'Now what can I make of that?'

'Nothing,' said Evelyn, more alone than she had ever felt. 'I'm going to wash.'

'Go ahead. Don't mind me.'

She wriggled away from him and got out of bed. There were bloodstains on her thighs and on the sheets but she was far too angry to feel embarrassed.

Quickly she pulled on her wrapper and poured some water out of the jug into the bowl. Sobered and satiated, Guy watched her drowsily, intrigued by the play of light and dark on her skin, the determined movements and the waterfall of clean, dark hair.

'You're working for the resistance,' he said without warning. 'Aren't you?'

Evelyn managed a creditable laugh. 'Don't be ridiculous.'

He bunched a pillow under his head and settled himself more comfortably. 'Oh, don't worry,' he informed her. 'It doesn't matter if I know. I don't care a toss about that sort of thing. I just want to know the truth. You and your masks have intrigued me for a long time.'

Who had mentioned masks a long time ago? John?

Evelyn's desolation deepened. She dried the inside of her legs. 'What do you mean?'

'Innocent or whore? Which are you, Mademoiselle?'

'Well, you now know it's not the latter.'

Guy gave a crack of laughter. 'No, indeed. Pass me the cigarettes.' Evelyn dropped the towel and reached for the packet on the dressing table. She tossed it to Guy and then turned to splash her face with water.

She heard the rustle of the packet and the rasp of a match as Guy lit up. Her body ached and her thighs felt as if they had been rubbed raw and she wished she could have another bath to wash him away.

By the time Evelyn remembered she had made a dreadful mistake it was too late. Guy snapped on the beside light and when he spoke, he sounded triumphant. 'You are a spy, Evelyn. An English spy.'

The harsh electric light made them both blink and bleached their faces. Guy held up a folded cigarette paper. 'Shall I read what it says?' He paused for dramatic effect. 'CONFIRM 3 JUNE OPERATION BAKELITE. STOP.' The message was in clear, not encoded. It was also in English. Guy drew on his cigarette, he had not had so much fun in ages. 'An English spy. I'll say this for you, Evelyn, I hadn't quite worked that one out.' He sounded impressed. Switching to English, 'Now, how are you going to keep me quiet? Got any ideas?' More than anything Evelyn hated his obvious enjoyment.

I deserve this, she thought, as she allowed the wrapper to fall off her shoulders, for being so careless and stupid. For ignoring every rule I was ever taught about security. It takes only one mistake, however tiny, however unwitting. That is all.

Guy settled back on the pillows. 'Give me some ideas?' he invited.

Evelyn bent over and pulled Guy's face towards her. 'Kiss me. I want you to kiss me.'

CHAPTER SIX

Paul was in hospital with pneumonia for the whole of April 1943. During that time the German *Wehrmacht* came under increasingly heavy attack; the most effective fighting machine the world had ever seen was being stretched beyond its resources – and proving vulnerable.

In Tunisia and Libya it was only a matter of time before the Allies destroyed the petrol-starved Axis armies. Not even General Rommel's brilliance was sufficient now. Disasters on the Eastern Front continued to accumulate. After the bitter defeat at Stalingrad, Hitler's frozen, hungry army faced continual and deadly harassment from Russian partisans. The spring brought the thaw and relief from the cold but it turned the ground into a quagmire, which rotted soldiers' feet and made it impossible for vehicles to move.

The ss continued to enforce their policies throughout the Eastern bloc and occupied Western countries, rounding up Jews from their homes and exterminating them in their thousands. In protest, Hans Scholl, twenty-four, and his sister Sophie, twenty-one, handed out leaflets at Munich University calling on the German youth to rise up. They signed themselves the 'White Rose'. Brother and sister were arrested, interrogated, brought to trial and guillotined in a Munich jail.

Meanwhile the Allies stepped up their saturation bombing of German towns and cities. One night in March 1943 1050 tons were dropped on Berlin in the space of fifty minutes. The idea was to pulverise the German nation into capitulation.

When he was feeling better, Paul lay in bed in hospital and analysed the news. His conclusions were depressing. There had been only one successful campaign recently; an *Abwehr* colleague passed on the information. In the Atlantic a total of

107 Allied merchant ships had been sunk by U-boat packs. But the Allies were striking back hard.

At home, a mania developed for daubing slogans on walls and buildings in public places. *Alle Halbheit ist taub* (Half measures are no measures). *Tüchtiges Schaffen, das halt auf die Dauer kein Gegner aus* (Strenuous endeavour will beat every opponent in the end). To keep Paul amused, Ingrid wrote down all the latest mottoes and read them out to him on her visits. The slogans made them laugh. Alone Paul concocted his own: German success lies in forging a future, not in repeating the past.

In his view uncertain, and probably a tragedy that would involve her people for decades, Germany's future was not something Paul wished to think about. Nevertheless, he knew it was necessary to do so and the more he reflected on it the more he knew he should act in some way. Less obviously than his father, because there was the family to consider, but act all the same. Act like Evelyn – his beautiful, unobtainable Evelyn – who had gone underground and whose duplicity, he now understood, had acted on him like a powerful aphrodisiac. Even so, the knowledge didn't make him love her any the less.

Paul looked around the hospital room. The walls were painted a dismal yellow. Despite the efforts of the nurses, the cornice was thick with dust and a layer had settled over the wash bowl and jug. It was no use trying to eradicate it; the bombing was too frequent and relentless. Nurse Gruber entered the room, stuck a thermometer under Paul's tongue and took his pulse. Starched and super efficient, she had scrubbed skin and hair stretched back so tightly under the nurse's veil that it looked as though the roots might spring out of her head. After she recorded Paul's temperature – 'The Herr Major is much better today' – and pulled his sheet savagely straight, he asked her if there was any recent news.

She flashed him a look of professional appraisal and replied, 'Nothing special.' In fact, the Allied Eighth Army had broken through the German Mareth line in North Africa. Then she remembered a piece of good news. 'The rising of the Jews in the Warsaw ghetto is being put down successfully.'

The nurse wrote the date on his notes, 1 May 1943, included her comments, clipped the chart back onto the end of his bed and measured a spoonful of medicine. Paul swallowed, lay back on the pillows and thought of the Polish Jews fighting it out in the rat holes and sewers of Warsaw. Concerned by his expression, the nurse bent over him, and a waft of starch mixed with the sickly sweet odour of medicine assailed him. 'You must take care of yourself, Herr Major,' she said. 'You've had a bad bout of pneumonia and you mustn't permit yourself to worry about the state of the war.' She stood back and folded her hands across her apron. 'The Fatherland needs its officers.'

The door clicked behind her. Left alone once more to stare at the ceiling, Paul flexed his bad leg under the sheet. It was aching. He concentrated on the lessons of self-persuasion he had taught himself once before in hospital and fell asleep.

A week later, Ingrid came to fetch him back to a suite in the Adlon Hotel, which she had wangled from one of her influential contacts. 'The beer is watered,' she informed him, 'and they are down to cold cuts of meat and potato salad at lunchtime, but it will do.'

'Anything's better than Nurse Gruber's bullying,' said Paul and slipped his arm through hers as they made their way through the foyer and up the stairs. True to form, Ingrid had arranged to stay in the suite across the corridor, so she was able to come and go discreetly without too many eyebrows being raised. She bustled around Paul's bedroom and then retired to her own to make some telephone calls. Paul sifted through the mail that was waiting for him. A letter from his father. Another from his brother Otto. A packet sent by special courier from France. He put the letters aside and opened it. Inside was his monogrammed paperknife and a note from Corporal Schwarz telling him that he had been detailed to send it on to him by Sturmbannführer Fleischer.

He looked up and frowned. Fleischer had evidently rifled through his old office and Paul did not like the idea. He had anticipated this move, of course, and had thought it prudent to extract his private papers from the files and bring them back with him to Berlin.

The door opened. 'Paul?' Ingrid sounded excited. 'Are you ready?' She hurried across the carpet in her green loden walking costume. 'It's so lovely to have you back. Look, the sun's out, and I've arranged for us to have tea at the Wannsee.'

That night they dined in the hotel restaurant. Both of them were flushed from spending the afternoon in the strong spring sunshine. Paul felt more relaxed than he had in a long time.

'You can have red cabbage, potato and roast meat – not horse, I hope. Or there is a fine selection of "field kitchen" dishes which, I'm told by the bell-boy, are barleymeal rissoles and Bavarian cabbage.' Paul tried to feel hungry and failed.

When the air-raid siren went off half-way through their meal, Ingrid grabbed her rissole and a roll, wrapped them in her handkerchief and put them into her handbag. 'I'm not wasting them,' she announced. 'It's the best meal I've had in weeks.' She adjusted the veil on her evening hat.

'Only you could wear a hat like that during an air raid.'

Ingrid smiled, a trifle smugly. 'Where is the cellar?'

'I imagine if we follow the crowd . . .' an undignified exodus was taking place through the door, '. . . we should get there.'

'Hurry,' said a white-faced woman who had been sitting at the next table. 'They are expecting lots more this time.'

Still a little weak, Paul's muscles were aching with the effort by the time he and Ingrid reached the cellar. Outside the bombs were already falling, and the building was shaking. Bits of plaster and grit shook from the ceiling and walls.

The cellars in the Adlon consisted of two rectangular rooms opening into one another. They were used for storage and were cluttered with orange boxes and crates of bottles. Along the ceiling and around the walls ran a forest of pipes of varying sizes. Weakened by previous bombings, some of the pipes had worked loose from their moorings, others leaked steam in spurts.

'Not there,' said Paul, as Ingrid settled herself under a steaming pipe. 'If it breaks . . .'

'What?'

'Never mind. Come over here.' He beckoned her over to a

pile of vegetable boxes. Stretching out a hand to help her, Ingrid clung to him. 'Got you,' she said lightly.

The cellar, already crowded, continued to fill up with guests and diners, the women mostly dressed in long evening gowns, with fur stoles, the men in uniform or black tie. Very soon the temperature in the claustrophobic cellar began to rise. There were muttered complaints and raised voices as people jostled for room to sit down and from behind the pile of boxes against which Paul and Ingrid were leaning came the deep, racking cough of a chronic bronchitic. In the inadequate light thrown from the single light bulb, the human forms dimmed into ghosts.

Ingrid shivered. 'I hate it.'

Paul touched her finger with his own. 'What do you hate?'

'This bloody war.'

The bombing intensified, and they listened to the booms and shudders of their beautiful city being reduced to rubble. The pipes hissed and spat. Trickles of dust and plaster swelled and avalanched down the walls. Some of it landed on Ingrid's hat.

'Take that damned thing off,' Paul said impatiently, and arranged his body against hers so that he would take the first impact if the ceiling came down. Ingrid obeyed and sat holding her hat in her lap as if her life depended on it.

'Wagner's Twilight of the Gods,' Paul remarked at the wisp of steam curling by his feet.

'Be quiet,' said Ingrid, bothered by his irreverent remark. 'Someone might hear you.'

Paul looked at the faces nearest him: frozen, frightened and verging on the hysterical, grim. A few couples were embracing each other. Paul watched as one man bent and pressed a passionate kiss onto the nape of his companion's neck.

'Don't worry, Ingrid, they are concentrating far too hard on their own affairs to pay us any attention.'

Ingrid snuggled against him. He squinted down at the dust-gilded golden head against his shoulder. She was a survivor.

Paul's chest hurt from inhaling dust and from his still-frequent coughing fits. A bomb whined directly overhead and then, to the hotel guests cramped in the cellars, seemed to hang poised for an eternally long second. Boom. A black circle hovered in the back of Paul's mind and expanded until it took him over.

The bomb had fallen on the building next door, tipped out at the last minute by a homeward-bound plane anxious to get rid of its cargo. The Adlon, however, sustained surprisingly little damage. The impact sent a fall of masonry across the cellar stairs, blocking the door. When it became apparent what had happened, some of the women screamed and one of them flung herself at the still-smoking pile of brick and rubble. A man in a white tie and starched shirt started to shout orders. He was told to desist by an officer in the uniform of the General Staff. The air became tropically hot, wrapping those trapped in the cellars in an airless, dusty blanket. Whimpering with fear, Ingrid hugged Paul's sagging body. He had been knocked unconscious by a wooden girder falling from the ceiling. The phrase 'Twilight of the Gods' ricocheted around her head.

The subject dominated her conversation for days until Paul grew weary of it, and in an effort to deflect her he asked, 'Did you lose your hat?'

'As a matter of fact, yes. And I won't be able to replace it very easily.' Ingrid patted her hair.

'Get in touch with Gehrbrandt, he'll organise a new one.'

There was a stunned silence as Ingrid digested the implications of Paul's remark. 'What are you suggesting, Paul?'

For a remark that had been intended as only a light gibe, it fell very flat, and Paul was sorry. 'Don't take any notice of me,' he said quickly.

Ingrid turned her back on him, and fiddled with the objects on a table by the window. They were in Paul's suite, as the Adlon did not close down after its near miss, and had returned to their rooms while he continued to convalesce. 'I can't think what has come over you.' She sounded bewildered and disappointed. 'It's not like you to be so cruel.'

'I'm sorry.' The mocking note she always dreaded, and which had been absent lately, was back in Paul's voice and its suggestion of restless dissatisfaction frightened her.

Ingrid stood very still; a figure in a grey costume, hair coiled into a roll above a white neck, as always, beautifully presented, the only incongruous note the darned stockings. Carefully, she replaced the paper knife on the leather blotter on the table. 'Oh, God,' she said suddenly.

'Ingrid, come here. I want to talk to you.' Paul indicated the space next to him on the sofa.

Ingrid obeyed. Close to, Paul saw that there were tear stains on her cheeks and that they had dissolved the powder, lending a clown's sadness to her face. When she put up a hand to wipe her cheeks, he saw with a shock that one finger was stained with nicotine.

'You're smoking too much, Ingrid.'

She snatched her hand out of sight. 'No lectures, please.' She had wanted Paul to say something quite different, and the disappointment made her feel savage. She sat miserably snapping the fastening of her bracelet open and shut, open and shut, while she waited for Paul to speak.

'You're wrong, Ingrid,' he said at last, guessing her train of thought.

'Am I?'

'I do care for you, very much indeed.'

'But you don't love me?'

He owed Ingrid the truth. 'Not in the way you want me to.'

'How do you know what I want?'

He knew this conversation of old. It would get them nowhere. 'Ingrid, I have fallen in love with someone else.'

Ingrid breathed out hard. 'Someone else,' she repeated in a quick breathy way. 'Who?'

'No one you know.' He would have given a great deal to replace the look of misery on her face. 'I'm so sorry.'

Ingrid straightened her back. 'You needn't pity me,' she said. 'I'm quite all right.' Tears were running openly down her face and she tried to wipe them away with the back of her hand. 'Oh, God,' she said for the second time, and turned her face away.

'Ingrid.' Paul put his arm around her shoulders. 'Don't,' he said. 'Don't cry.'

427

'What do you expect me to do?' Ingrid reared away from his touch. 'You tell me that you love somebody else in spite of everything we've shared. Just like that. Would you prefer me to laugh?'

'Please.' Paul stroked her hair. She allowed him to do so and then she sank against the scratchy uniform, absorbing the feel of him as she had done so often. Years ago, five years and a long journey ago, she had met Paul for the first time at a reception given by her friend the Italian ambassador. Someone pointed out Paul as an up-and-coming young officer. A flute of champagne in her hand, beautiful, expensive, assured and rather bored by clever, up-and-coming young officers, Ingrid turned round and fell in love. Fell in love with his golden head, long, rakish body and air of ironic detachment. And ever since then, her life had been spent waiting.

'This someone . . .' she began.

'Yes.'

'Where is she?'

'Not here. She's not a Berliner.' He kissed Ingrid's hand and got up from the sofa. 'After the war is over I shall go and look for her.'

It was only afterwards that it struck Ingrid what a curious thing that was for Paul to say.

The Annhalter railway station in Berlin was beginning to disintegrate. Each time there was an air raid another pane of glass fell away from the domed roof and the red and black propaganda posters on the platforms became a little more tattered – 'Führer, we thank you', 'To victory with our leader', 'National Socialist order or Bolshevik chaos?'

Paul arrived at the entrance to the station in the Admiral's car. Greatcoat shrugged over his shoulders, he waited until the chauffeur extracted his luggage and then made his way towards the train for Koblenz. At Koblenz he would pick up his own car for the drive to France.

'You're being posted to Bordeaux.' Von Bentivegni gave Paul his orders. 'The *Abwehrstellen* requires a communications expert. There are problems contacting U-boats in the Atlantic.'

'What about Ribérac, sir?'

Von Bentivegni made a face. 'I'm afraid you made an enemy there. The SD officer with whom you worked requested his headquarters to arrange it that you did not return. Apparently he insisted on taking over your job. A similar thing has happened to two other *Abwehr* officers recently.' Von Bentivegni adjusted his monocle. 'And you, I fear, won't be the last.'

Paul walked down the platform, past a party of children with labels round their necks attended by Red Cross workers and searched out his compartment. The chauffeur followed with his luggage. By now, passengers were used to waiting for trains that did not materialise or arrived a day late. Inconveniences like these were part of the erosion of everyday life and had to be suffered. Paul was amused to overhear one large woman say to her companion, 'Damn the lot of them.' A statement she quickly amended when she saw Paul to, 'I mean, damn those English and their bombs.' He stopped in front of his carriage which had 'Wheels must turn for victory' painted on the side. A pregnant woman was waiting to board and he helped her up the steps before boarding himself.

The chauffeur stowed his cases in the luggage rack of the compartment and left a picnic basket on the seat. It was already occupied by three children with stiff yellow plaits and identical tartan dresses, an exhausted-looking woman, who was evidently their mother, and a man with a suitcase on his knee. Deciding to wait a little longer before settling down with his travelling companions, Paul returned to the platform. The journey was going to be long enough.

Steam curled up over the edge of the platform and drifted in whorls towards the shattered roof casting a sprinkling of smuts onto the cast-iron pillars and roof arches. The chatter and crying of children mixed with the hiss of the engines.

Paul had not seen Ingrid since the conversation in the hotel room and he had moved out of the Adlon that day. He missed her more than he would have imagined. Yesterday he had bought a diamond brooch from one of the most expensive jewellers in Berlin and arranged to have it sent to her flat. Delicate, sensuous and exquisitely light, the brooch had six points pavé-set with rose- and brilliant-cut diamonds and a large brilliant set in a raised *collet* in the centre. 'It's English,' he told Paul. 'About 1895, and the diamonds are particularly fine. See . . .' He held it up. 'That white light. An exceptional refractive index.'

Paul had not bought it for the refractive index, he had bought it because it cost a lot of money but that was what he wanted. He wrote a note which said simply: 'Thank you for everything. Paul.'

The journey was due to take two days. Berlin to Leipzig. Leipzig to Frankfurt, where he would be changing trains, and then up to Koblenz to spend the night with his parents. After that he was scheduled to drive across France to Bordeaux. He would not be stopping at Ribérac.

'Paul!'

A familiar figure dressed in a dark suit and broad-brimmed felt hat was hurrying towards him, breaking into a run every so often. 'Paul! Wait.'

Paul had swung round at the sound of his name. 'Ingrid.'

'Paul.' Ingrid arrived at his side, a little breathless. 'Listen to me. You mustn't go without listening.'

She was wearing a white linen blouse under her suit which accentuated the curve of her breasts. There was a bunch of violets in her buttonhole and as she flung herself against him, he smelt their faint, troubling scent.

'What's happened?'

She raised one gloved hand and thrust it in Paul's face. In it she held the brooch between tightly clenched fingers. 'Take this back.'

Paul prised open her fingers and rescued the brooch. 'But it's for you.'

'I don't want your brooch. You can't buy me off, Paul, it's insulting.'

He bent over her and put his arm around the heaving shoulders. 'Yes, Ingrid, I'm sorry. I will take it back.'

She clutched him harder. 'You don't understand.'

She paused, turned her head away with a quick, embarrassed movement. 'I want you to exchange it for a wedding ring,' she said, and her hat brim hid her expression.

'What do you mean?' It took a moment for the implications

to sink in. Paul pulled her round so that she faced him. At that she recovered her courage and looked him straight in the face. 'I'm pregnant.'

The drive from Koblenz took Paul three days. He passed through the Rhineland, tipping the edge of Luxembourg before heading for Metz. Then he plunged into the heart of France towards Limoges. It was necessary to be watchful: a lone German car driving on unattended roads was at risk. In some areas the resistance had set up booby traps and, on the more remote roads, ambushes. Even so, Paul preferred to drive. He had missed his sleek, fast Mercedes and, anyway, he wanted to have his car at Bordeaux. At Limoges he was welcomed by the officer commanding the garrison and given an excellent dinner. The following day, he left the headquarters, drove past a string of horses, waiting patiently to transport men and equipment, and turned south-west towards Périgueux.

It was an interesting route. Green and lush, well cultivated and dotted with *manoirs*, *donjons* and the type of medium-sized *châteaux* that attracted Paul. He made a special detour to see the *château* of Puyguilhem. It was a charming, white-stoned Renaissance building with well-preserved stone carvings and machicolations on the towers. Paul would have liked to see inside and to inspect the chestnut-beamed roof built to repel insects.

At Périgueux the road dropped down towards the river valley and snaked along the rock defiles. But instead of driving into the city, Paul turned the car and headed north towards Ribérac. As he drove he thought of how he had soothed a sobbing and badly frightened Ingrid and told her he would, of course, stand by her. As the steam from the train had layered around them on the platform and Ingrid clutched him harder and harder, Paul tried not to feel trapped.

Attracted by Ingrid's sobs, a loden-coated *Hausfrau* stared at the handsome couple. She told her husband about it later. The girl was beautiful and expensive and he was a tall, blond soldier, bending over her protectively. It was an archetypal

431

farewell scene, just like the one she had wept over in *Die Grosse Liebe*. But instead of love or sadness registering on the man's face – the woman's was buried deep in his greatcoat – there was rage, bafflement and almost, she thought, disgust.

CHAPTER SEVEN

'Anything happening in Paris, d'you think?'

Tony Turner looked up from his desk and got to his feet as the visitor walked unexpectedly into the room. He was in the middle of stacking documents, ready to put away. The memorandum he had been studying read:

> You, Special Operations Executive, are the authority responsible for co-ordinating sabotage and subversive activities, including the organisation of resistance groups, and for providing advice and liaison on all matters in connection with patriot forces up to the time of their embodiment into the regular forces.

The memorandum had given the chiefs a great deal of satisfaction. It was the unequivocal authority from Whitehall for which soe had been waiting. Included in the memo was the directive from the chiefs of staff that the sabotage of industrial targets should be pursued vigorously and a recommendation that delivery of supplies should be increased to the resistance groups as quickly as possible.

He tapped the memo. 'This is tremendous,' he said to his visitor, and put it into a buff folder marked 'Top Secret'. It joined a copy of a report made by soe on the growth of resistance activity in France.

'So? Is anything happening in Paris?'

'Sorry,' he said to the visitor. 'I was taken up with the good news. Please sit down, sir.'

He went over to the window and pulled down the blinds on the bleached white-grey of late evening and switched on the light. 'Paris,' he said reflectively. ' "Prosper" is in place and working well. The circuit has received over two hundred containers.'

'Anything else?' asked the visitor.

Turner signed and opened a filing-cabinet drawer. 'It looks as though our chief escape line has been destroyed.' He straightened up. 'However, Armada might be able to produce something. Pimento and Scientist are functioning. Stockbroker is up and running under "César". In Lille Farmer managed to destroy a sizeable number of railway trucks and to close the Lille-Béthune line for a couple of days.'

'Two steps forward, one step back.'

'Yes and no. It's a bit like snakes and ladders sometimes.' He extracted a bottle and two glasses from the drawer.

'Nice.' The visitor approved the whisky with raised eyebrows. He was a senior figure in SOE and although the almost unbearable pressure of work did not allow him to fraternise often with his staff, relations were conducted along very cordial lines when they did meet. He accepted the glass proffered to him by Turner. 'I've come over because I need to know the date and time of the wireless station operation in the Périgord. You will understand I can't go into why.'

'Of course, sir.' The whisky was very pleasant after a hard, warm day's work. 'Well, the latest message from Astronomer confirms that the attack is planned for 3 June. Tomorrow. Other than that, I cannot say. Alouette appears confident and she has Tomas, a sabotage bod, with her. He's very good.'

'How's she done, this Alouette?'

Turner laughed. 'It's funny you should ask. Her initial reports were equivocal. Too young, too inexperienced, that sort of thing. But the chiefs had a hunch about her. They felt she had what it takes. She felt sound.'

When his visitor had left, Turner went back to work, stopping only to refill his glass. Once or twice he leant back and stretched to relieve the tension accumulating in his neck muscles. Then he looked at his watch. Half past midnight. Things would start to get busy now, as the radio messages came in between 1 a.m. and 3 a.m.

Later on, a colleague came in to talk to him. They discussed cover stories and shared the remains of the whisky. By the time he left it was 3 a.m., and Turner decided to get some sleep.

He stared at his fountain pen and then slowly screwed on the top. Not an imaginative man, he tried none the less to envisage the conditions under which 'his' agents would be working. How could they, the *attendistes*, tell what living with extremes of tedium and fear did to the morale? Or to the spirit?

He wished he knew. The map of France on the wall caught his eye. He imagined it stabbed with pencil marks and banded with tell-tale circles. Prosper. Scientist. Farmer. Pimento. Spindle. A landscape infested with secrets and traversed in blindness with only a few, damnably few, wireless operators with whom to maintain contact.

He got up from the desk, went over to the calendar on the wall and tore off the page to the date underneath – 3 June.

Operation Bakelite – 'Alouette's mission' – was on.

CHAPTER EIGHT

The last week in May had been glorious in central France. The rain had vanished and the temperature had inched its way into the eighties. Blood-red poppies bloomed in the growing crops and strawberries ripened in heavy clusters in the allotments.

By ten thirty in the morning, 3 June, Paul was in his old office at the *mairie* in Ribérac, hoping to check through the latest reports on Belle-Place. He had already had a quick word with his remaining former colleagues and greeted Corporal Schwarz.

'What are you doing here, von Hoch?' Sturmbannführer Fleischer flung open the door. He was livid. 'I wasn't aware we were expecting you.'

'You weren't.' Paul clipped out an answer. 'I am on my way to Bordeaux and I wished to check some details.'

Fleischer frowned. He had checked the signals files very thoroughly when he amalgamated them with his own – but perhaps he had missed a vital piece of information that von Hoch had come back for? 'I have all the papers, von Hoch. Perhaps I can help?' Fleischer had grown even plumper around the waistline since Paul had last seen him and the whites of his eyes looked bloodshot but he was a great deal more assured in his manner.

'No, thank you,' Paul replied.

'Since you are here, von Hoch,' Fleischer thought he might as well use von Hoch's expertise, 'we are expecting trouble. One of our informers tells us that the resistance is planning an operation in the near future. Have you come across anything about it in your reports?'

'I've been away, Sturmbannführer.' Paul moved over to the bookshelves. 'Are the sources entirely reliable?'

'Of course. But I imagine you have been keeping an eye on things back in Berlin?'

Paul took a chance. It wouldn't hurt Fleischer to think that his movements were under scrutiny of the *Abwehr*. 'Yes,' he said. 'Berlin is well informed.'

'Then the name "Alouette" must mean something to you.' Fleischer sneaked in the question without warning and Paul was surprised by the electric shock that streaked through his body. 'No,' he replied, as though he was searching his memory. 'It sounds like a code name.'

Fleischer's inflamed-looking eyes lingered on Paul's chest, his gaze travelled upwards and came to rest on Paul's mouth. 'A British terrorist,' he said. 'The name has featured in several terrorist radio transmissions we have recently intercepted. I have an idea as to the identity of this agent.'

'I see. What is your plan of action?'

'That's my business, von Hoch. As you know, she is exceptionally pretty— '

'What do you mean by that, Fleischer?'

'My dear Major, we shouldn't enquire too closely into each other's business.'

'Business!' Paul swung round to face Fleischer directly. 'Business! The whole of the Périgord knows what you get up to!'

Fleischer drew himself up to his full height, which easily matched Paul's. 'Yes?' He was a little nervous by the reaction he had provoked.

'Nothing,' said Paul after a pause. 'Except your methods are not mine.'

Paul's contempt infuriated Fleischer. 'Watch your step, Herr Major. I'm in a position to do more than put you out of a job.'

He regretted the words as soon as he said them, for Paul advanced on Fleischer. His mouth had gone white around the edge. 'How dare you threaten me?'

Fleischer retreated to the door. 'I won't forget this, Major.' He posed in the doorway and drew in his stomach. 'The sD is a very powerful organisation.'

'Your organisation', said Paul softly, and he articulated each word with precision, 'is nothing but a front for thugs and sadists.'

'Indeed?'

Paul had said far too much but it had been a relief after so long to articulate his hatred of Fleischer and his colleagues. 'You'd better think about it, Fleischer.'

'I'll denounce you.'

Paul took in the well-fed outline, the neatly pressed uniform, the puffy face and the nervous flutter of Fleischer's hands moving from his belt to his pocket and back again. 'I warn you, Fleischer, I will kill you first. It would, I assure you, be a pleasure.'

By now Fleischer was frightened. 'May I remind you that I am in charge and I order you to get out.'

'I intend to.' Paul picked up his cap. He walked to the door and pushed past Fleischer.

'You say you have no idea who Alouette might be.' Fleischer caught at Paul's sleeve and held him back.

'None,' replied Paul curtly, taking a huge risk and removing Fleischer's hand.

Fleischer watched him retreat down the corridor and tapped the gold filling in his front tooth with his fingernail. He had spent the last two months combing the signals reports: enemy radio traffic, enemy agent activity, damage to installations, railways. Estimated growth of resistance. Estimated resistance targets . . . It had not taken him long to see that the name Alouette occurred at least three times in different contexts – and like anyone else who scanned the contents Fleischer was forced to conclude that Major von Hoch knew exactly who Alouette signified.

Werner dumped the canvas bag onto the kitchen table. 'Here you are,' he said. 'Coffee and ham.'

'No cheese?'

Mariette had grown so used to the supplies of food that Werner channelled through to her that she could permit herself to make the odd joke. She dropped the saucepan she had been cleaning in the sink and went to inspect the haul.

'No cheese today, greedy Mariette. You will have to wait.'

'Greedy, am I?' she replied without taking offence. 'Wouldn't you be in my place?'

Werner checked to see that the children were occupied and pulled her over to him. 'Perhaps,' he nuzzled her ear. 'If you go on like this you will get plump.'

She went very still in his embrace. 'Everyone I know is so thin.'

'Not everyone.' Since becoming involved in undercover work Werner liked to imagine he knew more about the 'goings-on' than the average soldier. 'There are plenty in your country who do well out of the occupation.'

'Yes, but . . .' Mariette was reminded of her latest terror. 'What will happen to me after the war?' She didn't say when the Germans are beaten but Werner got the idea.

'I'll take care of you,' he said earnestly.

One of the nicer things about Werner was that he took her seriously and tried to understand her feelings. He whispered into her neck. 'Do you know what I think?'

But Mariette was too preoccupied by an unsettling vision of the sort of punishment meted out to a woman who slept with Germans. She pulled away from him and returned to the sink. 'What do you think?'

'I think . . .' he stated simply, 'I think you are beautiful.'

Mariette carefully replaced the saucepan in the sink and dried her hands on her apron. She did not want Werner to see that he had almost made her cry. 'Do you mean that?' she asked when she could manage it.

Werner wound his arms around Mariette's firm waist and leant his cheek on her hair. 'To me you are beautiful,' he said. 'You were too thin when I first met you. But now you are rounded out nicely. Your hair shines.' He lifted a strand between his fingers.

'Beautiful,' Mariette repeated, like a child with a new word, and turned herself round to face him. 'Nobody has ever said that to me before.'

All of a sudden, Werner was embarrassed. 'Please make me some of your coffee.'

Mariette noticed Werner was sweating. 'Are you feeling well?'

He avoided her eyes. 'Absolutely fine, but it's hot. Tell me what has been going on in the *château*.'

She stopped in the act of transferring the coffee beans from the tin to the grinder, suddenly remembering what Werner's visit was probably about, and her disappointment made her sound at her most sullen. 'That man sent you.'

Werner ducked his head. 'Yes.'

'You needn't bother to butter me up,' she said bitterly. 'What do you want to know this time?' She sounded so sad that Werner leapt up, kicked aside the chair and made a grab for her.

'Listen, I didn't come here just for that. I came for you too. Please believe me.'

Mariette stood limply against him, and shrugged her shoulders. In a passion of guilt, Werner leant over and kissed the sulky mouth. 'Just tell him something to keep him happy,' he begged. 'You've done it before. I reckon there's something going on and that's why he wants information sharpish.' He kissed her again, and nuzzled her bottom lip – and Mariette wondered again why it had been ordained that she should be so alone and why so little of what she had ever wanted had come her way.

Then she remembered her children. At least she had them. Men made wars. Women neither asked for them nor needed them. Women suffered, lost their men and struggled to hold their broken children and broken homes in some crazy whole, and she was entitled to make sure that her children had food in their stomachs.

Did it matter, then, what she did to obtain it?

Did it?

Werner pulled her tighter. 'Mariette, *liebchen*, listen to me. I love you and I want to take you home to the forest. You and the children.'

As he got dressed – and he was very late this morning – Guy pondered the future. The war wouldn't continue for ever. Now that American men and arms had been persuaded into the conflict, it was only a matter of time before the Germans were defeated. Guy wondered if Hitler the corporal would have been so ambitious if he had known the United States would be entering the war. The guy was mad, he thought. Because of the heat, he chose silk socks. What chance did a handful of dyed-in-wool Prussian generals and party lackeys have against the huge industrial resources of the American boondocks?

The war disposed of in this satisfactory manner, Guy felt at liberty to make plans for his future career. Naturally, it had to be New York. When last heard from before the fall of Paris, his gallery had pressed him to return, and he was sure they remained touchingly eager to accommodate his wishes. Actually – Guy rethreaded the laces through one of his expensive leather shoes – it wouldn't matter if they didn't. There was another equally well-sited establishment one block away, willing to provide the expensive show-case he required. Guy already had the theme of the exhibition fixed. Scenes of War: France 1940–5. *From where it happened, Guy Myers brings us his unique vision of the most cataclysmic event of the century, showing us the truth, and the horror at the heart of war* . . . Verbiage that was impressive in a catalogue, and the critics would cite it in their reviews.

A part of his life would be devoted to Paris, however, where he planned to keep his apartment. Paris was too beautiful, too voluptuous and too ready to cater for pleasure for him to abandon. He pictured the city – a woman lying on her back, one leg raised in lazy appreciation, skin a mass of exquisite tints and musky perfume. Experienced, corrupt, addictive. Who was it who said, 'Good Americans when they die go to Paris'?

Making plans put him into an agreeable frame of mind for the day. Perhaps he could persuade the newly compliant Mademoiselle Liegaux to figure in some of them. Having brought her around to his way of thinking it was a pity to waste her – and he certainly didn't care if she was mixed up with a bunch of spies. In fact, it added a certain frisson.

'You're so wonderful,' she told him that night when he seduced her – or was it the other way round? He couldn't remember. Her dark hair fell over her face and brushed Guy's shoulder with soft, butterfly strokes. Her lips were moist and inviting, a little hesitant perhaps, but he soon taught her a few tricks. 'You're so wonderful.'

Of course, Evelyn was a fool to think he believed her but it was nice to hear the words.

Guy drove himself to Ribérac in the Hispano and parked in front of the Café Mas. Inside the café, he went over to the bar and draped himself on a stool. He glanced at his reflection in the mirror behind the bar and was pleased to see that his skin looked healthy (unlike the half-starved look of the locals). The *patron* took his order for a morning cognac, and Guy settled down. He was curious.

Evelyn had told Guy that the message in the cigarette packet was nothing to do with her. She said the packet had been given to her by a stranger in the Café Mas who had taken pity on her tobaccoless state. Obviously – Evelyn flashed Guy a charming little smile – the stranger had given her the wrong packet by mistake.

Guy had been amused by this lie, but he was happy to continue the charade. When Evelyn implied that she was enraptured by her initiation in his hands, that she wanted to repeat it, he obliged. 'OK, Snow White. I look forward to our next assignation,' and they agreed that Evelyn would return that evening.

'Please don't tell Bessy,' she asked when she left. 'I don't want her to know.'

'Don't worry.'

Guy drank his brandy and ordered a second. So, the Café Mas was being used for undercover messages.

Behind Guy, Mariette, who had come for a chat with the barman, toyed with her *ersatz* coffee and observed him secretly. Her table was directly behind him and she was able to look at her leisure. The memory of her humiliation in his hands made her feel a little sick and she was glad she had told Fleischer about him. She watched as he placed an order and started up a conversation with a neighbour, and reckoned she could risk leaving the café without Guy recognising her.

She paid her bill and let herself out into the street and was arranging the contents of her basket when she noticed Hervé

Thuriot – a friend of her late husband – walking up the street. When he saw who it was, he drew his eyebrows into a frown, crossed over the street and spat into the gutter.

Mariette stared at the watery glob on the stone and felt as if it had landed on her own face. She looked at Thuriot's receding back and mastered the impulse to run after him and beat him with her fists. 'What do you know about it?' she wanted to scream.

She picked up her basket, held up her chin and began the walk home.

The Hispano passed Mariette as she trudged up the hill. Guy was at the wheel. Even though she could have done with a lift, Mariette was thankful he didn't recognise her. At the top of the hill, the road curved round to the left and she was put out to see that the Hispano was parked on the verge by the entrance to Collet's big field. Guy was perched on the gate, sketching the scene. Quickly, Mariette ducked behind a large chestnut tree.

The sun was very strong, and it had painted the sky a violent blue. Underneath lay the green fields, trees and grass, splashed with brilliantly coloured wild flowers. An expectancy invested the scene: a sense that the damp earth was surrendering to a new summer. Mariette leant back against the trunk and closed her eyes.

The big black Citroën had parked by the Hispano when she opened them, and when she realised what it signified Mariette's heart began to beat in thuds.

The passenger door of the car opened and two men in uniform got out. They stood blinking in the sunlight as if they were unused to being outside. The older of the two removed his black leather gloves and ran a finger round the inside of his collar.

Guy did not notice their arrival, but he turned quickly enough when one of the men poked him in the back. From behind the tree, Mariette watched as an animated conversation took place, at the end of which Guy shook his head. The man summoned his companion to help. Guy jumped down from the gate and made for the Hispano. He did not get very far. The old man pulled out his revolver and Guy

443

stopped. Mariette almost felt sorry for him as the confidence she had so envied drained visibly away, leaving him, she thought with a leaden feeling, like a collapsed puppet. Then he was pushed into the Citroën and driven away.

'Oh, my God.' Mariette was helpless as the shame flooded through her body. 'I did this.'

It had not required much persuasion, the senior adjutant reported to Fleischer. The suspect had been a walkover, very willing, very willing indeed to help after it was indicated what would happen if he should refuse.

'He didn't much like the idea of broken hands,' said the adjutant.

Fleischer laughed. 'Nor would I,' he said. 'Very sensible. Especially if you are an artist. A nice touch.'

'I suspect he isn't French, sir.'

Fleischer consulted his documents. 'Brought up, apparently, in Canada. That would account for the accent. These terrorists always say they have been born in Algeria or Canada. Did you check his papers?'

'They are in order. He is staying at the Château Belle-Place to catalogue the books and paintings. He has a weak heart.'

'I wonder,' Fleischer mused. 'They may all be in this. I'm pretty sure the secretary was involved. My contact tells me she left some months ago. I suspect she's gone to ground. My informant tells me that Maier makes a practice of going out alone for long periods. Who did he talk about?'

'A woman staying at the *château*. A cousin of the deceased Count.'

'Aha,' said Fleischer with satisfaction. 'What did he say? Quick.'

The adjutant produced a note pad and read from it. 'Maier declared that he always suspected this woman from the first and he also said he found some sort of message on her when she turned up unexpectedly. But he can't remember what it said because he was drunk.' The adjutant put away the note pad. 'Shall I bring him in, sir?'

'No.'

'What about the woman?'

444

'My dear Heinz, you have not been thinking. We know there are terrorists working in the area and it is more than likely they are planning an operation on a key target. We need to know who they are. Correct?'

His subordinate nodded unhappily. He thought he recognised the signs that Fleischer's temper was about to erupt.

'Tell me. If you wish to penetrate a terrorist cell, who is the best person to do it?'

The adjutant cleared his throat and gave the correct answer. 'One of their own.'

'Exactly.' Fleischer sat down at his desk. 'Ring Maier and tell him there has been a mistake and you are very sorry. Then put him under surveillance. He will try to warn his colleagues. Meanwhile, arrange for the *château* to be put under twenty-four-hour surveillance as soon as possible. Any sighting of the woman must be reported to me at once.'

Guy really needed this drink. Holding the glass to his chest, he walked over to the French windows and let himself out onto the terrace. A recently planted box bush by the lawn needed realigning and he made a note to talk to the gardener about it.

He did not care for the way his hand shook when he raised the glass to his mouth.

Bessy was out with Charles and Guy was alone. For once he was sorry: he would have liked to talk to Bessy and his hand was too unsteady to paint.

He never had any patience for people who held beliefs. Even worse, sacrificed themselves for them. He had no intention of immolating himself, like some blasted saint. Not for Guy Myers the altar and the bloody knife. In his view, it was not necessary. Things – history, events – repeated themselves in a cycle. The only way a man could put his stick in the wheel was to create something. There was no point in losing your skin over an idea. If only people realised that, unpleasantness could be avoided.

'We'll break your hands,' the older man had said. 'I'm quite experienced at it.'

445

The younger one was silent, and watched his senior flex his thick, powerful-looking fists. Guy's feet started to sweat inside his silk socks. Terror weighed in his chest and blood vessels constricted in his neck. At the front of the Citroën, the driver accelerated hard.

'What do you want?' Guy asked, too quickly.

'Information.'

Pause. More flexing of fists.

'Ask away.'

The gloved fingers rested on Guy's arm. The car swayed to avoid a pothole and the fields slid by. Guy talked.

What bothered Guy at this moment – he took another mouthful of brandy – was that he talked from fear, rather than the non-sacrificial principle. He turned and went back into the library to refill his glass. It was a pity about Evelyn and he hoped she wasn't in for too bad a time. With regret, he said goodbye to his plans for seeing her more frequently. After this episode, it was doubtful if she would live to see the end of the war and if she did she would not feel at all warmly towards him.

'We'll break your hands.' The hands that mixed paint, drew and brushed colour onto canvas so consummately well. He could not, under any circumstances, allow that to happen. Lying at the bottom of the ragbag of desires, confusions, betrayals and expectations that was his heart, painting was what Guy really cared about.

Damn the Nazis, he thought, and yanked the decanter towards him. Bessy mustn't hear about this morning. He knew what her reaction would be. Always, always, Bessy had been so mighty and high-nosed, insisting that Guy see through *her* eyes, respect *her* principles. It usually amused him, sometimes irritated him, and occasionally maddened him. But he loved Bessy as he loved no one else in his life *and he did not want her to know.* Actually, Guy could not remember precisely what he had said. A combination of terror and the brandies he had consumed had seen to that.

He looked into the brown liquid in the glass and it suggested guilt and disgust with himself – neither of which emotions he had experienced before. He did not propose beginning a career in them now. It also said fear. Fear of crushed, bleeding hands and swollen stumps of fingers.

Most of all, the brown liquid in the glass reflected fear.

CHAPTER NINE

'Please,' said the girl kneeling at Sister Hélène's feet. 'Please listen to me.'

Hélène bent over the figure kneeling on the stone floor. 'My daughter, what is wrong?'

Mariette eluded Hélène's outstretched hands and plucked at the skirt of the nun's habit. 'You must help me.' She sounded panic-stricken.

It was dim and cool inside the empty chapel, despite the weather. The candles on the altar were still lit from the office and St Euphonie's jewelled cross was outlined on the white-washed wall behind the altar.

'Mariette,' said the nun, resting her gaze on the brilliant points of colour. 'You had better tell me everything.'

'I have sinned, Sister.' The slight figure slumped back onto her ankles but she allowed Hélène to pull her gently to her feet and settle her on a pew.

'Mariette, I am here to help you. I will listen to you.'

'A priest wouldn't understand,' Mariette was beginning to gabble. 'They are men and they don't have families of their own. Once you told me to come to you. Do you remember?'

'Of course.' Hélène took Mariette's hand firmly in her own. Begin at the beginning.'

The girl turned away her face and pressed the knuckles of her other hand against her mouth. '*Ma soeur*, you will despise me.'

Hélène squeezed the hand in hers. 'Try me,' she invited. 'Now what is it?'

Mariette retrieved her hand and pulled off her cotton head-scarf. She began to pleat it between her fingers. 'I told Monsieur Fleischer that I thought Monsieur Maier was a spy.' Her voice cracked has she finished the sentence.

'Who is this Monsieur Maier?'

'He lives at Château Belle-Place. I don't know, I think he's an artist or something . . . They took him away this morning in a black car. I saw it happen.' She rolled the headscarf into a ball in her lap. 'It's my fault, Sister!'

'What, in the Name of Our Lord, possessed you to do such a thing?' Hélène was so appalled by the confession that it required the most strenuous self-discipline not to recoil from Mariette. 'You must know that was a foolish and wicked thing to do.'

Unnerved as she was by the older woman's expression, Mariette was not so distraught that she blurted out the whole story. 'The Nazis were threatening me, Sister.'

'If ever I had need of charity, Lord . . .' Hélène prayed silently beside her. She fingered the crucifix hanging on a chain around her neck and tried to summon the energy and compassion to help Mariette.

'Look at me, Mariette,' she ordered. The girl obeyed. 'We are all sinners. No one is exempt. And I am not going to sit in judgement.' Mariette looked a little more hopeful. 'But you must tell me exactly what you told them.'

The burden of her guilt was heavy and Mariette was desperate to lighten it. She started to talk. 'This man, Monsieur Fleischer, questioned me at the *mairie* and asked if I thought anyone at Château Belle-Place was behaving suspiciously. When I wouldn't tell him anything he took me down to the cells.' Mariette dropped her voice. 'It was dreadful, Sister . . . there were women down there with their faces beaten in. Their own children wouldn't have recognised them. He said if I didn't co-operate I'd be locked up with them. I was so frightened I told him about Monsieur Maier . . . that he acted suspiciously . . .'

It was not a very clear account but it was enough for Hélène to gather some facts together. 'Did you tell this man anything else? Think, Mariette.'

Standing in a patch of candlelight the jewelled cross sparkled. Blue, red and green pinpricks of colour danced before Mariette's eyes. 'No. I told him nothing else.' She paused. 'That was right, wasn't it, Sister?' Mariette could not yet bring herself to tell Hélène that Fleischer had insisted she spy for him at Belle-Place.

Hélène nodded. 'Certainly. The less said the better.' She folded her hands into the sleeves of her habit and assessed whether or not she could trust this girl to take a message to the *château*. 'Thank you for telling me, Mariette. It was a brave thing to do.'

Mariette jerked up her head. 'But you don't understand,' she said angrily. 'I want you to give me forgiveness.'

'Mariette, only God can forgive you. You must ask Him.'

The pew screeched on the stone floor as Mariette got to her feet. 'I should have known!' "Only God can forgive you",' she mimicked. 'Ask yourself, Sister. If He is so perfect, why does he let my children go hungry?'

'I wish I could answer that, except that we must have faith.'

' "We must have faith." What sort of answer is that?' Mariette pushed past the nun.

There are rare moments in a religious life which are luminous with meaning. A moment of discovery when the perfection of God is seen more clearly and the will to move closer to Him rededicated. In that instant Hélène's own guilt and uncertainty concerning her involvement in the resistance sloughed off and she could see her way forward.

'Stop! Come back.' Mariette hunched up her shoulders but did as she was told.

'Listen, Mariette,' said Hélène. 'What you have done, for whatever reasons, is hard for your countrymen to forgive and many would be unable to do so. You must live with that.' At the thought Mariette grew pale. 'But . . .' Hélène paused, 'I think I understand.'

'How can I make it up, Sister?'

Hélène sighed. 'That I cannot answer, except to tell you to put your faith in God.'

'He's never helped me before.' Mariette sounded a trifle less sullen. 'Would He now?'

'Try Him.' Hélène was very gentle.

Mariette glanced at the cross on the altar. 'I'm frightened,' she confessed. 'There *is* something else, Sister. I . . . I agreed to spy for Monsieur Fleischer at Belle-Place.' The truth came out, ugly and unpalatable. 'I give the information to Corporal Schwarz. He – he comes to visit me occasionally. The Nazis will arrest me if they find I've been talking. They might even harm my children . . . I couldn't stand that. I'd tell them everything I knew before they laid a hand on Jeannette or Jacques.' She smiled wryly. 'I'd make it up if necessary.'

'Mariette.' Hélène brushed the hair back from Mariette's face. 'You must face up to it. You can hide from me, from Monsieur Fleischer, from anybody, but you cannot hide from God. You must trust in His mercy.'

'The children! What about them?' Mariette had become shrill with anxiety. 'What do I do?'

Hélène checked that no one had entered the chapel. The candles still flickered, sending a St Vitus dance through the crystal chandelier, and the calm stone face of St Jeanne continued to gaze up the nave. 'Now, listen,' she said. 'You are to go home. Pack a small bag, not a large one, and bring the children and your mother to me here as quickly as you can. I will hide them in the infirmary. They will be quite safe but you must tell no one. When you have done that, I am going to ask you to go to the *château* and tell the Countess what you have told me. Tomorrow we will get you out of Bertric-Burée and send you south for safety.'

The speed and efficiency with which Hélène produced her plan surprised Mariette but she was not going to question it. She ran her fingers along the top of the pew, and then, gripped by an emotion she couldn't place – gratitude, perhaps, – she got down on her knees in the middle of the chapel aisle and bent her head. Hélène knelt beside her and began to pray.

She knew with a great, joyous surge of faith that the life she had chosen in God, and for God, was absolutely the right one.

Mariette almost shouted at her mother. 'Please don't ask any questions. Just do as I tell you.'

The older woman looked stubborn and too upset to understand fully what she was saying. Mariette bent down and picked up Jacques, who clung to his mother's chest in bewilderment. She put her other arm around Jeannette and mentally gritted her teeth. 'Go and pack your things, Mother. We're leaving.'

Her mother said something inaudible and did not move. Jacques began to cry.

'I don't understand,' said the old woman impotently. 'I don't want to leave.' She pulled her black shawl around her.

'You'd be quick enough if you knew your life was in danger.'

'Mariette,' quavered her mother. 'What have you done, girl?'

'Enough,' said Mariette shortly, experimenting with a prayer. 'Now do as I tell you.'

It did not take long to reach the convent, and as they trailed in through the gates a nun whose robes flowed out behind her like a figure in a dream, moved forward to usher them in. Jacques began to scream.

Mariette pushed past Marie making pastry at the kitchen table. 'Where's Madame de Bourgrave?'

Marie gestured with a floury hand. 'Upstairs, of course.' But as Mariette headed out of the room, she called after her, 'What do you think you are doing? You can't disturb the Countess.'

Mariette did not answer. She was up the kitchen stairs and into the hall before Marie could stop her. Uncertain where to try first, she hesitated in the hallway and then made for the Blue Salon.

Whenever she entered the Blue Salon Mariette was overwhelmed by the sumptuousness of the blue silk-hung walls, the antique furniture and oil paintings, and the lovely blue and white china.

Bessy sat on her favourite sofa embroidering. She looked up at the girl's entrance and her expression was not very welcoming. 'Is there anything wrong downstairs?'

For a second, Mariette's courage completely failed. Far from being a straightforward act which would bring her release, confession was proving a more difficult affair than she imagined. In her informal, rather foreign way the Countess was a formidable figure, and Mariette was terrified of what her response might be. 'I've come to warn you,' she said. 'Madame, you are in danger.'

Mindful of Evelyn's warning about Mariette, Bessy did not overreact. She inserted another stitch into the cornflower taking shape on the canvas, which depicted the de Bourgrave arms. 'I don't quite understand you, Mariette.'

'Madame, please listen to me. Sister Hélène sent me.'

At this, Bessy looked up sharply from the canvas on her lap. 'Why didn't you say so earlier?'

'They – I mean the Germans – I saw them take Monsieur Maier away in a car this morning.'

'Nonsense, Mariette. Monsieur Maier is upstairs. I saw him go up half an hour ago. It must have been someone else.' She drew a long blue thread through the canvas and added, 'Poor thing.'

'No, Madame. It was definitely Monsieur Maier.' Bessy continued sewing, a doubt beginning to insinuate itself into her mind. The girl was not to be trusted, but . . .

'How is it that you are so sure?'

'Because,' Mariette felt the throb of blood in the vein at the top of her thigh, which had varicosed from pregnancy. 'Because I told the Nazis about him. I told them I thought he was suspicious. They were threatening my children, Madame!'

'You did *what?*' Bessy rose to her feet and advanced on Mariette, her eyes blue slits blazing with shock and fury. Mariette felt her cheeks flush a harsh, painful red, but she stood her ground. 'I'm sorry. Truly sorry.'

'Why did you do such a terrible thing?' Bessy seized Mariette by the shoulders and began to shake her. Her French disintegrated and she shouted at Mariette in English. 'Do you know what you've done?'

'Stop. Please!' Mariette's teeth were chattering with the force of Bessy's shaking. 'It won't help, Madame.'

It took a second for the words to sink in, but finally Bessy stopped. 'No, it won't,' she said. 'You're quite right.' She turned away as if the sight of Mariette offended her. 'Now tell me exactly what you saw and what you told the Nazis about my brother.'

Mariette wiped her streaming eyes and nose with the back of her hand and, shocked into defiance by Bessy's rough treatment, said, 'I was being threatened. They were going to imprison me— '

'How *could* you?' Bessy interrupted. 'As if it's not bad enough having a German for a lover, you accuse an innocent person to save your own skin. And God knows how many more of us you've put at risk. People like you ought to be— ' Bessy did not finish her sentence.

Mariette's cheeks flamed ever deeper red as she took in Bessy's silk afternoon-tea frock in soft rose and her leather high-heeled shoes. Bessy's hair was brushed and shining, swept up into a coil around her head and when she moved her perfume spilled into the room. 'It's all right for you to say that,' she said from the depths of her troubled spirit, 'sitting here in your family *château* surrounded by luxury. I bet if you lived like me you wouldn't be so sure.'

Mariette had been cleverer than she knew. Her words acted like a slap on Bessy's face and she gave an audible gasp. Charles, she thought bitterly, why aren't you here to help me?

'Very well,' she said, and the hysterical note left her voice. 'I won't interrupt again. Tell me all you know.'

After Mariette had repeated the story she had told Hélène Bessy took a deep breath. 'Now what is it best to do?'

'If you don't mind, I've got to go,' said Mariette. 'I've done my bit.'

'No, you don't. I want to check a few things. You are coming upstairs with me to find Monsieur Maier.'

As Bessy was speaking, Evelyn was edging her way cautiously along the first-floor landing to her bedroom, where she had arranged to meet Guy. As usual she had used the wine-cellar passage. The door to the room was ajar. Evelyn closed it behind her and leant back. She saw that Guy was already there, sprawled out on the bed asleep. On the table beside the bed stood a half-empty bottle of brandy and a glass.

She hesitated before going over to him. Drink and sleep had slackened Guy's features and he was snoring softly. Evelyn dismissed the temptation to disappear without waking him: she had to make sure she had bought Guy's silence for a little while longer. Cautiously, she shook him. He sighed and shifted but did not wake up. She shook him again and he muttered something in his sleep, his hot, drink-laden breath hitting Evelyn. With a sigh of relief, she turned away. A search through Guy's jacket lying on the end of the bed yielded nothing of interest and she let herself out of the bedroom.

The bedside clock in Bessy's room said eight o'clock. It was not yet dark but the evening was drawing in. Evelyn looked around the room, at the elegant wall hangings, silver-backed brushes and shaded lamps. Bessy's dinner frock was laid out on the bed beside her lace-edged satin nightdress. Evelyn smiled as she pinned a note to it – *Love as ever*. Bessy would always be extravagant.

When Bessy hustled Mariette into the bedroom, she noticed the note immediately. She snatched it up, read it and tore it into bits. 'It must be tonight . . .' she said, and then remembered she had Mariette with her. Bessy went into the bathroom, threw the pieces of paper down the lavatory, and flushed it away while she tried to think.

'You will stay here for a while,' she informed Mariette, having calculated that it was just possible she might catch Evelyn. Locking Mariette into the bedroom, Bessy ran down the passage, flung open the door of Evelyn's room and, to her surprise, saw Guy.

'Oh, Guy!' Bessy felt exasperated. She bent over him and the smell almost sent her reeling. 'What have you been doing?' The inert figure of her brother did not respond.

Leaving him where he was, Bessy clattered on her high heels down the back stairs, forced herself to walk slowly through the kitchen, where Marie was still working, and let herself out of the back door. It was very warm and her unsuitable footwear made her stumble as she ran past the barn towards the maize field.

At the edge of the field Bessy halted and looked around

her. She noticed that a car was driving slowly along the lane at the bottom of the fields. It did not look French. Bessy turned round smartly and retraced her steps: it would look very odd if she was seen wandering around the maize dressed in a frock and high heels. Reluctantly, she faced the fact that she had missed Evelyn.

She hurried back the way she had come: the black Mercedes was obviously a patrol car and, if Evelyn was on an operation tonight, Bessy had to warn her . . .

When Bessy let herself back into her room she thought for a moment that Mariette had escaped. Then she saw that the girl had fallen asleep on the bed, one hand flung across the pillow, the other lying with a fold of Bessy's expensive dinner frock between her fingers, young and innocent-looking and not at all Bessy's idea of a collaborator. Bessy thought of Mariette's two children – once or twice the girl had brought them with her to Belle-Place and they had played on the lawns – and Bessy knew she could not totally condemn her or cast the first stone in punishment.

She woke Mariette. The latter groaned and sat up. 'Please let me go,' she begged, brushing the sleep out of her sore eyes. 'The children – they will be getting frightened.'

Bessy sat down on the bed beside her. 'Mariette,' she said urgently, 'do you want to make up a little for what you've done?'

'Well, yes, I do.' Mariette was dazed and a little unsure.

'Then I've got to trust you. I don't want to, but it will have to do.' Like a sleek and tawny lion, Bessy bent over the tousled girl and shook her firmly by the shoulder. Like a lion she was stronger and more determined than her captive.

'You've got to do this, Mariette. If not, I will let everyone know what you have done.'

Mariette woke up properly. The idea of Jean-Claude and her cronies taking vengeance was not a new one; she had dreamt of it often enough. 'It looks as if I'm caught between the lot of you.'

'Yes.'

Mariette dropped back on the pillow. 'Jesus, I'm so tired.'

'Listen, Mariette! Listen carefully. I want you to take the

bicycle from the shed by the barn and go to Jean-Claude's house. Tell him that the circuit is in danger. Violette is in danger. Do you understand?'

In the woods above the radio station at St Aulaye it was quiet and unusually still except for intermittent bursts of bird song. At the first hint of dusk, the guards switched on the search-lights, and their beams probed the dying daylight.

'Seems normal,' said Jack under his breath. He was lying prone in the forward position with Frisé and the other men ranged in a fan behind him. He did not dare to use his binoculars in case a ray from the setting sun reflected off the glass. He narrowed his eyes in an effort to see.

At midnight, they would emerge from the cover of the wood. Jean-Claude and Frisé would offer cover from the edge of the trees while Albert, Toni and Pierre set up a diversionary position in a ditch bordering the lane which encircled the radio station. Evelyn and Jack would aim to cut the first wire fence at 12.05 a.m., the second at 12.08 a.m. from where they would make a run for the central pylon, a distance of twenty metres or so. Up on the block they would plant the explosive, set the pencil detonators for seven minutes and return the way they had come. The whole operation was timed to take fifteen minutes; just under the time it took for a pair of sentries to patrol the perimeter.

It had been hurriedly formulated but it was a reasonably sound plan. Jack's stomach gave a nervous twinge. He looked at his watch. Nine ten. A long wait lay ahead.

Behind him the men, enshrouded in their private thoughts, hugged the ground and longed for forbidden cigarettes.

Where is Evelyn? Jack wondered uneasily for the tenth time. Where the hell is she?

CHAPTER TEN

Before she plunged between maize fields, Evelyn gave a last look at the Château Belle-Place. It stood solid and serene, painted onto the backdrop of a red-streaked sunset, the last rays of the sun gilding the windows.

A pinpoint of light moved across the sky overhead – an aircraft returning to base. Higher up, the evening star had appeared and a huge summer moon was slowly rising. It was very warm and the air was thick with the tang of herbs and peach blossom. Evelyn watched the aircraft's passage across the moon. It was worth it, her part in the fight to defend France.

Lit only by sidelights, the car was round the corner and coming towards her before she realised what was happening. It bore down, its lights tiger's eyes in the dusk. She had time only to think how stupid she had been to make such an elementary mistake as to dawdle. She began to walk briskly down the road towards the oncoming car.

When the car drew level with Evelyn the driver braked and stopped. Evelyn took no notice and continued walking but the driver leant across the passenger seat and opened the door. 'Get in,' said a well-known voice.

Evelyn stopped dead.

'I've been waiting most of the day,' said Paul, 'so I suppose thirty seconds more won't matter.' The wry, half-mocking tone was exactly as she remembered it.

Too shocked to say no, Evelyn got in beside Paul and pulled the door shut. She could not think of anything else to say except, 'I thought you were in Berlin.'

'I came to look for you.'

The old dark, disturbing fears shook her and Evelyn

thought, So this is it. He's come to finish what he left unfinished.

Paul read her mind. 'Trust me, Evelyn,' he said. 'Please, stay for a moment. Trust me.'

She removed her hand from the door handle and sat back. Hot and unmistakable, adrenalin streamed through her veins and her muscles tensed for flight, just in case. 'It was better left as it was,' she said.

Paul had not turned the car engine off and it was idling gently. For a reply he reached across her, felt in the glove compartment and placed a box wrapped in the sort of luxurious paper and ribbon she had not seen for years in her lap.

'The war can't be allowed to interfere with everything.' He watched her face as she examined the box.

Evelyn traced the frivolous curls of gold ribbon with a fingertip. She knew there was a more than even chance that Paul's motives for giving her the present were not innocent and this was one of the many ways he could choose to tunnel under her careful defences – and yet she was touched to the quick. *If he wanted to turn me in he could have done it months ago.*

Paul spread her fingers out between his own and caressed the nail on her forefinger. 'Still bitten, I see,' he said tenderly – the way she would have wished if her love affair had been ordinary and normal, as it might have been if she had fallen in love with one of those safe Englishmen who worked in the Foreign Office, and knew how to behave at cocktail parties.

'I've come all this way to give you a box of your favourite chocolate ginger and you've nothing to say. I had to search the length of the Kurfürstendamm.' Paul could have been describing a visit to Charbonnel and Walker in Bond Street – the sort of expedition they might have had. A quick dash into the chocolate-filled shop before hurrying on to the theatre and then to the slow, lingering pleasures of dinner.

'I'll save them for breakfast.' Evelyn made an enormous effort to keep the conversation easy to handle while she worked out what to do. Paul looked exhausted and there were lines around his eyes she could not remember seeing before. But his hair was still as fair, and she wanted to touch the nape of his neck where the hair was bleached.

He dropped her hands and the pretence at lightness. 'I can't do what I said, Evelyn.'

'You mean,' she prompted, accurately, because each word was held in her memory, 'when you said you would come back after the war was over?'

'I won't be returning – whether you are here or not. I am getting married to someone else.'

For many years afterwards Evelyn could recall exactly the snake-bite of anguish and jealousy, stinging at first, then gradually poisoning her body. And years later, she was able to look back on the young man and woman sitting together in a moonlit car and piece together the combination of idealism, desire and the sharp excitement of eating forbidden fruit that made them love each other.

But she was never able to remember whether her cry into the warm, still night, 'You can't!' was audible or silent.

'Yes, of course,' Evelyn did hear herself say as she fumbled for the door handle. 'I quite see . . .'

'No, you don't,' said Paul, and tossed the chocolates that had dropped off her lap onto the back seat.

But Evelyn had got the door open and was out on the road, running. With an exclamation, Paul let off the brake, drove the car up onto the verge and turned off the engine.

'Evelyn, wait.' He scrambled out of the Mercedes and began to run after her, wincing as his injured leg protested. Evelyn was fast and Paul had difficulty catching up. Panting, he caught her by the entrance to the field, pulled her to him and began to kiss her.

'I came back to say I'm sorry.' Hungrily, he kissed her lips, her eyelids, her neck. 'I have to marry Ingrid.'

Evelyn understood what he was saying. Her love for Paul, her need of him and the pain of what he was saying dissolved the final barrier. She gave in. Her fingers reached up to smooth the hair at the nape of his neck.

'How did you find me?'

'Let's agree to ask no questions, Evelyn.'

The headlights of an approaching car cut through the dusk and disturbed them. Evelyn pushed Paul away and fled into the hayfield behind them. For a moment, Paul thought he had lost her and panicked as he followed her over the crisp drying grass. Then, as he got his bearings, he saw she was crouched behind a walnut tree. He ran over and dropped down beside her.

'A patrol, do you think?' Evelyn whispered.

'Probably. Everyone's jumpy these days.'

Paul felt for her hand and gripped it as the car swept past, stopped and then with a grind of gears began to reverse up the road.

'Down!' Evelyn dropped flat on her face. Paul joined her with a soft thud on the grass. The black Citroën reversed back up to Paul's Mercedes and stopped.

'They're inspecting my car,' Paul hissed in her ear. 'Keep still. With a bit of luck they will think I am on some sort of patrol.'

After a minute, they heard car doors slamming and the engine note of the Citroën ebbing way into silence. Evelyn and Paul lifted their heads and stared at each other.

'Why are you risking so much for me, Paul?' she asked.

He reached out his arm and pulled Evelyn slowly towards him. 'The pact, remember?' he said, and swept the hair back from her face and kissed the soft exposed temple. 'Anyway, there is no law that can tell me where to love.'

Evelyn touched his cheek. 'No, I see that. I see that very clearly now. And you are right.' She helped him to undo the tiny covered buttons of her cotton blouse and he slipped it off her shoulders.

'You're so thin,' Paul said and kissed her collarbones. 'Is somebody taking care of you?' Then his lips were on her neck, her breasts and tracing the curve of her hips.

Washed in the moonlight, Evelyn lay and watched Paul undress. He was both unselfconscious and sure in his movements, his shoulders smooth and white and his stomach very flat. She leant over and ran her finger up the livid scar on his leg.

The ground under the walnut tree was hard and lumpy with clods of dry chalky earth. Wisps of drying hay prickled against Evelyn's skin and its new-mown smell drifted through the warm, heavy air. You are not dreaming, the sensations

461

told her, this is happening. Then, unfamiliar and urgent, Evelyn's feelings took over and she ignored the pinpricks of discomfort. As he took her into his arms and whispered her name, Paul's head blotted out the moon. The memory of that other time with Guy, which had haunted her, vanished. 'I love you,' she told Paul, over and over again, and kissed him on the mouth – and he drew her down.

Often, during the past year when she had lain awake at night or in the cold early mornings, Evelyn imagined telling Paul a lot of things. But now there was no time, and she was happy to lie quiet, absorbing as much of him as she could. Eventually, Paul lit two cigarettes and passed her one. Using his tunic as a cushion, he leant up against the trunk of the walnut tree. Evelyn lay in the curve of his arm and looked up at the moon hanging above her in the sky.

> *'Au clair de la lune,*
> *Mon ami Pierrot*
> *Prête-moi ta plume*
> *Pour écrire un mot*
> *Ma chandelle est morte*
> *Je n'ai plus du feu*
> *Ouvre-moi ta porte*
> *Pour l'amour de Dieu.'*

She recited the words in an undertone and when she had finished she turned her head and looked up at Paul. 'It's an old favourite of mine. The idea of it used to upset me as a child: "Please let me in for my candle has gone out, and I haven't any light." I had a vision of someone cold and hungry who was always on the wrong side of the door.' She stubbed her cigarette out in the loose earth at the foot of the tree.

He smiled and stroked the top of the dark head resting against his shoulder. 'You're a romantic.'

Reluctantly, Evelyn looked at her watch: it was ten thirty. She got to her knees and knelt in front of Paul. 'I'm sorry, but I have to go now. Do you understand?' She felt a hard lump gathering at the base of her throat.

Paul bent over and placed his lips on the crescent scar on her left breast. 'As much as I ever will.' He helped Evelyn to

462

dress, putting on her blouse and kissing the top of each shoulder before fastening it.

But already part of Evelyn's mind was ticking over what she had to do. Retrieve the bicycle at the end of the road, meet Jean-Claude, change . . . Operation Bakelite was scheduled to start in less than two hours.

Evelyn stood up, pulled on Bessy's blue serge skirt and did up the buttons. After she had finished she stood still. 'Paul, I don't think I can manage to say goodbye.'

'You must smile, Evelyn, and say something very English like "Till we meet again." ' Paul buckled his leather belt and searched for his boots.

Ignoring the lump that had spread to her chest, she took her cue. 'And then I promise that you will be indelibly engraved on my heart and no one will ever mean as much to me again.'

'Yes.' He considered. 'Yes, that would be the right thing to say.'

'Then I turn to face the camera with brimming eyes.'

'Yes.'

'We part and I find a good man and settle down but your shadow is always there, haunting me.'

'Yes.'

'Well, then, I've said it.' She was not going to allow herself to cry.

He pulled her roughly towards him and her arms went snaking up round his neck. 'Goodbye,' she said and clung to him, as his mouth hovered over hers – and she tried to say thank you for not giving me up and for not being what I expected. And for everything else that they had between them. Instead, she pulled away, ran along the hedge and disappeared out of the field.

Paul sat quietly in the car. Far from having the neat finality of a scalpel incision, his meeting with Evelyn had ripped open a new wound, a war wound which would earn no medals. And now that she was gone he had to ask the question: Where was she going at this time of night? And the answer was: In all probability, on an operation.

463

Still, if he took the journey back to Ribérac, slowly, he told himself, concentrated on the road, on driving the car and on smoking another cigarette, perhaps he could stave off the thoughts of Evelyn until he got hold of a bottle of brandy. The next morning he could make an early start for Bordeaux, and that would be the end of the episode. In three weeks, he would return to Berlin on leave to marry Ingrid, and start again.

He slowed the Mercedes as the dark mass of the beehive-shaped tower of Allemans village church came into sight. Beside the church, he remembered, was the remains of what must have been a large house. He craned his head to look and only just managed to avoid the cyclist ahead of him.

Whoever it was had no lights and, at the sound of the car, swerved towards the ditch. As Paul swung the wheel to the right, the cyclist gave up the struggle and fell off. With a sigh, Paul stopped the car. It was possible, of course, that this was an ambush but Paul could not bring himself to care very much. Even so, he reached for his Mauser and cocked it before getting out of the car.

'Are you hurt?' he addressed the figure slumped in the dust beside the bicycle with a crazily spinning back wheel. A sob of terror answered him and Mariette Maisson cowered at the sight of the uniformed figure. 'What are you doing here?' After a second or two Paul recognised her. 'Don't you know I could arrest you?'

Mariette sobbed harder. Paul tucked the gun into his belt and bent over to examine the bicycle. The chain had been dislodged by the fall. 'Would you like me to fix it?' he asked, and she stared at him with the helpless fascination of a rabbit trapped in a car's headlights. 'Look,' he said. 'Where are you going? I'll give you a lift.'

He bent down and helped her to her feet. At first, she flinched from his touch but then she permitted him to lead her towards the Mercedes and to settle her into the passenger seat. Still a little dazed, she stared through the windscreen into the night. Getting in beside her he tossed her a packet of cigarettes and a lighter. 'Where can I take you?'

Mariette looked blank. She had recognised Paul as the

464

German who had interviewed her the first time and given her the roll of francs and now that her initial fright was subsiding she remembered he had been kind once before. She flicked the cigarette lighter, the petrol flame flared into the car's dim interior, and she toyed with the idea of asking Paul to drive her straight to the convent and to forget about the message to Jean-Claude in St Aulaye.

'Tell him they are in danger, Violette is in danger.'

But more than anything, Mariette wished to sleep un-terror-ridden at night and to go with Werner if he still wanted her – and to feel free of the guilt that was growing inside her like a new baby . . .

'What do you want?' Jean-Claude's wife had been openly hostile when, finally, Mariette had wobbled up to the police-man's house at Allemans.

'Jean-Claude. Where is he?'

'Why should I tell you?' Jean-Claude's wife had gone even balder since the celebration lunch at Belle-Place and strips of grey hair encircled, tonsure-like, a pink crown speckled with pigment spots.

'You must tell me,' Mariette almost screamed in frustration. 'It's important.'

Madame looked at Mariette for a full thirty seconds while she assessed whether the girl was genuine. She was no fool and eventually she said, 'He's gone to St Aulaye to see a friend.' She banged the door shut.

Inside Paul's Mercedes, Mariette drew hard on the cigarette. Her rescuer was waiting for a reply but she had the impression he was in no hurry.

'Where do you wish to go, Madame?' he asked again.

'St Aulaye, please, Monsieur. I was on my way to see a friend there.' The car smelt of leather, tobacco and a tantalis-ing hint of expensive perfume. Mariette's nervous, sweaty body left a damp imprint on the seat as she shifted position.

Under Paul's hand the gear lever moved into first. As it did so, his thoughts assembled obediently into the correct formation and he understood.

St Aulaye.

Enemy radio messages piling up in the file. Reports of a

secret army gathering in the woods, living rough. Fleischer plump and self-satisfied. *'One of our informers tells us that the resistance is planning an operation in the near future.'* The radio station at St Aulaye with six aerial masts, beaming German radio traffic into the Atlantic where packs of U-boats waited for their instructions. One terrified French girl on her way there, floundering out of her depth. One English enemy agent codenamed Alouette. They were flashing dots on a cathode-ray screen, linked by threads to form a tangle of deceit and death, with Fleischer at its centre.

'Madame Maisson. Are you quite sure St Aulaye is where you wish to go? It's a long way.' Paul wanted to be quite certain.

'Pardon, Monsieur . . .'

'One English agent' equalled Evelyn's white shoulders gleaming in the moonlight. 'Alouette' equalled the woman he loved.

'She'll never make it,' he said out loud. 'St Aulaye, you said.'

'Yes, Monsieur,' replied Mariette uncertainly.

'Then I will take you,' said Paul, and let off the brake.

In bed at Château Belle-Place, Bessy was trying to concentrate on a book with little success. Her mind was on Evelyn and she was analysing feverishly whether she had done the right thing in sending Mariette off with a message instead of going herself when she heard the cars drive up to the front of the house. It was 10.30 p.m. by Bessy's watch and she had planned, in her organised way, for an early night and supper in her room on a tray. Bessy lifted the tray to one side and got out of bed. She padded over to the window and lifted the curtains back an inch or two. Two cars were parked by the front door. They were black Citroëns.

Bessy grabbed at the curtain material with fingers that had gone cold. Then, collecting her wits, she pulled on her dressing gown and ran out of the room to Charles's nursery. Her son was asleep, his small hands tucked behind his head in the curious way he had. The pose made him appear ridiculously grown up and Bessy's heart lurched at the sight. She scooped him up and permitted herself to kiss him once on his cheek before wrapping him in his blanket. He was so deeply asleep that he hardly stirred as she carried him as fast as she could up the back stairs to Marie's room.

'Marie,' she whispered outside the door. 'Marie.'

The door opened at once and Marie peered out, her hair already plaited for the night. When she saw who it was, her expression changed into one of horror, but she held out her arms at once to take the child. 'I'll look after him, Madame.' Explanations were unnecessary: the two women had long ago worked out an emergency plan in case the Nazis ever came.

Bessy was white and shaking as she handed over her son. 'You'll do what you promised and take him to your sister?'

'Yes.' Marie backed into the room, laid the stirring child on the bed and pulled off her dressing gown. 'I'll use the back entrance.' She kicked off her slippers and reached for the skirt folded over the back of the chair. 'You can trust me, Madame.'

'I must go.' Bessy turned away and then swivelled back to take a last look at her son. 'Take care of him, Marie.'

'Of course.'

Downstairs, the knocking at the front door was insistent and peremptory. Bessy picked up her dressing gown and ran as fast as she could to Guy's bedroom. It was essential that she warn him.

When she burst through the door, she was brought to an abrupt halt. Guy was packing. He had been in bed, for the sheets were rumpled; his possessions were scattered all over the room – shoes, shirts, ties, tubes of paint, books. Unable to take it in, Bessy stared for several seconds and then raised her eyes to her twin. Guy avoided her gaze and continued to throw objects into his suitcase on the bed.

Bessy endeavoured to say what she had come to say but the words would not come out. Guy threw a shirt onto the bed and picked up the half-full glass from the bedside table. 'Come for a late-night chat have you?' he said in a voice she did not recognise.

Out of the corner of her eye, Bessy caught sight of Guy's portrait of Evelyn with its horrible, vicious mouth, and she almost choked. She backed out of the room. At the top of the stairs she paused, ran her hands through her hair and then went down to face whatever was coming.

Fleischer was examining the blue and white china when Bessy was ushered into the Blue Salon by a shocked Gaston. A second man was standing by the fireplace, writing something down in a notebook. Fleischer stepped forward.

'Countess. How nice. Let me introduce myself and Obersturmführer Mundt.'

With a tiny nod, Bessy acknowledged the men and drew her dressing gown around her. 'Really, gentlemen, it is very late.'

Fleischer had turned back to the china and was fingering a rare Meissen-Augsburg pickle dish. He seemed to be making a mental note of its qualities and held it up to inspect the mark on its base. 'Just a few enquiries,' he said, and put the pickle dish down before moving on to a vase.

Bessy crossed over to Fleischer and removed the vase from his grasp. 'If you wouldn't mind,' she said. 'These are very valuable.'

'Oh, yes, I know that.' Fleischer was visibly offended that she should think he wasn't aware of that. 'I like to think I am something of an expert on porcelain.'

'Then you will appreciate I don't like the pieces handled.'

Fleischer smiled, revealing a neat filling. 'Don't worry, Countess.'

'Would you like some refreshment, gentlemen?' Bessy tried Evelyn's counting technique under her breath.

'No, thank you,' replied Fleischer. His tone changed abruptly. 'Sit down, Countess.'

Bessy remained standing until Mundt made a step towards her. She dropped back onto the sofa.

'That's better,' said Fleischer. 'Now. Mademoiselle Liegaux. Where is she?'

Bessy crossed her legs and arranged her dressing gown over them. 'If that's all you have come to ask me, I'm afraid I cannot help you. I cannot think why you thought it necessary to come and ask me such a question at this time of night. Mademoiselle Liegaux left my employ some time ago.' She

468

assumed what she hoped was a pettish expression. 'I was very disappointed in the girl. She let me down badly.'

Fleischer's laugh sounded genuine. 'Trouble with the servants, Countess? How tedious. So? Where do we go from here?' He sounded rather bored but Bessy noticed that he was fingering his belt. The sight gave her courage.

'Personally, gentlemen, I wish to go to bed.'

'What was your maiden name, Countess?'

Bessy got up from the sofa and went over to the cigarette box, where she lit herself one. She took her time over the operation. 'I don't wish to tell you.'

Once again, Mundt moved towards her.

'I think you should, Countess,' said Fleischer. 'It would be most unwise to drag out this interview.'

Bessy shook her head and blew out a stream of smoke into the room. Mundt pushed aside a chair and simultaneously drew his revolver out of its holster. He pointed it at Bessy's eyes. The knuckles on Bessy's hands whitened as she clenched her hands.

'Tell us,' said Fleischer. Tall though she was, he still managed to tower over her. The smoke from a cigarette curled over his fingers. 'Myers,' she told him after a moment.

'Ah.' Fleischer's gaze rested on the portrait of Charles and returned to Bessy's face. 'I think you have a Monsieur Maier staying here. A curious coincidence, don't you think? Would you be kind enough to have him brought down here?'

Bessy went over to the bell pull. Her initial panic diminished in the face of a steadily mounting fury and when Gaston appeared, she managed to ask him in a normal voice to fetch Monsieur Maier. There was silence in the room while Bessy nurtured her anger. The door opened and Guy walked in.

'For Christ— ' he expostulated, and then stopped.

Fleischer nodded. 'Good evening,' he said in his heavily accented French. 'I think you know Obersturmführer Mundt.'

Bessy's stomach lurched. The expression on Guy's face on seeing Fleischer had been craven. He turned red and then very pale, and his hand shook visibly as he loosened his cravat. Fleischer looked at his watch and gave a signal to

Mundt, at which the latter pushed Guy down into a chair and trained his gun at Guy's left temple.

'Where is Mademoiselle Liegaux?' said Fleischer.

Bessy could not watch. She turned her head to one side and stared at the portrait of her dead husband. *I'm glad you're not here to see this, Charles.*

'Right.' Fleischer nodded at Mundt. 'Perhaps it would encourage you to talk if you knew my men had surrounded the grounds.'

The muzzle of Mundt's revolver smashed into Guy's face and broke his nose. Thick blood began to stream from the nostrils. Guy gave a sickening grunt and Bessy screwed her eyes shut and dug her fingernails into her palms. Had Marie been scooped up by the cordon? Please, she prayed. Please, God.

After the second blow to his broken nose, Guy groaned and Mundt ordered, 'Hold out your hands.'

'No, please don't,' Guy implored him. Unwillingly she opened her eyes and turned to look at her brother. He was fumbling for his handkerchief. Mundt repeated, 'Your hands, Maier.'

Fleischer spoke to Bessy. 'Monsieur Maier was a lot more talkative last time he met Mundt.' He flicked a glance at the bleeding face. 'You could save yourself a lot of . . . trouble, if you just told us what you know of Mademoiselle Liegaux. The message you found on her, for example. You are an educated man, Maier, I'm sure you understood it better than you let on.'

The cigarette burned down to the stub and threatened to singe Bessy's fingers and she reached for an ashtray. No, she thought in disbelief. Please not –

Once again Fleischer looked at his watch. 'Hurry up, Maier. You have given us quite a lot of useful information about this mysterious Mademoiselle. You confirmed our suspicions about her. Correct me if Mundt reported it wrongly. You said you found a message on her that you did not understand. Now, come along, Maier, what did that message say exactly?'

Guy slumped back onto the spindly Louis Quinze chair. Dark stains began to spread over the blue brocade.

'Do you think your sister can tell us anything? She is your sister, isn't she?' Fleischer went on.

His face now a mask of bright blood, Guy nodded. 'Don't,' Bessy cried out sharply. 'Don't hurt him any more.'

Fleischer ignored her. 'Have you anything more to tell us, Monsieur *Myers*? You see, as you are an American citizen, technically you are the enemy. On the other hand, if you wish to help us with our enquiries concerning terrorists operating in the area, it is possible we could overlook this. I'm told,' he continued, 'that there are no such luxuries as paints and canvases in prisoner-of-war camps. Assuming that you could still use your hands, of course.'

Guy attempted to sit up. His hands were shaking and his face under its coating of blood appeared to Bessy to have collapsed inwards. As Bessy watched, sickened, he seemed to shrink – her elegant, brilliantly gifted twin brother.

'The message said something like "Operation confirmed 3 June",' intoned this shrunken Guy, and wiped his bloody nose with the back of his hand.

'Yes?' Fleischer breathed quickly and heavily.

Guy threw back his head and drew in a deep sigh. Blood and saliva trickled out of his mouth. 'I can't remember anything else,' he said. In desperation he looked towards his sister. Help me, he seemed to be saying. But Bessy was frozen and silent.

'More,' said Fleischer, and looked at his watch for the third time. 'I am getting impatient.'

'It said,' Guy dropped his head into his hands and winced as he touched his nose. 'It said: "Confirm Operation Bakelite, 3 June".' His voice was thick and muffled. Mundt lowered his revolver.

'Ah.' Fleischer kept his eyes trained on Bessy as if she could answer his question. 'Bakelite?'

Mundt shook his head. 'I don't understand, Sturmbannführer.'

'Fool!' Fleischer almost lost control. 'Radios are made of Bakelite. You should know that.' He walked over to the telephone on the window table and cranked the handle. After a moment he began to talk in rapid German and Bessy, who understood the language, grew colder and paler at what she heard.

Eventually Fleischer put down the phone. 'Good. That is under control. I must go at once to St Aulaye. See to those two, Mundt.'

With a cry like an animal, Guy heaved himself upright and swayed on unsteady feet. 'You can't do this.' He pointed a bloodied finger at Fleischer. 'You said if I talked . . .'

Fleischer went over to the pickle dish he had coveted from the moment he had entered the Blue Salon and picked it up. 'Then you are more foolish than I thought, Myers. Your sister has a better head on her shoulders.'

'No!' Guy screamed. 'No.'

Mundt pushed him towards the door and into the hall. Fleischer gestured with his revolver and Bessy followed her brother. Before Mundt hustled Bessy out of the door and onto the drive she managed one last, wild, despairing look at Belle-Place.

Charles will be safe, she repeated to herself, and hugged the words like a talisman as they tied her hands behind her back. Charles will be safe by now. Marie will have seen to it. And she repeated them over and over again during the drive to Ribérac.

As they were being led down the stairs to the cellars in the *mairie*, Guy sobbed out his sister's name. Bessy turned and looked at the broken nose, the purple bruise spreading across his cheeks, at the split, mashed lip and the blood-caked hands and spat so that her spittle landed at Guy's feet. Then she was led away to a separate cell and the door closed on her.

CHAPTER ELEVEN

Hotel Adlon
Berlin
3 June 1943

Darling, darling Paul,

I imagine you driving through France (my parents are horrified at the risk), stopping for glasses of wine and looking at houses. *Do take care.* I know you won't have got there yet but I'm writing to you because I am so happy.

I didn't think I could ever be so happy.

I don't mind now about the bombs or if I starve – except for the baby, of course. I can put up with anything because I have you and the baby to look forward to. My parents are delighted and will come to Berlin for the wedding.

When I was younger, I always dreamed that I would get married in my mother's tiara and old lace veil. I didn't ever think I would be a bride in a blue flannel suit and a borrowed hat. But I don't care. Truly I don't.

Do you miss me? I am aware that you are gone every moment – while I'm talking or eating, or just being normal. Everybody asks after you.

I promise I will be a good wife and mother.

Siegfried was furious when I telephoned him with the news and told me I was making a great mistake. But I'm not, Paul, I know that. I know I have the handsomest, most intelligent, the best man I could ever have or ever want.

Write to me as soon as you get to Bordeaux. I will be waiting every day for the post.

With all my love,
Ingrid.

P.S. The doctor thinks that I am doing well, and we should have a healthy baby.

P.P.S. I saw a painting in a gallery the other day that looked just like you. I'm going back to have another look tomorrow.

CHAPTER TWELVE

'Where have you been?' Jack was sharp with Evelyn. He lowered his binoculars and looked at his watch. 'It's eleven thirty. I thought there was trouble.'

'I was held up.' Evelyn wriggled forward on her stomach towards Jack's look-out spot. Through the trees the masts and cables of the radio station looked like a gigantic silver cat's cradle in the moonlight. A trickle of sweat ran down her back: she had changed from her skirt and blouse into corduroy trousers and a dark jersey in Jean-Claude's van, and they were far too hot. The policeman had parked the van a quarter of a mile away, just off the Échourgnac road running south-east from the radio station. He had turned it round in preparation for the get-away and the two of them camouflaged it with leafy branches. Then they pushed their way through the wood, thick with heavy summer undergrowth, to the rendezvous at the head of the tongue of trees south of the radio station.

Jack propped his gun against a tree trunk. 'Sorry. I was beginning to think you'd run into difficulties.'

Disconcerted, Evelyn looked back over her shoulder to the others. 'Anything to report?'

'Nothing so far.' Jack noticed how pale her dark jersey made her appear. 'You had better put some of this on.' He extracted a stump of charcoal from his pocket. There was something new about Evelyn tonight – a strange, exotic, almost wild quality. 'I wish we'd had more time to plan this operation. The moon's too bloody bright.'

'Are the others ready?' Evelyn turned and crawled back to the *maquisards*, brambles scratching at her knees through the corduroy. They were squatting in a circle with Pierre, passing a bottle around. Evelyn felt a surge of affection for them . . .

475

Frisé, what was left of his hair crammed underneath a beret, Toni, bottle in hand as usual, and the taciturn Albert. She loved them for their enthusiasm, for their prickliness, for their defiance of the Nazis, for their boozing and bravado, their fearlessness and for the loyalty which, once they had decided to trust her, they had given her absolutely. Checking over their weapons, they were talking in soft voices about what they would do once Operation Bakelite was over and how many more 'actions' they planned to notch up against the Germans.

Frisé undid the fastenings of his blouson and wiped the sweat from his neck. 'Just you wait,' he said. 'We'll show those pigs. You tell London from us, Violette.'

Evelyn gave him the thumbs-up and consulted her watch. Less than two hours ago, she had been with Paul. She could feel where his lips had rested on her shoulder blades underneath the chafe of her jumper. Frisé waved the bottle in her direction. 'Drink,' he ordered. 'To the end of the Boches.' Evelyn stretched out her hand and grasped the bottle. She took a large mouthful of brandy. 'It's nearly time,' she said, wiping her mouth on her sleeve.

Jean-Claude clicked off the safety catch of his Sten. 'None too soon if you ask me,' he said, and beckoned Jack over for the final briefing. 'Give us a swig,' he demanded and prised the bottle away from Toni.

The moonlight filtered down through the branches and threw a white *tranche* over the stretch of rough grass which lay between the edge of the wood and the back of the radio station. It was only fifteen metres across but it could as well have been fifteen kilometres.

A quarter of an hour before Operation Bakelite was scheduled to commence, Evelyn shook each of the men by the hand. All bravado had gone and their faces were grim and determined. 'Remember,' she warned, 'don't launch any diversion until it is absolutely necessary. Keep moving so they can't pin you down. Don't do anything we haven't agreed. Above all, don't go in. You must not be taken.'

'Do you understand?' Jack wanted to be sure there was no

risk of another incident like the one with Nicolas at the tyre factory.

Frisé punched him playfully on the shoulder. 'Of course, Tomas. You take after your namesake.'

The *maquisards* peeled off in separate directions, bodies bent double in the way Evelyn had trained them. Jean-Claude was the last to go. Unusually emotional, he grasped Evelyn by the shoulders. 'I want you to know I was wrong the other day,' he said, and his bulk seemed enormous. 'Strangers you may be, and English, too, but you have risked your lives to help us. I won't forget that.'

Evelyn wondered why it had taken her so long to like the policeman. 'It was nothing,' she said. 'It's all part of the service.'

'You'll have us weeping next, *mon vieux*.' Jack took Jean-Claude's hand and wrung it.

The big man lifted his gun and began to walk away. 'You English', he advised them in a whisper, 'need to cry more often. *Au revoir*.'

'Ten minutes.' Jack made a final check of the rucksack and his gun. 'Are you ready?' He stood close to Evelyn. Suddenly he bent over and kissed her lightly on the lips. 'Good luck, Violette.'

'Good luck, Tomas,' she replied, and smiled up at him.

He flicked her cheek with his finger. 'Let's go.'

The two of them dropped to the ground and began to drag themselves forward over the dry leaf mould. It was difficult to make rapid progress: the Stens got in their way and the rucksacks packed with explosive were heavy and cumbersome. At the edge of the tree-line, Evelyn glanced to her right and felt the erratic drumbeat of her heart. Jean-Claude and Frisé should have reached their position by now. She hoped the others had not encountered any difficulty taking up their places in the ditch on the other side of the station.

'Two minutes,' said Jack. He settled the rucksack more securely on his shoulders. The parcels of explosive rested between his shoulder blades. 'Your load secure?'

'I'm ready.'

Thirty seconds later: 'Sentries starting patrol.'

'Searchlight at six o'clock.'

'Go!'

Together they rose to their feet and, bending almost double, wove their way in and out of the shadows fracturing the open, turf-paved strip of land towards the east-facing boundary fence and dropped to their knees by the wire. Evelyn kept cover while Jack extracted the wire cutters from a pocket and, square by square, peeled back the mesh.

Concealed by the trees, Jean-Claude and Frisé held their breath and watched, their fingers poised on the triggers. In the uneven light, it was possible to see that Jean-Claude was grinning.

Jack and Evelyn squirmed through the first fence and pulled the wire back into place behind them. Grass and dirt embossed into their clothes as they snake-crawled across the no-man's land to the second fence. Evelyn whispered, 'Searchlight twelve o'clock.'

The wire of the inner fence was of a thicker gauge – a problem they had not anticipated. Jack wrestled with it for precious extra seconds. 'Searchlight two o'clock,' Evelyn hissed.

Jack wrenched the wire aside and they scrambled through, flattening themselves on the ground inches beyond the path of the swinging beam. From her prone position, Evelyn raised her hand and pulled the wire back into place.

With an eye on the patrolling sentries they ran towards the central pylon, espadrilles making soft squelching noises on the loose stones. At the foot of the concrete plinth, Jack cupped his hands together. Evelyn stepped on to them with one foot. 'One, two . . .' Arms stretched to catch hold of the top of the block, Evelyn used the impetus of Jack's push to help her spring as he threw her up. She caught hold of the rough concrete edge and hauled herself over, flinging herself flat on the top between the steel hawsers. The concrete was hard and cold against her cheek. Using her foot for anchorage, which she hooked around one of the hawser rings to give her purchase, she reached over the edge and held out her hands. Jack gripped them in his own and she pulled, while his feet scrambled for a firm footing against the concrete. In a couple of seconds he was up beside her.

From behind the block, they heard feet crunching on gravel and smelt the whiff of tobacco. 'Down.' They buried their faces in their arms.

The boots came to a halt under the plinth. Jack bit his lip. Go on, you bugger. A torchbeam sliced past their, wavered, and flitted up over the pylons. Then they heard the sound of the soldier sauntering away towards the guardhouse from where issued a murmur of voices.

Evelyn and Jack wriggled the rucksacks off their shoulders and extracted the packages. The parcels weighed about a pound each. The two of them worked together exactly as rehearsed, attaching a parcel to each hawser with a leather strap. Evelyn ran a length of fuse between each section, while Jack fixed a detonator to every third packet, setting them for seven minutes as planned. Just to be sure, he added a couple more set for ten minutes. It was not the most expert job but, providing nobody checked the pylons, it would do.

'Hey!' One of the sentries patrolling the inner fence had spotted a loose end of cut wire. His shout alerted his companions in the guardhouse and within seconds the compound appeared to be swarming with soldiers.

A volley of diversionary fire came from the edge of the wood and was taken up by Toni, Albert and Pierre in their hiding place on the far side. Their shots had the desired effect and drew most of the soldiers to the western edge of the compound. In the look-out tower the searchlight operator swept his beam from side to side in an attempt to illuminate the *maquisards'* positions.

Jean-Claude saw that the perimeter sentries were standing guard over the holes in the wire.

'They can't get out!' he exclaimed. At this distance he stood little chance of hitting them. Perhaps if he or Frisé could use the cover of the lane on their right . . .

'Frisé . . .'

Silence.

Jean-Claude swung round. Frisé had gone.

* * *

A quarter of a mile away, Paul and Mariette heard the first volley of gunfire. Paul depressed the accelerator pedal and the Mercedes gathered speed. Mariette leaned forward, her hand pressed to her mouth, emitting little moans of muffled fear. Suddenly, Paul put his foot on the brake and turned the car off the main road. 'There must be something going on up ahead, an ambush probably. We'll use the back route to St Aulaye.' Mariette said nothing. Instead she began to cry. 'You are very foolish to have come out, Madame Maisson,' Paul told her quietly.

The radio station was only a few hundred metres to their right. Up ahead Paul saw the dark shape of the wood. That was where Evelyn – and, he supposed, the rest of her team – would be heading for cover. However well she knew the forest, her chances of survival were nothing if reinforcements had already been alerted. Tracker dogs could hunt her down in minutes. Paul knew that Fleischer was anticipating a resistance action but would he have made the same connections that Paul had? He'd encountered no troop carriers on the road from Ribérac but that might mean there were already guns lying in wait. Paul looked at his watch. It was 12.15.

'Stop!' The scream made him ram his foot down on the brake. He had forgotten the girl sitting next to him. 'I want to get out.' Mariette was almost hysterical and groping for the door handle.

'It's dangerous out there. You'd be safer with me.' Before Paul could bring the car to a halt she had yanked open the door. 'Let me go!' she yelled, and threw herself out of the car, landing on her hands and knees in the road and rolling over onto the grass verge. Blood trickled down her legs, but she stood up, covered her ears with her hands and ran blindly through the nearest gate into a field.

'Get out,' Jack ordered and leapt off the plinth. Evelyn jumped after him. The ground rushed up at her and she landed with a jolt, almost winding herself. Jack pulled her to her feet.

Evelyn was the first to catch sight of the soldier running towards them. He stopped and raised his gun. Evelyn pulled Jack behind the block and they crouched, waiting. The soldier advanced more slowly and they could hear his breath coming in nervous little pants. Jack edged forward and then sprang, caught the man in a stranglehold and with his free hand administered a karate chop to his neck. The soldier's eyes rolled up with an expression of surprise and he slumped over.

Now for the double fence. But the two sentries stood guard by the break-in point. In the shadow of the concrete plinth Jack and Evelyn prepared to shoot their way out.

A slight figure in a leather blouson jacket ran out of the cover of the trees. He ran, a deadly, sacrificially generous figure with a blazing gun, straight for the two German sentries, shouting, *'Vive la France!'* as one of his bullets hit its target.

'Now!' Jack and Evelyn took the chance that Frisé had paid for so dearly. For Frisé had stopped in mid-flight, riddled with bullets from the gun of the surviving sentry, his body sprawled on the turf, like a broken puppet. Jack shot the sentry in the stomach as he swivelled round, and he and Evelyn threw themselves at the wire and propelled themselves through.

The *maquisards* were keeping up a steady stream of diversionary fire on the west side, and Evelyn prayed as she dashed for the trees that the ammunition was holding out. Could they keep up this sort of barrage until the station went up? In another minute they had rejoined Jean-Claude.

'Can we go?' he asked.

'We can't,' Evelyn panted. 'We must keep them busy until the fuses go off.'

'Pray to St Jude, then,' said Jean-Claude, the Catholic.

Jack said: 'Three minutes to go.'

It was too late to warn Evelyn. Paul snapped a magazine into his Mauser and got out of the car. Using the hedge as cover, he assessed the position of the *résistants*. If he could not prevent what was happening, then at least he could be there to help Evelyn get away.

The main fire was coming from the other side of the radio station but there was an isolated gun a few hundred metres away. The fire-power was light – obviously the resistance did not possess heavy weapons such as a bazooka. Paul considered the situation. The Germans were better armed and protected but the enemy held the advantage of knowing the terrain. Their main problem would be ammunition: sooner or later it would run out. Paul calculated that the officer in charge at the station would have rung through for reinforcements at the first sign of trouble and they would be arriving within quarter of an hour.

He was wrong. Within a couple of minutes he heard vehicles driving fast and turning up to the radio station. At the same moment he witnessed Frisé's wild dash and heard the shout, 'Vive la France.' Seconds later he saw Evelyn squirming through the wire and run to the wood, followed by a tall, dark man. Reinforcements began to flood around the perimeter fence and fire with disciplined precision into the trees.

By one of the strange coincidences that happen in battle, a silence fell and for two long seconds the landscape was at peace, seemingly untouched by the events taking place. The lull was broken by the arrival of a black Citroën accelerating up the back lane from the main road. Paul whipped round from his vantage point. The order had been given to encircle the station: Evelyn was trapped.

At the junction the Citroën slowed and a resistance fighter emerged from the cover of the trees and took aim at it. The bullets hit the front tyres and the windscreen. The Citroën shuddered like a wounded animal, slewed across the road and came to a halt. The driver's door swung open and the body of the driver crumpled into the dust, metres from where Paul was crouched behind the hedge.

'What are you doing here, von Hoch?' Sturmbannführer Fleischer recognised the face, as Paul backed away from the hedge, and leant out of the passenger window of the staff car, angry and alarmed that the rest of the convoy had not yet arrived. Paul ignored Fleischer. He was scanning the road and the wood to see if Evelyn and her team were making a retreat.

'Come and help me get this car out of the way.'

'Shut up, Fleischer, you fool.' Paul ran round to the front

of the Mercedes where he took cover. He thought fast, and then whistled the first bars of 'Au clair de la lune'.

He had to draw out Evelyn from her position and it was the only way he could think of to tell her. Fleischer leant forward out of the window. 'I've just given an order, von Hoch. I'll arrest you if you don't obey.'

Taking careful aim, Paul lined up Fleischer in his sights and shot him.

'Two minutes more,' said Jack. He had bitten his lower lip raw. 'Only two more minutes.'

The German reinforcements poured around the edge of the perimeter fence and Evelyn stopped shooting. 'Retreat, there are too many.' She turned and ran up through the wood. Jack followed and Jean-Claude brought up the rear.

'Car on the road. They've come already,' said Jack.

Evelyn looked in the direction of Jack's pointing finger and felt her mouth go dry. She knew that car.

Au clair de la lune. Paul's whistle filtered through the gunfire, a bizarre, haunting sound – a paean to battle, a song that Roland might have heard at the Ronceval Pass, an elegy to life.

He's telling me to come with him, she thought stupidly. He's calling me. Jean-Claude raised his Sten and aimed. 'There's a Boche there.'

Now Evelyn could see clearly the blond man crouched behind the Mercedes, alone and exposed.

It was the end of a dream. A dream that had led her to a moonlit field where she had experienced unimaginable sweetness. The dream was running out, ending with a lone man by his car, and three armed people advancing towards him. And, as in all dreams, Evelyn was powerless to change its course.

'What's that German bastard doing?' Jean-Claude struggled with his Sten which had jammed. 'You get him, Violette. Then we'll take the car.'

'There's more of them.' Jack suddenly sighted the slumped figure of Fleischer in the Citroën.

'Violette, shoot.' Jack raised his own gun and with a gasp Evelyn threw herself at him and knocked the Sten aside.

'What the hell are you doing?' Jack elbowed Evelyn roughly to one side. 'We have a chance to finish them off.'

From down the lane, there was a sound of vehicles accelerating towards them.

'No!' Evelyn shrieked as Jean-Claude wrenched his jammed trigger free and aimed at Paul. Inside the Citroën Fleischer was shuddering and sweating with shock from a bullet wound in his shoulder. He fumbled for his gun in the holster around his waist.

'You asked for this, von Hoch,' he shouted, and aimed it at Paul out of the window. At the same moment both Jack and Jean-Claude fired.

Paul staggered and threw up an arm. His Mauser fell into the road and spun once on the powdery dust.

Fleischer grunted with pain and fell back onto his seat, clutching at his shoulder. As if on cue, the radio station erupted with swirling tongues of flame. Twisted metal and burning wood spewed up into the night and rained down on the road and the wood. Burning debris fell onto the roofs of the two troop carriers racing up the lane. The light illuminated Paul's body on the road.

'Run!' said Jack, and pelted for Paul's car.

'Come on.' Jean-Claude pushed Evelyn towards the road, but, for ever on her conscience, she pulled away and ran round to the front of the Mercedes where Paul lay. When she reached him she flung herself down by his side and pulled his head into her lap. There was blood on his lips and streaking his fair hair, and she wiped it away with her sleeve as if she had all the time in the world. Paul stared up into the sky. He looked very puzzled. 'Are you safe?' he asked.

'Yes,' she lied.

With an effort Paul turned his head so that he could see her better. 'I love you.'

She bent over to kiss his cooling mouth.

'Tell me.'

'I love you, Paul.' She kissed him a second time.

Paul tried to smile. 'This is so stupid.'

With a cry, Evelyn pressed her cheek against his. He sighed and blood trickled out of his mouth. He raised a hand and touched her face. 'Go. Please.'

For a brief second, she buried her face in Paul's neck and listened to the harsh, painful breathing.

Someone was tugging at Evelyn and pulling her to her feet. 'You little fool, what the hell are you doing?' Evelyn clung to Paul.

'Go . . . please,' Paul managed.

Evelyn released him and Jack pulled her away towards the car. She held Paul's dying face in her sights – until a stinging red-hot pain flowered in her side. She staggered under the impact of the bullet and fell onto her knees. Jack caught Evelyn before she fell and dragged her to the back of the car.

There was no pain now. Only a panorama of trees and dazzling moonlight. Bullets and flames licked into the sky. Jack threw Evelyn's limp body into the back of the Mercedes, leapt in behind her and smashed the back window with the butt of his Sten. Jean-Claude took the wheel and accelerated the car towards Échourgnac. Jack fired repeatedly at the reinforcement vehicles blocked uselessly behind Fleischer's Citroën. Evelyn slumped on the seat and felt wetness soak her jersey, slither down her side and onto the car's leather upholstery. Trees rushed towards them and disappeared, and the inferno they had created faded into a nightmare.

The car bumped and swayed. Evelyn put out a hand to steady herself and encountered a box covered with splinters of glass. Carefully she lifted up the box of chocolate ginger, its ribbon still as pretty and frivolous as when Paul had given it to her. She closed her eyes, and held it tightly to her chest. Something in her – a strand of hope, of youth – fought for life and died.

CHAPTER THIRTEEN

The bandages in the infirmary were almost threadbare from constant washing. Sister Hélène checked through them, relegating one or two which were beyond redemption to the pile intended for dressings. After that, she moved on to the salves, calendula, arnica, comfrey, then to the flower essences and herbal *tisanes*. Finally, she checked the cabinet which contained the drug supply. It did not take long, and she shut the door with a snap on the virtually empty shelves.

Her log book lay open on the table. Recorded in her neat, nun's script were cases of a breech birth, a fractured arm and bad case of depression. The entries in the book, however, did not include everything with which she had dealt with in the last forty-eight hours.

Mariette had been terrified, so terrified that not one drop of colour remained in her face. When she finally dragged herself between the convent gates and stumbled through the courtyard to the surgery where Hélène was waiting up for her, she resembled an animal driven to the last ditch.

'Did anyone see you, do you think?' It took some time to calm Mariette down.

'No. I don't think so.'

'Tell me what happened.'

But at the thought of what she had just been through, Mariette retreated into incoherence and Hélène was unable to make out what had taken place since Mariette had left for Belle-Place to talk to Bessy. She administered a herbal sedative and led Mariette to the outhouse where Jean waited to take her out of the convent first thing in the morning. After that he would pass her on to one of the escape lines to Tarbes. Mariette's mother and the children were waiting for her in a safe house which Jean had arranged.

Mariette's arrival had put Hélène on the alert and when Jean-Claude's uniformed figure tapped at the infirmary door a couple of hours later she was not surprised. Evidently something big had taken place that night.

'This is Tomas,' Jean-Claude explained, as Jack inched his way through the door carrying an unconscious Evelyn. 'He's one of us.'

'Yes, indeed,' said Hélène, who recognised Jack. 'Put her down.' The nun was already taking a mental note of the vital signs: shallow breathing, clammy forehead, dull white complexion. 'Do you want her to stay here?'

The two men exchanged a glance. 'Can you risk it?'

'Yes.'

'Thank you, Sister.' Jean-Claude punched out his battered policeman's *képi*.

'You have blood on your jacket,' Hélène said. 'You must wipe it off.' She handed Jean-Claude a rag and pointed at a bowl of water.

'I'm off, then,' said the policeman after he had cleaned up his clothes. '*Au revoir et merci*.'

Jack, who still held Evelyn in his arms as if afraid to put her down, looked up. 'Good luck,' he said to Jean-Claude and laid her gently on the examination couch.

'Do I need to know anything?' asked the nun as she cut off Evelyn's jumper. Jack dragged his gaze away from the wound in Evelyn's side and bit at his raw lips. 'She was shot from a distance of about fifteen metres. Is she going to be all right?' Hélène appraised the dark, tense face and made her own judgement of the relationship between the two. 'Will you keep a watch at the window, please?' she said, avoiding his question. She worked in silence.

'She has lost a lot of blood but luckily the wound is superficial. You will have to help me. Are you up to it?'

Tomas had the look of a man carrying an intolerable load, but he came over obediently and held the unconscious Evelyn while Hélène searched for any splinters in her side.

'We'll have to get out tonight,' he said, and looked away as Hélène's instrument probed the cleaned wound and brought out a fragment which she dropped into the kidney dish beside her.

'Not till morning.' Hélène rearranged the red ribbons of flesh. 'But I will have her taken out first thing.' The nun placed her instruments as noiselessly as possible into the kidney dish and felt for Evelyn's pulse.

'They'll be searching for injured,' Jack told her. 'It's possible more might come in for treatment tonight.'

Hélène threaded her suture needle. 'Thank you for the warning.' She bent over the wound. Evelyn twitched and her breathing appeared to become shallower and more laboured. Once or twice she gave a little moan. Hélène worked on. 'Could you hold down this dressing,' she asked once, and a little later. 'Raise her up a bit, please.'

While Hélène worked, Jack made plans. He must retrieve his wireless set and then travel south until the furore had died down. First, though, there was Evelyn. How could he get her out of France? Did the nun know of an escape line? Jack's contacts would take some time to alert and Evelyn had to be got out by this morning at the latest.

'Where will she be taken, Sister?'

Hélène understood Jack's train of thought. 'I can arrange for her to be kept in a safe house until she is fit enough to join an escape line. It means crossing the Pyrenees, but she is young. She will recover quite quickly.' The nun studied Jack's expression. 'That is the best I can do, I'm afraid.'

Against the white pillow, the bruises of Evelyn's face appeared deep purple. Jack had the impression that she had shrunk. He bent over her. 'Violette.' Her eyelashes moved, flickered, and then opened. 'You're safe,' he told her.

Evelyn's vision was blurred and Jack appeared to be talking to her from a long way away. Something was hurting her badly and she was very thirsty. She wondered if she was having a nightmare. 'What?' The question took all her energy.

'Listen,' said Jack gently. 'You've been wounded but it's all over. You're safe for the moment. We are going to get you out of France as soon as possible. Very soon you are going to have to walk so don't think of anything other than getting better.'

'Bessy?' she whispered.

He bent over so that he could hear and his lips brushed her hair. 'I'll find out for you. Operation Bakelite was a success. The station went up. Do you remember?'

Evelyn remembered a lot of things. Fire. Noise. Pain. Paul. 'Did you . . . ?' Her mouth was so dry that it hurt to speak. 'Did you see . . . ?'

Jack gazed down at the drained face on the couch while he battled to master his jealousy of a dead German officer. She looked up at him with trust in her green eyes and Jack could not find it in him to accuse her. She was barely conscious, in pain and what was done was over. 'I saw nothing,' he lied. 'Nothing at all.'

The words percolated through Evelyn's consciousness and roused her and she had to put her hand over her mouth to stop herself screaming from pain and despair. Jack brushed his fingers down her cheek and she remembered afterwards how comforting the gesture had been. 'We're burned,' she said with difficulty. 'You must warn the others and get out.'

'That's enough,' said Sister Hélène, checking Evelyn's pulse a second time. 'You must lie still.'

By now a hot band had settled down over Evelyn's forehead and she tried to turn on her side. The pain was excruciating and she felt herself beginning to lose consciousness once more. Hélène was ready with a herbal pain killer. 'It is the best I can do,' Evelyn heard her say.

An overwhelming fear shot through Jack. 'Don't die on me, Evelyn,' he cried out.

Hélène gave a disapproving click of her tongue and shook her head at him. Evelyn's head turned towards him. 'Paul?' she questioned, her voice filled with such tenderness that Jack was forced to look away, guilty that he and not the owner of the name stood there.

'Don't worry, Sister,' he muttered to Hélène. 'I won't say any more.'

All the same, before he left, Jack found himself saying, 'I'll come and find you when I get home.' He kissed her slowly on the lips. 'I promise.'

Evelyn did not appear to hear him but the words found

their way into her subconscious because later she was able to recall them quite clearly.

Jack stepped back. Evelyn was lying on her back, her hair, matted with blood and dirt, spread out in a dark stream over the pillowcase, her face blotted into the white of the linen. The nun was holding a wet linen rag to her forehead. Evelyn sighed and moaned. Jack took a last look, turned and left the room.

By morning Evelyn was fully conscious but so weak that Hélène was forced to hide her in the outhouse for the day, with Jean mounting guard outside. They were terrified the Germans would search the convent but there was nothing else Hélène could do until dark had fallen. At dusk, Jean carried her gently from her hiding place among the garden tools and put her in the back of his cart. Covered with sacks, Evelyn left the sanctuary of St Euphonie's without having the opportunity to thank or even say goodbye to Sister Hélène.

Jean reported back to the nun that the first leg of the journey had gone according to plan and that Evelyn had not suffered unduly during the trip. If all continued smoothly, she could rest for a couple of days at the safe house in Pau before tackling the long march over the Pyrenees to Spain. She was young and strong and Hélène had faith that Evelyn would survive.

During the next few days. Sister Hélène's surgeries were full of talk about the latest resistance coup. She also heard that Madame de Bourgrave and Monsieur Maier had been taken from Château Belle-Place and were due to be transferred to the prison in Bordeaux. Hélène passed the information on to Jean and told him to find and tell the policeman Jean-Claude. A day later, Hélène heard that the Countess had been freed by a *maquis* ambush as she was being transferred in a German car to Bordeaux. The gun battle resulted in three German dead, one of the *maquis* Jemaye boys and Monsieur Maier. It was reported that the latter's body had been left lying in the road with a large 'C' – for collaborator – pinned to it.

Sister Hélène finished writing her notes, replaced her log book in the drawer and looked out of the window. Outside the sun was shining, hot and strong. Good weather, she reflected, for climbing mountains. Something caught her eye over by the stone cross in the garden. Curious, she let herself out of the infirmary door, crossed the courtyard and walked onto the square of lawn in which the cross stood. Someone had placed bunches of wild flowers around its foot. There were daisies and bright cornflowers, wilted poppies, and the bright blue of wild chicory – all flowers from the fields – tied with lengths of twine. Sister Hélène bent down and touched one of them with her finger. While she was standing there Jean-Claude detached himself from a group standing by the gate and came over. 'For Violette,' he whispered in Hélène's astonished ear.

Sister Hélène never had time to question the man because when she straightened up it was to see Reverend Mother in the courtyard, flanked by two men in uniform. One of the men had his arm in a sling, the other carried a pair of hand-cuffs. Reverend Mother pointed in the direction of the cross and the Nazis began to walk towards her.

As she did so, Hélène prayed, lifting her face to the sun. 'Thy will be done.'

All those summer weeks, the sun climbed high into the sky and dried everything under it. The men working in the fields grew thirstier. The soldiers sorting the wreckage of the radio station burnt their fingers on the twisted remains of the pylons. At the *mairie* in Ribérac Sturmbannführer Fleischer grew increasingly bad-tempered from the heat. The bullet wound in his shoulder was taking a long time to heal.

All summer German vehicles drove up and down the main roads of France and the teleprinters between Paris and Berlin were never silent.

On the back road where Paul had died, a dark stain sank into the hard-baked earth and on the place where Sister Hélène faced the firing squad, splashes of blood encrusted the hot stones.

The sun shone down on the cross in the convent garden and the bunches of wild flowers arranged around it dried and whitened in the heat. Nobody moved them.

CHAPTER FOURTEEN

In memory of the lives given in the fight
against the Nazi invader, 1940–5

CHARLES DE BOURGRAVE
SR HÉLÈNE MARIE DE BOURGRAVE
JOHN DUNNE – 'GEORGES'
PATRICE RIEUX – 'FRISÉ'
ALBERT RIEUX
ANTOINE DUPREUX – 'TONI'

Erected in grateful memory by
their friends and *camarades*

EVELYN PICKFORD – 'VIOLETTE'
JACK PICKFORD – 'TOMAS'
BESSY DE BOURGRAVE
JEAN-CLAUDE SOISSONS
THE MEMBERS OF THE MAQUIS JEMAYE

ELIZABETH BUCHAN

Consider the Lily

PAN BOOKS

*'An excellent story . . . strong imaginative power . . .
wonderful sense of atmosphere'* Joanna Trollope

Consider the lily . . . waxen, exotic, doomed to bloom for its short, sweet season. Consider the rose . . . tenderly beautiful yet resilient, twining its way into the English garden . . .

Winner of the 1994 Romantic Novelists' Association Novel of the Year Award, *Consider the Lily* is a glorious fusion of love and gardening, of family life and coming to terms with loss. A haunting, passionate story played out between three people, it is also a poignant and beautiful novel of England between the wars that propels the reader into its own rich and nostalgic world.

'Wonderfully stylish and absolutely compulsive reading'
Penny Vincenzi

'A gorgeously well-written tale: funny, sad, and sophisticated'
Independent

'The literary equivalent of an English country garden'
Sunday Times

ELIZABETH BUCHAN

Against Her Nature

PAN BOOKS

'A *modern day Vanity Fair . . . brilliantly done*'
Mail on Sunday

Love, money, children . . . Life is a risk, however much we try to protect ourselves . . .

Unlike the Frants living their quiet ordered lives in the village of Appleford, Tess and Becky are of the generation that reckons it can have everything. High flyers in the high-octane world of London's high finance, they move through the opportunists, the short-termists, the sharks, the bullies and the very, very rich to face many choices, not least the one presented by biology: children.

How they and an older generation balance the texture of their lives is offered in a story with universal themes. Brilliantly and beautifully combined with a tender and unexpected love story and a journey to maturity, it is the work of a fine and courageous writer.

'With her customary understanding and compassion,
Buchan nudges Tess and Becky towards the recognition
of what really matters when the chips are down.
A satisfyingly easy but never facile read'
Daily Telegraph

'She refreshes the parts other writers don't know about'
Daily Mail

ELIZABETH BUCHAN

Perfect Love

PAN BOOKS

'*Modern marriage and its compromises . . . a terrific, compassionate, compelling novel*' **Daily Mail**

Let me tell you a story of a family, an adultery, a child's anger and forgiveness . . .

Twenty years of marriage to Max has seen a busy, contented Prue through the stresses of a resentful stepdaughter and motherhood. Now, Violet has returned with her new husband from New York and, suddenly, Prue is precipitated into a secret life.

The small village of Hampshire and the city are very different places and, as Prue moves between the two, she traces the boundaries between innocence and difficult knowledge, between the gluttony and surrender of desire and the stark realities that result. Pinpointing the battleground of the modern – and second – marriage, the author offers a blisteringly truthful and tenderly observed picture of the extraordinary bargains and accommodations that are struck between people who love one another.

'Adultery . . . handled with care and moral intelligence. What a good writer Buchan is' *Daily Telegraph*

'A powerful story; wise, observant, deeply felt, with elements all women will recognise with a smile – or a shudder. Very highly recommended' *Good Book Guide*

OTHER BOOKS

AVAILABLE FROM PAN MACMILLAN

ELIZABETH BUCHAN

CONSIDER THE LILY	0 330 33991 5	£7.99
AGAINST HER NATURE	0 330 34685 7	£7.99
PERFECT LOVE	0 330 34473 0	£7.99

ANITA DIAMANT

THE RED TENT	0 330 48796 5	£6.99
GOOD HARBOR	0 330 49166 0	£6.99

JUDITH LENNOX

MIDDLEMERE	0 330 48001 4	£6.99

All Pan Macmillan titles can be ordered from our website,
www.panmacmillan.com, or from your local bookshop
and are also available by post from:

Bookpost, PO Box 29, Douglas, Isle of Man IM99 1BQ
Credit cards accepted. For details:
Telephone: 01624 677237
Fax: 01624 670923
E-mail: bookshop@enterprise.net
www.bookpost.co.uk

Free postage and packing in the United Kingdom

Prices shown above were correct at the time of going to press.
Pan Macmillan reserve the right to show new retail prices on covers
which may differ from those previously advertised in the text
or elsewhere.